The
HERO
of the
SLOCUM
DISASTER

For:
Donna & Phil:
who also ~~serve~~ serve: who
stand with loads of books

6/30/97

The
HERO
of the
SLOCUM
DISASTER

by
Eric Blau

Mosaic Press
Oakville, ON. - Buffalo, N.Y

Canadian Cataloguing in Publication Data

Blau, Eric
The hero of the Slocum disaster

ISBN 0-88962-615-4

1. General Slocum (Steamboat) - Fiction.   I. Title.
PS3552.L393H4 1996   813'.54   C96-930827-2

Published by MOSAIC PRESS, P.O. Box 1032, Oakville, Ontario, L6J 5E9, Canada. Offices and warehouse at 1252 Speers Road, Units #1&2, Oakville, Ontario, L6L 5N9, Canada and Mosaic Press, 85 River Rock Drive, Suite 202, Buffalo, N.Y., 14207, USA.

MOSAIC PRESS, in Canada:
1252 Speers Road, Units #1&2,
Oakville, Ontario, L6L 5N9
Phone / Fax: (905) 825-2130
E-mail:
cp507@freenet.toronto.on.ca

MOSAIC PRESS, in the USA:
85 River Rock Drive, Suite 202,
Buffalo, N.Y., 14207
Phone / Fax: 1-800-387-8992
E-mail:
cp507@freenet.toronto.on.ca

MOSAIC PRESS in the UK and Europe:
DRAKE INTERNATIONAL SERVICES
Market House, Market Place,
Deddington, Oxford. OX15 OSF

Mosaic Press acknowledges the assistance of the Canada Council, the Ontario Arts Council and the Dept. of Canadian Heritage, Government of Canada, for their support of our publishing programme.

Copyright © Eric Blau, 1997
ISBN 0-88962-615-4

Cover and book design by: Susan Parker
Printed and bound in Canada

PROLOG

The New York Times

THURSDAY, JUNE 16, 1904

1000 LIVES MAY BE LOST IN BURNING OF THE EXCURSION BOAT *GEN. SLOCUM*

* * * *

St. Mark's Church Excursion Ends In Disaster In East River Close To Land And Safety

* * * *

606 BODIES FOUND—HUNDREDS MISSING OR INJURED

* * * *

Flames Following Explosion Drive Scores to Death in the Water

* * * *

FIERCE STRUGGLES FOR ROTTEN LIFE PRESERVERS

* * * *

The Captain instead of Making for the Nearest Landing, Runs the Doomed Vessel Ashore on North Brother Island in Deep Water–Many Thrilling Rescues–Few Men on Board to Stem the Panic of Women and Children ....

* * * *

This front-page story in *The New York Times* was also the front-page story in all the dailies in the City of New York and nearly every single newspaper in the United States of America. It was the front page of almost all the newspapers in Europe, Australia, and New Zealand, and it appeared in many other newspapers around the globe.

In the months following, the many issues surrounding the burning of the excursion boat were dealt with extensively by almost every magazine and periodical in the United States.

The *Slocum* Disaster, was either, scholars agree, the largest or the second largest *inland* sea disaster in the history of the world. It was certainly one of the greatest disasters in *maritime* history. Merely regarded as a fire, it resulted in more fatalities than any other fire in the history of New York City.

It was an event which shook the world.

The *Slocum* Disaster occurred on New York City's East River. Less than a third of a mile wide, the East River is, in fact, not a river at all but a salt-water estuary or straight, dividing Brooklyn and Queens from the Bronx and Manhattan. It connects Upper New York Bay with Long Island Sound.

The tragedy of the *Slocum* had been witnessed by thousands of New Yorkers who had lined the piers and the rooftops fronting the river. Those on the Manhattan side could see see the faces and hear the screams of the women and children on the boat. Engulfed by the uncontrolled fire, her whistles piercing the air, the *Slocum,* at full steam, cut into the head wind which bellowed the flames up toward the blue and cloudless sky. Avoiding the east and west shores, the *Slocum* screamed north.

The river pilot of the burning boat kept steadfastly on that course into the wind-North. North past Blackwell's Island toward North Brother Island, a mile and a half ahead. The high-pitched terror of women and children trailed in the wake of the *Slocum* on the snapping wind.

> *I had some kind of crud I picked up in Tahiti from one of the girls. It wasn't the clap and it wasn't syphilis either. It made me dog sick. I had loose bowels which came out green. When we docked in New York, they sent me here.*
>
> *I was walking around the grounds watching some of the hospital people, nurses, doctors, bathing in the water and sunning on the beach. I wasn't near well enough for that.*
>
> *I could see this white boat, like a dot, down river. Flames were rising up from it. The boat got bigger and bigger as it came on. I could hear voices. Bigger, bigger, you know, as the boat came. It was like I was in a dream. It was like I was in the middle of the flames and the flames were in the middle of the dream. The white boat kept coming, burning, screaming. It hit the beach. The whole island shook. I fell down.*
>
> Charles Allen Jr., an Able-Bodied Seaman confined to The Hospital for Contagious Diseases On North Brother Island. June 15, 1904.*

The Irish novelist James Joyce was so shocked and moved by the event, which had been featured daily on the newsboards of Dublin, that he incorporated the *Slocum* into his novel *Ulysses.*

In Joyce's view, the fact of the *Slocum* might pass but not its meaning nor its burning entry into contemporary myth and history.

Here are some excerpts from *Ulysses:*

> *...Terrible affair that* General Slocum *explosion. Terrible, terrible! A thousand casualities. And*

---

*From an unpublished statement given to a reporter on *The New York Evening World.*

*heart rending scenes. Men trampling down women and
children. Most brutal thing.
What do they say was the cause? Spontaneous combustion:
most scandalous revelation.
Not a single lifeboat would float and the fire hose all
burst.
What I can't understand is how the Inspectors ever
allowed a boat like that...
Now you are talking straight, Mr. Crimmins. You know
why? Palmoil!
Is that a fact?
Without a doubt.
Well now, look at that. And America, they say, is the
land of the free.
I thought we were bad here.
I smiled at him. America, I said, quietly, just like
that. What is it? The sweepings of every country
including our own. Isn't that true?
That's a fact.
Graft, my dear sir. Well, of course, where there's
money going there's always someone to pick it
up.....
...In America those things are continually happening,
Unfortunate people to die like that, unprepared.
Still a perfect act of contrition..
...All those women and children, excursion, beanfeast,
burned and drowned in New York.
Holocaust.
Karma.
They call that transmigration for sins you did in a
past life..Dear, dear, dear, pity, of course....*

In the first months of the summer of 1904, more space
was devoted to the *Slocum* than to the Russo-Japanese War. The
day after the burning, *The New York Times* devoted many of its
sixteen pages to the catastrophe.

It continued to be a journalistic point of interest for many
decades to come. More than three-quarters of a century later,
newspapers were writing I-still-remember stories about the *General Slocum* told from the point of view of some survivors. By
1991, New York's *Daily News* had reported that there were four

known survivors. New Jersey's *Newark Star Ledger* reported two living survivors in June, 1996.

Like other German American survivors, their families had fled the old neighborhood. Perhaps there are none today. Perhaps, there will be no more *Slocum* stories until the next century when the 100th anniversary occurs in 2004. Aside from the loss of lives the *Slocum* Disaster brought into question maritime safety laws which were changed as a direct result of the happening.

The new legal instrument, "The Corporation," was seriously challenged following the disaster as an immoral device which had sheltered those criminally responsible for the loss of more than a thousand lives.

Then, too, the *Slocum* Disaster permanently changed the ethnic composition of the Lower East Side by decimating the German-American community, "Little Germany" (*"Klein-deutchland"* or *"Deutchlandle"*), whose women and children were the main victims of that holocaust. After the *Slocum* Disaster, the smell and the fresh memory of death compelled the remaining German population to relocate to Yorkville, some three miles north, and elsewhere. Little Germany had gone down with ship.

The excursion boat *General Slocum* is no longer a household name. After the *Titanic,* the *Lusitania,* World War I, The Great Depression, the Hula Hoop, the Lindy Hop, World War II, Korea, Vietnam, Grenada, and other wars, the event of the *Slocum* seemed less important and has been crowded from popular memory.

But the *Titanic* is remembered, sometimes for the tragedy and the terror, sometimes as the subject of ironic humor: *It's like rearranging the deck chairs on the Titanic.*

Was the *Titanic* more important than the *Slocum* ? No, but the passengers of the *Titanic* had been richer, drawn to a large extent from the glamor of the Social Register. The voyagers on the *Slocum* had been mainly members of the families of blue-collar workers.

Of the 2206 passengers on *the Titanic,* 1,500 perished. Of the 1,358 passengers on the *Slocum,* at least 1,031 were lost.

Sixty-eight per-cent lost to an iceberg in the Atlantic as against seventy-six per-cent lost to a caldron of soup heating on a faulty galley stove or to a cigar butt dropped on some kindling in a storage cabinet in the hold of the *Slocum.*

Time erodes history. The event remains known, but understanding and detail move out of focus.

The Encyclopedia of New York City, published in 1995 by Yale University Press and The New York Historical Society, is aware of the existence of the *Slocum* disaster. It receives one and a quarter columns of space. Written by the editor of *The Encyclopedia*, the article correctly says of the *Slocum* that it was "the worst single disaster in the history of New York City and one of the worst in all maritime history."

While employing the services of almost one hundred advisers and forty editors, the chief editor observes that encyclopedias, while alphabetical, are also subjective.

This is undoubtedly true.

It explains, perhaps, why pornography in New York gets almost a full page in *The Encyclopedia*, ferry routes (1812 on) are given three full pages, and the Mayoral Electoral Returns from 1834 to 1993 receive eight and a half pages. Major Fires within the Current Boundaries of New York City, 1741 to 1990, is presented in less than a single page. In all these fires, 2,205 people died. Almost half these deaths are attributed to the *Slocum* disaster. Two hundred forty-eight years of fires, half the deaths having occurred in one single day, in perhaps fifteen minutes of that day.

The Encyclopedia, however, does not consider the burning of the *Slocum* to have been the Great Fire of New York. Here the big book nominates a conflagration which took place in 1835, one of three listed under Great Fires. The 1835 blaze, at the southern end of Manhattan, destroyed 674 wooden houses in an area of twenty square blocks. The cause is unknown. In The Great Fire of 1811, 102 buildings were lost, one fireman killed. In The Great Fire of 1845, 300 buildings were consumed, thirty-three people died.

In *The Great Fire* of 1835, *The Encyclopedia* does not account for any deaths. The 1835 *Great Fire* had been chosen on the basis of property destroyed although the value of the property is only poorly approximated.

While taking note of these 59 major fires, *The Encyclopedia of New York City* omits the category of Shipwrecks in and around the Port of New York and its waters. Between the years 1880 and 1938, alone, there were well over 600 shipwrecks. A subjective omission? An error of experts?

The Christodora Settlement House was established, according to *The Encyclopedia*, on Avenue B in Manhattan. The address is given as "1637 Avenue B" a number which never existed. According to street maps of the time, Avenue B terminated before 21st Street. The numbered addresses barely reached the 300's. Avenue B, veering eastward beyond 21st Street, if continued, would have fallen into the East River.

A typographical error? Probably. However, there were forty editors and proofreaders who read this account. Any knowledge of Manhattan precludes such an outlandish number as 1637 as an address on Avenue B. It would seem that neither editors nor advisors knew much about the streets of Manhattan. Yet, "1637" has the full force of a major source book behind it.

While hundreds of personalities indigenous to New York City are properly included, dozens are clearly absent. Others, as the *Encyclopedia's* editor has observed, are quite subjectively chosen. Still others, while present, seem to be cited for lesser reasons than they deserve.

For example, under the heading Boxing the name of the prize-fight promoter Mike Jacobs appears [born circa 1885 at the Battery, the southern tip of Manhattan, New York City. His father had earned his living as a ship's chandler.] The bracketed data is missing from the account. In *The Encyclopedia,* Jacobs is cited for his association with the great heavyweight champion Joe Louis. It is a benign reference omitting, however, a few useful facts. Jacobs, by promoting Joe Louis, flaunted the prejudice of the time against black fighters, especially heavyweights. The cloak that prejudice wore was that white boxing fans would not buy tickets to see black fighters no matter how talented. Jacobs, a great promoter, made Louis not only the best boxing draw of the time but the best loved fighter of the era.

Before he had become a successful ticket broker and fight promoter, Mike Jacobs had been a candy butcher who held concessions on day-liner excursion boats. The *General Slocum* was one of the ships on which he had hawked his candy and novelties. However, Jacobs was not aboard the *Slocum* on the fateful day. He had had a business conflict. His brother, Jake, took over for him that day. Jake, who could not swim, leapt overboard to escape the *Slocum* flames. He had held onto a floating piece of *Slocum* lumber until rescued. He was one of some three-hundred-odd survivors. The fact that Mike Jacobs was not selling candy on the decks of the *Slocum* on June 15, 1904, may have made the career of the great black champion, Joe Louis, possible.

The absence of this more complete account of Mike Jacobs is not the fault of *The Encyclopedia* but the accomplishment of Jacobs vis-à-vis racism might have provided a more expert and certainly more interesting account. It merely underscores that history is a very large and daunting place and New York is a very big and complicated city. Was it Thomas Wolfe who wrote, "Only the dead know Brooklyn"?

A great deal of *The Encyclopedia of New York City* is often based on direct excerpts from other books and lists. By using secondary and tertiary sources, *The Encyclopedia* seems to endorse their veracity. But the reader has no way of knowing the truth. Acceptance is, therefore, an act of faith.

Yet to peruse *The Encyclopedia* makes a reader wonder what is true and what is untrue. After all, in the matter of the *Slocum*, we are not certain of precisely how many passengers were on the boat, how many crew members there were, nor how many members of the band. Nor are we sure of how many people died. Over a thousand is the consensual number.

On the day when the *Slocum* burned and New Yorkers gazed horrified upon the event, a young man, a teenager, was seen shinnying up the ships flagpole, where its burgee (a small, swallow-tailed flag identifying the boat) flew. He was frantically waving a free arm to the shore. He seemed to be trying to signal the people on the piers that the ship was in danger.

The on-shore watchers became aware of the thickening smoke billowing upward. Then they saw a rage of flame.

The boy continued his signaling. He seemed to be shouting but those on shore were unable to hear him. The flames, leaping up, enveloped him. He was no longer seen. Those on the shore, who had witnessed this, called the boy on the mast a Hero.

His identity was never determined.

A half-century later, on June 15, 1954, an elderly man wearing the clothes of a seaman and a ship's officer's cap appeared at McHooley's Bar and Grill on the Upper West Side of Manhattan. He sat drinking silently through every Happy Hour of the week, all seven, after his first mysterious appearance.

He let McHooley's late-afternoon revelers know that he was a survivor of the *Slocum*. The drinkers did not recognize the *Slocum* name nor did they know it was an excursion boat.

The elderly man spoke, sometimes aloud and sometimes to himself, of a holocaust on the East River, the casual horrors, the casual heroics, and the indifference of the nation.

Sometimes he made the other drinkers uncomfortable. *People got burned alive. I saw them die in the middle of a scream. I saw them get mashed up in the paddlewheel. Ach!*

In his early days at McHooley's, the old man often told the comrades of the Happy Hour that he had been celebrated, even revered, as the Hero of that sad event. Although the drinkers heard bits and pieces of the man's narrative, they paid only enough attention to decide that he was a character--a nut, a kook--whose brain had been softened by a lifetime of alcohol. The old man certainly could drink.

Only McHooley, about the same age as his rambling customer, seemed to listen. McHooley listened because not only had *he* heard of the *Slocum,* but the McHooleys in County Sligo had heard of the ill-fated ship. Sometimes he had asked questions of the man with the close, yellow stained white beard. It was he who first addressed the man as Admiral.

Joseph Patrick McHooley sometimes tried to draw the old man out, but with no success. Asked almost any direct question, the Admiral became furtive and mumbled; growled, really.

McHooley had almost become convinced that the Admiral had no real association with the *Slocum* Disaster. One of those poor demented people in New York City who believes he had walked and talked with Jesus, and who could describe the wounds of Christ quite convincingly.

But the Happy Hour people simply thought the man was an annoying bore and crazy, without a doubt. Occasionally someone was rude to the Admiral and he would lose his temper. McHooley would have to calm him down, sometimes coming out from behind the bar to physically restrain him.

The years went by and McHooley died, passing on the Bar and Grill to his nephew James Timothy McHooley, who sometimes called himself Jimothy. The drinkers, the companions of the Happy Hour, were not the same. One had died in a subway accident and the rest had moved on to other, more stylish bars. Others, of brief tenure, came and went. The old man, however, remained and had claimed a permanent seat at the bar, where he drank and mumbled.

His connection to the *Slocum* had become well known to the latest set of Happy Hour regulars. The Admiral was more comfortable with this new crowd than with those who had preceded them. McHooley said it was good chemistry. The drinkers accommodated themselves to the old man who was now very, very old, although hale and hearty.

Yet, like his uncle Joseph Patrick, James Timothy was not convinced that anything the old man said was at all true. There were bold contradictions in the disconnected tale told through the years.

McHooley thought it was easier to dismiss the old man as an aberrant than try to pin him down to one truth or another. Still, there was the story of the song, "The Slocum Waltz", which weighed heavily against the old man in McHooley's judgment.

The Admiral had claimed the music sheets of "The Slocum Waltz" had washed ashore at North Brother Island in the fiddle case of the conductor of the band, whose name no one knew nor remembered.

One afternoon, when they were alone together, the old man showed McHooley the handwritten music of "The Slocum Waltz", laminated between folded plastic sheets. McHooley held the cracked plastic in his hands as the old man sang the song.

"The Slocum Waltz"

When you waltz on the deck of the *Slocum*,
When you dance on a rare day in June,
leave your cares in a basket at home
and you'll laugh at the waves and the foam,
yes, you will...
Oh, you'll sing and you'll dance
to the fiddler's tune,
yes, you'll sing and you'll dance
and you'll laugh like a loon
and you'll whirl and you'll twirl
and your skirts will all swirl...
Oh, your long hair will throw off its comb
and you'll wish you'll never go home
and you'll wish you'll never go home.
on the *Slocum*,
on the *Slocum*,

> on the merry ship the *Slocum*,
> one, two and three
> were waltzing
> on the very, merry
> *Slocum*...

But McHooley knew the manuscript was a fake. He knew because the manuscript had a small copyright line dated 1960. He challenged the old man by drawing a black circle around the telltale copyright year.

The Admiral hung his head for a long moment. When he looked up he was smiling broadly, splitting his beard and showing his yellow teeth. He acknowledged that the song was a fraud and that he had paid a young songwriter to compose it based on an idea that he had harbored for many years.

McHooley slapped the old man on the shoulder and said it took guts to tell the truth.

But now, McHooley wondered if anything the Admiral had said about the *Slocum* was true at all. And this saddened him, although he didn't know why.

The Encylopedia devotes four pages to popular songs about New York City, or songs inspired by it. Of course, "The Slocum Waltz" is not there.

Nor is the name Edward Francis Knittel, which was the name of the oldest member of the Happy Hour crowd at McHooley's Bar and Grill. This is is quite logical, of course. *The Encyclopedia* cannot be required to deal with the 1,358 passengers on the *Slocum* nor its 321 survivors, nor the boy who climbed the burgee-topped pole. Nor every song the waves washed up on shore.

But McHooley had become fond of the old man and had refrained from challenging him further regarding "The Slocum Waltz" or any other matter pertaining to the *Slocum* Disaster. Still, he wondered, as did the other companions of the Happy Hour, what was true and what was not. Or, if indeed, it mattered.

No one at McHooley's considered the ideas of relative or absolute truth, which encyclopedists and historians often do. For his part, Edward Francis Knittel believed throughout his entire life in the existence of absolute truth and immutable history.

The Slocum Waltz

when you waltz on the decks of the

Slocum   when you dance on a   rare day in June   leave your

- 1 -

cares in a basket at home

and you'll laugh with the waves and the

foam (yes, you will!) and you'll sing and you'll dance to the fiddler's tune

and you'll

sing and you'll dance and you'll laugh like a loon, and you'll

- 2 -

whirl and you'll twirl and your skirts will all swirl Oh, your long hair will throw off its

comb and you wish you'll never go home and you

wish you'll never go home On the

- 3 -

Slo — cum, on the Slocum, on the merry ship, the
Slocum

rit -- Tempo

One, two and three, we're waltz — ing, On the

merry, on the very merry Slocum

When you

2nd verse: When you dream on the decks of the Slocum
Of the time when you first fell in love
You remember your very first kiss
and the taste and the feel of that bliss
(yes, you will!)
Oh, you'll sing and you'll dance to the fiddler's tune
Oh, you'll sing and you'll dance and you'll laugh like a loon
and you'll fly through the sky and you'll never ask why
and your heart will sing out a poem
and you wish you'll never go home
and you wish you'll never go home

-5-   (Chorus)

Yet, Edward Francis Knittel, like his companions, was content to allow the *General Slocum* to get lost on the seas and rivers of libations and laughter.

However, an incident occurred on the Eightieth Anniversary of the tragedy of the *Slocum*, which caused the emotions of Edward Francis Knittel to spill over. His single desire now was to set the record of the *Slocum* straight.

What follows is his attempt to do so.

LOG

June 15, 1984, 5:30 p.m.
80th Anniversary of The *Slocum* Disaster
McHooley's Bar and Grill
The Upper West Side, Manhattan

1

Poyfidy! Poyfidy! It's goddamned poyfidy, the corruption of the woild! the old man shouted at the top of his voice.

He pushed people aside as he hurried uptown along Broadway, rattling the fully opened *New York Times* in Manhattan's warm spring air.

Poy-fi-deeee! Step aside! Move Move! Plunkerbrote, bastard! May her skinny ass freeze to ice and shatter into a million pieces! Poyfidy! And *The Times* is in it up to their fuckin' necks! Did you see her picture on the front page? The old cunt put lipstick on! May the Lord God give her His woist case of Alzheimer's! May she choke on her dentures, that lousy, lying Margie Ann Plunkerbrote! Revisionism, that's what it is! Bring her here! Strangle her! Break her goddamn neck! Poy—fi—deeee!

Edward Francis Knittel, his tongue hanging out, panting like a dog, slammed the door of McHooley's behind him. With his quick, hobbling gait, he crossed from the bar and took his place against the wall where the bar ended its short curve. The old man beat the bar top with his heavy, gnarled, black briar cane. A drink, McHooley, a double, now! Move your ass!

James Timothy (Jimothy) McHooley smiled. He placed two brimming shot glasses before Edward Knittel. Now, you take it easy, Eddie, he said.

Knittel's voice rose. Take it easy, take it easy! You tell me to take it easy, you sonuvabitch! No one's pissing in your face!

McHooley, his smile fixed and benign, said, Just take it easy, Eddie. Have your Glenlivet, darling.

The old man, hand trembling, spilled some of the whiskey as he lifted the glass. He tossed the first drink down and wiped his beard with his large rough hand. When his thumb and forefinger pinched the second glass, his hand trembled again. He lifted it to his mouth, spilling some again, and tossed it back.

My life is saved, he said. Yer an angel of moicy, McHooley.

His close white beard was stained yellow around his lips from the crooked guinea stinkers he chewed but rarely smoked. He waggled a finger at McHoooley for another drink, took it from the bartender's hand, and threw it neatly back.

Goddamned *New York Times!* All the shit that's fit to print! Edward Francis Knittel growled.

Halfway down the bar, Joseph Cortin, his handsome, olive-toned face, weather beaten like a road company Marlboro Man said, Try the *News*, Eddie.

Shut up, you fag!

Cortin laughed.

That's not nice, Esther Lieber said, not taking her eyes away from her glass of white wine. If you don't watch that big mouth of yours, Eddie, you won't have a single friend left around here.

You can shut up too, you yenta.

Esther the yenta. Good, very good. You have such a way with words, Eddie, Cortin said and clapped his hands in slow sarcastic beats.

McHooley put another shot glass before the old man, who swallowed the whiskey quickly. Knittel looked at McHooley intently. He opened his mouth to speak but said nothing. Then lowered his head to his arms on the bar and cradled it there.

Oh, boy! He'll have a stroke! At his age can you believe the temper? Esther Lieber said, allowing her chain-attached eyeglasses to fall to her ample bosom.

You know what it is? said Vilma Rakos, exhaling a blue column of smoke from her full lipped mouth. It's another *Slocum* anniversary. That's what it is!

So what? said Cortin. He goes off like a volcano, about anything he doesn't like. He doesn't need the *Slocum*. One day there's no morality in the world, or there's no truth, the perfidy of *The New York Times*, et cetera, et cetera. (Here Cortin imitated Yul Brynner as the King of Siam.) Perfidy is everywhere. The woild is filled with poyfidy. Right, you old fart?

Edward Knittel raised his head. That's right. *The Times* lies. *The Times* stinks. I'm sorry I called you a fag, you fag.

I only object to the tone of your voice. When you call me a fag, podner, smile. I prefer "gay" myself. Esther is right, Eddie. Keep it up and you'll have a stroke. Soon, I hope.

It's the *Slocum* anniversary, isn't it? Vilma Rakos asked softly, fixing her large gray eyes on the old man. Is it the fiftieth?

Knittel snorted. The eightieth, he said.

McHooley whistled. That's a big one! Calls for another drink, lad. The bartender poured.

Eddie held the shot glass with his thick fingers. I'm already one over my sworn limit, he said. I promised God never more than two. The old man swallowed the drink.

You lied, said Milt Oster, stroking his shaved bald head. You already had four. Plus one makes five.

Let him lie. It's better than a stroke, Esther Lieber said to Oster. Turning to the old man she asked, Did *The Times* say something bad, Eddie?

It was the same shit they print every five years. Where are the peanuts, McHooley? You balancing the budget on peanuts?

Yes. On peanuts and pretzels, the bartender said, spraying himself a glass of cola. Here's to the Big Eighty and to our very ancient friend, Edward Francis Knittel. Cheers!

Here! Here! Here! the comrades of the Happy Hour said, glasses held high.

They waited for the old man to speak. But Knittel stared down at the damp bar and said nothing. The silence was interrupted only by the departure of a man and woman who had finished eating.

Mindy Lewton, the waitress, who wore a long skirt to cover her thick legs, came to the bar with the check and some money. She handed them to McHooley. Two-fifty is mine, please, she said. McHooley rang up the transaction on the old Burroughs. He handed Mindy her tip.

Edward Knittel looked up. You know what gets me, what drives me crazy?

What? Joe Cortin asked. Something we don't know? Something besides everything?

Knittel gripped his cane. His knuckles were white.

Cortin laughed. See, see! Old Vesuvius is going to blow again!

The bones in the old man's tight fingers seem to glisten beneath his skin.

Be calm, Edward, Vilma Rakos said. Just tell us what's upsetting you, okay? Calm, okay?

Knittel looked directly toward the woman who, in her early thirties, was younger than the others. He said, It's this: they always interview fucking Marjorie Ann Plunkerbrote. Every five years they ask her to remember what happened on the *Slocum.*

Why should that make you so crazy, Eddie? So they ask her. So what?

I'm not talking to you, Oster. I only talk to accountants when it's taxes. I'm talking to Ms. Rakos.

All right, Eddie, please go ahead and tell Ms. Rakos all about Margie Ann Plunkerbrote, Milton Oster said with a thin smile.

I'm listening to you, Eddie. Really, go ahead, okay? And be calm, okay?

Okay. It's this: what can she remember? She was three years old when the *Slocum* burned. I wasn't ten feet away when her mother threw her into the river. Close as I am to you. That close when the flames took over Plunkerbrote's mother! Little Skinny Ass flew away and saw nothing except maybe clouds in the sky. But it was me who saw her mother burn up! Ach! Ach! Ach!

Knittel covered his eyes with his large hand. He wept.

Would you offend God and have another short one? McHooley asked. The barkeep pushed a Glenlivet before him.

Knittel raised his head. His eyes still held the last of his tears. He knocked back the shot. It's funny in its way, he said. When they asked her thirty years ago what she remembered—Plunkerbrote had her senses then—she told *The Times* the truth. She said she didn't remember anything except for flying through the air and splashing into the river. A man in a rowboat fished her out of the water. But ain't it a miracle? Every five years she remembers more and more. Now she tells *The Times* what happened in the engine room! In the engine room! Now Margie Ann is already the Shirley Temple of the *Slocum*! Tap dancing! Tap dancing through the smoke and the ruins. Ach! A three-year-old biddy with white hair and her ass grown big as a horse!

Has it really, Eddie? I have a big bottom but you don't know about Plunkerbrote, Esther Lieber said.

A figger of speech, yenta, Knittel growled.

Well, you know, Edward, maybe you could speak to *The Times.* Tell them the truth, Vilma said.

Knittel guffawed. Tell *The Times* the truth? No one can tell *The Times* the truth! They own the truth! All they have to do is look in their own records and see how Margie Ann Plunkerbrote remembers more and more the older she gets. It's all shit! A boatload of shit! He was shouting. He slammed his black stick to the bar top.

You'll have a stroke! Esther said, shouting almost as loudly as Knittel. Straighten it out! Talk to *The Times!*

No, said Knittel, I haven't talked to those whores for fifty years and I ain't going to do it now! I won't do it! I swore to God!

Have another drink then and forget it all, Eddie! Jimothy McHooley said. There's a time to put your anger away!

Edward Francis Knittel locked his teeth and spoke through the slash in his beard. Yes, he said, that's what I want! To put it away! To sink it down in the deepest sea!

Good! said Vilma.

But I can't do it! I can't do it! I hate them! he shouted and again beat the bar top with his black briar stick.

Who? asked Cortin. Who's catching the fire and brimstone today?

Them! shouted Knittel. *The Times!* The Plunkerbrotes! You! Those who never listen! Those who always lie! And I hate you especially, you fag.

You'll have a stroke! Esther admonished. A stroke, you'll see!

You can't be angry all the time, Eddie! Vilma Rakos said quietly.

Knittel softened. You're right, I know you're right! I must give it up. No more anger! Sink the *Slocum!*

That's the spirit! said Jimothy. Sink the *Slocum* and drinks all around! You pay, Eddie.

⋄ 2 ⋄

McHooley thought peace had descended.

Eddie, in his corner, stared down at the damp wood of the old McHooley bar. Sometimes he seemed to talk to himself, his yellow-stained beard twitching. The old man mumbled, Rosy! Rosy! and McHooley asked, Did you say something, Eddie?

No, the old man said, no.

I thought I heard you say Rosy. Is it Rosy you said?

Knittel stared at McHooley. Nothing, he said.

Shall I get you some coffee?

Tea. That *Red Zinger* piss.

Mindy, McHooley called, *Red Zinger* piss for Eddie Knittel!

At their places at the bar, they whispered to each other. Milt Oster, the C.P.A. whose psoriasis had wrapped itself around his penis, was saying to Vilma Rakos that the whole thing was amusing. To which Vilma, the taxi driver, said, He's an old man. We should just let him alone.

Esther Lieber, sipping her third white wine, was asking Joe Cortin, the stage manager of an off-Broadway show, how it was going. Cortin shrugged. He told her the musical was sinking like the *Slocum*, the trouble being that the singers thought that each was God's gift to the stage when none of them was much above summer stock. When Esther hinted she'd like to see the show anyway, Cortin said he'd put aside a pair of tickets for her. She thanked him.

Knittel, his tea cup empty, said in his loud voice, I will not be angry anymore. If anybody here catches Knittel getting angry I will give him a hundred simoleons.

What's a simoleon? Esther asked.

Shhh! said Cortin as Knittel continued to speak.

Not even for a Plunkerbrote will I let my gorge come up! I will not turn red like beets. I will not have a stroke!

The four at the bar and McHooley applauded.

Knittel smiled and put up his arms like a victorious boxer. I need you to help me! he said to the Companions of the Happy Hour.

The four booed, except for McHooley, who razzed. Knittel's face darkened. His beard seemed to narrow.

We're kidding, Eddie, you know that. How can we help? Jimothy asked.

You wouldn't help a drowning man unless he paid you cash on the barrelhead, McHooley, Knittel said.

That's not nice, Vilma said. What is it with you, Edward?

I know you'd help, Vilma.

Well, so would I, Cortin said, although it depends. Give us a few particulars, Eddie.

Milt Oster said, That's right, a few particulars, Eddie. That's not unreasonable.

What I said to McHooley goes for you too, Oster.

Edward, cut the shit, Vilma said, just cut it out!

Okay, have it your way. You need our help but you think we won't give it to you, Cortin said, laughing.

Except if I pay you, is what I said.

You're a little hard in the arteries, Knittel.

And you're a fag.

"Gay", Eddie. Don't be so homophobic. You want a kiss?

Edward Knittel pulled at his beard, which widened with his smile. You're not going to get me, Joey. No, sir, Joey! You're not going to get a hundred bucks so easy.

Cortin laughed again. Okay sweetheart, what is it I have to do that will make you want to pay me?

Edward Francis Knittel became silent. Finally he said, I want you to listen to me.

Vilma Rakos walked up behind the old man and put her arms around him. Eddie, she said, we always listen to you because you're such a sweet thing.

Ach! said Knittel, I mean *listen* to me. I want to tell you the whole story, what really happened. What's in my heart, y'know.

What's he talking about? Oster asked as McHooley filled his glass with another seltzer from the bar dispenser.

It's the *Slocum*, I imagine, said McHooley. Is that it, Eddie?

You know fucking well it's the *Slocum*! I want to tell you the whole thing.

What is there to tell? Cortin asked. We know all about it. We read *The Times*.

You know shit! You know shit! Knittel screamed.

You owe me one hundred simoleons, Cortin said, with a cool, contented smile.

Knittel reached into the inside pocket of his powder-blue cotton jacket and pulled out a thick stack of bills. He slammed it on the bar. Come here, fag, and I'll give it to you, Knittel said.

Up your ass! Cortin said.

You are a total idiot, Eddie, Vilma said and returned to her stool. I don't know why we let you hang out with us.

We shouldn't, Esther said. I don't want to be here when the real explosion happens.

You're a schmuck, said Oster. Old and a schmuck!

McHooley was about to say something but didn't because Eddie Knittel had begun to weep again. McHooley turned on the radio. The Drifters singing "Save The Last Dance For Me" filled McHooley's Bar and Grill.

♪ 3 ♪

Edward Francis Knittel finally spoke. I'm sorry, he said. I lost my control. Everything is crushing in. I'll leave. I'm sorry.

You will not leave, Vilma Rakos said. You promised to tell us the story. We all want to hear it. We really do, Edward.

Also, said McHooley, you mentioned money. You can't deny that, Eddie. I'll do anything for money, y'know. As will Milton, Joseph, and Esther there. I don't know about Vilma. She only takes tips when she's driving.

Come off it, McHooley. What the fuck are you, a torturer? Vilma said. The man's hurting. I'll listen to the story, Eddie. Whatever you want to tell me.

Now there's an offer, Ms. Rakos, will give you a freebie, said Oster the accountant.

McHooley said, Speaking for myself alone, I want to be paid because the way I see it, Eddie, lad, you're a drowning man.

You're a son of a bitch, McHooley, Vilma said very softly.

He's old and he's mean, McHooley replied.

You forgot demanding, Cortin said.

I don't think we're being awfully nice, Esther said. I'm going to finish this and go home.

But I love the old darlin', Cortin said.

You're mocking me, Edward Knittel responded. I haven't cried in a hundred years and when I do it's in front of you shits!

A hundred years? said Esther. You cry every day!

A hundred years without a tear? Oster said. C'mon, Eddie, you're not that old.

Almost. I was ninety-five two weeks ago. I never cried in eighty years. Not once! Now all I'm doing is blubbering.

Well, Eddie, it's the Happy Hour, Esther Lieber said, so cry a little.

Knittel took a large white handkerchief from his back pants pocket and blew his nose into it. He took some deep breaths, exhaling with whistles. All right, McHooley, milk me a Glenlivet and I'll tell the story. But I want to pay you for listening.

It was as if Edward Knittel had not wept at all. He squinted at McHooley and said, Didn't you hear me? I want a drink. God doesn't always go around counting. He's watching the sparrows.

McHooley put the shot glass before the old man. Now you be careful, he said. I will not be carrying you home.

Eddie downed the whiskey. I would like to tell you my story. The real story, the whole story, from beginning to end.

How long will it take, Eddie? Oster asked. I have an appointment.

I don't know. I've never told the whole thing before. It's a long story. It's eighty years.

Can't stay, Eddie. I've got to be somewhere by Christmas, Oster said, laughing at his joke.

I've got to leave for the theater, Cortin said. He looked at his watch. I'm already late.

McHooley said, You can't just spring this on us, lad. I'll be here, but I must tend the bar. The beer swillers will be here later. I can't stop to listen to you all night.

I must tell my story, McHooley. I must tell it! Knittel's voice tightened and climbed.

Down, lad! Don't make trouble. Be a good boy.

Please. I have to get it out of me, McHooley. Please!

Christ, I have a business to run! I'm not a retired man yet.

Close the place, Jimmy! Close up. I'll pay you to close the place down.

Jimothy McHooley shook his head slowly.

Twenty-five hundred! Close! I'll give you twenty-five hundred!

McHooley ducked out from behind the bar and went to the door. He turned the door sign over. CLOSED in large red letters faced the street. I've taken you at your word, Eddie, McHooley said. I don't want to be losing any money now.

As McHooley returned from the door, Edward Knittel, wetting his thumb and forefinger, counted off twenty-five hundreds and gave the currency to the barkeep. McHooley smiled. Well, it was a slow night, wasn't it?

Vilma said, McHooley, this is like fucking rape. Give him back his money!

No way, lass. I've already closed the inn.

You're a prick, McHooley.

I'll not be denying it but you must add to that, my darling girl, a supporter of free enterprise.

Cortin got off his stool and turned from the bar.

Where are you going? Knittel asked anxiously.

To work, Eddie. You tell your tale to Jimothy.

A thousand, I'll pay you a thousand to listen! Stay! Joey, please?

You bought me. I'll call the theater.

You're just as bad as he is, Joey. You're taking advantage of him. I had respect for you, Joey.

I'm a snake.

Do I get paid? Esther asked.

Yes. And you too, Oster.

Well, well, well, I think I can delay my appointment until Easter, Oster said, looking at his wristwatch

Okay, that's it then. We'll all stay and listen, Vilma said with a sigh.

Thanks. I want you to have the money, too. Are you going to turn down a thousand dollars?

Let's say you'll owe it to me, Edward. Okay?

Look at it this way, Vilma, McHooley advised. Old Eddie could walk down the street and get mugged. Then the money would serve no purpose except for crack or other evils. Now tell me, Admiral, how much cash do you carry on you?

Well, it's the Anniversary. I take out five thousand every June 15th except every fifth one I take out ten.

What do you do with ten thousand dollars on your person, lad?

Tips, gifts, and emergencies, McHooley. Would you close if I wrote you a check?

All that cash! Esther said.

You got something against cash, yenta? the old man condescended through his bearded smile. Cash wins respect, y'know. I bought your big ass!

Eddie got off his stool with the stack of currency in his hand and approached each of the four. Wetting his fingers frequently, he counted out ten bills for each of them and to each of them he said, Thank you.

Oster said, You're getting a lot of respect, Eddie.

Joey Cortin turned to Vilma Rakos. Hey, Rakos, he said, you used to be Miss Hospitality and now you've become Miss Altruism.

Lay off, Vilma said brushing her thick blond hair back with her hands. Just get off my back, okay?

Hey, I can understand you're not taking Eddie's money. But if you stay, you also lose a night's pay. That's double jeopardy, babe.

What do you care? It's my business and it's my cab.

That's a lot to do for free, Vilma, Cortin added.

Nothing is for free, Joseph. I'm staying to make sure you don't take advantage of him.

No, no, Vilma. No one is taking advantage. It's a favor, they're doing me a favor. I must tell the story. It's been eating me up.

Drinks on the house, said McHooley.

If I don't call the theater, Cortin said, walking to the pay phone in the rear, the curtain won't go up.

Sink the *Slocum*! said Oster. One thousand times!

Yes, that's it! Knittel said as he returned to his stool. I'll give you the story. I'll be rid of it. It'll be your story, see. Then I'll go to God in peace.

Jesus Christ, said McHooley. If you die at my bar, Eddie, I'll never forgive you.

Knittel giggled. No, no. I feel good, James. I'm happy! I want to begin! Drinks around! Knittel pays!

The drinks dispensed, Joseph Cortin offered a toast: To God! And may the *Slocum* ply the river forever!

No! said Eddie. Tonight she takes her last excursion. Then let her sink!

And sink *The New York Times*! said Oster, raising his glass.

Yes! said Knittel.

And sink Miss Margie Ann Plunkerbrote, said Jimothy McHooley, whereever she may be!

Cortin, returning from the phone, shouted, Let's have that old Plunkerbrote cheer! The first two lines are Rah, Rah, Rah, Sissboombah. Here we go: everybody!

      RAH RAH RAH
      SISS BOOM BAH
      PLUNKERBROTE PLUNKERBROTE
      YAAAAAAAAAAAAY

Yes, yes! said Knittel. He reached out and touched his glass to McHooley's then Lieber's, Oster's, and Cortin's. Vilma, seated now on the farthest stool, did not offer her glass.

I'll go make a wee-wee, said Knittel, then I will tell you the whole thing. I'm already happy.

Well, Merry Christmas, said Miltie Oster. Bartender, take me off the seltzer and put me on the Glenlivet.

♪ 4 ♪

But Edward Francis Knittel was not happy. He was frightened.

As he had gotten older, fear burst in on him for no reason, no reason at all. It was not unlike his out breaks of weeping. One minute he was calm and steady and the next he was blubbering without control, filling the world with tears.

But he had gotten exactly what he had wanted: an audience to hear his story. Now he was not certain he wanted that and he was afraid to even begin. Fear tightened his heart. And then, he had no idea of how to begin because it was not just what had happened on the boat but everything else before and after; and what had happened to himself. The old man knew it was not the *Slocum* which was so important. It was himself. Or himself inside the *Slocum*. Not on the damned boat but twisted and tied into the thing, *into* the damned *Slocum*.

How to begin, how to begin, how to begin!

Poised over the white toilet bowl, Knittel, his penis between his fingers, waited. It took a few minutes before the urine stream emerged weakly. There was practically no color to it.

Knittel regarded the soft entry of the stream into the bowl. It isn't bad, he thought, pretty much the way it's been for years. The prostate was not bad either for a man of his age. He wondered how many men at ninety-five still got erections, had a sex life, or even thought about sex?

Knittel looked down at his cock, held lightly by two of his thick fingers. Was that the symbol of a man's life? Was that what they called manhood. If it died, would he die? He thought that was true. Dead cock, dead Knittel.

Not the common death, where strangers take the corpse away for burial or burning. The sort of dying that old plants do: a leaf, a stalk going brown while other parts remain green. Enough consciousness to be able to look from brown to green, from death to life.

Ah, Knittel thought, looking down at himself, thinking of an old joke about the one-eyed man wearing a derby who would spit in secret intimate places. You're alive and well, old boy. Still got that old git up and go!

The urine ceased to flow but Knittel did not shake off the drop which quivered at the end of his penis. He knew there was more to come. He waited.

Was he doing the right thing? Telling them the story? Paying them for listening, not being sure that they'd listen anyhow. Money would buy only the first minutes of their attention. He knew that. He could imagine their eyelids drooping after a time. Then he would be talking to himself, as he did more and more often now. Sometimes out loud, too. He could not be sure that even Vilma Rakos would listen to the whole story. He smiled when he thought of her. Protective of him, she was. He liked that. He didn't need her protectiveness but he liked it. She had a good soul.

Sometimes he thought he would like to have sex with her but his feelings toward her were fatherly. He wished he had had children. But that could only have happened with Rosy; only with Rosy.

He thought, I can always start off with: It happened on June 15, 1904. No one can object to that: It happened on June 15, 1904. Or: I was fifteen years old and I worked as a plumber's apprentice.

Maybe there was a better way to start. A way that would make them all lean forward and forget to drink.

The urine flowed again. He shook the last clinging drops into McHooley's toilet bowl. It was a clean men's room. Fresh odor. Well, it was early in the evening. He washed his hands, dried them on the brown paper sheet cranked out of an enameled dispenser.

He had to make it interesting for them, exciting. Especially for Cortin. The fag was a real wise guy and could kill you with a laugh line. He had a better chance with the others, he thought.

They all knew the *Slocum* was real. They understood the disaster had occurred. That was the most important thing. But that was long ago and did it matter now?

Edward Knittel became extremely anxious. He wiped the light sweat from his forehead. He breathed deeply. He had never told the entire story before. Never! Not in the eighty years which had passed, passed in a dream inside a dream. And how do you tell such a story anyway? A story nobody had been able to tell. Not those who survived, not all the newspapers in the whole world.

You sit down on the stool and you begin, that's it, you begin: Once upon a time...

The most important thing, Edward Francis Knittel reasoned, was not to lose his temper. To be pleasant, to keep his voice soft, mellow, even when Cortin swiped at him, which the fag would certainly do. He felt his anger prickle over the burn scars on his arms.

The old man closed his eyes to calm himself. He thought of his childhood, Sundays at St. Mark's Lutheran, listening to Pastor Haas preach. He recalled the odor of the church and the light echoing of the sermon.

His temper, the old man knew, rested on his anger. His anger was the deeper thing. In a way it was the anger, the flame, which kept him together and alive. He knew this without understanding it. Anger was in him, part of him, like his kidneys or his balls. There, and not to be done without.

When it came to the *Slocum* and to Margie Ann Plunkerbrote it was anger alone that allowed him his sanity and survival. Anger which allowed him to overcome betrayal, tragedy, and, most of all, the love denied him, wrenched from his blistered hands.

Yet he wanted to get rid of it because the anger was becoming poisonous bile. Survival and sanity were now being overrun by poison.

This thought troubled Edward Knittel. It went two ways at once and he had no control over it. He needed his anger to survive; he needed to get rid of the anger because it was poisoning him. He trembled. If he told the whole story, told it as he knew it, would that kill the anger? And, if the anger in him was killed, would he die?

I don't have to go ahead with it. Let them keep the money, have a good time. Fuck it!

Yet, he knew he could not back out. He could make it brief, get it over with. Ach! he said. I'll just open my mouth and see what comes out.

He flushed the toilet, sighed, forced a smile through his beard and walked briskly back to his place at the bar.

♪ 5 ♪

The old man sighed. He looked from face to face. It's such an old business, he said, I thought I would open my mouth and the story would speak itself. But instead it's a dream which comes back, a dream I've dreamed a thousand times.

Knittel stroked his beard. When he spoke his voice was caught in the palm of his hand, which covered his mouth.

I can't hear you, said Oster.

Knittel removed his hand from his mouth and looked down at it as if it were a foreign object.

Then he began again. He shifted his buttocks on the stool, cleared his throat, and spoke. It's the dream of a white, white seagull in a blue, blue sky, he said.

Louder, please. I'm right next to you and I can't hear you! Esther Lieber said.

Circling. Crying, y'know, the way seagulls cry. I'm in the river floating on my back. Looking up, y'know. I'm sloshing on the lift and the fall, y'know. Up and down. Up and down. I'm between life and death but I'm not feeling pain. Sometimes I see my left arm. Sometimes my right. Burned. Badly burned. I feel the flesh pulling away from the bones. My left leg is twisted. The bone has come through the pants leg. But I feel no pain. It's like it ain't my body. My eyes open. My eyes close. I see the seagull. It's like a thousand miles up. It circles. I drift. The bird follows me. Between life and death, y'know, between life and death. I think, I feel, if the seagull goes away I will die.

Jaizus! said McHooley.

I'm sloshing on the water. Up and down. Up and down. When the river lifts me up I touch the sunlight. Then the gull seems so big, y'know? Then down. Miles down, deep, cold, like I'm touching death. Life is up. Death is down. The bird gets small. Now it's not white. It's black. My head feels like my brain is falling out through my nose. No pain—dreams are so amazing--no pain! Life is nice. Death is nice. My eyes roll away into my head where everything is pink, soft, heavy pink. The dream ends.

Knittel breathed deeply. The black plastic clock nestled among the back bar brandy bottles ticked. The Happy Hour people waited for Knittel to continue.

Finally he said, Now I'm on the beach of North Brother Island. They had a hospital there for contagious diseases. We used to call it Leper Island.

No pain. That was the important thing, no pain. I can't move. I'm on my back. The seagull is still up there, y'know. The sun is shining down. I'm in bad shape. I know it. The sunshine is burning my arms. Pain, all of a sudden, is coming into me.

Doctors from Leper Island and nurses are running around. I see pieces of white pants, white stocking. Voices. Like insects, crickets maybe.

The first thing I hear clearly is this man's voice. It says, She's dead. Put her in that pile.

You know how it is when you lie on a beach in the summer? You hear the sea sounds and pieces of voices. And in the middle of that, whole sentences, y'know?

Give me the syringe, Miss Oliphant. A doctor is talking.

How many were on the boat?

Millions. Look, the river is filled with bodies.

Shall we put the babies in a separate pile?

Doctor Littleman—isn't he on duty today?

A woman's voice is asking, Am I blind? I can't see. Help me, please.

A child's voice: Mama! (Knittel imitated the cry of the child.)

I can't work if you don't get them out of the way!

Doing the best I can, Doc. There's only a half of this old guy. Where do I put that?

Mama! Knittel imitated a child's cry again.

Esther Lieber stuffed a paper napkin between her lips.

This one's gone, Oliphant. That one?

Still alive, Doctor. He's moaning.

Not for long. Have you got a full syringe? Let him die in peace.

They stick the needle into me. I feel nothing again. Opium, it is a blessed thing. I'm lying on the sand and feeling good. The dead are all around me and I'm singing:

Oh, the boy stood on the burning deck,
His feet are full of blisters,
He caught his pants upon a nail
And now he wears his sister's.

Jaizus, said McHoolley.

⚘ 6 ⚘

It gets mixed up, y'know: what is the dream and what ain't? But I think most of it was real.

You got a little poetry into it, Eddie, Oster said.

Dreams are like that, Miltie. And the colors are very bright. Here's something else: my eyelashes felt thick and heavy. The sun made the hairs like little jail bars. This is important: through the bars I can see most of a man. He's got a seersucker suit and wide hips. He's splashed all over with sunlight. He's like an angel. His voice is very high, like a girl's.

Homophobia, Eddie, Cortin said.

The man, the angel, says, I'm Melvin Honeycuitt of *The New York Times.*

A real guy from *The Times* is in the dream and he's an angel? C'mon!

Cut it out, Esther, Vilma said softly, let him tell it.

Eddie nodded toward Vilma and continued. He squats down next to me and pushes his flat straw hat up from his pink face. A doctor and a nurse are working over me.

Is he alive? Who is he? Honeycuitt asks the doctor.

The doctor says, I don't know. Go away.

What is he singing? Honeycuitt asks.

That's crazy! Esther Lieber said. What a dumb question!

I *was* singing, yenta. Don't interrupt me!

Yes, Oster said, you got your pay, now hear the man.

I'll answer her, said Edward Knittel. *The Times* can ask anything it wants.

But what he's singing ain't so important, Eddie, Esther said.

If *The Times* asks, it's important. Don't you understand that, yenta?

No, I don't!

Oh, shut up, Esther, Cortin said. Let Eddie get his money's worth!

Thanks, fag!

Up yours, Eddie!

After a silence, McHooley said, Get on with it, Edward! It's damned interesting.

Edward Knittel rubbed his beard but remained silent.

Vilma Rakos said, Please, continue. Edward, don't sulk.

Knittel looked at Vilma and said, All right. I want to. I'm sorry if I was sharp with you, Joey.

I'll give you a kiss, said Cortin.

The others laughed. Knittel continued. So, Honeycuitt said, What's he singing? The nurse says, The boy is out of his senses! Go away!

Honeycuitt stands up and yells, Does anybody know this boy? Right away I know the voice that answers. It's a neighbor in my house on 9th Street. It's Bruni Neumann.

Gott, she says, that's Edward Knittel!

Honeycuitt asks for her to spell her name. And my name. I can see half of him writing it down on a piece of paper.

Bruni is standing over me now. Her dress is a pattern of big white and pink flowers. I can see all the way up to her bosom. Her garters. Her corset. She says to Honeycuitt, I am a friend of the family's. Oh, Edward! Look at him! Look at him! He was the one who climbed up the pole to save us all! Oh, poor Edward!

Are you sure he was the one on the mast, Honeycuitt wants to know.

Sure. It was Edward. I wasn't far and my eyes are sharp, she says to Honeycuitt.

Another voice says, Yes. That's him, all right. The same kid who swam right onto the beach with the two infants on a piece of wood!

It's some kind of hospital worker who says that. I can see all of him because he's crouched over, dragging a body on the ground, an old woman. Her dead hand brushes against my broken leg. Even with the opium, it hurts like hell.

Honeycuitt is writing all this down very fast on his folded piece of paper. He squats down by me again. His face looks red now. He's sweating.

You're going to be all right, kiddo! he says.

I can hear Bruni Neumann weeping. She says, A hero, a hero! Doing such things for us, not even thinking of his own life! A hero! God spare him!

The doctor says, I'll have to straighten out his leg.

The nurse holds my head still. The doctor pulls my leg straight. I scream. A scream that chases seagulls out of the sky!

And Honeycuitt, he sits down on the ground with a plop. Oh, sweet Jesus, he says and turns away. I can hear him throw up.

They give me another needle. It's like I'm going up and down on the water again. Like black seagulls come down and crowd into my eyes.

7

They all looked toward Knittel, waiting for him to continue, but the old man was looking vacantly up at the ceiling. He scratched his beard.

Cortin said, Don't fall asleep now, Eddie. It's getting good!

Are you tired? Vilma asked.

Knittel shook his head slowly. Nah, he said, all the memories! Ach, ach! What did I say when I shut up?

On the beach, said McHooley, black seagulls flew into your eyes.

Yes. You know why I stopped? I was thinking: How did I get off the island? Damn, I don't know till this minute how I got off Leper Island.

You passed out. You were taken off the island. That doesn't seem to be very important, Edward, Rakos said.

Vilma, listen to me: it's very important. It was things like that that they used against me!

Who did that? asked Esther.

What things? asked Oster.

Everybody. Honeycuitt. Bruni. Helga. Wolf. Everybody around me. Confusion, y'know. If I said anything they didn't want to hear they'd say I was confused. Confused because of the skull fracture, the pain, the drugs, the shock. I was not confused! Knittel shouted, slapping the wet bar with his big hand.

There you go, Eddie! If you don't get a stroke you'll get a heart attack.

Oh, shut up, yenta!

I was joking, Eddie! You get so agitated!

Okay. Why was it so important? Oster asked.

Because anything I forgot, anything I didn't know, they used it to kill what it was I did know. They said I climbed up the pole to signal for help. I swear to you right now I never climbed up the that pole, never! They said I saved those infants. I didn't save any infants. They say I was running all over the *Slocum*, through the flames, helping the women and children. I didn't, I didn't! So if I said, Hey, please, I didn't do it!, they said, you're confused, it disappeared from your mind. You know why?

McHooley said, Why, Edward?

Because they needed a hero. They needed a fucking hero to prove how good they were. That there was some good that came out of the disaster. Out of evil comes good. The plan of God, y'know.

I'm beginning to like this a lot, Oster said.

Well, then return his money, Vilma said.

I didn't say I liked it that much! But did you notice there was a philosophical turn there, Vilma? The invention of the hero. The creation of God's design. Out of Evil comes Good.

Cortin clapped Oster on the back. The accountant philosopher speaks!

Fuck you!

I'm putting you back on seltzer, Oster, McHooley admonished. All right, Eddie, my lad, continue spinning your yarn.

Knittel said, I never could remember how I got off the beach there. So it proved to them I could blank out, see? When I didn't remember something it was my Achilles heel. I woke up in Lebanon Hospital in the Bronx and I didn't know how I got there.

I'm looking up at the ceiling. It's a tin ceiling with a design stamped onto it. It's green. But where did it come from? Where is the sky? The seagulls? The voices? The smell of the river? When I look down I can see my leg, in a cast up to my ass. It's held off the bed in what they call a "cradle", a canvas sling. My arms are also in these slings, in loose bandages, loose but thick, in layers, y'know. I can smell medicine all around.

And my head! Like a mummy, I was! The nose sticking out! The eyes not covered. All of this sinks in slowly and I think, oh, boy, you got it good!

I hear the doctor and the nurse talking. The doctor says, Keep him comfortable. If he has pain give him more laudanum.

Not heroin? the nurse asks.

Alternate them. Just keep him comfortable. Be careful of his arms. Drip on the solution. Keep the bandages moist. Keep the cotton batting loose and the top gauze, too. Most important—no pain. I don't want him squirming.

Will he be all right? the nurse wants to know.

He'll live. We won't have to amputate his arms. Scars will be thick. The leg will be shorter.

Poor boy. He's the one they say is the hero.

They say.

He's a good-looking fellow.

Don't get any ideas, the doctor says, and laughs. And don't let that reporter in.

He's from *The Times*. He came with the boy. He was in the ambulance.

Only family, please. And not before seven o'clock.

Then they leave and I'm lying there counting the flowers on the ceiling. The only pain I feel is Rosy, my girl, my love.

The old man fell into another silence. He stared ahead, past McHooley. He didn't move. The others, after a while, fidgeted.

I warned him about dying, McHooley said.

Don't worry, said Esther Lieber, you see he's blinking. His mind wandered.

You people are so unbright! Vilma said. Rosy was the love of his life.

How do you know that? Maybe Rosy was a sled.

Joseph! Haven't you ever been in love?

A hundred times till the plague came, Cortin said, getting up suddenly. He left the bar and walked to the rear, where the rest rooms were.

Vilma got off her stool and came to the old man. Are you all right?

McHooley called out, Mindy! Bring us a plate of chicken wings.

In the silence, the door to the kitchen squeaked on its hinges.

Cortin returned. He glanced at the faces at the bar. Aha! he said. You were waiting for me! Let the saga continue! Speak, Eddie, or I'll drop a quarter into the juke box.

The old man's beard twitched on his buried smile. Yes, he said, where was I?

In the hospital, Oster said.

Did I say it was Lebanon in the Bronx?

Yes, you did, Eddie, Esther said. Go on.

Did I say they put me in a private room?

You were a celebrity, Oster said, his sarcasm resting on his smile.

Milton, stop it! Vilma said with patient annoyance. Please, continue, Eddie.

Well, I have no pain. The first groan out of my mouth, in goes the heroin or the laudanum. So I'm sailing away. It's like that until my father comes. My father, Tammuz Hans Knittel.

The old man rubbed his beard and took a deep breath. That was something to remember, believe me.

I'm peeping out of my bandages. I hear this deep breathing. I move my eyes. I see he's standing there in his work clothes looking down on me. His big hands, bigger than mine, hang down by his sides like hooks. My father's hands always scared the shit out of me. They were made in the foundry where he worked. Big. Hard. Asbestos. My throat chokes. I can't get out a word, a sound. Maybe ten minutes he's standing there, looking down on me.

Finally my father says, Where is your mother?

The old man touched his throat below his chin where his beard was especially white and soft.

My father says again in his deep voice, Where is your mother? The sisters? The brother?

I let out a scream. Dead, Papa. Dead. All dead. They burned up in the fire.

My father, quiet, five more minutes, says, And you're alive? What did you do to help them?

I couldn't do anything, Papa. What could I do?

You could have died with the rest!

I'm sobbing, Papa, I swear to you I couldn't help them. The fire came on like waves, Papa!

He puts his hands together and raises them above his leather cap. I think for a second he's going to pray, although he was an atheist. But then his fingers lace themselves into a knot and his arms come down like an axe and smash my face. It's funny. I'm so doped up I can't feel a thing.

I scream not because of the pain. But because I know my father is going to kill me. The whole hospital comes running. Doctors, nurses, orderlies. They jump on top of Tammuz and drag him to the floor.

He is bellowing like a bull: Where is your mother? Where is your mother? WHERE IS YOUR MOTHER?

And Melvin Honeycuitt is standing there in the madhouse, scribbling on his folded sheet of paper. The bandage on my head is off. My nose is spilling blood all over. My leg in the cast hangs off the bed.

They stuck my father in the neck with a needle. They drag him away. Then they look after me. Honeycuitt asks the doctor, Is it bad?

Oh, he's not in any real danger. A bloody nose never killed anybody. What this boy has endured, nothing will kill him. He'll live forever.

In the newspapers they write: "Grief-Maddened Father Attacks Hero Son", "Father Beats Hero Son in Hospital". "Hero's Father Confined to Madhouse"

Honeycuitt didn't write about my father in *The Times*. He wrote a story about how I was taken from North Brother Island by boat to the hospital. He went over all my wounds, describing each one, and reporting that the prognosis was good. The headline says: "Slocum Hero Receiving Excellent Care. Will Survive".

Give me a drink, Joe Cortin said.

After I have a wee one myself, said McHooley. I suppose you're paying, Joseph.

Eddie Knittel said, This is my party. I pay.

And all the time, McHooley said, I thought that flat nose of yours was the result of youthful fisticuffs.

Knittel rubbed his large flattened nose with his forefinger. My father's gift to me. Whenever I touch it Tammuz springs up into my mind. He was a powerful man.

Nothing wants to be simple, Edward Knittel said. They were fixing it so I had to be the hero. They were framing me. They were forcing me to keep my trap shut. Now they had two more things on me: my father was a loony and they put him in the loony bin. If I keep on saying I didn't climb the pole, I didn't save the infants, maybe they'd say I'm crazy like my father, y'know. I'm trapped, I'm trapped, I gotta be a hero. No way out. It's easier to be a hero than to be locked up or filled with shame. My father filled me with shame.

I'm fifteen! I'm hurt! I'm scared. I don't want to be put in the nut house with my father. He'd kill me in a minute, y'know.

Even so, what's so terrible being the hero? asked Oster.

Nothing. Except it's a lie. Not even my lie, Oster. I had to live their lie, and that ain't easy. After Tammuz tried to beat me to death, I was glad they gave me a needle. For almost a whole day I was out of the world.

The hero slept, said Oster.

I slept, all right, and when I awoke I was more than ever the hero. In a million newspapers, in a thousand magazines, in a hundred different languages, all over the world I was Edward Francis Knittel: Hero in Flames.

At the top of his lungs Knittel sang:
>   The boy stood on the burning deck,
>   His feet were filled with blisters....

⸜ 8 ⸝

Knittel seemed to have lost his thought. He chewed a fresh cigar.

Where was I?

In the hospital unconscious, bloody, and dressed like Boris Karloff. Tell me, who paid the bills?

Knittel snorted. Who paid the bills? That's a good one, Joey! Who paid the bills? I was in the Lebanon there, not too long, but you're right. Somebody paid.

Oster stroked his glistening shaved head. Nobody paid, he said, it was on the house, a hero perk.

Knittel laughed. In those days there were perks all right, more than today. You couldn't count them. Letters came from all over, from every state in the Union and foreign countries, too. A sack or more a day, the letters came. Checks and cash. Checks from the rich. Cash from the poor. Almost nine thousand dollars for the Hero of the Slocum Disaster. A lot of moola in them days, right, Miltie? At bank rates what would that be right now?

Off the top of my shiny head, I'd guess in the millions. Sonuvabitch, you'd be a rich man on that alone, Eddie.

Knittel laughed softly. I'm a lot richer than that, though, he said. Melvin Honeycuitt took care of the money. He opened an account for me in the Corn Exchange Bank on Tenth Street and Avenue D. He also made what he called prudent investments. For me Melvin was alway prudent and proper. He read me lots of the letters that came to me. He got people at *The Times* to write thank-you notes in my name. Almost every day he and my Aunt Helga came to visit. Wolf, my uncle, Helga's husband, he came once or twice. He had to work. He was a master plumber, y'know.

That's where the money is, Oster said.

And I got flowers too. Flowers and plants. The room was so filled they had to put them in the hall. The nurse took bunches out of the room because they were sucking up all the oxygen.

I never heard of a guy getting killed by a gladiola, Esther Lieber said.

Knittel looked toward her. Ay, yenta, yenta! he said. One plant with red and yellow tulips came from Nellie Melba with a card saying she'd sing a private concert for me when I got better.

Did she do that? Cortin asked.

Knittel scratched his beard. Nah, he said. I appreciated the sentiment anyway. Lots of big shots say things but don't do them, y'know. Tell you the truth, I don't care for opera music.

I hope you saved the card, Cortin said. I'll buy it. Give you a profit on it.

Nah, I had it in a pile somewhere. There were thousands. Stacks of them. But I got drunk on the Fiftieth Anniversary and angry, smoke was coming out of my ears. I burned them. Letters, telegrams from famous people, all that shit. Set my place on fire, too. The fire engines came. It was in the papers.

Now, said McHooley, I'm not going to ask you what you were angry about, Eddie, but didn't you see it was a dumb thing to do, burning up letters from celebrities? Dumb!

That's true, McHooley. It was dumb, all right. James J. Jefferies, the heavy weight champ, y'know, he sent me a set of boxing gloves, with his name on each one written on it and a letter. "You are the true champion of the world. Your pal, James J. Jefferies." I burned up the gloves, too. I wish I hadn't done that. That was the worst.

I was wrong, Eddie, you'll never get a stroke—you'll become an arsonist. I'll bet you burned up the letter you got from God, Esther said.

You didn't! Oster said.

No, but the one from Roosevelt went up.

Oster said, You're talking about Theodore, I presume?

"I'm proud to be your fellow American. You inspire us all."

Verbatim?

Yes. That one. There were so many.

Drop a name, Cortin said.

Irving Berlin. George M. Cohan. Thomas Edison, George of England.

We're talking kings here, Cortin said.

Can't say I care for that one, McHooley said, would you have another?

Kaiser Wilhelm, on very heavy paper with a wax seal at the bottom. It was written in German, naturally. Helga translated it. "I grieve with you for the innocent German women and children who lost their lives in the flames of the *Slocum.* I praise you for your courage."

Well, said Cortin, I know from fan mail—that's fan mail!

Eddie, you must kick yourself in the ass when you think you could have saved all that. Real treasures! Vilma Rakos said. Tell me, you don't regret it?

I don't regret it. I'm not fooling. That was 1954. In '54 maybe a hundred-fifty survivors were still around. I wasn't the hero anymore, thank God. Everybody was already a long time dead. My family, Honeycuitt, my wives, everybody, dead, gone.

I didn't know you were ever married.

I don't tell you every thing, yenta. And don't anybody ask me any questions about my wives. They had nothing to do with the *Slocum*. They had nothing to do with me, either.

And Rosy?

Shut up, McHooley, Vilma said sharply.

Knittel, hard eyed, ignored McHooley. He spread the collar of his pale-yellow shirt. A tarnished necklace of Indian head pennies hung around his neck. From a little girl, Knittel said, June Kaslow was her name. When I got it every penny was new and shiny. In her letter she said I would be all right. "I love you, Edward. Junie." Eighty years it was lying in my drawer with my socks. I just put it on today. If it had been from Rosy it would have been around my neck every day of my life and shining all the time. I have nothing from Rosy, nothing.

Knittel covered his eyes with his big hand.

The kitchen door swung open and Bo Wang stood in the frame with a cleaver in his hand. What happenin'? No business. Is Yom Kippur?

We're closed, Bo. You can go home if you like.

Need the pay, McHooley.

Right you are, Mr. Wang. You'll be paid.

Bankrupt, boss?

No, Bo. Plenty of money. You can have the night off.

No, no, said Bo Wang, somebody want more chicken wing or steak-ah-power? Bo fix. Work ethic. No work, no pay.

Give that man a raise, McHooley! Cortin said as the kitchen door closed behind the cook.

Wee-wee, said Edward Knittel, getting off his stool and walking toward the toilets.

In the porcelain confines of the men's room, Eddie Knittel breathed deeply and leaned against the white-tiled wall. He had no need to urinate, only the need to escape for a moment. He smiled. I have their attention now, he thought. He watched the sweep hand of his wristwatch go round three times before emerging. Let them wait, he thought, whet their appetite.

♪ 9 ♪

His back straight and stiff the old man with his hobble marched from the toilet toward the bar. Brrrooom! Brrrooom! Brrrooom! Knittel barked as he beat the imaginary drum which hung from his neck.

What the hell are you doing? Cortin wanted to know.

Drumming, you fool, I'm drumming!

Oh, said Cortin, drumming.

Daft! said McHooley.

Well, I told you, said Esther Lieber. What have I been saying, huh?

Cut it out, Vilma said. He's all right. You okay, Eddie?

Brrrooom! Brrrooom! Brrrooombrrrooombrrrooom! Eddie said as he marched in a circle around the empty tables of the dining section. Sure, I'm okay! he said, I'm feeling good! While I was making my wee wee my Aunt Helga's story about the first funeral came back to me. The great funeral for the one hundred fifty-six Unidentified Dead, y'know.

Eddie Knittel hobbled and brrrooomed his way back to the bar. Helga did that brrrooom business when she told me what had happened that day, that day of the funeral out in Queens. Honeycuitt and Helga had gone to the funeral. My Uncle Wolf couldn't go because he was working over on Fifth Avenue. My aunt and Honeycuitt wouldn't get to see me until after the burying. So it was me and the ceiling and the bedpan, y'know. Nothing to do but think, which was a good thing. It gave me a chance to put together the picture, to prove to myself that I was not so confused and that my memory was not drowned in the river.

He didn't mean any harm but Honeycuitt didn't always believe me. Like he'd say, "Just a few questions about those infants."

I was floating on my back, sloshing. Ach! I didn't even see the infants. I saw my bone and my burnt arms and the white seagulls. I didn't save them. I didn't try. You know what it was? The board with the dead infants got washed against my head and me and the board floated in together.

So I tell this to Honeycuitt and he wipes his glasses with his skinny necktie. He smiles and says, Edward, there were *hundreds* of eyewitnesses who saw what you did. You probably don't remember because of the shock you endured, the awful events that erased your memory. Alienists accept that as a fundamental truth. But you must believe me, Edward, there is no doubt about what happened. You swam with one hand holding the board on which the infants lay and you stroked with the other. Only when you had placed the babes safely on the shore did you pass out.

What shit that was! Eyewitness and all that. I never even saw these innocent babes and I told Honeycuitt so. What does he do? He gets up from his chair near my bed and keeps on cleaning his glasses for a long time. He says to me, We'll talk about it another time when you have the strength to think clearly.

I'm lying there in bandages and casts and I'm working up an explosion you wouldn't believe!

I believe it, Esther Lieber said. You were frustrated because you couldn't get out of bed and sock him!

I controlled myself until he went home. Then I let out a yell. You know what I said?

What? said Esther.

You're a sonuvabitch and a bastard, Mr. Honey*cunt!*

That's no way for a hero to talk, Edward, Oster said.

Knittel held up his arms like a victorious athlete, smiled, and said, I'm telling the truth, y'know. I could have killed him but I liked Mr. Honeycuitt from *The New York Times.* I wanted him to believe me, that's all.

Knittel sucked up the whiskey left at the bottoms of the shot glasses which clustered before him.

I want to tell you what happened after the funeral for the Unidentified Dead. Knittel stared vacantly past McHooley. The old man drummed the bar top with his long, thick fingers. Brrrooom. Brrrooom. Brrrooom.

We're listening, Mr. Knittel, McHooley said.

Knittel reached over and took Cortin's drink. He swallowed it.

It's past eight o'clock, after visiting hours, when they let in Aunt Helga and Melvin Honeycuitt. They're like a couple of damp dishrags. There are no legs under them at all, y'know. They don't say hello, how are you, or anything. They just sit until Helga talks.

Over a hundred degrees, she says, and the air wet as a bathtub. Look at me! Und I smell like your Uncle Wolf when he comes home from work. Phew!

Oh, Edward, it's a day I never want to see again, but how will I ever forget it? I will tell the story all in a row and if I miss a part, Mr. Honeycuitt will fill it in. Most of the time we were together, no?

Let me confess to you, Edward, when it happened, the tragedy, I was shocked like everybody. Jah, I cried like the whole world but I could not let myself give in to the grief in my heart. Your mother and the children, no one knows, ashes maybe, but for sure not identified. You in the hospital, Edward, and your poor father taken away to the madhouse because of God's grief upon him! I went to see him there but they sent me home. I did busy things to keep the tragedy from eating me up. You understand what I'm saying, Edward? So this morning when I go out of the house, what do I see? Gott! Gott! Gott!

Helga sobs. Her body shakes. To calm her, Melvin Honeycuitt puts his arm around her shoulder and she leans her head on his seersucker chest. It's a good cry and when she finishes, she goes right on with her story. Helga was like that: she could cry her eyes out then stop in the middle of a yowl and say, I forgot to buy the meat for the roast.

When Mindy breaks into tears, said McHooley, there's nothing to be done but send her home. Mindy, where are you? The wings are getting low.

As I walked out on Ninth Street, Helga says, as I walked past Brumer's saloon on the corner, you know where it is, Edward? Black ribbons, flowers, and wreathes were hanging on every door. On so many doors the names of the dead were written. On the door of the Schwimmers, all seven names I knew. Gott! And messages! *We mourn our family. We mourn our Gretel and Hans. We mourn our mother and grandmother.* Every door! In windows, also, German and American flags hanging in the middle—

Half-mast, Honeycuitt says in a low voice.

Yes, that's it! Half-mast. When I got to Avenue A it was the same. Wreathes and ribbons, white ones for babies, and messages to break your heart.

If anything, says Honeycuitt, Avenue A was worse than the other streets. There was the funeral parlor, Braun's Funeral Parlor.

In front of Braun's on the sidewalk there was the coffins, Helga continues, one on top of the other. As high to my shoulder, Edward. My skin ran up and down with cold. I could not walk a step in front of me. From the inside the funeral parlor two men carried out another casket. They said, One, two, three and swung it up to the top of the pile. By the arm muscles and back muscles you could see it was not an empty box. Ach, it frightened me so! Was the world ending? Were they burying the world?

Then Helga begins to speak German until I say, In English, Aunt Helga, in English.

She looks at Honeycuitt and blushes. Excuse me, please. I didn't mean to be rude. My English is still stiff yet.

Your English is very good. Please continue, Honeycuitt says.

A man came out of the funeral parlor, white like a sheet. Mr. Braun was holding him up by the elbow and he's saying, I'm sorry. Anything to help I'd do, but I have no caskets left. I have some on order from Yonkers and New Haven. Maybe I'll get them in a few days but I don't know. The highest bidder. There's a chance I'll get a few from Philadelphia. The man cried, but it's for my daughter, Mathilda. She's lying in the morgue. Mr. Braun, you knew her, my daughter, Mathilda...

And that man was lucky, says Honeycuitt, because most of the dead are lying under canvas covers on the piers or in horses' stalls—the horses are tied to the lampposts outside. Would you believe, in a city like New York, the morgues are full and there are no coffins to be had? Not a hearse unspoken for! And, Edward, the price of black crepe ribbon has increased ten fold if it is to be had at all. Everyone in New York wants to join in the mourning with a little piece of ribbon or an armband.

Honeycuitt lights another Fatima Turkish and I think if I ever went to smoking I would smoke those, Knittel said. Fatimas had class—ivory tips and oval shapes, y'know.

Honeycuitt blows the tobacco smoke up toward the ceiling and saiys, Holden Waner, the alderman from the infamous sixteenth district, was run down by a motor car on Madison Avenue and 20th Street. Instantly killed. There was no room for another body at the Bellevue morgue not at the funeral homes, either. So his bloody corpse was delivered to the flat of his daughter. They had to put the Alderman in a packing crate with the name of a fish market on it and rush it over to New Jersey for burial in the cemetery where his parents are buried. The dead ain't got no political clout, y'know. Good thing Mr. Waner was not very much liked. You're lucky to be in the hospital and spared the sight of all of these dreadful things.

I'm wondering why Honeycuitt thinks I'd be interested in this Waner. I don't find it sad when a politician is killed. And Helga isn't listening to Melvin Honeycuitt anyway. She's just waiting to go on with what she was saying.

Ach, Edward, when I could find the strength to walk again I went into the middle of the street so I wouldn't see anymore caskets or wreaths or ribbons. Others walked in the middle of Avenue A, eyes straight ahead like soldiers. When I got to 6th Street I turned in toward St. Mark's church. Before me all of a sudden, like an ocean, the people appeared und a sound came from them like a moan. Thousands, thousands!

How could I get through, Edward, to pray for the dead, the unknown dead? But, no matter what, my mind was made up to be inside St. Mark's with our dead family und all the other souls from the neighborhood. I walked into the crowd saying, Excuse me, Excuse me, all the time.

Like an ocean, yes, but packed und hot, Edward. I pushed und pushed. The people were standing there, quiet, not crying or praying. They are not church members, of this I am sure. There are Italians und Jews und some coloreds, too, all come to stand there. I said more Excuse Me's and pushed step by step toward the church. Already I'm feeling dizzy so I close my eyes and push my steps. I don't open my eyes until I bump the head of a horse with a black feather, his mouth covered with slobber. He made that funny sound horses make sometimes und he raised his feet in the air. I fainted.

When I came awake I'm inside the vestry of St. Mark's. Two men look down on me. One rubs my hand. The other is putting smelling salts under my nose. The one with the smelling salts I could see right away is Mr. Honeycuitt. The other one is a man with a long red beard, on his head the little black cap Jews wear. Ach, ach, first I think I am dead und put in hell but how could it be? What would Mr. Honeycuitt from *The Times* be doing in hell? Also, was I such a big sinner?

Honeycuitt glances at Helga and smiles. I was doing the story for my paper about the first burials, Honeycuitt says to me. The Unidentified Dead. I happened to be in the crowd when I saw Helga faint.

Where it is you got the cold water to make a handkerchief compress for my neck, I can't imagine, but soon I am myself again. I looked down from the vestry window at the crowd. The police are holding the people to one side of the street und on this side, the side by the church, stand the horses with the hearses. The horses on their heads, all black, had black, black— is there a word, Mr. Honeycuitt?

Plumes, smiles Honeycuitt as he picks up Helga's story. The horses, he says, pawed the cobblestones and struck up sprays of sparks which you could see in the shadow cast by the church. They sparked and snorted as if they were anxious to get on to the cemetery.

Helga turns to Honeycuitt. How many hearses are standing? Fifty?

Honeycuitt smiles, Actually, one hundred fourteen for the one hundred fifty-six unrecognizable bodies. The small white caskets were for infants, of course. They were put on top of the others. The intention of the ecumenical committee of clergymen was to have a hearse for each body. They didn't want to show disrespect for the dead even if they were not identifiable. But there were simply not enough hearses and they considered themselves fortunate to have been able to acquire the number of caskets they did have. There was a waiting cortege with flower filled *barouches* in the line of hearses, which extended east up 6th Street and then along Avenue B. I don't know for how many blocks.

Helga puts a finger into the air and says, Flowers covered the hearses. Heavy with flowers they were, Edward, like it was a day in May in Bavaria! Ach!

Details are important, Honeycuitt says. When I write my story tonight I'm going to describe the bees and the yellow jackets diving into the thick masses of flowers. And the acts of nature the horses performed while they waited, if I can find appropriate words for you-know-what, Honeycuitt says with a high, polite laugh. Girlish.

Finally, word came, Helga says, in five minutes the hearses will start out for the Lutheran Cemetery in Middle Village in the Queens Borough. Also, word came Pastor Haas would go to the cemetery. Go there out of his bed with his burns und wounds. His wife dead, his daughter dead, lost among the unknown.

Tears traced down my aunt Helga's cheeks. Oh, Edward, just the same as your mother, your brother, und sisters! It was only a picnic, Edward! It was only for happiness, Edward, only for joy!

Believe me, tears came down my cheeks too, but because of the bandages they could not see them.

Then, Helga continues, there is a great commotion. The first horse with the first hearse moves und a sound comes from the crowd. I cannot tell you, Edward, what that sound was but for sure it was awful, awful. Not a sob, not a moan, but such an awful sound from thousands of throats came up. Ach, ach, it was like from ten thousand mouths the souls of the dead flew out und went up to God in Heaven. Oh, Edward, I cried out such a heavy cry I scared Mr. Honeycuitt, so he put his arms around me to calm me.

Then it was the drums, Helga says. The whole air got filled with the drums. Brrrooommm, brrrooommmbrrrooommm-brrrooommmbrrrooommm! It was The Bugle and Drum Corps from the Police Department, the Fire Department, und der Boy Scouts. So, with the drumming, the parade for the dead turns onto Second Avenue. The crowd is very quiet and what you could hear is only the iron hooves and the drums. Brrrooommm!

Except where an anguished cry pierced the air, Honeycuitt adds. He talked that way, y'know: *an anguished cry pierced the air.*

It was with no end these hearses, Edward, and through the glass of the hearses you could see the coffins, the black ones und the brown und the little white ones to break the heart. God in His Wisdom knows why all of this is, God in His Wisdom!

I was so filled up with everything, Edward, I didn't even think how I am to go to the graveyard, so it was lucky that I fainted und Mr. Honeycuitt found me.

Well, says Honeycuitt, I had my roadster parked on 7th Street. I invited your Aunt to ride with me since I had to cover the burial at the Lutheran Cemetery. I managed to nose into the cortege behind one of the *barouches.*

He lit another Fatima. When he talked you could see he was writing a story, Edward Kittel said, speaking to Vilma Rakos.

Honeycuitt says, continued Knittel, With a slow and steady pace we went down town toward Delancey Street. People were a dozen deep on the sidewalks. Black armbands and white handkerchieves. The sun beat down without pity. The drums were muffled, of course, with black cloth tied about with purple ribbons. The sound, if I might describe it, was like distant thunder. This accompanied by the iron cadence of horses.

Knittel's voice had changed. He was producing the remembered sound of Melvin's speech. Somewhere behind us, a band was playing "The Funeral March". On Delancey Street the cortege turned east to the Williamsburg Bridge. As we ascended the bridge, I felt that we were high up in the air with no support beneath us. The horses' hooves sometimes struck the iron-work of the bridge and sometimes the stone. Iron on iron. Iron on stone. Somber and beautiful.

I could see the silent crowds on the rooftops and on the streets below us. Over that arc of gray came the long, rolling dignified display of death drawn along by the black-plumed horses. The drums. The hooves. The stately funereal music.

Jaizus, said McHooley, a clerichaune has seized him! He's speaking with the dead man's voice!

Cut it out, McHooley. I listened to Melvin for more than a quarter of a century. It's the way he talked.

In the voice of Jimmy Durante? Cortin said. What an actor!

Fuck you, fag, Knittel said and continued in Honeycuitt's voice.

Only after we had left the bridge behind did the heat take over. It was very hot and humid for June. I would have been embarrassed by my perspiration—I was soaked through—if Helga had not been in the same condition.

In Brooklyn, on Myrtle Avenue, the cortege seemed to pick up its pace a little. All along the way there were the mourning crowds. More than three hours passed before we arrived at the cemetery.

You fag, Knittel said to Cortin, the last part I didn't do so good. You made me selfconscious. I lost his voice.

Sorry, Eddie. Really. I should have known better. Go on, please.

The night nurse comes into the room and gives Helga and Honeycuitt a glass of cold tea with ice. Drinking, Helga says, This is very good, Edward. Don't you want some? I tell her I had had plenty before they came.

It's such a beautiful place, the Lutheran Cemetery, Helga says. One day, your father, Wolfgang, und me also, will lie there under the beautiful ground. There's also a space for you, Edward. Did you know that?

I didn't know and I was not too happy to hear of it. My mother and my sisters and brother were with the Unidentified, but I was sure that I didn't want to lie near my father. Maybe he'd reach over and clobber me, y'know. But for my Aunt Helga, I could see, a nice green graveyard was as close to heaven as you could get. Like a waiting room for eternal life, y'know.

Honeycuitt, says to me. Does all of this disturb you?

No, I say, I want to hear it. If I could've gone, nothing would've stopped me. Everything you can tell me, Mr. Honeycuitt, I would be glad to know.

Another Fatima.

In front of the high, iron gates of the cemetery, Honeycuitt says, there was a large band of boys and girls from churches throughout the city. Perhaps two hundred in number. They played hymns and all kinds of appropriate music.

Inside the gates three men in black suits stopped each hearse and instructed the driver where he was to take his burial wagon. I identfied myself asked where the sermon would be given. I drove to that section and we got out of the car.

Edward, Helga says, there was like a big pit, a square hole the grave diggers had opened. The brown earth was piled up. The hearses came by the gravesides und the grave diggers reached up for the caskets. How quick it was! Came the hearse, out the casket, und down.

They were certainly quick, says Honeycuitt, and we were all thankful for that. In less than an hour the caskets were laid, double decked, in the mass grave. The small white ones on top and in the center. You could not hear a sound except for the grunting of the grave diggers as they handled the coffins. Not a sound, not a breath, from the several hundred people ringed round the open earth. When the last coffin was put down the silence continued. The weeping did not disrupt the silence. From the ring of people Pastor Haas, his hands in bandages, stepped out. His Bible was open and he read from it in a voice so low I could not hear it.

Gott! Gott! Helga sobs and rocks in her chair. His wife and daughter were in the pit! Your mother und Oscar, Kathryn, und Mary. In which caskets we did not know. Pastor Haas was praying. The tears were running from his own eyes until he finished. We could not hear him but we knew he was finished when he closed the book. Like it was a signal, people began to move off. The hearses also. I did not move until the grave diggers began to shovel the earth onto the caskets. Then I went quick to Mr. Honeycuitt's car. When we drove through the gates the school children's band was playing *Wehre Waiss Wie Nahe Mir Mein Ende.** Then we drove to the hospital.

Edward Francis Knittel drummed his fingers on the bar. Brrrooommm, brrrooommm, brrrooommm.

⤝ 10 ⤞

Esther Lieber stared down at her wine.

I'm very glad there was a funeral for those people, she said. I wouldn't want to think that they just burned to ashes and blew away on the wind. No matter how tragic, that was a great funeral.

I think I remember how Helga and Honeycuitt told it as clear as anything I remember myself. The one regret is that I wasn't there.

Didn't you ever go there? asked Vilma. That's a dumb question. You must have gone a hundred times.

At least. But not in the last fifty years or so.

It must have opened wounds. Your family. Pain like that never leaves, Vilma Rakos said rubbing one of her eyes.

There was no pain anymore, believe me, Vilma. They were gone, my mother, my kid brother and my sisters. Feelings die, y'know. Knittel paused. That's not honest, what I said. There was pain but it was for Rosy. I never got over Rosy. Never.

Knittel moved away from the bar and did a broken, hobbling waltz among the empty tables. As the old man danced he whistled a tune.

* Who knows when my end will come.

Cortin, beating a tempo with a spoon on the ashtray before him, sang the words. *Rosy, you are my posy. You are my heart's bouquet.*

Together they sang the entire song, Cortin's sweet tenor wrapping itself around Knittel's low, breathy gargle. They finished with Cortin holding out the last note for a long moment. Everyone applauded. Knittel came to Cortin and hugged him. You can sing, you sonuvabitch!

Now, let's have "Danny Boy", Joseph, McHooley requested.

Another time. I think Eddie was about to tell us about Rosy.

Don't push, Joey! Vilma said.

It's all right, Knittel said. I want to. She's part of the *Slocum*. And I won't have a drink while I speak of Rosy and I'll say it to you motherfuckers plain and simple and out loud: I loved Rosy more than anyone in the whole world.

Mindy set two platters of onion rings on the bar. No wing, give ring, she said. Compliments of Bo Wang. Is it all right if I sit in the back? she asked McHooley and seated herself without getting his answer.

Knittel was deep in thought. Finally he said, What is Love?

Accountants always eschew that question, Oster said, as should mankind in general.

Is it a debit or a credit, Miltie? Vilma Rakos asked.

A debit or a credit is in the mind of the beholder, Oster answered. How can a man get rich buying the losses of his enemies?

You're some kind of nut, Oster, Esther said. A computer said that, right?

Friends, said McHooley, we've stopped Mr. Knittel dead in his tracks. Love—you were making an inquiry about Love.

Knittel stroked his beard. I never have understood it. Why should I remember Rosy after eighty years? Smell the lilac smell she had, and her hair like a woodland and even the odor of her sweat. Ach! Ach! The faces of my sisters and my brother have faded with the time. My father, I remember his hands, cruel hands, and the anger when he lifted them above his head. That doesn't fade, that picture.

My mother I remember only because she came to check on me when I was sleeping on the roof one night. She was in her nightgown and her long heavy hair was hanging down around her. She was brushing it with strong strokes. She said, Edward, you're acting funny. Is it you have found a girl somewhere?

How could she know? It was only a few days before I had met Rosy.

My mother said, I think you're in love with someone. So, *liebschön*, be careful.

Now, why should I be careful of Love? Why should my mother come to me and almost warn me to be careful. I remember my mother so exactly because of that night on the roof, because of the smell of her. She smelled of lilacs mixed with perspiration. Like Rosy, she smelled. What is Love? I don't know, but it ain't lust.

Knittel looked up to the ceiling. A tear tracked down from the corner of his left eye.

Cortin grinned. Vilma Rakos put her hand over his mouth. Just keep it shut, Joey! she hissed into his ear.

You can let the fag talk, Knittel said gently to Vilma. Maybe he'll learn about how real men feel.

Sorry, said Cortin Don't get me wrong, Eddie. You said Love isn't lust. You happen to be right. But how do you separate one from the other? I always stumble over that one. Am I making sense?

You're making sense all right, Joey. I didn't know Rosy a month, and for half that time I was sick in bed. I dreamed of her. I wanted her in my bed. But even in my imagination I could not do it to her.

Because you were a virgin? Esther asked.

Knittel cocked his head toward Lieber. No, he said, I had lost my cherry three times in the month before. A present from Uncle Wolf. A secret between us. That was lust. Well, not the first time. That was fear and shame.

My Uncle Wolf brought me to this whorehouse on Avenue C near 5th Street. A white, chalky whore with peroxide hair.

I was sitting on the bed and she says to me, Y'wanna take yer pants off? I just sit, y'know. She looks annoyed. She comes to the bed and opens my fly. Just take it easy, kiddo, I ain't gawnna hurt you. She gets her hand inside my underwear and handles it.

It? What was *it?* Did you have a turtle in there?

Joey, there are ladies here.

Oh, excuse me. I didn't mean to offend. *Continuez, mon ami!*

Well, she takes *it* out.

I'm leaving, Esther Lieber said as she laughed I didn't know you were going to tell dirty stories.

Well, said Edward Knittel, also laughing, nah. After that it was a whore's routine. She did a little of this and a little of that and in less than five minutes I was no more a virgin.

Oster said, You skipped all the good parts.

I was trying to show the difference between love and lust, y'know. It was different with Rosy, y'see. Oh, I wanted to do it to her, believe me, but I didn't want to mix up Rosy with the whore.

Vilma kissed Eddie's flat nose. You're sweet, she said, you were showing respect.

Ach, if you were in my brain, Vilma, you wouldn't say that. I wanted her so badly and I already knew what a man can do together with a woman. Eighty years, Vilma, and I still want her! I dream! I dream!

Knittel sobbed and put his head down on the wet bar.

While Knittel wept, Oster said, Maybe the entire *Slocum* affair was in reality the story of Edward's love for Rosy? Perhaps an unfulfilled and unrequited love? Perhaps that's the reason Edward cannot allow the *Slocum* to fade. Rosy is the governing passion of his life and he will not let Rosy go down with the ship.

Knittel's white head rose from the bar. He looked at Oster and said, Maybe you're full of shit, Milton. You love to hear yourself talk.

All right, Eddie, I'm full of shit. It was my thought.

You're not a hundred percent wrong but, Mr. Oster, you make it so simple. You drown it, Eddie said.

By overstating, Milton, you trivialize, Cortin said. Love is the glory and the ruin of the world.

Oh, boy! said Esther Lieber.

Vilma Rakos said, half-mumbling, If this keeps up, I'll ask to be paid.

Knittel pushed his stack of currency before her. She got off her stool and went toward the back. When she returned McHoolley's private bar radio was playing "Teenager In Love".

It's a tribute to Mort Shuman and The Golden Age of Rock, McHooley said.

Oh, yeah, Vilma Rakos, said as she got onto her stool. Were you waiting for me, Eddie?

Yes, I was. I don't expect these cynics to understand shit about Love. You, yes.

You see, Vilma, if a man doesn't tell his secrets to a bartender, McHooley said, he'll dump them on the first taxi driver he rides with.

Except, McHooley, a cabbie might listen, right? But a bartender with his ears plugged just polishes a hole in the wood, Vilma answered with an anger close to rage.

What's got into you? Esther Lieber asked.

Vilma Rakos shrugged.

⌁ 11 ⌁

Knittel closed his eyes. He was silent. The small movements beneath his beard indicated that he was thinking, perhaps in coversation with himself. The bar people waited.

Esther Lieber fidgeted. Makes me so nervous when he shuts up like that, she said. Maybe he already had the stroke. He's alive but just twitching.

He's dead again, said Oster, but soon he'll be reborn. Take my word for it. Change to QXR.

No way, said McHooley.

You have the queerest Happy Hours, Mindy said. It's like a seance.

Wake up, Eddie, wake up, Joe Cortin said, the dawn is breaking.

Fuck you, fag, the old man said, his eyes still closed.

What are you dreaming? Vilma asked.

Eddie's eyes snapped open. You're the smartest of them all, Vilma. You're right on the money. I was dreaming, all right.

The same dream? asked McHooley.

No. It's the other dream. I've only had two dreams. This is the other dream, Knittel said and sighed deeply. Then he closed his eyes and became silent again.

Phenomenal! said Oster. The only man alive who can have a dream and then dream the dream he had. Are you going to speak, Old Hero?

Knittel remained silent, his beard working.

Cortin snored dramatically.

Fucking fag, Knittel said, his eyes still closed.

How'd you know it was me?

I guessed, he said and continued to speak with his eyes closed. It took me almost eighty years to understand it, almost understand it. I lived my whole life in one month, y'know. Before that there was nothing. After that there was nothing.

Knittel opened his eyes. It's not the dream yet. I'll tell you when the dream starts.

He spoke again.

Wolfgang, my uncle, had a fight with old August Stimmler, who had the plumbing contract on the Flatiron Building on 23rd Street. Wolf wanted more money. Stimmler was very tight-fisted and said no. So Wolf said for him to stick the Flatiron Building where the sun doesn't shine.

The pain and the passion of the Flatiron Building, said Oster.

Yes, Miltie, but Uncle Wolf had another job waiting in his tool kit. A graystone on east 63rd Street, to change the iron plumbing to copper. It paid better than the Flatiron job, it goes without saying. It was there I met Rosy.

An heiress? said Esther Lieber.

Nah, said Eddie Knittel, a house maid with a black dress and a white lace thing on her head and a little white apron also trimmed with lace. A thousand volts of electricity went through me.

Ohboyohboy, said Esther.

Smitten, said McHooley.

I'm looking at an angel. I'm frozen in my tracks, y'know. I'm looking at a miracle.

And there was music?

Of course there was, Joey, said McHooley. The pipes, the pipes were playing!

Wolf had to take me by the arm and shake me. The sonuvabitch whispers in my ear, That's quality pussy, Eddie

"Put powder on her ass, give the boys another pass, give her five if she won't take two..."

I didn't even get angry at him. All I knew is if she asked me to lier down on the trolley tracks, I'd say yes. Love at first sight. I'm talking like a cheap love story, but that was it: I belonged to her.

Knittel searched each face at the bar defiantly. On this I don't want shit. I'm emptying my heart.

Vilma Rakos wiped her eyes. She lit a cigarette and inhaled deeply.

It wasn't until two days after that I said my first word to her. She was serving us in the kitchen where we took our lunch. She asked, Would you like some coffee? I said, Please. That was the first word. The same day I asked her for a match to light the blowtorch. She gave me a couple. Our hands touched. I got up the moxie to ask, What's your name? She says, Rosy and I know your name is Edward. The way she said it, it was the first time I really liked my name, the sound of it. The way it came from her lips, her mouth, it was a good strong name. That's how it was, she could change my life with a word, a smile.

Smitten, McHooley said.

Smitten, said Eddie Knittel. I asked her if she'd go on the Fifth Avenue bus with me on Sunday. She said, Yes, without a hesitation.

So there we are on the top of the bus, the sun shining down on us. We're laughing. We're pointing at buildings we pass. We're saying silly things about people in Central Park. We're holding hands. It's ecstasy. When we breathe it's ecstasy. When we move our bodies on the slatted wooden benches, it's ecstasy. Ach! Ach! They say when a hurricane comes or a volcano explodes or a person dies for no reason that it's an Act of God. Tragedies like that are Acts of God. But to ride on a Fifth Avenue bus when every single ordinary thing you do becomes ecstasy, ain't that also an Act of God? My whole life in one month, that was an Act of God.

Quality time, said Oster.

Quality time, Knittel repeated, quality time. Even so, y'know, if God puts everything in one package there is still the other side of ecstasy. I want to kiss her, hard. Our legs touch and I want to touch her legs. I see her breasts pressing up inside her lavender blouse, I want to put my hands inside that blouse. Ach! Ach!

I scare myself to death with the thoughts I'm thinking: what if Rosy knows what's going through my head? I'm so scared of that that I begin to talk like crazy. You know what I talk about? I talk about plumbing! Until a 110th Street I am a professor of plumbing. And Rosy is laughing like a genuine nut case.

She did know what was going through your head, Vilma said, waving her finger at Knittel.

Oh, yes, she knew all right. We got off the bus and walked through the park. She took hold of my hand and squeezed it, Knittel said, grasping his fingers. We walked along like that. I remember how there were patterns of light on the paths, leaves y'know, which moved and changed when the breeze blew, like a kaleidoscope.

Were we speaking to each other? We must have been doing that, y'know. It was a long walk from a 110th down to the zoo. I'm saying One day I'll be a Master Plumber and make a good living. She's studying typing and shorthand and one day she will be a secretary for a fine company. Then she says, Orphans must rely on themselves. She's an orphan from the Hebrew Orphan Society of Ohio. HOSO, they called it.

Rosy was Jewish! Esther Lieber cried. She was Jewish?

But not a yenta. She had a little gold Jewish star around her neck. Her name was Farkas. In Hungarian that means fox. So she was a red fox. Her hair was brown, though.

Esther turned to Joey. Did you hear that? Jewish!

That changes everything, Cortin said.

All through the park people had blankets and were lying on the grass. Rosy said. Next Sunday we should do that. Have a picnic.

Next Sunday! My heart was like a balloon floating over my head, pulling me up to tiptoe, walking on air.

Just like in songs, said Joey Cortin.

Yeah, exactly like that. I'll tell you this: if I had had to wait the whole week and not see her I don't know how I would have stayed alive. But I was at the graystone every day. We'd find corners to kiss in. We'd feel each other up in the big closets they had there. She let me get to the naked flesh of her breasts. Until the next Sunday came it was murder and wet dreams.

Eddie, Esther said, you're turning me on!

Drop some ice in your panties, yenta, Eddie said. That's not my idea. It's just that we were on fire.

But it wasn't lust, Vilma said, it was really Love.

I wish you were my older sister so you could explain it to me, Esther said. Tell you the truth I haven't got anything against lust either. Maybe if I lost twenty, thirty pounds somebody would want to lust with me.

Fat is in the mind of the beholder, Oster said, and I behold.

That's not kind, Miltie, Esther said, without hiding the hurt Oster had inflicted.

Forgive me?

I forgive. That's my job. I always forgive, Esther said with a laugh. On with the dirty stories, Eddie. So it's next Sunday.

It was a very nice picnic. She made little tiny sandwiches—white bread with the crusts cut off. I never saw such sandwiches in my life. I'm sure that in the graystone they ate sandwiches like that. Damp lettuce, a slice of tomato or pickle. I ate them with little bites and said, Wonderful!

And when I ate one Rosy would give me a kiss. On the mouth, on the eyes, on the nose.

How many did you eat? McHooley asked.

At least a thousand. Rosy said I was the first beau she had had in New York. And in Ohio? I asked her. She said, Edward, you are my first beau in the whole world, in the universe.

Now we're kissing like Central Park is empty, not even squirrels watching. No laughing now, the old man said, but on the blanket there I thought, My God, this is how angels made love in heaven!

Vilma blew her nose. Her eyes were red.

Melvin Honeycuitt once explained to me that, when a newspaper had a little story to write which was part of a bigger story, they called it a sidebar. This is a side-bar. We were already kissing and feeling like crazy, y'know, but I had to take a pee and I held it back because I was ashamed to say I had to go. Rosy, too. Finally we had to go into those restrooms. The Men's had those gray-slate urinals, y'know? Anybody here ever piss in a gray-slate urinal?

Not me, Esher said. What was it like in the Ladies'?

I never asked Rosy. Pissing is a private thing. It was a thing you didn't talk about in those days.

Très délicate, Oster observed.

Very *très*, Cortin added.

Knittel chuckled. Then we took a walk through the zoo and when we went past apes in their cages there was this baboon masturbating and people were laughing. Embarrassed, maybe. Rosy and me felt disgusted and ashamed. Now why the fuck was that? Ecstasy. Paradise. A day made by God for Rosy and me, and a baboon jerking off!

I once knew a day like that, Cortin said.

Don't tell us, Joey, said Vilma. Another time, okay?

Okay.

Eddie Knittel chewed on a fresh, crooked cigar. Eighty years and even now I remember a gust of wind and leaves spinning and dancing. Then boom, boom! A cloud buster and cats and dogs coming down. The next day we both had bronchitis.

God? McHooley asked.

God, said Knittel. It had to be, right? We wrote little notes to each other. Wolf was our messenger, y'know. He teased me without mercy. My mother has an idea of what is going on and she says, Nobody ever died of Love, Edward. Which the whole world knows is untrue. Everybody dies of Love.

Eddie, Vilma said, don't say that!

Knittel shrugged his shoulders extravagantly. He said, My mother wouldn't let me go back to the job. The doctor said for me to stay home. We made a compromise: I would go with her and the kids on the *Slocum* and after that, if there was no fever, I could go back to work. But I couldn't wait.

The *Slocum* was moored at the pier on West 54th Street, getting ready for the excursion on the coming Wednesday. On Friday I wrote a note to Rosy to meet me on the pier there on Monday at noon. I wanted her to see the boat before it came around to the 3rd Street Pier on the East River for the St. Mark's Excursion and Picnic to Locust Grove.

She sent back her answer with Wolf. She wrote: I'll be there for sure.R.

⌐ 12 ⌐

Now it's here the second dream begins, Edward Francis Knittel said. He got off his stool and walked a few steps away. He returned to the stool and sat down again. He shook his head slowly. His mouth opened as if he wanted to speak. What the hell, he said, it's the second dream.

Still, he seemed uncertain. Then with a rush of energy, his voice rising, plunging defiantly into his thoughts, he said, I told my mother, Mama, I'm going out to take a walk down to the dock.

There's a buzzing in my ear. I try to get rid of it. I shake my head. It stays. Maybe it will go away by itself.

In stead of going to the dock. I walk down to Avenue D. The horse trolley stops for me. I get on. I pay the fare: one cent. The driver kicks the gong board. The bell has a good sound. The trolley is going uptown. On 42nd Street the horses turn west. It's eleven o'clock. I'm the only one onboard. The driver uses the kick board. The gong sounds along the empty street. Where is everybody? I wonder. The trolley stops across the street from the Hudson piers. Ocean liners are in the slips. I squint at the light. The sun is sharp in my eyes.

I get on the northbound trolley. This trolley has two white horses. One horse has a sore on the back of his leg. It's healing but it's red as if the scab has fallen off. The driver is singing "Funiculi Funicula".

At 51st Street the *Leviathan* blasts its horn. The city shivers. The huge ship is sliding out from its berth.

54th Street. I get off. My legs feel weak. I have never felt this way in my life. I say to myself, It's a little fever. Even with a nice breeze there's still sweat on my forehead. I think: It's okay, it'll pass. I cross over to the pier where the *Slocum* is moored. To me it seems to be as big as the *Leviathan*.

The 54th Street pier is very long. It goes out and out and out, maybe to New Jersey. But I can't see New Jersey. From the street end of the pier I can't even see the river. I feel I'm made of air and I am tall, tall, very tall. I wonder if I can walk all the way to the end of the pier. The pier is printed with the shadow, almost the silhouette, of the *Slocum*. The shadow feels cold. I tremble a little. On the river end the pilings are in full sunlight.

I walk on my long, weak legs toward the pilings. I want to sit inside the piling curve. I want to be warm.

There are seagulls sitting in the sun. There are seagulls sitting on top of the piling poles. They have a squattish shape. They have no necks. I sit down they fly up. There are many green-and-white gull droppings on the poles and on the dock ledges. There is a clean space. I sit there. I sit down, the seagulls fly up. In the sun my trembling lessens.

The sun warms my eyelids. I smell the river. The Hudson smells of salt and laundry waste water. I like that smell. I like the sounds. The river slaps against the pier. It sighs when it ebbs. The gulls cry. A stinkpot putts northward. I see it pass. On the street, Twelfth Avenue, the sounds are far off, tiny. Motor lorries. Horse-drawn lorries. Voices. Far away.

The *Slocum* is very still in the slip. It does not rock. Slowly, so slowly, it rises up and sinks down. It is like a great, white animal breathing in its sleep. I cannot see where the prow reaches. I see the black wooden plaque where, in gold, the name is printed: the *General Slocum.* The letters slant. There are two gangplanks reaching from the *Slocum* to the gray dock.

I hear a man singing. I think the singing comes from the *Slocum.* I don't know the song. It's about when the stars begin to fall. I look toward the sound of the distant voice.

I hear another voice. It's saying, Edward, Edward! I look into the place of the voice. It's Rosy. She's like the kaleidoscope on the path in the park. Filigree of light and shadow. She's wearing a hat. A straw hat. I'm startled. She looks like a ghost. Edward, Edward! the ghost says.

I shield my eyes with my hand. Rosy? Is that you, Rosy?

The ghost laughs. Of course it's me. Did you expect your old girlfriend, Edward? She laughs again.

I laugh, too. I hope she doesn't hear the hollowness in my laughter.

Rosy kisses me. I feel better. I stand up and hug her. Her body is real, her breasts are real. We sit down together in the pilings' curve. She sits close to me in the space which is clear of gull droppings.

A great horse-drawn lorry thunders onto the pier. Very loud. The lorry rolls alongside the *Slocum.* The driver stands up and pulls on the thick leather reins. I can see that he's yelling something but I can't hear him. The lorry comes to a full stop.

I hear him now.

Rastus! Rastus! You in there? the driver's helper shouts.

The distant singing stops.

Raaastuuus!

A thin black man appears on the Main Deck. He walks slowly down the gangplank toward the lorry. The helper offers the black man a sheet of paper.

The black man takes the sheet of paper. He stares at the lorry assistant. He takes a pencil stub from behind his ear. He squats, spreads the paper on the dock planking and signs. He hands the paper back to the assistant. He goes back to the boat. He stands on the lip of the gangplank.

The driver scrambles over some crates on the lorry's flat bed. He rolls a barrel toward the tailgate of the lorry. The assistant unfastens the gate and lets it flop down.

One at a time the assistant lifts the heavy barrels down to the dock. He wraps his muscular arms carefully around each. He huffs and he puffs. His cheeks and his neck swell out with the strain. When he's done he lifts the tailgate to its hasps. He goes up front, climbs onto the seat. The reins crack. The horses move, the lorry wheels around. The wagon with the seated teamsters leaves the pier.

The black man comes from the gangplank. He inspects the barrels. He removes some straw packing. He takes off his cap. His hair is white. He sings, *When the stars begin to fall...* He rolls the first barrel toward the gangplank.

Rosy says, Can we go on the boat?

I don't answer but she takes my hand. Pulls me after her. We're over the gangplank and onto the Promenade deck.

We walk slowly along the rail. There is the river below us. Garbage is floating. There's a raft tied to the opposite pier. There is a man without a shirt sleeping on the raft. The raft bobs up and down.

We follow the black man below to the Main Deck. He's taking beer steins from the straw-packed barrel. He places them on the saloon bar of the Main Deck. He knows we're there but he doesn't look at us.

There are more stairs going down. I follow Rosy. We go to the boiler room. There are piles of coal. Shovels stick out of the piles. Rosy picks up a piece of coal and eats it. Her mouth and lips become black.

In the dream, the boiler room goes away. We're standing in another room. The whole room is yellow. There are five beds. No bedding. Just beds. On one bed there's a captain's hat.

It's made of fire. Rosy puts it on her head. The fire doesn't burn her. She smiles at me with her black lips.

A big room. Giant machinery with axles extending into the paddle wheels on each side of the *Slocum*. I have never seen such huge axles. I wonder what kind of foundry could make such big parts?

Another room. An oil lamp burns on a table. The table is a made of two boards laid across three saw horses. The floor is covered with cigarette and cigar butts. Cans of white paint are against the walls. Pots of rusty nails and screws. Tools. Under the table, two blowtorches with their flames turned down to little blue spouts. Rosy picks a cigar butt from the floor and puts it between her black lips. I don't know why she is doing this but I'm afraid to ask her.

We go back upstairs, past the Promenade Deck, then to the Hurricane Deck at the very top. Rosy's mouth is clean. We walk along the rail. The sun is very strong. Everything is very white. We look up the length of one of the black smokestacks. I can't see the top of it. I take my knife from my pocket and I scratch a heart into the smokestack. I carve our initials into the black. Rosy weeps.

Rosy takes off her clothes. She is naked. She is very beautiful. I also take off my clothes. Arm in arm we walk to the back of the boat. Rosy says, Edward, we will now get married before the one and only true God. My manhood is swollen and sticking out in front of me. We kneel down. We pray. We stand up. We are made of gold from the sun. We kiss each other gently. We get dressed.

Rosy takes a coin from her purse. She says, I must make a wish. She closes her eyes. She puts her hands together. She smiles and throws the coin into the green, smoky water. It will come true, she says.

The sky is wheeling over my head. Dizzy. Hot. I'm sitting in a deck chair. Rosy is pouring water into my mouth.

We leave the boat. We stand on the pier and look at the *Slocum*. Like a white mountain it rises up and fills the air. It touches the clouds and the sky.

The whole world can fit onto that boat, Rosy says, the whole world!

I'm looking at the boat. I gasp. Rosy, I say, look, it's turned gray!

Clouds have come over, Rosy says. She touches my forehead. You have fever, Edward. I will take you home.

How, I don't know.

I remember my mother opened the door. She saw me shaking like an empty shirt on the line. She let out a scream. Edward, where have you been! Look at you, you're burning up!

I stagger into the apartment. My mother holds me up and helps me to my bed.

 13

You gave me such an eerie feeling, Eddie, Vilma Rakos said. Did you know something was wrong, that something was going to happen?

Foreboding? asked Oster.

I don't go for things like that. It was the bronchitis coming back. A little relapse. I was weak and shaky. I just wanted to leave the pier. Hey, what's going on here? Why so quiet?

After a moment, Esther said, I ain't crazy, Eddie. You gave me the feeling that you had a vision of what was going to happen.

Naw. You read sometimes about someone who won't get on an airplane because he has a premonition it's going to crash and that gets printed in the papers when the plane goes down. I put a lotta salt on those stories. Same thing with the *Titanic* or the *Lusitania*. My feeling was...it was the bronchitis. I was trembling.

Ah, but you're not quite sure, Edward, lad, are you? You said it was a dream. Perhaps it was a foreboding, McHooley said.

Ach, Timothy, it's not like we're sitting around a campfire telling ghost stories. If only I had had a vision! Everybody would've been alive. My mother and the kids, the boy who climbed up the flagpole, the hundreds and hundreds. And Rosy. Alive, alive, everybody alive! Give me a drink, please, and no lecture. I'm as sober as Bo Wang.

I still say it was an omen, Eddie. The whole thing was just one big omen, Vilma said.

Well, Oster said, it wouldn't have mattered. Who would have believed you?

No one. No one believed me anyway. It's the Marjorie Ann Plunkerbrotes of the world who get believed. I wanted Rosy to see the *Slocum* because she wasn't going on the Excursion -Wednesday was a work day for her and she had already snuck out on that Monday before.

Why did you want her to see it? asked Cortin. Why did you? You had a feeling, a foreboding.

No, Joey, it was Love, the way of Love. Ain't it strange Love has no tomorrows? It's all today, now, y'know. Ach, Rosy, Rosy, she took me home. And I was shivering and shaking, so much so we didn't even kiss.

A thought occurred to me, said Oster. Maybe it was Rosy who had the vision. That's why she wanted to join you on the *Slocum*.

Knittel pushed himself away from the bar. He walked to the front of McHooley's and stared out on Broadway.

Not a single building he could see had been standing when he had been born. Not a building standing when the *Slocum* had sailed. There probably had been small farms here and they were long gone. It was the way of the City: build it up, tear it down. No monuments. No memories. Ach, thought Knittel, I shouldn't have brought Rosy into the story. Now she'll be in everybody's mouth.

But Knittel was certain it was all a matter of fever and that Rosy had had no vision. If she had, she wouldn't have boarded the *Slocum*. If she had, she would have told him and he would have stopped the *Slocum* from leaving the pier. Maybe there was such a thing as destiny.

Knittel turned away from the street. He spoke from where he was standing, his voice low.

I remember when my mother opened the door and saw me shaking she yelled at me, Where have you been all day, Edward? You were not supposed to go out; just to the dock! Into bed! You'll miss the picnic! Ach, ach, Edward, Edward, she said. I can hear her voice. I wish you people could hear her voice.

So, hot tea and schnapps. So, the mustard plaster. So, three blankets in the middle of June. A sweat bath you wouldn't believe! And then sleep. In the middle of the night, soaking wet, I woke up. I kicked off the blankets. The fever was broken. Then something very strange happened.

I'll tell you about this because I remember it. Don't you tell me what you think it means, all right? When there had been no response, Knittel turned back from the doorway and walked to his place at the bar. All right?, he asked again.

It's all right, Eddie, Vilma said, everyone will let it go. Go on.

Without looking toward the others, Knittel continued.
Two crows flapped down onto the windowsill. They startled me. I jumped. My heart went like a triphammer. I wondered if they would fly into my room. Would they fly into my face and pluck out my eyes?

Where did crows live in New York? Nowhere, I said to myself. Crows don't live in New York. I took some deep breaths to calm myself. Why should I be scared of them; crows or pigeons or whatever. They couldn't do me any harm. If they flew into the room I could swing at them. I could smother them with a blanket. They couldn't get close enough to pluck out my eyes, y'know.

It's dumb but I asked myself, Could they be giant sparrows? They hopped around. I studied them. No, they were not sparrows—their heads were too big. They were not pigeons—their feet were too long. What else could they be, I said to myself, except crows?

I knew if I ever told Honeycuitt of the crows in the window he would have wiped his specs with his skinny tie and said, You're confused. There are no crows in New York.

Knittel laughed softly and drummed his fingers on the bar top.

But I must say this to be fair. In my fifteen years I'd never been outside New York City. I had never seen Staten Island or Queens. Had I ever seen a crow in my whole life? And let us say if I had ever seen a crow who was it who told me it was a crow I had seen?

But none of this mattered to me. I knew they were crows. Maybe I had seen a picture? Four and twenty blackbirds baked in a pie, or the Aesop fable of the crow that dropped pebbles into a jar to make the water rise up. Some things you just know. Not sparrows, not pigeons, crows.

Finally, I had the courage to talk to them. I said, with real authority, What do you want here? Go away! Be gone! Go back to Hell whence you came!

Whence? Joe Cortin said, whence?

That's right. Whence. It was a word I knew from church. I said Hell so up came whence. Wait, Joey, I'm not finished yet. I said, Tell me why you're here or go away! Are you birds or are you omens?

When I said omen the birds stepped inside the window. They looked this way and that. They made sounds—not like caw, caw but like words. The words were mumbled and slurred. They hopped around in tight circles, like a dance, then they hopped back outside the window and flew into the night.

Then it came to me what the crows had said. It was, Never forget! Never forget! But what I shouldn't forget I didn't know on that night when the fever broke. Now I want to tell all you motherfuckers it was not a dream.

Eddie, I must comment on this, Oster said.

No, said Knittel.

A question then, said McHooley.

No, said Knittel.

You sure you just want to let this pass? asked Cortin.

Yes, said Knittel. Have you a question you want to ask me, yenta?

No, said Esther Lieber.

Eddie, said Vilma Rakos, you are one aggravating sonuvabitch.

How can you say such a thing, Vilma? I swear on the Bible they were real crows!

Bo Wang stepped into the room and announced, Fresh Irish New Zealand Lamb Stew for dinner. One hour twenty minutes. Compliments Mr. Wang and Mr. McHooley.

Very generous of you, Mr. Wang, said McHooley.

Proper Christian hospitality. Acquired manner of Boxer Rebellion.

Wang assumed several martial arts positions in quick succession, bowed, and retreated behind the swingingdoors.

❧ 14 ❧

Vilma Rakos could see that a change had come over Edward Francis Knittel. It was as if he had moved away from the bar although he had not. He was there, sitting in his corner. He seemed to have gotten smaller inside his blue jacket. At the same time he was more intense. He had intertwined his fingers and was wringing his big hands. It was not only that the old man had seemed to move away from the bar, he had moved away from all those who lined its edge. The others, too, could see the change in Knittel.

Vilma thought it was not exactly like Jekyll and Hyde but certainly as profound. Knittel had moved into another space. She hoped the space was all right for him, that he would not die there. She wanted to shout something to break the mood but Knittel, his voice tense, his pale eyes moving from face to face without seeing them, had begun to speak.

On the day of the Excursion, Knittel said, I was miserable. Loss, I had the deepest feeling of loss. I wouldn't see Rosy. Not on this day or the next day. I would be on the *Slocum* and Rosy would be on 63rd Street. How lonely I felt!

It was before the sun had come up. I couldn't sleep so I went out ot the flat, sneaking like an indian.

❧ 15 ❧

I walked onto the 9th Street dock, which was not more than fifty yards from the foundry where my father worked. The moment my feet touched the weathered planking I felt good. My spirits rose up in me with a great warmth. This was my dock. This was my place, y'know.

I went out to the far end of the pier, where the sun was just coming up out of the river. It was warm in the special way of the early morning. The river was grayish green and very still. The stick buoys were almost straight up. It was dead high tide. When the tide had begun to flow again, the face of the reflected sun shimmered.

I was an apprentice that summer so I did not get much chance to swim in the river. The summer before it was almost every day off the dock. Even when it rained. When it rained the river was warmest and softest. That's how childhood ends, not being able to go off the dock, and falling in love.

It was my choice, y'know. If I had wanted to go through high school I could have. My father put it up to me. You want to use your brain or your back? he asked me. I said I wanted to use my back because it would make money for me. How many fellows my age could get to learn the plumber's trade and knock down six dollars a week at the same time? What could you learn in high school that had anything to do with real life? Plumbing was the goods, something wanted and appreciated.

I had no regrets. Especially since I had met Rosy. In two years I would be a journeyman plumber. Then we could get married. In five years I would be a master plumber, at the age of twenty! Then Rosy and I could buy a house like Wolf and Helga, unless we had too many children like Mama and Papa.

The morning river, soothed your spirit. You felt the world was good and you were lucky to be alive.

Between the 9th Street and the 10th Street docks, you could hear the heavy sound of the wooden door being slid back on the stable side of the Knickerbocker Ice Company. The door was being pushed open by a man in a leather apron. Grunting, lifting, and putting his shoulder to the door edge, he drove the huge black barrier into the rough sleeve, which took it in and hid it out of sight.

I could hear the sound of the horses neighing and the rattling of the hitching chains. And, even though I knew it would happen, there was the full surprise of the horse and wagon coming through the wide opening onto the cobblestoned street. Then another one and another one, turning and going to their routes, loaded with blocks of ice.

Smoke was up from the ironworks. You could hear the drop forge hitting down. I could smell bacon and eggs cooking. Voices came up like choirs along the street.

The day passed like that. Seeing things in new ways, y'know, things I had known all my life. It was hard work squeezing the minutes out of the day, trying to keep Rosy out of my mind.

When I came back from the dock I lay down on my bed. My mother was up already. I came out to the kitchen only after my father was gone. I didn't want to hear another lecture about socialism, about his meeting with Samuel Gompers. Not at breakfast. Not on that morning.

Should I wake the children? I asked my mother.

Let them sleep, she said. There is nothing to do. All is cooked. All is packed. The day has come out beautiful. Beautiful!

She brushed back her long, blond hair so it lay on her back. She sipped from her coffee mug, half milk and three sugars. She was still in her slip, which was white with openwork lace at the top and bottom. The slip reached the middle of her legs.

Mama's arms were heavy and round. On her left arm there was a wide black-and-blue mark. Her broad forehead, like her face, had many pale freckles, and her eyes were a warm brown color, maybe hazel. She smiled and said, You are staring at your Mama, Edward. Well, that's all right. You are a man already. You have a very good-looking Mama, no?

I lowered my head. She did that a lot and she knew she embarrassed me.

The strap of her slip moved off her shoulder, showing the strap of her brassiere. Mama was a woman with a large bosom. Very large. I wondered if her breasts hung way down as Wolfgang had said of big-breasted women.

I was glad that Rosy's breasts were modest. Not small, not flat, like some girls, just nice. Then I thought that maybe when Mama was Rosy's age she was not so big. Maybe it got bigger as you had children who sucked the milk and all.

The thought of that made me shudder inside. I thought of Rosy with such huge breasts and I swore to myself that I would not hold it against her. It would be okay. I would always love her, no matter what. For better or for worse.

Oscar was the first to come from the bedroom where he and the girls slept. He was wide awake and wanted to know what time it was. I told him 7:15 and we were plenty early. We did not have to be on the 3rd Street pier until nine or even later. Mama made some eggs and sausage on the gas burner. Oscar, who never had much appetite, had no more than two half-forkfuls of eggs and a sliver of sausage and a glass of milk. Mama said he'd grow up to be a stringbean and be the skinny man in the circus. She finished off what was on his plate, which was almost everything.

Kathryn and Mary came into the kitchen fully dressed. Katy's dress was what she called Robin's Egg Blue with a sort of checkerboard blue-and-white scheme on the neck part and the collar. There were gathers at the waist and wide curvey pleats all around the skirt.

Mary's dress was exactly the same except in Blushing Baby Pink.

When Mama saw them she yelped and told them to get out of those dresses and not to put them on before they had washed themselves. So back they went to the bedroom.

They returned in their slips, which they let down to their waists, and washed at the kitchen sink. Katy had pretty pink nipples which she did not try to cover up. Mary had nothing more than Oscar.

Mama said, They think on the *Slocum* they will meet the princes from the fairy books and they will be carried away to a castle in Bavaria and live happily ever after. I hope their wishes come true, but I don't know.

With profound disgust Katy said, Mama, how can you think such a thing!

When we started out, I insisted on carrying the two heaviest baskets. Mama protested that I was still too weak from the bronchitis. I told her no, and not to bother me because it was bad enough I was being forced to go on the excursion. At least people should see that I am a man and doing what any man would do.

So everybody carried something. Oscar and Mary carried towels and blankets folded across their arms, Katy a basket of napkins, silverware, salt, pepper, pickles, and things like that. Mama carried a large jug of lemonade, cold from the icebox, a basket with a ham in it, her large purse, and a parasol. She wore her cameo brooch on its gold chain and on her hand, in addition to her wedding ring, a wide gold band which she always wore, there was the ring with the square-cut diamond: my father's gift to her on their tenth anniversary.

We walked to Avenue D, which was the first corner from our building, then we turned downtown toward the 3rd Street pier.

From each house along the Avenue, and from the connecting streets, people came out, like us carrying baskets and bags.

From one building a mother with an infant would come. From another building a whole tribe of a family—eight or ten— would join the parade.

I was surprised by my feeling. I was sure that I would be embarrassed being one of the few men going to the pier. Instead, as the parade swelled, the sun shining on the women with their pretty dresses, the children in their Sunday clothes, I felt excited and pleased.

At 6th Street and Avenue D there was singing. A group joined the march to the south giving full voice to "My Old Kentucky Home" and all the walkers joined in.

When that song ended, almost like magic the tune changed to "Home, Home On The Range". Those who were left behind—and there could not have been very many because the men were already at work—opened the windows and smiled at the columns of singers on Avenue D.

On 3rd Street the parade turned. Ahead was Lewis Street. And then the Third Street Recreational Pier, with its double-decked structure of decorative wrought iron. The sun poured through the delicate iron filigree, which threw lacy shadows onto the stones before the dock.

It's like you're speaking poetry, Eddie!, Esther Lieber said.

Shh; said Vilma Rakos, Don't interrupt him.

Knittel continued.

Again like magic the second song ended as the first marchers reached the pier. In its place there was a roaring cheer: Hip, hip, hooray! Hip, hip, hooray!

Hundreds of people were already on the pier. Pastor Haas from St. Mark's Lutheran and Mary Abendschein, his assistant, were there. Miss Abendschein had a little bunch of flowers pinned to her dress. She and the Pastor put up a small folding table. They stood behind it and waved and smiled to the picnickers pouring onto the dock.

There were signs tacked to the table's edge. One, in neat black-and-red hand lettering, said: *Those wishing to purchase tickets may do so here.* Another said: *Those who have lost or forgotten tickets may apply for duplicates here.* A third sign said: *Any problems, Information, Ask Pastor Haas or Mary Abendschein.*

There was lots of activity at the table and from the money being passed you could see tickets were still being purchased.

Not far from the church folding table, we parked our bundles. My mother said, Children, stay close to me. I don't want to hunt and chase.

I was sure she didn't mean this for me, so I added very sternly, y'know, You children, listen to Mama, hear me? Katy, I'm holding you responsible. Katy punched my arm.

I walked to the pier's end. There was a group of men standing there smoking cigars. They all had mustaches neatly cut, not bushy, not handlebars. This would not be so unusual although, by average, you expected about half the men to be clean shaven. My father, for example, had a pretty heavy mustache, which used to be a handlebar mustache but he had clipped the ends because he was always burning them in the foundry. Wolfgang, when he had come to America from the old country at the age of fifteen, had a thin mustache, which had not yet bloomed. But he was very much impressed by the new dandies who were shaving clean. So he had no mustache at all. What I'm trying to say is that both styles were equally in fashion.

As for myself, I didn't know which way to go. It didn't matter too much since I was light haired like my mother and I didn't think my mustache would show for years. Even so, for the last few months I had been shaving off the fuzz.

The men with the neatly cut mustaches all wore tan suits. They had thick, knotted maroon neckties and, under their jackets, broad maroon-striped shirts. Each of them had a hard-black case with him and from the shape you could tell he carried a musical instrument.

The sound of whistles and horns came from down river. It was the *Slocum.* A murmur started up and people reached down for their baskets and bundles. They formed a line.

No one had to say, Form a line! They did it by instinct. We were Germans. It's in the Cherman chenes. In a few minutes the line stretched to the foot of the pier and a long way out on the cobblestones.

The horns and whistles got louder. Like a great white iceberg the *Slocum* slid toward the pier, the paddlewheels going in reverse to slow the boat as it came in.

Four crewmen leaped from the *Slocum's* Main Deck to the dock. Heavy ropes were thrown after them. The ropes were wound quickly onto the iron pier cleats and the iron stanchions, which looked like giant thumbs sticking out of the dock planking.

The *Slocum* horn gave a final blast to tell us that she had moored. The people gave a great cheer. I cheered, too, I don't know why.

The gangway came down. The first on board were the nine musicians with mustaches. You could see the tan suits going quickly from lower deck to higher deck until they were on the top. They went to the stern. Against the rail they set chairs. They took their instruments from their cases and began right away to tune up.

The people gave that a cheer too.

From the gangway one of the *Slocum's* men shouted through a megaphone, In one minute, you ladies, gentlemen, and children will come aboard the good ship the *General Slocum*. [Cheers.] Thank you. Now Captain William Van Schaik wants you to enjoy this excursion to Locust Grove on Long Island. He wants you to enjoy his ship as if it were your own. [Cheers.] the *General Slocum* is, as you know, the Queen of the New York Harbor waters. It is the most modern, the most beautiful, and safest ship afloat. [Cheers]. To the children I say, Do not be too wild! Walk, do not run! To the parents, I say, If one of the little darlings falls overboard you will find that there are twenty-five hundred cork-filled life preservers on board. You will see them over your heads on each deck, where they are held in place by slats. Give a pull and you will have more life preservers than you can deal with. One of these you can throw into the river for your darling. [Laughter.] There are twenty-three crew members and five officers aboard. While they are all busy doing their duties to give you a nice smooth ride, they are never too busy to answer your questions or help you in any way whatsoever. On each deck–this is mainly for the gentlemen among you, although ladies are also invited–on each deck there is a saloon with a bar where a schnapps can be purchased for pleasure or medicinal purposes. [Great laughter.] Finally, please have your tickets in your hands as you come up the gangway. The *Slocum* has room for all of you. Come aboard! It will be a wonderful cruise and a great day! [The biggest cheers of all.]

ꙗ 16 ꙗ

The line moved very quickly. We got up to the Hurricane Deck and found places on the benches at the stern, nearer to the band. Mary and Katy sat so close to the trumpet player! It was like they were part of the orchestra. Mama pulled the hairpins from the braid around her head and let her hair fall down. So the river wind can play with it, she said. She opened her silk parasol and smiled to no one in particular. She was so happy; so happy!

Young Oscar had already found a piece of the rail to hang over and from which he gave mysterious instructions to the *Slocum* crew to begin the journey.

The line was near its tail end when I saw Rosy, her skirts swinging as she walked right by the people in the line. She smiled at them and they smiled at her. The ticket takers stopped collecting to watch her go by as if it was natural, y'know. As if Rosy Farkas was someone they knew, someone who came aboard the *General Slocum* whenever it sailed. I watched her, her curls bouncing, her hips swaying, the cotton sunbonnet which matched her dress held high in her hand like a banner. I watched until she was on the *Slocum* and out of my sight.

Then I ran down the ship's broad staircase to meet her.

Halfway up to the Promenade Deck we met and I took her into my arms. I kissed her and she kissed me. Right there on the staircase, with women and children going up and going down. I never in my whole life until I met Rosy thought I could kiss a girl out in the open like that, before the whole world.

You're here! I half-shouted, You're here!

Yes, don't get so excited. I can't help it, I can't believe it! You're here, Rosy, here on the *Slocum!* How did you do it?

I told the housekeeper I had a boyfriend on the *Slocum.* She said, The Captain, no doubt. I said, He isn't the Captain but he is more important than captains. Since no one was going to be at dinner tonight, she said for me to go and have a wonderful time.

With no ticket? You just walked on, Rosy. You are a wizard!

I knew they'd let me, she said. You must be bold, I said to myself. Besides I'm wearing such a pretty dress. Mrs. Ames, the housekeeper, loaned it to me. I never thought old women could be the same size as girls!

Oh, Rosy, I'm so happy! We'll be together hours and hours. Until eleven o'clock at night!

Already in my mind I was thinking, Should I bring her to say hello to Mama? I knew I couldn't stay away from Mama and the children all day to be every minute with Rosy. Of course, I would have to introduce her. Besides, that way she would get plenty to eat—capon and ham and all. But not yet, I decided. I would just go to Mama and tell her I was on the Main Deck talking to a friend, which wasn't a lie. So she wouldn't worry and come looking for me, which she would certainly do, what with my broncitis.

I told Rosy what I would do, feeling wonderful I didn't have to hide anything with her.

It was not crowded on the Main Deck, since everybody wanted places on the Promenade and Hurricane Decks. We agreed that she would be standing aft of the paddlewheel, by the rail, and I would be back in three minutes.

It took five, the boat was so packed. You couldn't take a step without knocking somebody down. When I returned we held hands and looked down at the river. The big boat rocked slightly.

I looked into her beautiful eyes; there was such a smile there. I said, I don't know what to say, Rosy.

You don't have to say anything, she said.

All day together! I can't believe it! This is the luckiest day of my life. I said to Rosy, squeezing her hand.

She says, This is our ship, Edward. I decided since yesterday that this ship belongs to us. By the way, have you seen that colored man with the strange eyes?

No. I guess he's working down below. I don't know if I'd recognize him, anyway.

His eyes, Edward.

It would be crazy if I went around looking into every nigger's eyes, I said. That was funny to us so we laughed.

Under our feet we could feel the engines begin to throb. Two of the crew unwound the hawser lines from the cleats and stanchions, while another two on the boat pulled the lines back onto the *Slocum*. The crew on the dock came quickly on board and helped pull the gangway up. The *General Slocum* moved away from the 3rd Street pier. Ten yards out on the river you could see the full view of the wrought-iron, double-decked pier. It was something, y'know.

Slowly, slowly, the great pistons turned. Slowly, slowly, the paddlewheel boxes began to sink into the river and go round, come up with water, and pour it out on the other side. Slow, slow, lift, rise, and pour. The *General Slocum* moved up river, toward Locust Grove.

The whistles and the horns blasted out and shivered the city. The river wind caught the flags and pennants which flew high from her masts.

From a pole off the stern hung the American flag. It was large and of light silk. The wind billowed it out. Below the stars and stripes flew the imperial flag of Germany. The wind took that, too.

The orchestra struck up "Eine Feste Berg Ist Unser Gott" - "A Mighty Fortress is Our God."

I could almost cry for the beauty of that moment. Rosy slipped her arm around my waist and put her head against my chest.

The man tending the bar on the Main Deck wore a white shirt with a little black bow tie. He came out from behind the bar and went to the stairway and shouted down into the well, C'mon up a minute, will you?

He went back behind the bar, which was made of mahogany and had a high shine to it. In a few minutes the small thin Negro man came up, went to the bar, and said, You been calling?

Don't play dumb, Rastus. You know I've been calling you.

There's lotsa racket down there with the engines. You can't hear nothin'.

Well, you could have come up without my yellin' after you. Act like a white man!

Yassuh, boss, the black man said, wiping his hands on his apron. How about a little one? he said.

How about a little one? the bartender mimicked. I get you the nice easy jobs on this boat and all you do is get uppity. Can't you wait until we're underway? You get nothing from me until you have that chowder ready.

Chowder ready, Mr. Pelham. It's on the stove, heatin'.

How much is there?

Fifty gallons. I got ten on the stove now. It be hot soon. How the Knickerbocker Steamship Company going to feed all them fifteen hundred people clam chowder when all we got's fifty gallon? What we need is loaves and fishes.

They all ain't going to want it.

How about it, Mr. Pelham? I got a bad tooth back in my mouf.

How about it? How about it, Mr. Pelham? Shouldn't even be giving you goddamn Indians any of this fire water, the bartender said, pouring some whiskey in a glass and sliding it over to the Negro.

Hard to please you, Mr. Pelham. First Mate's a lot easier. He give me five dollars, you hear that, Mr. Pelham? Five!

Well, that's cheap enough for getting him deck hands. How much you cuttin' those poor niggers for?

I only got but six; less than a dollar a head. Then the small Negro man said to the bartender, I got to tend to my clam chowder. He smiled broadly showing the gold teeth in front of his mouth.He had hazel eyes and three gold teeth in the center of his mouth. He went down below.

Rosy and I walked aft. No one was at the rail there. We looked down at the white wake the *Slocum* churned up. We held hands tightly. It was like eternity, and like we were holy.

Oh, how I loved her. So much! So much!

Softly, almost under his breath in his gravelly voice, Knittel sang, *Rosy, you are my posy, you are my heart's bouquet.*

♪ 17 ♪

My brother, Oscar, found Rosy and me standing there holding hands.

Mama wants to see you. She can't open the lemonade, Oscar says, a little snotty, y'know.

Rosy, this is my brother, Oscar. Oscar, this is my friend, Rosy.

Rosy shook his hand. I'm pleased to meet you, Oscar. Edward spoke of you but he didn't say you were so big.

I'm nine. Oscar said without taking his eyes from her face. Mama can't open the lemonade.

Oscar, will you do me a favor and not tell Mama about my friend Rosy?

Why?

I want to tell her myself, later, when I introduce Rosy to Mama and the girls.

Okay, Oscar said. She wants you for the lemonade.

With Oscar by the hand, I went up to the Hurricane Deck, where Mama was in a lounge chair near the orchestra, which was now playing waltzes.

Were they playing the "Slocum Waltz"? McHooley asked with a grin.

Knittel, annoyed, glanced toward the bartender. As a matter of fact, they were, Knittel said. It was written especially for the excursion.   —

Did they do things like that in those days? Vilma Rakos asked.

Yes, they did, Knittel answered with his eyes locked on McHooley. McHooley, grinning still, ducked his head.

Knittel continued, Katy and Mary were dancing in a little circle. Mama was brushing her hair, watching the girls dance, saying, Very nice; very nice. That's it. That's it. Und step, und turn.

I found the lemonade jug. The top had been screwed on very tight. By Papa, I guess. I didn't think I could get it loose but I was so anxious to get back to Rosy that I pressed the jug to my chest and with a new strength I gripped the lid, twisted, and it was off in two turns.

Here you are, Mama, I said, but she was so involved with the girls dancing I handed the jug to Oscar, gave him two bits, and said, Shhhh!

It seemed everybody was on the Hurricane Deck. It was not so easy pushing through to get to the staircase. But it was all friendly and gemütlich.

The women, all nicely dressed, and many with parasols, gossiped. Their fingers were heavy with rings, their necks gleamed with chains dangling pendants and cameos. In Little Germany, the neighborhood where we lived, the people did not believe so much in banks and paper. They believed in land, gold, and diamonds. You had your wealth to use and to show that way. Even my father, a socialist, who could not afford to buy a house like Wolf and Helga, understood the practicality of a diamond on the hand.

After a pause, Knittel rubbed his flat nose. He continued.

I stepped over the feet of this mongoloid—slanty eyes, big head, silly smile, y'know. The boy sat against the railing. He had an army of paper soldiers between his thick, hairy legs, and his eyes kept darting upward to see his mother, checking on her, sort of.

One of the crew was talking to one of the mothers who had opened the top of her blouse to let the sun peek in. The man had his eyes stuck to the tops of her breasts. She was bigger, much bigger even, than my mother. The crew man made a little salute to her bosom before he moved on.

Although it wasn't near ten o'clock it seemed all the food hampers were open and everybody on the boat was eating. Germans can eat, y'know. The orchestra was playing the "Blue Danube".

That's the first cliche of the night, Joey Cortin said.

Knittel continued. It's the sea air. It makes juices in my mouth—like a lion in the jungle! I heard Bruni Neumann say. Before I could move on she called to me. I turned and gave her a little wave and with luck escaped without letting her talk to me. She could talk and talk, y'know.

Rosy had not moved from the rail. She still watched the wake of the *Slocum.*

It's much cooler down here, she said. Much better too. You can hear the music. You can see everything and you don't get crushed. Do you dance, Edward?

No. I'm sorry. But don't you worry I'll learn.

I'll teach you.

Not here, I'd be too embarrassed.

Ah, but not too embarrassed to kiss?

Rosy!

She laughed. Did you open the lemonade? I nodded. She pointed toward the shore on the Manhattan side. Is that 34th Street there?

Yes. I don't think the boat is up to speed. It's not much of a trip to Locust Grove so they have to make the most of the ride.

It's nice this way. Look, you can see along 34th Street almost to the Hudson. I would like to meet your mother, Edward.

Sure, whenever you want, I said. I was blushing but Rosy didn't notice.

Ah, Eddie! That's sweet! Esther said.

Thanks a million for nothing, yenta, Eddie said and returned to his story.

At the bar the deck hands and the crew took quick drinks. The bartender said, Better be careful if any one of you gentlemen is steering the boat through Hell Gate. Ha, ha, ha!

A yacht lay off the portside of the *Slocum.* It was fifty feet from us as we passed. All the men on board wore very dressy sailor's clothes with smart white hats and shoes. Round soft hats for the crew. White-braided billed caps for the officers. A bunch of swells! Rosy said I'll bet they're from Fifth Avenue.

We waved. They waved back. They were waving at Rosy. That's what I thought.

There was loud cursing and swearing which came up from the hold below.

The bartender shouted, Hold your mouths, you damned animals! There are ladies and gentlemen up here!

Then a laugh and a giggle came up and kept on for a time.

The bartender looked toward Rosy and me. From the half-smile on his mouth I could see that he was enjoying himself with the bad language, and the way he was looking at Rosy, I knew what he was thinking.

Rosy saw my anger coming up. By God, I wanted to punch that bartender. She squeezed my arm. Don't be silly, she said and led me to the ship's prow. There was a breeze strong enough to bring a spray into our faces. It felt good. I calmed down. But I marked the bartender down for getting even.

New York is so close to us, I said to Rosy, George Washington could throw a dime onto the dock.

⚓ 18 ⚓

Knittel ground his teeth. Although he sat perfectly still, a light sweat coated his forehead.

Are you all right, Eddie? Vilma asked the old man, who looked straight ahead, his eyes fixed on something beyond the far wall. He continued to grind his teeth. Eddie, Vilma said, look at me, here, look at me!

Knittel didn't respond.

Esther said, I hope this ain't it!

Hallucinating, Oster said, I think he's hallucinating.

Hey, there, you with the stars in your eyes! Joe Cortin sang.

Now, friends, if any of you are looking for an example of stoned, there y'have the perfect example, said McHooley.

Vilma dipped a paper napkin in a glass of water and walked to Knittel. She reached toward him with the napkin. Without looking or changing his position, the old man grabbed her wrist and held it.

Okay, Eddie, let go. You're hurting me.

Cortin and Oster got off their stools and walked toward Knittel's corner. There was no sign that the old man had seen Cortin and Oster coming, but he released Vilma Rakos's wrist and began to speak, his voice tense, his body taut.

The little girl, he said, came out of the toilet. Blond hair like Mary. Didn't see her. Didn't hear her. She tugged at my pants leg. I was looking into Rosy's eyes. Deep, deep bottomless eyes, y'know. Filled with love.

The little girl tugged again. Mister, she said, smoke smells in the toilet.

Yes, I said without looking at her.

It smells, Mister. A burning smell.

I looked down at the little face, which was like my sister Mary's. Sure, I said, it's from the galley. They're cooking chowder. In a little while we'll all have a cup of chowder.

I kissed Rosy lightly on the lips. The girl went away. *I told her there would be chowder.* Ach, ach, ach! Knittel said without moving, his voice now as lifeless as his face.

Rosy was teaching me how to dance. There were not too many people on the Main Deck. A few old men at the bar. Men and women coming down from the higher decks. Getting a

schnapps. Going to the lavoratories. Rosy teaching me to dance.
She could have taught me to bark, y'know. You're graceful,
Edward, she said. I told her my mother had taught me a little.

One two three four, one two three four. We're waltzing.

The music can be heard where we are. In the back of my
brain is the little girl. Is it chowder burning? I should look in
that toilet. Why doesn't someone else say there's the smell of
something burning?

One two three four, one two three four.

She was only a little girl. Maybe seven. Maybe eight. I
should look in that toilet!

One two three four, one two three four.

I'm thinking: the ladies' toilet. I can't go inside the ladies
toilet. Rosy can go inside the ladies toilet.

One two three four, one two three four.

Rosy, would you go sniff in the ladies' room? Her laugh
like porcelain.

You're acting so funny! But I will go, Edward. I will go
when the music stops.

One two three four, one two three four.

The music stops. Rosy goes. I wait.

She returns. There is trouble on her face. There is the
odor of something burning, Edward.

Chowder on the stove?

She shakes her head. No, she says. Maybe we should tell
someone, Edward.

The crew must know. Shouldn't the crew know?

I'm sure the crew knows. I hear laughter. It's my laughter.
At the back of my brain I think: If I tell someone from the crew
maybe they'll laugh and call me a girl.

I say to Rosy, Let's wait a minute or two. If there's still a
smell we'll go to the Captain. Rosy smiles. All right, she says.

We go to the rail on the port side. The _Slocum_ moves up
the river. The paddlewheels turn. The little girl. Rosy. The
chowder. Let's wait a minute or two.

One two three four, one two three four.

We lean over the rail. My arm is around Rosy's waist. The
paddlewheels churn. I turn my head to the starboard. Blackwell's
Island–Roosevelt Island today–is sliding by.

I turn back. A man on the shore is waving to us. Rosy
returns his greeting. I wave. The man waves at us with both his
arms. Agitated.

One two three, one two three.

Ward's Island, Randall's Island. We are hissing toward Hell Gate. We must go through Hell Gate.

Is it dangerous, Hell Gate? Rosy asks.

Not when the Captain knows the way.

Rosy says, I'm not worried, Edward.

But she is worried, I can see it in her eyes, y'know.

Some men on the pier are waving very hard. One jumps up and down while he waves, like a monkey on a string.

One two three, one two three.

Rosy gives me a kiss.

We go back to the prow. The wind and the spray take us over. I have to shout: We are going through Hell Gate now!

Everybody on the boat cheers! It's like that boat is cheering; like the boat has a voice.

The *Slocum's* horns sound. Her whistles blow. Bells.

The smell of chowder burning. Something burning. Rosy sniffing. The little girl. There's the smell of smoke burning. The *Slocum* hisses through Hell Gate. We are dancing again. Why the fuck were we dancing!

One two three, one two three. I should go to the Captain. ONETWOTHREE AND ONETWOTHREE.

Heavy pounding of work shoes coming up the stairs from below the Main Deck. A crewman. A haze of smoke sits on his shoulders. There is soot on his face. Rosy's grip on my arm tightens.

He hurries to the speaking tubes. On the wall on the starboard side. Forward of the stairwell where smoke rises. He whistles into the tube.

Captain Van Schaik! Captain Van Schaik! Flanagan! There's a fire! We have a fire! Yes, damn it, a fire! In the storage cabin. Don't know. Some flame. Mainly smoke. Packing straw. I'm doing all that. I ain't losing control. It's a fire, Captain!

Flanagan drops the speaking tube. It bangs against the wall. He races back to the stairwell. He scrambles down.

In a minute, in the blink of an eye, Flanagan comes up again. Two men race up behind him.

Flanagan gets to the fire stand. He jerks the pleated hose from the wall. It opens like a dried-out accordion.

O'Neill, Flanagan yells, grab the end of it. Stretch it out. Fast, fast! Get it down the stairs!

O'Neill, the large brass nozzle in his hands, pulls the hose toward the stairwell. The hose is so dry, it creaks. To Conklin, the other man, Flanagan screams, Find us some buckets! Conklin runs.

The people on the Main Deck, frozen in place, stare at the crewmen working with the hose.

Flanagan, using both hands, screws the back end of the hose with its brass coupling onto the water pipe sticking out from the wall. He opens the valve with quick turns. The pressured water rushes into the hose. The hose swells. For one blink, the hose swells. Then water fountains break through all along the gray hose. Then the brass coupling explodes from the wall pipe and crashes onto the deck. The water from the pipe, like it was a big kitchen faucet, splashes down onto the deck.

From the Hurricane Deck the music seems very loud.

ONE TWO THREE . . .ONE TWO THREE.

At the bar, a woman with an infant held to her breast with one hand and a stein of beer in the other, drops the stein, screams. She runs to the staircase.

Water is washing over the Main Deck.

A tongue of flame from the stairwell shoots up on the back of a cloud of thick, black smoke.

Mother of God! screams Flanagan. He runs up the stairs to the Promenade Deck.

ONE TWO ... ONE TWO ... .

19

Rosy's nails are digging into my arm, harder. I couldn't feel it.

Hip, hip, hooray! hip, hip, hooray for Captain Van Schaik!

I hear the passengers cheer. Hell Gate is behind us. There is joy on the Promenade and Hurricane Decks. They sing "For He's a Jolly Good Fellow".

On the Main Deck the tongue of flame is sucked back down below. The cloud of smoke sits heavily in the stairwell. Two old men on bar stools remain seated. They look hard toward the stairwell. Pelham, the bartender, is not behind the bar.

ONE TWO...ONE TWO.

A shaft of flame pierces the smoke again. It stays there. Then it bends itself in the middle. It reaches toward the bar. One of the old men slides off his stool. The flame reaches for him. He walks backward slowly as if the flame is a monster animal he does not want to arouse. The flame touches him. He springs backwards, loses his balance and falls to the deck. The flame retreats.

ONE TWO...ONE TWO.

On the Promenade Deck above, there are shouts.

IT'S A FIRE! THERE'S A FIRE DOWN THERE! OH, MY GOD, THE *SLOCUM* IS ON FIRE! THE CHILDREN, THE CHILDREN, WHAT SHALL WE DO WITH THE CHILDREN!

I DON'T SEE ANY FIRE!

THERE'S THE SMOKE! IT'S COMING UP! OH, MY GOD, THE *SLOCUM* IS BURNING!

The voices are as thick as the smoke now. Feet are pounding over our heads. The smoke is filled with names. People calling names. In German and in English. The name called most is Mother, in German and in English. Mother Mutter Mommy Mutti Mama Mama Mutti Mutti . . .

To Rosy I say, They'll put the fire out. They know how. I know you're scared but it'll be all right. I love you, Rosy, listen to me. There's a lifeboat over there. I'm going to see if I can get it down. You stay here. The fire is not on this side.

I pull her hands from my arm. I go to the lifeboat. I don't see any ropes or handles to loosen or turn. The lifeboat is tied to its place with heavy baling wire. I can't find a loose end. It's like it's soldered in place.

ONE TWO...ONE TWO.

The thing to do is to jump into the river. That is the thing to do.

Overhead are the life preservers. I reach up and pull down a few of the varnished slats. Life preservers tumble out. I grab one. It comes apart in my hands. The cork is a gray dust. I grab another. Dust. Dust runs out of my fingers. In my hand I'm holding a square of iron. I tear the life vests apart. Dust, rotted cork, gray dust, and in the dust a little iron bar!

I hold the dusty bar between my fingers like a little dead animal. How did it get into the cork?

ONE TWO ONE TWO ONE...

My heart is pounding. What can I do? Tell me, God, what can I do?

There is one long scream. Louder than the ship's horn.

ONETWOONETWOONETWOONE...

The *Slocum* is going up river. Why is it doing that? Doesn't the Captain know his boat's on fire?

On the Main Deck the fire is on the starboard side. Everybody is crowded to the port side. On the Manhattan piers crowds of people screaming. I can see their faces. I can hear their voices.

A man shouts across the river to the Captain, You're in flames! Turn into the shore! Turn into the shore! Get your head out of your arsehole! Turn it! Turn in!

The *Slocum* hisses up river. The paddlewheels turn faster.

A man in a tan linen suit, holding a tuba, flies down from above and splashes into the river.

I say to Rosy, You must jump over.

She shakes her head. She is trembling. I can't swim, she says. There is the dust of the life preservers covering her black shoes. I notice how small Rosy's feet are. Ach, ach, ach!

Only a few jump from the Main Deck. The others are old or can't swim and the life preservers are rotten. Do they know that? The fire is on the other side. They are against the rail. Some pray, some cry.

I say to Rosy, You stay here. I'll go up. Maybe I'll find some good life jackets.

She grabs hold of me and sobs, No, no, no, Edward, don't leave me! I don't want to die, Edward!

You're safe here for a while, Rosy. I'll run up quick. If I don't see good jackets I'll come right back. A few minutes, that's all, Rosy.

I force her arms down. I take a deep breath. I run up the stairs.

The staircase is burning on one side. It is heavy with smoke. The smoke and flames are sucked up the well.

When I reach the Promenade Deck I remember my mother and the kids. They are on the Hurricane Deck. I must go to them. Rosy will be all right.

At the top of the stairs lies the body of an old lady. Her white hair is singed. I step over her.

More people are jumping overboard. Those wearing life jackets sink like stones.

Fire is everywhere. Islands of fire. A woman with a baby in her arms is trying to put out her burning dress. She is screaming. She leaps over the side.

All around the burning *Slocum* there are boats. Rowboats, tugboats, pleasure boats. Shouts of Jump, jump, we'll save you!

Such screaming! Ach, ach, Ach! Oh, my God, such screaming!

The fire is eating through the Hurricane Deck.

I can see the Captain on the bridge. The river pilot stands next to him. He has one hand on the wheel. The Captain moves from side to side. He looks one way and then the other.

I see the mongoloid boy. He's standing at the bottom of the burgee pole. I notice for the first time he's wearing red suspenders like mine. He's waving his free arm like crazy. He's yelling for his mother. In German, he's yelling. He is shinnying up the pole screaming Mutti, Mutti!

Bruni Neumann is looking up at the boy on the pole and yelling, Edward, where is your mother? Why does she think the boy is me?

A man, an old man, grabs her arm and pulls Bruni to the rail. Together, holding hands, they jump over.

Now I hear myself yelling, Mama, Mama, where are you?

A woman throws a child overboard. The child is caught into the paddlewheel. There is a noise like a big water bug being crushed.

The fire is sawing the deck apart.

The mongoloid boy is halfway up the pole. His hairy legs are badly burned. Flames are chasing him up. Above his head the blue swallow-tailed burgee flaps.

Wind hits my face. A hot wind. The Captain is not turning into the shore. He is going full speed up river.

I must go back to Rosy!

I think I see my mother. I have to get around the flames. I push to the rail. I step over it. On the outside edge of the deck I am away from the panic. Hand over hand, gripping the rail, I begin to move toward my mother. I am a few yards away.

I see her and the kids through a wall of flame which opens and closes.

Opens and closes.

It's me, Edward! I'm coming!

Opens and closes.

They don't hear me. They don't see me. Great waves of flame break over them.

The wall opens and closes.

Mama has no hair. In her hand there is the handle of her parasol.

Opens. Closes.

They look all red. A big blister blows up on Katy's cheek. Oscar's face is pushed into the fire on Mama's dress. Mary, her face so red, so red, looks angry. She's screaming but I can't hear her!

I'm coming! Wait!

There are two soft explosions. The flames and the smoke leap high into the wind. The Hurricane Deck collapses down to the Promenade Deck. The pole with the boy clinging to it is pulled into the red pit. Burning people fall into the burning pit. My mother, Mary, Katy, Oscar, are like statues of ashes. They are pulled into the pit!

My shirtsleeves are burning. Rosy! Oh, sweet Jesus God, Roseeeey!

Knittel emitted the name like a scream. His voice filled with breath, gasping, he continued.

I try to swing down from the railing of the top deck to the one below. An explosion. There is a great shudder. I lose my grip. I'm falling. My foot catches in the space under the railing. I'm hanging upside down. Upside down I see the Bronx, where all the piers are lined with people. I twist my body so I can look inside the *Slocum*.

My leg snaps. I scream.

Did I scream because of my leg? Or did I scream because I was looking inside Hell? For the eternity I could see inside it, nothing but red embers and shafts of flame.

The flagpole, resting in the fiery pit, is like a red line, redder than the embers into which it is stuck like an arrow. The mongoloid boy is a black clump melted onto the pole, a burnt marshmallow.

Prow first, the *Slocum* collides with the shore of North Brother Island. I am torn away from the boat with the section of railing still holding my broken leg.

Whistles and horns, screams from everywhere.

I go deep into the river with the railing pulling me down like an anchor.

How my leg gets dislodged from the railing I don't know. I drift upward toward a small cloud. My head hits the cloud. It is not a cloud. It is the corpse of a fat lady dressed in white, her dead eyes open, staring into the river. I flop myself across her back. I float with her.

I see my arms. Badly burned. I see the sharp end of my leg bone sticking out through my pants leg.

Beached on the shore of North Brother Island, the hull of the *Slocum* reaches out a long way into the river. People are still jumping, jumping, jumping to death. The boat is smoking and burning. It is surrounded by small craft. Larger boats with hoses have turned them onto the burning *Slocum*.

The river is covered with gray powder and corpses. Among the corpses, the living swim. From the boats, with hands and poles, the living are pulled from the water, the dead are pushed away. Men in their underwear are diving into the river to save people.

I am floating on the back of the drowned woman. The corpse is pulled to the rowboat of a man with a hooked pole. He pokes at me with pole. I moan. From inside the boat he takes an iron pipe and smashes it into my head. Go drown, he says.

I black out for a minute. I open my eyes. He has turned the corpse over. He has it hooked alongside his rowboat. He searches the dead bosom and pulls out a knotted bluecloth. He tears the gold earrings through the dead lobes. He cannot remove the diamond ring from her finger. He cuts the finger off.

No, no, I blubber.

He pokes his hook into my forehead. I close my eyes. I am going to die. My head bumps into a floating board. There are two infants, badly burned, dead, lying on the board. I cannot bear to look at them. I roll over onto my back. The board with the infants supports my head. I am filled with pain but I am beyond pain.

I am sloshing in the crowded river. Up and down. Up and down. I see my arms, floating by themselves. I see my legs floating. One has no shoe, the one with the bone sticking out.

I am floating. I am sloshing. Up and down. Up and down. The sky is so blue, you can't believe it. Horns and whistles and bells and cries and voices.

And high up in the sky two snow-white seagulls are gliding over the river.

PART II

1

When Knittel had finished there was silence at the bar. McHooley turned up the radio volume as if it was a fan meant to disperse the sounds of the *Slocum* burning. Mort Shuman was singing in French "Brooklyn sur La Mer".

Knittel continued to stare into space as if he did not know he had finished speaking. Vilma Rakos asked, You okay, Eddie?

Knittel blinked and grimaced. He shook his head vigorously. He rubbed his beard with both hands. Another taste, McHooley, and keep the water on the side, he said in a soft voice.

Bo Wang came through the swinging doors with a galvanized iron dishpan and a large wooden spoon in his hands. He struck the pan with the spoon. Somebody die? Bo Wang asked.

Everything's fine, Mr. Wang, McHooley said.

Too quiet. Wang know that sound. The voice of mourning. Very Zen concept. Fire at sea story finished, Honorable Old Man?

You goddamned heathen Chinee, Knittel said, I ain't finished my story yet. Get back into the kitchen and stir your woks. Who invited you to listen?

Mindy, standing behind Bo Wang, said, He wasn't listening. I told him a little about the story you were telling. Don't be so mean.

No, no! Mistah Knipshun good Christian soul. Wang begs two thousand pardons!

McHooley hurled an ashtray toward Wang, who caught it clattering in his iron dishpan.

Good shot, boss! Bo Wang said with a smile. He struck the dishpan again. New Zealand Irish Stew ready for delivery in thirty-five minutes. Meantime, courtesy McHooley Bar Grill, Chu Lo Dim Sun served at once.

And what is that, Mr. Wang? Cortin asked.

Mini-pizza pies.

Everyone laughed except Knittel, who was stroking his beard and thinking.

Mindy and Bo Wang went through the doors and re-turned almost before the doors could swing through two arcs. Each held a large tray of mini-pizzas. They placed the trays on the bar.

Bring that tray closer to me, Wang, Eddie Knittel said sharply.

Dropping his Chinese accent, Bo Wang said, As Confucious once said, Fuck you, Knittel. Eighty-year-old boat rides don't require reverent attention. And I'm not into elder worship, you prick.

That's not nice, Esther Lieber said.

I'm not trying to be nice. He's a pain in the ass.

You're way out of line, Wang, said Oster. The old man is trying to tell his story. It's very important to him.

McHooley added, Lots of people died on that boat, Mr. Wang, and I think it's proper to remember those poor souls.

As I understand it, evesdropping, that was eighty years ago. Also, what seems to you to be lots of people would hardly be noticed in China.

You smoking something, Wang? Rakos asked.

Why must I be smoking? Because I'm Asian? Captain Knipshun there could tell you any bullshit at all because he's old and white. But if you've been listening with half an ear, he's been saying that nobody believed him when the *Slocum* burned. And he knows no one believes him now. So the old bum has turned to a new jury, being careful to bribe it to guarantee the verdict.

Raising his walking stick above his head, Knittel screamed, I'll kill him! I'll kill that slant-eyed sonuvabitch!

Vilma Rakos grabbed hold of the black cane and shouted, Please get back to the kitchen, Wang!

Wang smiled. Heathen Chinee go back to place, he said.

I think you can go home now, Wang, McHooley said. I'll see you tomorrow.

Wang slammed through the kitchen doors.

I went to a mah-velous party, Joe Cortin sang.

Beer! shouted Oster.

McHooley snapped the caps off six bottles.

I hate to ask this question, said Esther Lieber, but what's going to happen to the New Zealand Irish Lamb Stew?

♪ 2 ♪

It ain't easy to love you, Eddie, Vilma Rakos said. Why did you do that to Bo?

Because I hate fake Chinks! He's always putting on that ass kissing Stepin Fetchit stuff.

I'll allow that he was in full flower tonight, said McHooley. It comes out of frustration. He's an architect making stew when he should be building palaces of culture.

It's a problem, said Oster, when you don't know if you're a New Democrat lugging around the Statue of Liberty or the heir to the Ming Dynasty.

You give him a chance and he always does shit like that, Knittel said. I'm telling a serious story here.

Maybe he was bringing us comic relief, Eddie, Joe Cortin said. You were pretty intense.

Knittel snorted. Yeah, I was intense. It took me eighty years just to say what I said. It was like shitting a brick. Then out comes Mr. Bo Wang with that Charlie Chan crap. Sonuvabitch.

I can understand how that made you feel, Eddie, but you were overreacting, Vilma Rakos said. Bo is not Margie Ann Plunkerbrote.

I think he was overreacting with Margie Ann Plunkerbrote too, Esther Lieber said.

Maybe not, said Milton Oster, In *The Times* story today they also printed one of her poems.

A poetess?

Yes, McHooley, a poetess. The oldest poetess and regular reciter at the Angry Squire. Here it is: "On the Eightieth Anniversary of the *Slocum* Disaster," by Marjorie Ann Plunkerbrote.

> Into the burning air I took wing,
> A frightened bird who could not sing,
> Flung by mother from smoking nest,
> The fledgling did her very best.
> Her tiny wings beat upon the air
> While in her heart she said a prayer:
> Dear God, listen now to your daughter,
> Save her from flame and chilly water.
> And God responded to my plea
> And said to me, What must be, will be.
> And so forever my thanks I give
> That in His Wisdom He let me live.

She should have gotten roasted and drowned, Knittel said with a hiss. That cunt is becoming the admiral of the fucking fleet of history. I told you, she was only three years old when she got heaved overboard. She doesn't remember anything, nothing, zip, nada. She can't remember any of it!

Esther Lieber said, clearing her throat, I know you don't like Margie Ann Plunkerbrote, Eddie, but three-year-olds can remember a lot.

I see, said Knittel, the yenta wants to tell us something, is that it?

Yes, I do, Esther Lieber said. What did Margie Ann remember? she asked the companions of The Happy Hour. Eddie keeps telling us she remembered nothing. Just flying through the air. Clouds. Well, I say after eighty years that's something.

Esther dropped her glasses to the porch of her bosom and looked into Knittel's eyes. Maybe, if you weren't so angry all the time, Eddie, you'd take Plunkerbrote out to dinner and ask her, really ask her, what it is she remembers or what it is she *thinks* she remembers. Then you can be the judge of what's true or what's made up.

I don't want to be a judge, Knittel said, turning his head away from Esther Lieber.

All night so far you've been the judge, Eddie, and you know it. About everything.

Only about what I myself saw, what I myself remember.

Okay, so you're the judge of memory and no one else counts.

My memory.

Your memory, okay. But is Plunkerbrote entitled to a memory?

Christ, she was only fucking three years old!

Is it against the law to have memories of when you were three years old? Two even. I was also three once and I remember.

Flying through the air?

Esther smiled and, still facing Eddie Knittel, she put on her eyeglasses again. Oh, yes, she said, flying through the air. I remember that too.

Eddie slapped the bar top. Don't fuck me over, yenta! What are you saying? You were on the *Slocum* when she burned?

I ain't fucking you over, Eddie. I wasn't on the *Slocum*. I was in Buchenwald.

McHooley hurriedly wiped the bar top in front of Esther Lieber. He hesitated a moment before going to the radio and turning down "The Golden Age of Rock".

Almost embarrassed, Esther Lieber fidgeted, stroked her eyebrow, and said, Yes, I was in Buchenwald, and I remember. Not because of eyewitnesses. But because *I* remember. Even the name Buchenwald. It's a name I heard a thousand times when I was three.

THE YENTA'S TALE

The first thing I remember is the door of the freight car opens. The light hurts my eyes. A band is playing. The musicians are in rags. An officer in a black uniform with a skull and crossbones on his hat says, *Welkummen auf Buchenwald! Arous, arous. Schnell! Schnell!*

Where is my mother? I was holding her hand. Now she's gone. My father had gone away long before. I had brothers—I think I had brothers. I don't remember for sure.

I go to the man with the skull and the crossbones. I look up at his faraway face and I say, I'm hungry.

He looks down at me standing there in a dirty blue dress– a jumper, I think. He laughs. He points at me with his riding crop. He looks at the soldiers and the people who have just got out of the boxcar and he says in a very loud voice, She's hungry!

Everybody laughs. They laugh. Hunger and laughter.

He shouts again, She's hungry! Well, well, when someone is hungry in Buchenwald, what do we do? We feed them!

Corporal Kleiner, he orders, take her majesty here to the kitchen, feed her, and then bring her to me!

You'd think I'd remember eating or something about the kitchen, but I don't. I remember a lot but it's very blotchy. Some things I remember and I wonder what they mean. You know what I mean?

One memory is this: I am walking. I am always walking. I'm walking behind Bruno's high-polished black boots. Bruno, that's the name of the skull-and-crossbones guy.

Sometimes I look around. Maybe I'll see my mother. I don't. Maybe she'll come out of one of the barracks doors. She doesn't. Maybe I'll hear her call out my name. She doesn't.

So I'm walking after Bruno. Sometimes he looks down and pats me on the head. There's a pink ribbon in my hair. Where it came from I don't know. My blue jumper has been replaced by a little brown dress. I'm wearing patent leather shoes. From where?

At night I remember the stars over Buchenwald. Bruno smokes a cigar. He's sitting on a chair. The chair is on a porch like. Bruno looks up at the sky. Clear, he says. Tomorrow will be a wonderful day.

I think I'm sitting at his feet wearing a white nightgown with little bumpy knots of flowers around the neck and at the wrists. I'm one hundred percent sure about the white night-gown.

Bruno pats my head. He talks to the sky.

I think he carries me into his room, his quarters, and puts me to sleep in a box fixed up for me. It was on the floor but it's still not easy for me to get into. The sides are too high.

Bruno would take a bath in a big porcelain tub. I'm in the tub with him. He washes me. When he finishes he says, There you are, clean as a German. No more dirty Jew.

Did I go inside the barracks with him and see all the living skeletons? Or did I see them in the movies years later? I don't know for sure. But I remember a smell. I remember holding my nose, Bruno laughing.

Dead people—isn't that strange—I know they are dead people. They are piled on carts. They are naked. Skinny people in rags push the carts to a long row of little doors in a wall like.

Of course, I know what the iron doors are. I know that now. But at that time I wondered.

In Bruno's room there are two boxes of dolls and children's clothes: beads, hats, dresses, shoes. He says to me, Take what you want.

But I don't know how to dress myself or what to pick out from the boxes. Bruno says, Dumbbell! Where are your Jewish brains? He dresses me. He is so gentle, so patient.

I remember I am singing a song to a porcelain doll. Bruno applauds. I sing all the songs I know, Applause, applause. Bruno teaches me new songs.

I am dancing before Bruno. My little Jewish ballerina, he says. I will present you in concert.

I am in a large room. I am on a small stage with big lamps shining from the sides. The big room is filled with soldiers sitting on boxes and chairs. I sing and dance. Applause, applause.

Bruno teaches me a trick. He puts me on top of two wooden boxes. All right, he says, When I say alley-oop you jump into my arms. He shows me how. Alley-oop! He says. I dive into his arms.

The boxes get higher and higher. I climb up and up. Alley-oop. I dive into Bruno's arms.

Bruno says, All right, now we will give a gala circus concert.

On the stage in the big room boxes go up and up. I am wearing a tutu. Bruno is on the stage with me. He cracks his riding crop against his leg. I dance around in a circle, crack! I jump through a burning hoop. Applause, applause.

I climb to the top of the boxes. Very high. Oh, boy, it was very high!

There's a drum roll..

Bruno says, Ready? One, two, alley-oop! I dive into the air. I float down into the arms of the soldiers.

Cheers! Applause! Applause! Applause!

Bruno gives me a piece of candy.
Jesus Christ, McHooley said.
Bruno calls me the Virgin of the Sky. He finds an old woman with deep wrinkles who makes me a uniform like Bruno's. Skull and crossbones on the hat, iron swastika over the heart. I am so proud of that uniform! And my new, black shiny boots. Who made those boots? Sometimes I still wake up at night with a start—I've been dreaming about those boots. What comes before the little black boots in my dream, I don't know. I wake up sweating. The boots. What comes before the boots? What happened to the old lady?

So much music at Buchenwald. I dance and sing. And, best of all, I march right behind Bruno with my little riding crop under my arm like him.

Whenever a soldier salutes Bruno, he also salutes me.
Heil Hitler! Loud and strong. That's a soldier.
Heil Hitler! Like a bird. That's me.
The Virgin of the Sky parades after Bruno of Buchenwald. Heil Hitler! Heil Hitler!

Esther Lieber looked toward Knittel. Consider it, Eddie, Margie Ann Plunkerbrote must have remembered something.

She remembered shit! Shit! Knittel said and turned away.

Sometimes you're just a dope, Eddie, Esther Lieber sighed. Listen, I remember one day in spring. It's a little warm. Winter is gone. The sky begins to buzz. High up there are planes. On the ground and all around there is also a buzz. American planes.

The people in rags look up.

Bruno, smiling, looks up. He says, Well, here's something new.

Eddie, I can hear the guns faraway. Then closer, closer.

The soldiers are running to put things in trucks. Bruno is shouting: Do this, do that. *Schnell! Schnell! Schnell! Hoop-la! Alley-oop!* No, he didn't say *Alley-oop*. Not then.

I'm scared. I hold Bruno's hand. He walks and yells. He walks too fast. I stumble. He picks me up and holds me in his arms. He smiles at me. His face has the odor of cologne. The odor is still in my nostrils. I can still smell his cologne. Just as you can smell the fire.

I see the earth exploding.

Bruno says to me, I have to go away. The Americans are coming. You will stay here. The Americans will take care of you.

He puts me on the ground. He salutes me. Heil Hitler! he says. And what do you say? he asks.

Heil Hitler! I answer.

Stay! he orders.

Jaizus Christ! said McHooley.

Bruno strides away. I run after him. I grab his hand, his leg, I'm crying and screaming.

Bruno calls to one of the soldiers, who runs off and in a minute comes back with a rope, a hammer, and a piece of wood. He drives the wood into the ground. He ties me to the stake.

Screaming and crying. Bruno! Bruno!

Bruno pins a note to my breast with a little gold swastika.

Screaming and crying! Bruno! Bruno!

There is great cheering: the Americans had arrived.

Jaizus! said McHooley. You remember all that?

Yes!

You poor kid, said Vilma.

Hey, I was lucky. I'm here with you.

Joey Cortin said nothing. His cheeks were wet.

Oster asked, What did the note say? Did you ever find out?

Oh, yes. The note said, "This is the Virgin of the Sky of Buchenwald. She is a Jewish child. Take care of her. Her parents are dead. Colonel Bruno Gunther, Second Regiment, *Totenkopfferbande.*"

◄ 3 ►

Milton Oster had taken off his tie and removed his seersucker jacket, which he draped over the back of the stool. Put the air conditioner on, Jimothy. Eddie will pay.

Knittel was regarding Esther Lieber, who had moistened her eyeglass lenses with some white wine and was now polishing them with one of McHooley's bar napkins.

Vilma Rakos, who had left the bar, re-entered through the side door. No ticket, she said. I think the meter ran out an hour ago. I bought a fresh sixty. Did I miss anything? Eddie kill anybody?

No. Just a lot of breathing going on, said Joey Cortin.

I wasn't really taking Margie Ann Plunkerbrote's side, Esther said, and put on her eyeglasses.

I ain't going to be a schmuck and say Plunkerbrote couldn't remember anything. But she exaggerates, Knittel said in a conciliatory tone. Does anybody think she was down in the fucking boiler room?

No one replied. Knittel met their silence with his own.

Finally Esther spoke. You quit, Eddie, or you going to continue?

Continue. I already paid for the privilege. I hope you don't think I'm bribing you, do you? You think Wang was right?

There was no response.

McHooley grinned.

Knittel sighed. Maybe he's right. I want everybody to believe me and I'm afraid you won't. Like the early days, y'know, when Melvin didn't believe me. Helga didn't. I didn't care if Wolfgang didn't believe me but Helga and Honeycuitt, I wanted them to.

My father once said to me, If one man says you're drunk and you don't think so, stick by your guns. If three men say you're drunk, think it over, but if you don't think so, stick by your guns. If ten men say you're drunk, lie down.

But how could I lie down? Knittel asked, his tension rising. I knew, I believed what I saw with my own eyes! But that's how it is with delusional people, right? What's that word?

Schizophrenic, Oster said.

Right, that's it: schizophrenic. Another world, real to me but to no one else, Knittel said and thumped the bar with a closed fist. Ten men. A hundred. A million eyewitnesses. If I lie down I'm a liar. If I stand up I'm crazy.

How about a combination of amnesia and confusion? Oster suggested.

There you go! That's what Honeycuitt always said. Amnesia, confusion, the eyewitnesses, confusion, amnesia! Lie down, Eddie, you're drunk! I just couldn't lie down, y'know. Couldn't do it!

One stubborn kraut, said McHooley, as stubborn as any Irishman I've ever known.

If Helga didn't believe me—all right! I just wanted Honeycuitt to believe me.

Because of *The New York Times*? Vilma asked.

No, because I wanted one person to say he took my word and because I liked him, respected him. Here it is, Knittel continued. I'm back from the hospital. They let me out early, y'know, because Helga is a nurse and I'll be at her house and under her care. So now I'm there and Melvin Honeycuitt is sitting by my bed smoking a Fatima.

Honeycuitt says, Mayor McClellan told me he'll visit you tomorrow. He's confided to me that he will declare July 30th as Edward Francis Knittel Day. Aren't you pleased?

I don't answer. He smiles, y'know, as if he's reading my mind. Edward, he says, you can't keep hiding behind this false sense of modesty.

I close my eyes to get control of myself. Honeycuitt notices this. So he says, Are you in pain, Edward? Do you need your medication?

No. I can go a few hours yet.

That's a good sign. Sometimes people become addicted to opium. They live their lives in a dream world.

Is that bad? I said. I was teasing him, y'know.

Edward! he says. Have you never seen pictures of those Chinese opium smokers? They become absent human beings. They dissociate from life. They exchange the joy of a thousand pleasures for the pleasure of an empty, painless dream.

Yes, I said, I know. Sometimes I feel like that.

You look tired. Are you?

I didn't sleep too well. I was thinking of all of the things that happened on the *Slocum*. You're wrong, Mr. Honeycuitt. If I was up the flagpole I'd be dead now. That pole fell into the fire when the top deck collapsed.

Yes, I know that, Edward. But you vaulted off the mast even as it tilted and fell. You vaulted right into the river.

No! It didn't tilt! It went straight down! I yelled. What Honeycuitt was saying was pure shit, y'know. Vaulted into the river!

He comes right back at me and says dead serious, You're wrong. I'm sorry but it's my job to sort out truth from untruth, Edward. That's what journalists do. It's not a simple thing when more than a thousand people die to find out why or how, to substantiate everything, to make the details, the facts, fit. Can you understand that?

Not really, I say to him. The truth must be the truth all the time, not just sometimes. I ain't going to agree with the eyewitnesses, and especially with Bruni Neumann. You can write what you want a hundred times. If anyone asks me, I will say I was not on the pole at all. I was *never* on the pole.

You're stubborn, Edward! Honeycuitt said with a little impatience. He changes the subject.

The Coroner's Jury trial begins today, he said.

What's that? I asked.

It's the job of the Coroner to sift out the facts for a jury to determine who may be responsible for the tragedy. If the jury feels some parties are responsible, those parties will be brought to trial in civil and criminal courts, depending on the exact nature of the findings, of course.

Who do you think is guilty? I ask him.

I have my own ideas, but let's see what the inquest finds.

It won't help the dead, I said, and turned my head away. You'd think I was thinking of my mother and the kids but I wasn't. I was thinking of Rosy. Who cared about the thousand others? Rosy!

True, he says. The dead can't be brought back. But, I believe, Edward, the guilty still must be punished. If we avoid that, morality will simply crumble. How many thousands of years did it take mankind to seek justice through law? Not through opinion, not through passion, but through law, the language of justice. It's the process of law and you will be part of that process.

I can remember what Honeycuitt said and I can repeat what he said because I thought, y'know, the way he said it was so beautiful.

You will appear before the Coroner's Jury, Honeycuitt says. Then he spread and smoothed a copy of *The New York Times* across his lap. It says so right here.

I can't help laughing. It was the first time I had laughed since the disaster. Honeycuitt laughs, too. At the end of his laughing he wheezes.

It's not completely definite, he says, after he gets his wind. Bill O'Gorman, the Coroner, says it's up to you. Here I quote him, "Surely we will hear from Master Edward Francis Knittel, the young hero of this awful disaster. Master Knittel can affirm many of the facts alleged by witnesses. If his health allows it, we will ask that Master Knittel be brought here on Wednesday July 17th . . . ."

No one asked me, I say.

They will.

I won't go.

That's up to you, Edward. He takes a fresh Fatima from its box, puts it to his mouth and lights it. Don't you want justice done?

Asking me about justice, Honeycuitt makes it sound like my father talking. My father always talked about justice and injustice. The ruling class, which was always unjust to the laboring masses, would one day be brought to justice by the workers of the world. Unlike the justice of the bosses, the justice of the workers would be fair. Even the bosses, as they walked before the Revolutionary Firing Squads, would say, We have been tried fairly. We have been found guilty fairly, and the punishment is just. Then they would be shot down.

When I asked my father what would happen if the bosses didn't say the justice of the workers was fair, he slapped my face. That's what would happen, he said. He was a prick, my father. So I don't answer Honeycuitt's question.

From the river we hear a loud explosion. I almost jump out of my skin. Honeycuitt leans out the window. Then there is another explosion, so loud it bounces off the buildings and bridges. It comes again. I count twelve explosions.

Honeycuitt pulls his head in. He's smiling. Cannon! he said. They have actually brought the cannon! What nonsense!

I asked him why nonsense?

They've brought a coast guard vessel to fire cannon along the route of the *Slocum*, close to the river surface and down into the river, he explains to me. The booming is supposed to cause deep vibrations under the water. The vibrations are supposed to free any corpses caught on the bottom and bring them to the surface. It's some kind of military theory. They used it during the Civil War. I have no idea how it works but I think it's nonsense.

What if it does bring up corpses?

I'll be greatly surprised and mildly astonished, he says.

My feelings about this cannon shooting, bringing the dead to the surface, were very confused, y'know. I thought: what if Rosy floats up? I didn't want that at all. What would she look

like rising from the bottom after so long in the river? I shudder.
My arms tingle under the bandages.

Will you know if the cannon brings up anything? I ask.

I'm sure that one of my colleagues is there, witnessing the
action. It'll be in tomorrow's *Times.* I think they've found all the
bodies they ever will. They've done a very good job there and
it's an ugly business. Takes very strong stomachs to do that.

He lights another Fatima Oval. He takes a drag, blows
some blue smoke. He picks at his lips for a piece of tobacco,
which he can't find.

There is nothing so mysterious as the thousand parts of a
catastrophe, Edward. I think about it a great deal. I've written
many stories for *The Times*, but I think I will always remember
this one. No, that's not saying it well enough. There are other
stories I will always remember. But this *Slocum* business is
something I keep thinking about, mulling it over and over. It's
an event I know more about than any other of which I have
written. Yet, at times it slips away from me and I have to think
about it over again. Almost as if I don't know what happened.

I think I have him there so I snap, Then why do you keep
saying I'm the boy who climbed the pole? Why do you keep
saying that?

Because it's probably true.

I look at Melvin Honeycuitt for a very long time as he sits
under a pile of Fatima smoke. He's troubled. And me, I'm
wondering which is better–to know the truth or not to know the
truth? Then I have another thought which disturbed me a lot:
What difference does it make if you know the truth or you don't
know the truth?

Did it make any difference to the whole world if I had
climbed up the flagpole or if another boy had? Did it make any
difference to the whole world if I, Edward Francis Knittel, was
alive or another was?

But it made a difference to Melvin Honeycuitt, y'know. I
decide I won't bring up the boy anymore. Let him think whatever he wants to think. I wouldn't say yes and I wouldn't say
no. And, as for the boy who had fallen into the fiery furnace, it
wouldn't mean a damn thing to him. So, let it be, I say to
myself, let it be. Let Bruni Neumann be, too!

It was the beginning of a new thing, my learning to keep
my big mouth shut, to hide my real thoughts, y'know. I will go
to the Coroner's Inquest if they want me, I say, more to break

the mood than anything else. It has some effect on Honeycuitt because he smiles and nods. He's pleased.

There is a knocking at the downstairs door and a voice calls up from the street, Eeooh, Mr. Honeycuitt! It's Peter!

I'll be right down, Honeycuitt answers from the window. As quickly as he can with his bad legs and his big butt, he goes downstairs. In a few minutes he comes back reading from a sheaf of papers.

Some copy on the *Slocum*, he says. Nothing much. Unimportant but curious. Two bodies, children, have been retrieved at the Fulton Street Pier. The current pulled them that far.

What he says gives me a chill. I look toward him. Jesus, I say, the tide could pull them out into the bay. Out into the sea. They'll never know how many died!

That's possible. If the tide brought corpses out to sea we may never know how many actually died. There can be no accounting. Tickets for the excursion were not issued for children, only for adults. A mother could have said she would have two with her and then for whatever reason come with five. Her ticket would get them all aboard. There was no way of knowing exactly how many—not to the final body count, anyway.

Honeycuitt waddles around the bedroom as he thinks out loud. The Unidentified Dead. Now that makes for a perfect quandary, you see. There are one hundred fifty-six Unidentified Dead. If bodies have been washed out to sea—even a hundred bodies—those whose lost ones were assumed to be among the Unidentified Dead would have to be uncertain that their relatives had been buried in the Lutheran Cemetery. There would be no way to ever know, no way.

My stomach turned. Was Rosy in the ground? Or did she fall so deep under the waves that no grappling hook could find her and no cannon could make her rise. Caught in the undercurrents, was she pulled through the mud? The dirty mud of the dirty river? The river into which the toilets of the city emptied? Oh, God! Was she surrounded by scumbags and goldfish? God! Would the river bump her into the green legs of the docks? And the wakes of ships shake her and turn her and tumble her? And the big water rats take bites of her flesh? Oh, God! Oh, God! If the river tides took her out into the deep water, were there huge sharks? Rosy! Rosy! Rosy!

Then I begin to blubber. Whenever I thought of Rosy it tore me apart, y'know.

Honeycuitt says, You don't look too well, Edward. You've lost color. Are you in pain?

Yes, I'm in pain, I cry and ask for my medicine. A few minutes after the laudanum I feel much better. Honeycuitt feels better himself seeing that my color has come back.

The likelihood is that the bodies found at Fulton Street were the only ones to get down that far, he says. They were the bodies of infants. If indeed bodies did get out into the bay and into the sea, some will wash ashore at the Statue of Liberty and at Governor's Island. They would be sighted, of course. It's logical to believe that the Fulton Street corpses were accidents.

Accidents? What did that mean? The laudanum had smacked me good. I hadn't taken any for a while. Despite my horror, I feel happy. I'm in an empty, painless dream.

Honeycuitt, reading the papers which had been delivered to him, says, It seems that the Coroner's Jury trial will be a grand success. They've had to delay it because of the mobs waiting to get into the armory. Second Battery of the New York National Guard. When they were admitted, they came on in a great stampede, and trampled each other. Some had wild donnybrooks, men as well as women. Thirty have been arrested.

He lowers himself into the narrow chair which is almost too small to surround his rump. He pulls the chair close to my bed and says, Here's a question for you. Why are they holding the trial in the Bronx? Why not in Manhattan? I surely would have thought they'd hold it near City Hall, wouldn't you?

I am very high now. I giggle. I say to Honeycuitt, Gee Whiz, sure, City Hall!

I'll explain why, Edward. It's because Bill O'Gorman, outfoxed City Hall. Mayor McClellan would have preferred the trial in one of the downtown court buildings or in one of the larger assembly rooms of City Hall itself. But Bill O'Gorman wanted to hold it in the Bronx armory so the great unwashed might see him preside. He's an impressive man with a gavel. He wants to get as much attention as possible. Why? Our Coroner wants to be a judge one day. Or perhaps mayor? He's just as happy that our District Attorney, Mr. Jerome, has refused to conduct the Bronx inquiry and has turned it over to the Assistant District Attorney, Francis P. Gavin, Gavin is less flamboyant than Jerome, which pleases O'Gorman a great deal. O'Gorman doesn't want anyone to shine more brightly than him. Gavin, of course, bless his boyish heart, is as happy as the proverbial, because this is his big opportunity. One day he dreams of being District Attorney. Even if that does not transpire, Gavin is on the front page of *The New York Times* and the press all over the world, and that will lead to some good for him.

I giggle. Everybody is going around the mulberry bush, I say with a dopey grin. I remember that, Knittel said, and stroked his beard.

Did you go to the trial? McHooley asked.

I had to, the bastards subpoened me. So much for the hero shit, y'know. They didn't invite me, they didn't ask me, they subpoenaed me! Hero!

Weren't you still in bed in your mummy outfit? Rakos wanted to know.

Yeah, but they put a smaller cast on my leg so I could move it a little. The bandages on my arms were the same except there was more room for the fingers. The bandages were off my face, Knittel said, as he touched his bearded cheek, the burn was there but it had ointment on it. My head was still heavily bandaged.

Still, Rakos persisted, you couldn't go to a courtroom like that.

Ah, Vilma, when the time came they sent a crew to Helga's house and carted off the whole fucking bed! When they want you, they want you. Hero! Honeycuitt was pissed off even though he said he wanted me to testify. How could they do this to Master Knittel? He protested to the Mayor, he protested to the Governor. Sympathy, y'know. But there is law and there is justice, and we are the Land of Laws and the world is watching. No one is above the law and that includes Our Hero, Master Edward Francis Knittel. So the crew came and they lifted up the bed. They had to remove the doorframe to get the bed out into the street where the ambulance, a Toledo, was waiting. Honeycuitt and Helga are in the ambulance with me.

Honeycuitt is sore as a boil so he talks a lot as the ambulance bounces its way up to the Bronx with Helga yelling for the driver to go slow over the cobblestones.

I don't get it about Honeycuitt, Esther said. What made him change his mind?

I don't know, Knittel said with a smile, Maybe I had changed his mind. Who knows? But he was mad all right.

⌐ 4 ⌐

The Bronx? Oster said, his voice filled with amazement. The
Bronx? The Hero is abducted to the Bronx?

Well, said Eddie Knittel, it was politics. In those days the
Coroner held his own jury trial when there was a death. If they
found cause against you at the coroner's trial you got put before
a regular court. The Coroner acted as the judge, y'know. It was
a great shot for O'Gorman to bang the gavel while the whole
world looked on. And in the Bronx the spotlight would fall on
him, not on McClellan. Honeycuitt thought that O'Gorman
was very clever. Quite clever, is what Melvin said. "Quite" was
one of his favorite words. Sometimes I found myself waiting for
him to say it.

In that minute the Bronx was in the eyes of the world. It
was the big stage of history, y'know. If you went to the Bronx
that July, went to the armory, you would be standing on the
stage and your name would be known forever. That's what
people thought. So the mobs came and fought to get in.

Mayor McClellan couldn't afford not to show up.
O'Gorman gave him a ringside seat. From Washington come
representatives and senators. Both senators from Mississippi
came. Sitting right behind the Mayor was Police Commissioner
Bill McAdoo, Fire Commissioner Nick Hayes. There's the Lieutenant Governor of New York, but I forget his name.

Philander C. Knox, the Attorney General of the United
States, is there. He lets everybody know that the City of New
York has no jurisdiction over the East River. All rivers belong
to the United States y'know. He promises to put the whole
thing before a United States Circuit Court.

Philander. How can a man with a name like that be allowed to hold public office? Cortin asked.

I think it's a great name, Oster said. Politicians should be
named Greed, Plague, Theft, and Pestilence.

George Cortelyou, Secretary of Commerce, appointed a
blue-ribbon investigating committee, all generals and admirals.
All the foreign press was in the Bronx. A special table was put
up for them. I remember all that, Knittel said.

The United States Inspector of Steamboats is also there.
Everybody wants to speak to him but he will not say a word,

y'know. They say that the Administration has put a clamp on
him because the Democrats are screaming that the *Slocum* is
being white washed to protect the criminal role of the shipping
industry. The Republicans are screaming back that this is a
Democrat attack on Teddy, who will run for re-election in the
fall.

And outside the armory there are prayer vigils with pas-
tors, priests, and evangelists standing on chairs and packing
crates. The crowd is bigger outside than inside and is laced with
half the whores in New York. Plenty of hotdog and hamburger
sellers, ices and ice cream, and booze peddlers–denounced by
the priests and ministers. And there are men with megaphones
shouting out the news coming from inside the armory. With
each announcement they yell: And be sure to watch your
pockets and purses! Pickpockets are everywhere!

The ambulance splits the crowd and rolls up to the armory
doors. They lift my bed out and a roar goes up and my name is
in it: Eddie! Eddie! Hero! Hero! I shiver.

Why? asked McHooley.

Don't ask dumb questions, Knittel snapped. It was all out
of hand. Blood, blood, they wanted blood.

Not yours, Oster said.

Eddie, said Vilma Rakos, if you were lying down, how
could you see the booze peddlers or the ambulance splitting the
crowd, or any of that other stuff?

Honeycuitt. He's my personal reporter, y'know. He tells
me what I'm missing. But I know one thing on my own: I'm
scared. What am I doing here at the center of the world? When
they call on me what will I say? But there's another thought I
have as they carry me into the armory that's as important as all
my other thoughts: What if I have to take a piss? Did Helga
bring the jar?

⁊ 5 ⁊

I'm flat on my back. I'm looking up at the ceiling of the
armory. It's a mile up there. The light from the outside comes

through these slits in the walls. They are the windows. There are no lights in the high ceiling. On the walls of the armory there are gas lights sticking out on metal arms. On the floor there are electric lamps on stands.

They carry me down a long aisle. I hear voices: It's Eddie Knittel. Look at the bandages! Guts, the kid's got guts!

Everywhere there are chairs, wooden folding chairs.

There's a space cleared for my bed. They put it down. Helga holds my hand. Honeycuitt says, Don't get excited. When they call on you tell the truth. I nod.

Helga leans over the bed to straighten the thin blanket which covers me. She's got a shiner on one eye. It's been covered over with powder.

Helga and Melvin adjust the bed so that it's in the highest sitting position. I can see pretty good now, the whole armory.

Coroner O'Gorman bangs the gavel. On this day, at this hour, the Inquest is in session, he says. Everything becomes quiet. From almost a thousand people sitting there, there isn't a sound.

O'Gorman is reading from a paper he holds. He reads, This Inquest has been called to determine the facts in the burning of the steamship the *General Slocum*. We have determined that, thus far, one thousand, three hundred forty-six people died in the fire which consumed the boat. It is, to my best knowledge, the largest sea catastrophe in the history of the world. It saddens me that this holocaust has taken place in the environs of the great City of New York, on our own East River, in full view of tens of thousands of New Yorkers. How did this happen? Could it have been prevented? Above all, who is responsible and to whom does guilt fall? To these ends the Inquest is dedicated.

He raps the gavel again.

I look toward the jury. They are all men. They sit very erect. Only two of them are without mustaches. One of them has a straw fan, which he is using. It's getting very hot on the armory floor. I am feeling pain. I close my eyes.

Helga whispers into my ear, I have some medicine. I'll put a half-dose in some water. Helga gives me a tumbler. I drink it. I feel better.

Assisstant District Attorney Gavin has called the first witness. It is Frank A. Barnaby, President of the Knickerbocker Steamship Company, Incorporated. He wears a gray suit. His shirt is white with a high collar. His necktie is gray. There is a pearl stickpin in it. His mustache is waxed stiff.

Even the half-dose of laudanum makes me groggy. I don't hear the first part of Gavin's questions to Mr. Barnaby. Whatever Gavin and Barnaby are saying it makes Honeycuitt very tense. No smoking is allowed so he keeps touching his lips with a damp handkerchief. Helga asks if I'm all right. I nod.

It's not word for word what I tell you now, but I remember how it went because I was there and I heard it. And later, I talked about it with Honeycuitt, who had a great time imitating Barnaby and Gavin. And I had a bound copy of the Inquest, which O'Gorman gave me after the Inquest was complete.

Which you burned up, McHooley said.

That's right, Knittel said with a smile. But my memory holds on to it like a tape, y'know.

Knittel took out one of his stinkers and this time he lit it. Here's Barnaby, he said and produced a deep, unctuous voice.

Cortin guffawed, Here's Knittel imitating Honeycuitt imitating Barnaby imitating the president of the Knickerbocker Steamship Company, Cortin managed to choke out through his laughter.

Knittel laughed. Fag humor, he said.

Eddie! Vilma admonished, Cut it out!

Hey, let him, said Cortin. It makes him happy, doesn't it, dear?

All right, it just slipped out. I like you, Joey. I apologize.

Sweet, said Cortin and blew Knittel a kiss.

Knittel blew some smoke from the side of his mouth. He pushed his chest forward, pulled his shoulders back, waved his arms, for attention and continued in the deep unctuous voice.

I want to say immediately that the *General Slocum* was the finest—the finest, I want to emphasize—the finest paddlewheeling steamship ever to ply these waters. The *General Slocum* was constructed according to the highest standards of the art of shipbuilding in the year of our Lord, eighteen hundred ninety-one. It was this great ship which was chartered by St. Mark's Lutheran Church. Chartered, I say, in full confidence of the *Slocum's* safety. Full confidence in the experience and leadership of Captain William Van Schaik, who has sailed these waters for forty years carrying thirty-six million people on sunfilled voyages of joy. I salute Captain Van Schaik. The officers of the Knickerbocker Steamship Company have reviewed every available fact and have come to this conclusion; The minor combustion which occurred on that fateful day would have been easily brought under control–I repeat–easily brought under control if the passengers had not fallen into a panic and become an unruly mob.

Then Gavin says, Knittel continued in a higher voice with a slight stammer in his delivery, Are you telling us, Mr. Barnaby, that the *Ssslocum* disaster was the fault of its passengers?

Yes, I am, Knittel said in his deep Barnaby voice. In my experience we have never, I repeat never, had any trouble on our boats when there were no passengers on them.

Stop, said McHooley, no man could have said such a mindless thing. You know that, Eddie. You're joking.

Yes. But it was all a joke, y'know, because that's what Frank Barnaby meant. And when Gavin, astounded, y'know, caught Barnaby up and said to him: You are condemning the women and children on the *Ssslocum* as a mmmutinous mmmob?

Barnaby answers him like a cannon shot: No, sir! Not at all! I loved those people. They acted out of ignorance and without malice. They were as my own family, for that is the way Knickerbocker Steamship thinks of its passengers. Why, Mr. Gavin, on the day of the signing of the agreement with St. Mark's, I promised Pastor Haas and his assistant that I would provide every man, woman, and child fresh clam chowder at absolutely no charge. I wanted them all to have a good time, a joyous day.

He really said that? asked Esther Lieber.

Knittel's face suddenly became a mask of sadness. In essence, Eddie Knittel said, in essence. After that Barnaby cried. Really cried. Real tears. Real nose honks. The sonuvabitch.

It was a good time for the Coroner to call a recess and he did. Few if any left the Armory because it was another hot day outside. Also they didn't want to lose their seats. You could get into a fistfight over a seat, y'know. There was plenty of ablutions in the house–I could see the bottles pass around. O'Gorman poured himself a schnapps from a silver flask.

Knittel cocked his head, smiled, and then laughed softly. Fucking circus, he said, and Frank A. Barnum was in the witness chair!

I think Eddie is pulling our leg, the old smartass! Cortin said.

I don't think so, said Oster. You laugh to keep from crying.

Look at Eddie—I don't see him laughing, Vilma Rakos said. You an accountant or a psychologist?

Oster shrugged.

* 6 *

Helga whispers in my ear, You have to pee?

I see her swollen eye again so I ask her, How did you do that?

She says, An accident. It's nothing.

But I got a flash and I knew how she got it. Wolf. So I say to her, I know it was Wolf. She shakes her head.

Thirty years later she told me the story. In the meantime Wolf had left her and gone back to Germany. After that Helga and Melvin got involved. They lived together for years before they got hitched. The divorce was not easy because Wolf was in Germany and he wanted a lot of money for his half of the house they owned. Helga got her Cherman up and wouldn't give him what was not fair. It took time to settle all that.

Wolf and Melvin both got into World War I. Melvin was a volunteer ambulance driver. He got killed all the same. Wolf made sergeant, lost an eye, and joined Hitler and Roehm. But I'm getting off the track. I was telling you about the Inquest. How did I start with Helga?

She asked you if you had to pee, Esther said, and you saw her swollen eye.

Some shiner! Yes, said Knittel, but that's another story.

I want to hear it, said Vilma. What happened?

It's too long, Knittel said and patted her arm. I'm in the trial and I got Barnum sitting.

I want to hear it, just quickly. What happened?

In a nutshell, said Oster.

In a thimble, said Cortin.

Knittel blew some smoke. It's like this, he said. Wolf began to get fixated by the *Slocum*. Not the *Slocum* itself, but by the dead, y'know. He'd go to the morgues and say he was looking for my mother and the kids. On the 23rd Street pier, where they put a hundred or so bodies which the morgues couldn't take, he found Duseldorf's wife, half her face gone. The thing is, Wolf is going from corpse to corpse, inspecting. Then he goes to Brumer's Saloon and tells morgue stories to the beer drinkers. It excites him and when he comes home he can't wait to do it with Helga. He has her under him and he tells her about the dead he's seen. Details. This woman's breasts, that woman's heavy thighs, Mrs. Duseldorf's varicose veins, and their eleven-year-old daughter already had good-sized tits. Helga turns to ice. She will not do it with him. He goes crazy and beats her up.

That's it. Everybody satisfied? I shouldn't have told you about it. I broke a confidence. I don't think Honeycuitt knew about it. Now back to the Bronx.

McHooley said, What about Honeycuitt and Wolf in the war? Hitler and Roehm?

Nah, said Knittel, I'm back in the Bronx. Let me get my train of thought.

The old man stroked his beard and continued. Assistant D.A. Gavin gets real close to the witness stand. He looks into Barnaby's eyes. I think Gavin was a little pissed off. No preliminaries, he gets right to it. He says to Barnaby, I want to talk to you about firehose. You know what firehose is, sir?

Yes, sir, I do. Barnaby answers in Knittel's low voice.

This firehose on the good ship *Slocum* was very old, did you know that?

No, I did not.

Old and dry. Technically, Mr. Barnaby, it was not firehose. It could not hold water. It was made of cotton material so thin you might have made stockings of it.

I don't believe that, Mr. Gavin. You're being dramatic for effect.

Gavin adds, the *Slocum's* firehose was so useless it might just as well have been painted on the walls!

There is lots of laughing on that.

Frank Barnaby smiles and looks at Gavin. He says, I have no knowledge of the nature or the condition of the ship's firehose. It is not my job. I delegate such tasks to others. I rely on others in such matters.

Can you tell us, sir, on whom you relied in this case?

I relied on the Steamship Inspection Services of the government of the United States of America.

Lots of laughing here. Gavin is taken aback. He stammers, Ddddid you know, sir, that the lllife pppreservers were rotted through, the cccork ttturned to pppowder? Useless?

I had heard some rumors regarding the life vests but I have no direct knowledge. The life preservers passed inspection, he says and glances at a slip of paper in his hand. Passed inspection on May fifth.

Gavin snaps at Barnaby, May fifth of what year, sir?

Barnaby tries to surpress his smile. May fifth of nineteen aught four. Yes, aught four, he said.

Gavin is spraying spit at Barnaby, who leans to one side. Dddid you know, sssir, that the cork in each life preserver panel was not only rotten but contained an iron bar at its center? Did you know that?

Barnaby's face becomes stern. He says, I am shocked to hear such a thing! That is shameful and criminal! It should be called immediately to the attention of the Steamship Inspection Services of the United States Government!

Honeycuitt almost has a fit. He jumps to his feet. Helga has to pull him down. When I ask Honeycuitt if Barnaby had lied, he says, No, and that's the damned part of it! For the record he told the truth . For the rest of it he is worse than the devil quoting scripture! He's only the major stockholder and the president of a little corporation which owns two steamships, yet, damn it, Edward, he owns the world, and the government of the United States comes to serve him at his bidding. I'm dying to have a smoke. I'll be right back.

I watch him waddle away toward a near exit.

Honeycuitt misses the next questions by Gavin. I remember this part: Gavin asks if the *Slocum* carried insurance.

Of course, Barnaby said.

How much insurance?

Seventy thousand dollars.

Seventy thousand dollars? Is that all? The grand total?

Yes, sir.

That's less than ssseventy dddollars a cccorpse!

You misunderstand, Mr. Gavin, that amount insures the ship, not the people. Our contract with St. Mark's clearly states that passengers come aboard at their own risk. It is also printed boldface on every ticket.

Then Barnaby says, The Knickerbocker SteamShip Company has suffered a tremendous loss since the cost of a new ship comparable to the *Slocum* would be at least three hundred thousand dollars. The ship burned right down through the Main Deck. After the investigations are complete and the *Slocum* released to us, we have arranged to sell the hull to the Erie Coal Company for eighteen hundred dollars. The *Slocum*, sturdy ship that she is, will spend the rest of her days hauling coal through inland waters. In this way the spirit of the *Slocum* will sail on.

When he says this Barnaby chokes up and I think he's going to blubber again. It was all funny, y'know. I was enjoying it. A trial was like a circus, I thought. But all the fucking clowns are serious.

⹂ 7 ⹂

Honeycuitt comes back, still very angry. Did I miss anything important? he asks.

Helga says, Ach! and swipes at the smoky armory air with her cologne-soaked handkerchief. Why are they doing all this trial business? The dead are dead. Let us have some peace.

I don't want peace, Honeycuitt says, I want justice.

It gets hotter and stuffier in the armory. Someone farts. It hangs in the air all day. Handkerchieves and hats and caps are waving like fans. Helga is fanning me. I'm dozing off. Every once in a while she whispers in my ear, Don't sleep now, Edward. People are looking over here. It's not nice.

I doze anyway.

I wake up when Mr. Walter Payne takes the stand. He's the colored man the wagon drivers had called Rastus, the colored man with the hazel eyes, the nappy white hair, and the gold teeth. He's wearing a white shirt with a blue tie and looks uncomfortable sitting in the witness seat. A little scared. Mr. Payne looks toward me. I think he recognizes me from the day Rosy and me went on the *Slocum* when it lay in the slip at 54th Street. Nah, how could he recognize me when I'm in all the bandages?

You're Walter Payne? Gavin asks.

Yassuh.

Porter on the *Slocum*?

Yassuh.

How long have you been employed by the Knickerbocker Sssteamship Ccccompany?

Seems like since May before last, suh. Since I move up from Georgia.

How old are you, Mr. Payne?

Upwards of fifty, I do believe, he says after hestitating a moment.

Not sure?

Well, suh, there are four years after the century come on. Thirty-five years since the war end. I was a little boy then. Eleven, twelve maybe. That put it upwards of fifty.

You were a ssslave?

Yassuh.

Assisstant District Attorney Gavin clears his throat and asks Mr. Payne about his duties aboard the *Slocum*. Then he gets to the straw-packed barrels of glassware which had been brought onto the ship the day before.

What did you do with those barrels?

Emptied them, suh.

There was a roll of laughter.

You emptied the barrels. Then what?

Put the glass where they was needed. In the racks behind the deck bars.

Then?

I was finished with the glass.

A voice in the back somewhere yells, How about a little dance, Walter? More laughter. O'Gorman bangs his gavel.

Did you have other duties?

Yassuh. Put the barrels in the hold. Fill the oil lamps. Polish the bar spittoons. Clean the pilothouse, captain quarters, crew quarters, and all like that.

Where in the hold did you put the barrels?

Storage cabin.

What is kept in the storage cabin?

I'll tell you, Walter Payne knew where everything was stored, Knittel said. He began with tools, nails, rope, screws, paint, varnish, blowtorches—and right there Gavin cuts in.

Did you say there were blowtorches in the cabin?

Yassuh.

What were the blowtorches doing in the cabin?

They wuz being stored, suh.

Lots of laughter. O'Gorman is heavy on the gavel.

They were not used?

'Cept for light.

Light, Mr. Payne?

Yassuh. The 'lectric gen'rator ain't on but sometime. When a crew gen'emen comes needin' somethin' he light up the torch to see 'round the cabin.

Crew members used the open ffflame to illuminate the cabin, is that right? Am I understanding you correctly?

Yassuh.

Mmmister Payne, did you ever use a blowtorch in that manner?

Yassuh. For lookin' 'round and for lightin' my seegar.

And the cabin was filled with oil, sssolvents, pppaints, scrapwood, packing straw, and the like?

Yassuh.

Mr. Gavin drinks from a glass of water. He looks down at a sheet of paper for a minute or so.

On the day of the excursion, June 15, 1904, did you have any other duties aside from those of a porter?

Gang Boss for six boys.

Gang Boss. What did your boys do?

Pick up the garbage on the decks where passengers wuz droppin' it. Keep toilets clean. Be handy if someone needed somethin'.

Mr. Payne, was the sssstorage room used for sssmoking by the cccrew?

Yassuh. That was the smokin' place for the crew and the deck hands. Everybody.

Cigarettes and cigars were smoked there, Mr. Payne?

Yassuh.

Was the gggalley in ppproximity of the sssmoking rooom?

Two cabins aft, suh.

Was the chowder provided by the Kickerbocker Steamship Company being heated in the gggalley?

Yassuh.

How many stoves were in the gggalley?

Two coal burners.

Were you in chchcharge of the chchchowder?

Nossuh, 'twas some other nigger. I boss him that job.

Did you know him?

Knew him only to see him. He was on the *Slocum* sometimes. Other times he be on The *Grand Republic.*

Where were you, Mmmister PPPayne, when the fire broke out?

On the Main Deck, chippin' up a cake of ice for the bartender.

When the fire gggot underway and threatened the ship, what did you do to help the ppppassengers?

Nothin'.

A murmur of discontent rolls through the warm humid air of the armory.

Gavin looks up from his notes. He asks, Why did you do nothing, Mmmister Payne?

Well, suh, no one ever told me what to do if fire comes on that boat. I just think how it's best to save myself.

Now, said Knittel, I'm looking at Payne and I'm saying to myself: Here's an honest man. He's in this white man's court and he's taken an oath to God to tell the truth, the whole truth, and the rest of that bullshit line. But when he says that about saving himself, you can hear "Black Bastard, Nigger, Coon" rumbling around the armory. O'Gorman, smiling, bangs on his table. Gavin stares out at the audience. He's a little pissed.

Did you want to help anyone? The women? The children? Didn't you have any feelings of compppassion?

Yassuh, powerful feelings inside my liver. They's all goin' to be burned up! Womens, childrens, old folks, they's all goin' to be burned up. I'm a Christian man. I prayed for the word what to do. I got no guidance. Best I could do was make folks jump overboard.

Did they?

A few but most I had to th'ow. They was old or babes or afraid of the water.

How many? How many did you throw overboard?

Walter Payne pauses. He puts his hand to his mouth. You could see he is thinking, y'know. Then he says, Upwards of twenty. Most of those being children and the rest being they mothers and old folks.

You threw them over?

Yassuh.

How did you do that?

There was a gate in the railing. I opened it and walked them through. I say as they go, Keep your faith in God.

Then what did you do?

The fire was comin' on. I jumped over myself.

Gavin looks at his notes again. Why did you not cccontinue to help the passengers?

Payne sighs, his face contorted. No one else was heppin'. Deck hands was gone. Crew was gone. I was afeared to die. The fire was eatin' up the deck. I jumped. I swim over to the Bronx, a marble yard there. I pull a lady and her child with me.

♪ 8 ♪

You had a great accent there, Eddie, Cortin said. Real South. Just right!

Knittel slapped the bar. I should have had the brains to tell Honeycuitt, Maybe Walter Payne was the hero of the *Slocum!*

C'mon, Eddie heros never know they're heros, McHooley said.

Bullshit! I knew. *I know.*

I like trials, Esther Lieber said. Are you going back to the armory or is that it?

No. There's more. They call lots of people to the stand. Technical stuff. She's eleven hundred feet long, like the *Grand Republic,* her sister ship. A great and worthy vessel. Opened up, she can do fourteen knots. The paddlewheels are thirty-two feet high, nine feet across. Gavin wants to know if the paddle-wheels can scoop up people. The answer is Yes. Nine children and three adults were mashed up inside. At least that's how many were found inside the paddlewheel boxes.

There was more of that stuff, but I nod off a lot. Little snores. Helga jabs me to keep me awake. Honeycuitt, listening to the testimony and snapping his yellow pencils in two between his pudgy fingers, keeps saying, Lies, lies, fatuous! Lies, idiocy!

When they put First Mate Flanagan on the stand my head is clearer. Gavin is more exasperated. He's mopping his face with a wet handkerchief. He's disgusted and angry. He stammers even more.

Mr. Flanagan, you are the First Mate of the *Slocum?*

Yes, I am.

How long?

More than a year, less than two.

How did you become First Mate?

The Captain asked the company to give me that promotion.

Was being First Mate different from being Second Mate?

Better pay.

Laughter. O'Gorman gavels. The gaveling is getting weaker. The heat, y'know.

Flanagan says, Not too different, except for experience, it being my thirteenth year. I started out as a deck hand and worked my way up. I was part of the *Slocum's* first crew.

Were you trained for the sea?

No, sir, Flannagan said. I just liked the idea of being on a boat.

Do you have First Mate's papers, Mr. Ffflanagan?

No, sir.

Second Mate's pppapers, Mr. Ffflanagan?

No, sir. As I say, it's experience.

I see. With a little more experience do you think you might become Ccccaptain?

Laughter.

It's not for me to say.

Wouldn't you agree, Mr. Flanagan, that you are not even an able-bodied seaman? That you are incccompetent to serve as First Mate on the *Slocum* or any other ship?

Flanagan squirmed a little. He says, No, sir, I'm not incompetent. I just haven't got papers. It's experience that I've got.

Given proper examinations for First Mate status, could you pass such an examination, Mmmister Ffflanagan?

Flanagan takes a minute or two. Now he's really squirming, leaning forward in the chair. That's just schooling and paperwork. Nothing to do with real knowing or doing.

Mr. Flanagan, under the requirements of the regulations and the law you are inccccompetent. Did Captain Van Schaik know you did not have your pppapers?

I can't say. I never told him. He never asked me and the Captain is the best Master in New York Harbor, as every seaman knows. He had no quarrel with my ability to do my duties.

In the thirteen years you have served on the *General Slocum*, Mr. Flanagan, have you ever seen a fffire dddrill?

Flanagan pulls back into his seat. The air is going out of him. No, sir, he said.

A lifebbbboat dddrill?

No, sir.

Did you ever order or conduct any fffire dddrills? Lifebbbboat dddrills?

No, sir.

Why not?

It would have done no good. The fire hose was worthless. The life preservers were worthless. What good would it have done to have a drill?

You knew about the condition of the fire hose and the life pppreservers, did you not, Mmmister Ffflanagan?

Yes, sir. Everybody knew about them. When the old hose fell apart and hung there in shreds on the wall I told Mr. Barnaby.

The Pppresident?

Yes, sir.

What did Pppresident Barnaby do?

He ordered new hose. It didn't look right to me, it was kind of thin. Mr. Barnaby told me it was a new kind and strong enough.

I see. Did you tttest this hose? Put water through it?

No, sir, that wasn't my job. I relied on the inspection fellows. They saw the new hose and they passed on it.

Did you ever call the new hose to the attention of Captain Van Schaik?

I don't think so. He has bigger things on his mind.

It's not your jjjob and it's not the Captain's jjjob. Is that it, Mmmister Ffflanagan?

The way I see it, that's right, sir.

What happened after the hose burst? What did you do then?

Went aloft and joined the Captain in the pilothouse.

And then?

What do you mean, sir?

Did you aid the passengers? Did you ask your men to aid the pppassengers?

I don't remember. There was panic.

Yes, Gavin shouts, there was pppanic! There was ffflame! Pppeople were dddying! Bbburning aaalllive! Dddrowning in the rrriver! And what were you doing, Mmmmister Ffflanagan?

I don't remember. It was like I said. Panic.

How many members of the crew were lost on that ddday, Mmmmister Ffflanagan?

I don't know, sir.

None! *Nnnnone!* Did you know that? *NNNONE!*

No, sir, I didn't know that.

And, you, Mmmmister Ffflanagan, how did you get off the ship? When did you get off the ship?

I don't remember, Flanagan says in a voice which could hardly be heard. If I hadn't been so close to the witness stand, I wouldn't have heard him either.

⁊ 9 ⁊

They didn't tell the truth, did they? McHooley said.

Nah, but in a way they didn't lie either, Knittel said and looked with distaste at his dead cigar, which had been soaked through with saliva. Honeycuitt was right: when a thousand people die in twenty-five minutes it's pretty hard to know what happened. Even if you want to tell the truth you ain't sure what it is. And let's say you sit there on the witness stand and lie like a bandit, you might be telling some of the truth.

C'mon, Eddie, Vilma Rakos said, you didn't lie. You told the truth when you said you didn't go up the pole.

Yes, I told the truth. I *say* I told the truth. But will that convince the eyewitnesses? They saw what they saw. I'll tell you the answer on that one, though. It's red suspenders.

Red suspenders? C'mon Eddie! Cortin laughed. Red suspenders, party hats, paper horns, c'mon!

Honest! Eddie said and stuck a fresh crooked cigar into his beard. Red suspenders was it. Anyone here ever hear of Hearn's Department Store on 14th Street?

There was no answer.

Aha! Well, take my word for it, there was a Hearn's and my mother dragged me there the day before the picnic. On the main floor there was a big close-out on all kinds of items. My mother bought some garters and some hairnets. And there was a whole mess of suspenders on sale. Every one of them was red. Red wasn't selling worth shit that year. They all had these metal snaps. Some of the snaps were silver-plated and some were gold. My mother bought me a pair. Gold snaps. The poor kid who climbed up the mast had silver ones. His Mutti probably bought his red suspenders the same day my mother bought mine.

So the truth hangs by red suspenders? Esther said.

That's right, ain't it? But I can't prove that the kid on the pole had red suspenders on, which he did, they burned up with him. But everybody knew that Eddie Knittel had red suspenders. And ain't that the truth?

Other people are called to the stand, Eddie continued.

Marjorie Ann Plunkerbrote? Cortin asked.

Fuck you where you breathe, Joey! Knittel said.

Wrong place, dear.

Ach, I can't ever get the best of you, you sonuvabitch, Knittel said. You always get the last word.

Go on, said Vilma, you shouldn't let him distract you. Joey, lay off!

Most of the other witnesses are not so important, Knittel continued, rolling the cigar around in his mouth. Some of them were heros on that day, though. They did good things. Put out some of the fire. Saved people. And they testified to that. But the crew all lied under oath except Payne. They did shit, took care of number one.

Gavin has them on the stand, Knittel said, five minutes for each. He's building up a case, y'know. Honeycuitt wrote about them, too. The damned thing was whenever he wrote about someone, he wrote about me. Edward Francis Knittel was everywhere, not only in *The Times,* everywhere.

But there were good guys, right? said Esther. You said there were heroes.

That's right. There was a fireman named Mooney, fireboat *Zophar Mills.* He almost drowned saving people from the river. There was a fellah named Jim Duane, who rowed a skiff right up to the burning *Slocum.* They kept a hose playing on him so he could stand the heat and also to keep the skiff from burning. He pulled in ten people. Albert Rappaport, like Duane, was from the Department of Charities boat *Massasoit,* swimming around in his underwear. He fished out seven and then he had to be fished out himself. When the *Slocum* beached on North Brother, a nurse name of Pauline Pelz kicked off her shoes and uniform and went after children in her bloomers. They were all heroes.

But you were the big hero, Oster said.

I was *their* big hero.

You're in a steady state of denial, Eddie. You are *my* hero.

Knittel threw his cigar at the accountant. It spread sparks across Oster's shirt. He brushed them away. Temper, temper, he said.

Why are you so crazy! Vilma shouted at Knittel.

Because he burns my ass. Then, as if he had done nothing offensive, Eddie Knittel continued, Gavin puts Henry Lundberg of the United States Steamship Inspection Service in the witness seat. He refuses to even say his name. Fifth Amendment, y'know.

Gavin finally says, You're a thief, Mr. Lundberg. Didn't you take bribes in the course of your duties as an inspector? Dddidn't you? Dddidn't you? You were on the pppayrrroll of the Knnnickerbbbocker Sssteamship Cccompany.

Gavin is spraying spit right into Lundberg's face. Gavin screams at the inspector, You're nnnothing less than a mmmu—mmmur–mmmmmurderer!

Lundberg just stares ahead of him. As Gavin waves him from the witness stand a voice comes up from the armory, You tell that sonuvabitch!

It's pretty exciting now and I'm hardly groggy at all anymore, Knittel said, and the next witness makes it even more exciting. There was a real stir when they bring Captain William Van Schaik into the armory. Every ass in that big room shifted.

He's in a wheelchair. Hot as it is, he's wearing his Captain's uniform: the coat with metal buttons and a white hat with designs on it. Gold-braid designs. Something like the Navy but not the Navy, y'know.

When they wheel him up to the witness stand, he struggles out of his chair. He gets into the witness seat without help. He's a good-looking guy. He's tall. He looks like he just stepped out of the Old Testament.

He snaps off his hat. He's old. Over sixty, easy. His hair is silver. It shines in the armory light like it's lit by a silvery halo, y'know. His white mustache has little hooks at the ends. His face is like he's standing at the helm in a helluva storm. Deep grooves around his mouth. Around his starched white-wing collar there's a black cravat, more a bandanna. Very natty, y'know. And, oh, yes: he's wearing these little round glasses with black lenses, like a blind man. Honeycuitt tells me he's gotten some hot ash in his eyes, stuck right onto the irises. They cleaned his pupils with castor oil. Now the light bothered him.

Gavin is calm with Van Schaik, polite. He asks, What is your name and occupation, please?

Van Schaik answers all the routine questions. Gavin takes a big guzzle of water and then he asks, You have been the Master of the *Slocum* since she was put into service?

Yes, sir. Since 1891. I was there at the launch. I took her out on her maiden run.

Tell me, Captain, was the *General Slocum* a good ship, a safe ship?

She was the best vessel of her class in the New York Harbor. I have not heard of a vessel better. No ship built for the purposes of the *General Slocum* was safer.

Yet, she caught fffire and ccclaimed the lives of more than a thousand women and children.

I can see the way Van Schaik's back stiffens when Gavin says that but his voice doesn't tremble when he answers, Yes, sir, that is the sad and damnable fact.

I assume, sir, that the two great dangers for a ship like the *Slocum* are sinking or burning. Is that correct, Captain?

Yes.

What are the chances of ships like the *Slocum* sinking on the East River?

None.

Burning?

Van Schaik is silent for so long, I think he'll never speak again, y'know. Finally, he asks for some water and then he says, Fire is an ever-present danger on boats of her type.

Why is that, sir?

They are made entirely of wood. There's lots of paint and varnish on a ship of that size.

Have there been many fires reported aboard the *Slocum*?

It was not uncommon. Small fires. They were put out almost immediately by the passengers themselves. Cigar fires. Trash fires. Small.

Nothing ever larger?

There was a somewhat larger fire last year. A trash fire started near a freshly varnished staircase banister and it blazed up.

What happened in that case?

It was smothered by a deck hand with a large piece of tarpaulin. He threw the tarp over the banister and slid it down over the flame.

Was the dddeck hand instructed in fire-fighting?

No, sir. He was a man of good common sense. He saw the blaze. He put it out.

Have you ever conducted a fire drill for the crew of the *Slocum*? Instruct them in the management of the pppassengers in case of fire?

Not this crew. There were other priorities. I had fallen behind in some of my other duties.

Are there more important duties, Captain? Mmmore important than fffire dddrills? Garvin asks. He takes a deep breath and then he says, Never mind that, Captain. All right, there were other priorities. Did you conduct a fire drill last year?

No, sir, Van Schaik says strongly. Not directly, not personally. I have fully expected that the men are assigned to their fire stations, are told where the hoses are, the water outlets, the water and sand buckets, the lifeboats, and so forth.

Who is in charge of that?

The First Mate.

Mr. Flanagan. Is that his duty?

Yes.

Did Mr. Flanagan ever report to you, sir, that he had indeed put the crew through a fffire dddrill? Or that he had not put the crew through the dddrill?

Mr. Flanagan is an able mate. I assumed he had complied with his duties.

You assumed?

Yes, sir. The *Slocum* is not a naval vessel at war. I always allow for honesty and trust.

There were twenty-three men and six porters in the crew aside from the officers. Is that right?

I believe that's correct.

The twenty-three deck hands, did they have any sea experience?

I can't say. I didn't hire them.

Did you know that the crew were ordinary day laborers, a few coloreds, and many hardly more than boys?

It is the company policy to employ itinerant labor. Some are with us for a single day. Very few are aboard for more than a season.

Then there is neither time nor pppurpose in tttraining them, is there?

Captain Van Schaik doesn't reply. He sits there stiff as a board.

Gavin walks around in a crooked circle. You can see that he is calming himself. Finally he says in a low, level voice, without a stammer in it, May I say, sir, that it is not unlikely that there has never been a fire drill on the *Slocum* since the day she was launched in 1891? Is that a fair statement to make?

Van Schaik says nothing. Sits there. His black eyeglasses stare out. I tell you, I felt sorry for the old man. I wished I could help him.

Gavin counts on his fingers and says loud and clear: Rotten life preservers with iron bars, worthless fire hose, fire buckets empty of sand but filled with trash, life boats wired to the davits and to the decks.

Gavin asks if Van Schaik knew that only the crew had acquired serviceable life jackets. He yells, Did you know that? Did you know that, Captain of the *General Slocum*?

Van Schaik says, I relied on my First Mate.

Gavin, spitting, yells, And the First Mate relied on the United States Steamship Inspectors! And the Knnickerbbbocker Sssteamship Cccompany relied on Inspector Henry Lundberg, who nnnever fffound one sssingle rotten lllife vest and not one sssingle bar of iron !

Esther, Eddie Knittel said, if ever there was a guy who was going to have a stroke it was Assisstant District Attorney Gavin.

I think that's why Coroner O'Gorman called another recess, during which time Van Schaik remained seated in the witness stand, staring out through his black glasses. His coat was buttoned but he sat there cold as ice.

⋄ 10 ⋄

Knittel belched loudly and grimaced. McHooley, he said, you got some Tums back there?

Alka Seltzer?

Any port in a storm. The booze is backing up.

Tsk, tsk, said Cortin, you've had a fifth. You've got a cast-iron gut, Eddie.

McHooley placed the foaming glass before Knittel, who drank it down. He belched again. I needed that, he said.

Oster said, So you liked Van Schaik?

Yes, I did.

Ain't it great that you liked somebody? You're a genuine human being, Joe Cortin said and slapped the bar top for emphasis.

Knittel belched again and turned his grimace toward Cortin. Don't let your feelings run away with you, he said. Sometimes I even like you.

The trial doesn't end there, does it? Vilma Rakos asked.

No, said Knittel, getting off the stool and stretching. If anybody has to pee let him do it now or forever hold his bladder. Anybody?

When no one left the bar, Eddie Knittel belched again and continued. Gavin gets himself in hand and doesn't raise his voice again.

When did you first learn of the fire, Captain Van Schaik? he asks.

As we came by Sunken Meadow.

You heard of the fire from First Mate Flanagan on the speaking tube?

Yes.

Then what, sir?

I looked from the pilothouse to the port side. I saw the flames shooting up from below.

Knittel cocked his head and said, But that was not true, y'know. When Flanagan was on the tube there were no flames, just smoke.

Then Van Schaik says, I turned the wheel over to the riverpilot. I left to see what the situation was. It wasn't good. The passengers were unruly and in a panicked state. I returned to the pilothouse.

Then? Gavin asks.

My first thought was to run the *Slocum* into the Manhattan shore at once.

You didn't.

No, sir. We were at 134th Street. The river bottom there could not take a boat the size of the *Slocum*. I might not be able to get her into a pier. The ship might get grounded and still be on the river burning. More people would be lost then through fire and drowning. And if I were able to get close enough to the shore I might set the piers ablaze. There were oil storage tanks along the waterfront there. I had no idea what kind of catastrophe might be caused to the city itself if the oil went up. The safest harbor was the north shore of North Brother Island. It lay two or three minutes ahead. It was my judgment that the least damage would be done to the *Slocum* and fewest lives lost by putting into North Brother. I went full speed ahead.

Was this also the judgment of the pilot? Gavin asks softly.

No, sir. He was no longer in the pilothouse.

Where was he?

I do not know.

You do not know?

No, sir.

The decision to go full speed ahead to North Brother Island was your decision alone?

Yes, sir, it was.

You were running into a head wind, were you not?

I was unaware of the wind. I reckoned the time: I'd beach in two minutes. It was the safest.

The headwind whipped the flames into a blazing torrent. In that wind people were burned alive in an instant. To escape that wind of fire, people wearing rotten life vests, people who could not swim, women and children, leaped to their deaths. Did you know that, Captain?

No, sir. I had set the course. I looked ahead to North Brother.

Two minutes ahead at full speed?

Yes, sir, that is right, sir.

Two minutes. What course would you set, Captain, if North Brother were, say, six or seven minutes distant?

Captain Van Schaik lowered his head. The silence in the armory is deep. When he looks up, Van Schaik's black lenses focuses on Gavin, whose eyes grip the Captain's face. Gavin waits. I think for sure the armory is going to explode.

Van Schaik finally speaks. Simple. Dignified. Strong. Back straight. Fewer than three minutes to North Brother, he says.

He says that very softly and Gavin, just as soft, says, Thank you, Cccaptain. That will be all.

♪11♪

Right after that Coroner O'Gorman says, I call the next witness, Edward Francis Knittel.

Center stage for the kid, said Cortin applauding. Rakos pinched his arm.

Even though I had been in the armory all the time, a roar went up like a football game. Scared the shit out of me, I want you to know.

Four cops lift up my bed and place it on the floor in front of the witness stand.

Gavin says, I will be as brief as ppposible. It is an honor to meet you. I apppologise for detaining you so long. I have only a few questions to ask of you, sir.

I was impressed that he called me sir. His first question to me is, Did you see any crew members aiding any of the passengers?

I heard what Mr. Payne, the colored man, said. He helped lots of people. I guess there were other crewmen who also helped.

That's very generous of you, Master Knittel. But we have come to expect such conduct of you.

I tell you the whole armory applauds. Makes my eardrums dance.

Did you witness, did you pppersonally witness, any member of the crew in the act of aiding any of the stricken pppassengers?

No, sir.

Thank you for your answer. My next question. Do you remember where you were when the fire broke out?

On the Main Deck, I said.

Will you tell us, as best you remember it, if you saw the start of the fire?

First, I said, I smelled smoke. I thought the smell came from the chowder cooking. Then when Mr. Flanagan came up the stairs I saw that he was dragging smoke with him. Smoke was all around him.

Yes?

He went to the speaker tube and whistled into it. He was talking to the Captain. He told the Captain there was a fire. Then he went to the firehose stand with two other crewmen. They stretched out the hose and turned the water on. The hose couldn't hold the water and it fell off the water pipe.

Were you surprised by that?

Yes.

Now, Edward, will you please think carefully about your answer to my next question.

Yes, sir.

Can you recall, can you remember, where the *Slocum* was when the hose fell to the deck?

I take my time before answering because until Gavin had asked me the question I had not thought about that at all. Where was the *Slocum* when the hose came off the pipe? I squeezed my brain and the Manhattan shoreline came back to me. I had looked away from the pipe stand to the shore.

I answer. It was 89th or 90th Street.

How do you know it was 89th or 90th Street?

Because 86th Street is a broad street and I had just caught sight of it going by when Flanagan went to the hose.

Couldn't you be mmmistaken?

It's hard for me to get it out but I says, No, I was looking over to the shore with my friend Rosy. I was telling her about the different streets because she came from Ohio.

Where is your friend Rosy now?

My eyes fill with tears but I do not cry. I says, She died on the *Slocum.*

Everybody waits, the whole armory, until I get myself in hand. Then I say, We talked about 79th Street, what a nice street it was. It was after that.

So you are certain about that?

I nod and say, I'm sure, but even if I was confused–I look toward Honeycuitt when I say that–I knew the *Slocum* hadn't gone through Hell Gate, yet.

Would that be seven, eight, nine minutes before North Brother Island?

I don't know, I say, but more than two minutes.

Can you guess as to how much longer?

I don't know why I said it, but I say, *Forever*.

Gavin takes his time before he asks me the next question. When did you see flame?

Right after we got through Hell Gate. Smoke and flame came up with a roar from the stairwell and everybody on the Promenade and the Hurricane decks was singing "For He's a Jolly Good Fellow".

Could the run to North Border have taken possibly six or seven minutes from Hell Gate? Gavin asks me.

Possibly, I answer.

Four days after that Honeycuitt showed me his story in *The Times*. The jury had come in with the verdict. Indictments for Henry Lundberg of the United States Steamship Inspection Services, Frank A. Barnaby and the whole Board of Directors of the Knickerbocker Steamship Company, Incorporated, First Mate Edward Flanagan, and Captain William Van Schaik.

I asked Honeycuitt what that meant. Would they go to jail?

He explained that being indicted by the Coroner's Jury meant that now they would go to trial in a criminal court.

I hate trials, McHooley said fiercely, smashing the wineglass he had been wiping into the metal sink before him.

I didn't know I told the story that good, Knittel said with a smile. Anyway, Jimothy, I'm finished with the trial. It's over.

There's the damnable trouble, Eddie, trials are never over. McHooley looked intently at Knittel. The truth, Eddie, and be careful with your answer. Was the trial truly over? Was the trial over in ten years? In fifty? Will it ever end?

Jimothy, I don't know what the fuck you're talking about!

Jaizus, Eddie, and it was my thought that you'd be the one man on Broadway who'd understand such a question.

Knittel shrugged. Sorry to disappoint you, McHooley.

THE INNKEEPER'S TALE

Trials are never over, nor do they ever begin. They exist. We are born in the middle of the proceedings and we die before the verdict is achieved.

It is said in my country that the trial for Irishmen was already underway a thousand years ago, give or take a century or two.

Nor is it for me to tell you all the history of us. There are books to do that, some of them true and some of them written by Englishmen.

I will tell you only a small part of what has befallen the Clan McHooley and myself, James Timothy, who might have been like Ould Edward Francis Knittel, a hero. But instead, as the Gods demanded it, with deep sadness in their eyes, I was, indeed, a craven coward.

My God, are you plastered! Esther said.

Only to loosen my tongue.

You're lost, McHooley, Oster said. You know there's a special place in Hell for blotto bartenders.

I'll find my way, said McHooley, holding the edge of the bar with both hands, I'll find my way.

After a moment, McHooley's mouth twisted into speech.

Long ago, before the Church, before the damned English, when faeries, leprechauns, demons, banshees, and clerichaunes, roamed the green night, the tribe was first assembled under the leather shield of King William Cooley.

You a fucking prince, McHooley? Knittel asked.

In thim times there was no England to taunt us. And under William there were wars without end: wars against the McGraths, the Connails, the Mallons, the Morrisons, the Cuskers, against all who hunted the wood or whose women were comely. Good wars.

I don't want to listen to a story that takes a thousand years, Oster said. You're drunk. This is Eddie's night. He paid for it, didn't he? You'd better get his okay, McHooley.

McHooley swished a shot of rye inside his mouth and swallowed it by occluding his fine white teeth. He grimaced. Have I got your permission, Eddie?

Knittel grinned. You're asking me to yield?

Aye, that.

How long?

I don't know.

Approximately.

I can't say exactly or approximately. Half an hour?

No way, said Cortin. Come on, McHooley, you'll disrupt the *Slocum.*

But Esther was given time to speak, McHooley protested. Give me ten minutes. Eddie invited her, Cortin said. You're buttin' in, Jimmy!

McHooley looked toward Knittel. Can I have yer invitation?

Knittel shrugged and looked toward the others.

Five minutes? Oster suggested. Will that be all right? he asked the others. They nodded. Eddie? Oster asked, turning to the old man.

My mouth is dry anyway, said Knittel, and five minutes— that's fair enough.

McHooley swished another whiskey, occluded, and swallowed. He exhaled. Five minutes it is, he said.

In the interest of time and the constraints of inebriety, I will excise-tax a thousand heroic years.

This tale has an excise tax? Oster asked.

Yes, it does.

You're cookoo, McHooley, Esther said. But I like it when you're cookoo.

McHooley, gripping the edge of the bar still, continued, 'Tis now the time the English are upon the land with their iron hands and handsome horses. They steal our cows and pigs, our grains and greens.

Do you mean, Jimothy, that the English brought the famine? Vilma Rakos asked and then quickly apologized, I didn't mean to be a wise guy.

It's all right, lass. Famines are trials, don't y'know? And Jewrispudence—sorry, Esther—is a magna English invention.

Four minutes, said Little Joe Cortin, looking at his wristwatch. Step lively there!

You're cheating him, you fag! Knittel said.

Ah, Joey, Joey, if only they had said a kind word! If only our lords had had a drop of pity in their hearts! But they stole our final pig in payment for the rent due them. And when we stole a little from their gardens to feed our wee ones, they dragged us in chains before their magistrates.

Women who still had breasts on them turned to whirring— to *whoring*, McHooley said, correcting himself painfully with his wooden lips. Young men with pistols turned to the highways, leaping out before stagecoaches, purloining jewels and gold.

McHooley laughed very hard, lost his grip on the bar, and fell to the duck-boarded floor. Esther Lieber gasped. Vilma Rakos reached toward the vanished McHooley. Joey Cortin climbed over the littered bar top and, jumping down, pulled McHooley to his feet.

I missed the joke, Eddie Knittel growled.

McHooley laughed his hard laughter again and fell backward into Cortin's arms. Cortin pushed McHooley to the bar edge. McHooley steadied himself again.

As he climbed back over the bar, Cortin said, Don't let go, now, Jimothy. Will you be all right?

Sure he will, said Oster. He was just down there looking for the jewelry.

What was the fucking joke that almost killed you? Knittel growled again.

Well, Eddie, lad, what could a starving, thieving Irishman do with jewels and gold?

All right, what could a starving, thieving Irishman do with jewels and gold? Knittel repeated.

Why, McHooley said, pointing a wavering finger in the general direction of Knittel, he could find an honest Englishman who might buy the boodle at a tinth of the fair market value. Oh, praise the English!

Symbiosis, said Oster.

Then somehow—who knows how? them thieves were betrayed and brought before the Judas courts, tried, and found guilty.

It's not fair! said Vilma Rakos.

Why, lass, smiled McHooley, justice delayed is justice denied and a speedy trial was had all round. And Guilty! said the Magistrates, and Guilty! said the Judges, and they dropped us through the gallow traps six and eight at a time!

That was a hundred years before you were born, Oster observed.

No, lad, I was there. I was on trial. Ongoing, McHooley said, his words losing form.

McHooley lifted the bottle of rye to pour a drink. Cortin reached over the bar and had no trouble taking the bottle from his hand.

If you want to tell your tale, get hold of yourself, McHooley. Your time is running out, Cortin said. Your mouth is filled with mush.

McHooley took the hose of the water dispenser and released a shower over his tight, wavy hair. His shirt and pants soaked through. He shook his head vigorously, wetting everyone at the bar.

Bo Wang got behind him with a handful of towels. He removed McHooley's shirt, dried him off, and helped him on with a fresh one, which he had brought from McHooley's room in the back. Jimothy got out of his pants, and struggled to get into the dry ones, which had also been brought by Wang. Unable to get the pants on, he held them in his hand and, bare-legged, continued.

Sorry, said McHooley, got carried away. Mr. Knittel, I don't want the bathing time charged against me speaking time. I simply won't have it!

Adjust the clock, said Knittel to an imagined Time Keeper. And will you bring your tale into modern times, you sonuvabitch.

All right, said McHooley after a lengthy pause. My father's dead and my mother's dead and Sean and Seamus, my brothers, twins, are dead. And I am here, as you see, alive.

At the top of his voice McHooley shouted, I am a coward! I am a traitor! The gallows're too good fer me!

You're not going to do something drastic, are you, Jim? Vilma asked.

Yes! said McHooley. I'm going to stay alive and burn in the hell of my sins!

What did you do, McHooley, fuck an Irish Setter?

Vilma threw a balled-up wet napkin at Knittel's face. You are simply awful! she yelled. After tonight I'll never speak to you again!

Okay, okay, that was bad. I have a big mouth. It's a plumber's joke. I apologize, Mr. McHooley. I ask everybody here to forgive me if I offended anybody.

You're on probation, Edward, Vilma Rakos said. Continue if you want to, Jim.

McHooley nodded and went on.

It's about trials, I'm speaking. My Da was a great fighter for the freedom of Ireland.

I.R.A.? Oster asked.

Of high rank, McHooley replied, and respected. Now, something happened one night at The Claw of The Eagle. No one knows what, but there was a donnybrook. An Ulster constable came in to restore law and order. Someone shot him through the head. Everybody scattered except my father, who sat at his table drinking his quiet whiskey.

The police came. He was arrested and brought to trial for murder. With a platoon of constables surrounding him, they

brought him from the cold cell where he had taken up resi-
dence for sixteen months without bail.

And a great troubadour he was, too! All day long he sang
the glories of Ireland to the delight of prisoners and jailers alike.

My kind of guy! Cortin said.

They found him guilty, of course, said Oster.

No, sir! said McHooley

Innocent? Vilma Rakos asked.

No, sir! said McHooley. The trial just continued and
continued. My Da, his own attorney, said you can't convict a
man for having an innocent whiskey. And in his defense he
recited the crimes of England and those of the lackey brutes of
Belfast. The crimes of a thousand years, he recited. And, at
regular intervals from the witness dock, he entered a song into
evidence, singing it always from beginning to end, verses, re-
frains, choruses, and all. "The Singing Assassin", the London
tabloids called him.

Each day the courtroom was filled. At the end of each
day, they took him back to his cell. One morning a guard found
him dead, tattooed by an automatic firearm.

It was on that day me mother's hair turned white, and her
rosy skin ashened and wrinkled like a land of rivers. But the
trial, though foreshortened, did not end.

Sean and Seamus swore to our mother they would not do
it, but they continued the struggle all the same. They'd blow up
a police station on a Friday and, our weeping mother between
them, kneel before God on the Sunday follering.

Bombers? Vilma Rakos asked, looking up in wonder at
McHooley.

And the very best! Like ghosts they were, Sean and Seamus,
gliding through the nights and fogs with their deadly bundles
and their clocks counting time in the dark!

It's for Da, they said, and took me along with them to
learn the liberty trade.

McHooley turned to the back bar and took an unopened
bottle of rye from the shelf.

Cortin said, Jimothy, put it down. If you break the seal,
I'm gone.

Me too, said Lieber over the murmur of the others.

McHooley, his hand coming away from the bottlecap,
sighed, It's damned hard, he said, and yer not having any
mercy at all.

Knittel stroked his beard. Maybe, he thought, he should not have given Jimmy the five minutes. He did not want to know what McHooley's pain was. He had enough of his own. The old man pointed to the bar clock behind McHooley. Go on, he said.

I learned the trade, McHooley said. The red wires and the blue. The batteries in their place. The proper setting of the time.

Innocent people, innocent people, McHooley! Rakos said. People just sitting in a pub. Shit!

As if he had not heard her, McHooley continued speaking. Sean and Seamus would not let me place a package then. I was too young. But after an explosion they'd bring me into a pub and buy me a short, triumphant beer.

Oster broke the small silence. What did they do, your brothers? I mean, what kinds of jobs did they have?

McHooley chuckled. Unemployed, he said. The unemployed Catholic underclass of Ulster.

Knittel asked, And where did they get the beer money and the bomb money?

McHooley smiled widely. God provides, he said, and crossed himself. He breathed deeply and pulled at his nose.

The first time I saw London, we were blowing up Victoria Station. I was the lookout. If something was wrong, I had a high whistle to warn them. Well, after we blew Victoria, we had a good dinner. The next day we went home to Ulster.

D'ya remember when Lawrence Olivier was doing *Lear* at the National? The Prime Minister, half the cabinet, and some of the R'yals attended opening night. We planned three plastique packages, enough to bring the theater down. Our intelligence lads had given us the architectural drawings with the proper placement of the packages marked with red X's. The placements were to be made the night before.

Since I was the lookout, I went ahead and walked the perimeter of the theater. Sean and Seamus sat in a Ford van a block and a half away, waiting for my high note.

The van blew up. Just blew up. The street was filled with fire. I ran away. It was agreed that way. "Anything happens, y'run, lad". They were twenty-three. I was not yet seventeen.

I'd ask for a shot, Knittel said, except that would get you a shot, McHooley.

McHooley patted Knittel's arm. Eddie, the hard part is yet to come. "Twin Sons of The Singing Assassin Die in Blast", the tabloids wrote.

Out in a lonely piece of Ulster woodland, the I.R.A. had a ceremony for the twins. They fired rifles in the air. I stood there at attention, my eyes dry.

But, oh, how my mother wept! She ordered me to America to stay with the ould McHooley who had prospered here. In her hand she held a heavy pistol. It had belonged to me Da. She said to me, If ye ever return to this Ireland I will leave my bloody brains on m'pillow and it will be you, James, who've pulled the trigger.

Knittel bit through his cigar and removed it from his mouth. He hobbled toward the toilet in the rear. He heard McHooley's fading voice saying, And what good was it? Two years after I arrived in New York, she blew her brains out anyway.

Knittel, listening still, held onto the open toilet door.

God, McHooley, Vilma Rakos said, it wasn't your fault. You did your best.

No, no, lass, Mea Culpa, Mea Maxima Culpa! I should have returned to Belfast and taken up the work of freedom again! They had invited me often enough.

It ain't easy to go against your mother, Jimmy, Esther said.

But she's been dead all these years and I'm standing here before you. I will be forever in the dock. My trial will never end.

Well, go back to Belfast and make bombs then, Cortin said unsympathetically.

Joey, yer not understanding, lad! No Irishman can turn his back on a cause that is holy.

Cortin shrugged and said softly, Jimmy, you sound like a Muslim in a minefield.

But it comes with my mother's milk, lad! Freedom!

Easy, Oster said, it's all right, Jimmy. You can go back whenever you want.

Sure, said Esther, you can go back.

McHooley's large-jawed head nodded in grave movements. No, I cannot, he said, I like it here. Ah, America, do you know what a wonderful country it is?

McHooley searched their silent faces.

Knittel closed the uni-sex door behind him. Over the small bowl of the sink he scrubbed his beard with cold water. He thought, Trials don't go on forever. Nothing goes on forever. Why should anything go on and never end? Maybe for McHooley.

Ach! Knittel said in a loud voice looking into the mirror above the white enamelled sink basin he said. Old fool! You started all of this! He thought of Esther; the flying virgin and Jimothy, the craven coward. And he thought of himself talking, jabbering, about the *Slocum* and Rosy. Talking, talking! and what was the truth of it?

Knittel squinted at his white-yellow bearded face and said aloud, softly, I don't know any more.

PART III

1

Mindy had pushed four tables together to make one long one and covered it with three small, pink tablecloths. She had placed chairs around the table and had set it with plates, silverware, and napkins. There were two baskets of bread and two small bowls of butter. At each end of the table was a carafe of white and a carafe of red wine.

There was the sudden banging of a large spoon on a galvanized dishpan. The kitchen doors swung open. Mindy and Bo Wang came through carrying steaming pots. Bo announced, New Zealand Irish Lamb Stew, Forbidden City Style!

Knittel said, I thought you got the night off, Wang.

I decided to stay, Bo Wang replied in his straight American voice. You got me hooked on your sea saga. I'm waiting for the part where you drown.

McHooley told you to go home.

I know that, Methuselah, but I decided to stay.

Knittel laughed and recited:

> You can always tell the Irish,
> You can always tell the Dutch,
> You can always tell a Chinaman
> But you can't tell him much...

Fu Man Chu say, Fuck you, Eddie Knittel.

Kiss and make up, said Cortin as he seated himself at the table and immediately spooned some stew onto his plate.

Bo Wang and Mindy also took seats. Finally, McHooley came from behind the bar and sat down opposite Esther Lieber.

Boy, this sure smells good, Esther said. Thank you, Bo. Let's not have any arguments, okay? Bad for the digestion. Can you pass me the bread, Milt?

Oster looked up and said, I'd like a tall glass of coke, lots of ice, please.

You'll have to duck behind the bar and get it yourself, Mr. Oster. The bartender and the help are off duty, McHooley said.

The eating was intense and noisy.

You're a slob, Eddie, Vilma Rakos said. You've soaked your beard in the gravy.

To make it grow, Eddie said, as he wiped his face. Better? he asked.

Vilma glanced at Eddie Knittel. I like light-red beards, she said.

No slob like an old slob, Cortin said, filling his plate again. You never made it better, Bo. I mean that.

Thanks. You can always count on the stew. It's McHooley's recipe, handed down by an ancient Irish king.

Is that right, McHooley? Eddie asked,

Bo Wang never lies.

Is there dessert? Esther wanted to know.

Only last night's rice pudding. Bo and me thought, with the place closed, it wouldn't be needed, Mindy said. I can cut up a few melons. Anybody?

There was a sharp rapping on the front-door glass.

Jaizus, said McHooley, why don't they read signs? No one in New York ever reads signs. We're closed! he shouted.

The rapping came again, this time on the side window. A woman was pressing her face to the glass. I know you're in there, Eddie Knittel! the woman shouted. If you don't let me in, I'm gawna bang and bang till the glass breaks. Eddie, you open the door, hear?

Oh, my God, it's Linda! If you like your glass, McHooley, you'd better open up and let her in.

You know her? Cortin asked, mopping some gravy from his plate with a piece of bread.

It's Linda Fernandez, Vilma said. She's Eddie's housekeeper and stuff.

And stuff? Oster asked, touching his cheek, pretending amazement and shock. God, McHooley, let her in!

McHooley held the door wide for her as Linda Fernandez squeezed through, carrying two shopping bags. She placed them on a vacant table.

Excuse me, she said, every Tuesday I'm at Eddie's place to do a little work.

You're a night worker? Cortin asked with a smile.

Linda stared at Cortin. Who's this gringo creep? she asked Knittel.

Joey Cortin. He doesn't mean any harm, Linda. I left a note on the door. Didn't you find it?

You got company here, Eddie. I'm not going to say you're a liar. So I'm going to say a wind blew it away.

Agitated, Knittel rubbed his beard and the back of his neck.

I apologize, Linda. I forgot. Something special came up.

The Eightieth Anniversary of the *Slocum* Disaster, Vilma said.

What the fuck is that? Linda asked. She turned to Eddie. You didn't say nothing to me about no disaster. Who died?

Everybody, Esther said. Why don't you join us for some terrific Bo Wang New Zealand Irish Lamb Stew?

Linda ignored her.

This was in front of the door. From *Party Cake Bakery*, Linda said, and put the bakery shopping bag before Knittel. Knittel stared at the bag.

What's in it, Eddie? Esther asked.

A cake, said Knittel.

Hey, dessert! said Cortin.

They bake it for me every fifth year. It's a standing order with *Party Cake*. I just forgot it was coming.

McHooley reached into the shopping bag and lifted out the large, white box tied with string. He pulled the loose end of the bow and opened the box. Jaizus, he said and smiled. He placed the cake on the table.

It was iced in white. In the center was the confectionery image of a three-decked paddlewheeler. Chocolate smoke swirled from the smokestack. Red-icing flames curled up from the Main Deck. On the side of the boat chocolate letters said: the *General Slocum.* Above the boat there were the blue shapes of clouds and birds flying. Below there was a wavy river of blue icing.

Knittel hung his head. Shit, he said, it's a private thing.

It was Bo Wang who broke the silence. Hey, that's real neat, Eddie. Do you want me to cut it?

Knittel rubbed his beard, took a deep breath, and cocked his head. Yeah, cut it, Bo.

Wang cut the cake. The inside was a dark, moist chocolate.

Mindy said, Devil Food, my favorite!

Heaven! said Cortin.

What's a few more pounds? said Esther.

When Mindy returned with a pot of coffee, Knittel said, Let me tell you about the cake.

You don't have to tell us anything, Eddie, Vilma said.

Linda Fernandez said to Eddie in a voice the others could hear, Who's she? You got something going with her?

No, he's got nothing going with me, lady. Don't lose your pantyhose, Vilma said with a cold fierceness she seldom displayed.

Eddie lifted Linda's hand to his mouth and kissed it. Don't be foolish, Linda, he said. You know better than that. You're the only one.

Turning to the others, smiling, Knittel said, Now since you've eaten it, I'm going to explain to you about the cake.

Knittel held Linda's hand as he spoke. Most of her anger and edginess had abated.

Vilma thought that Linda could not have reached forty. Esther thought she was very pretty. Oster wondered if Linda Fernandez was Knittel's mistress. Cortin had no doubt about it. Neither did Wang, who wondered how an old man like Knittel could be so lucky. Mindy wondered how much Linda's emerald ring cost. McHooley was astounded by the idea that Knittel could make it with any woman, and he had no doubt he could get his Irish up for Linda on demand although he knew right now he was too depressed to try.

In those days, Eddie Knittel said, when I was the hero, I got tributes from all over the world, which I told you about.

Which you burned up, said Cortin.

I was a damned fool. But what is done is done. One of those tributes came from Luchow's on 14th Street until it went out of business. Ten, fifteen years ago. They used to have a big glass case which was a tribute to the *Slocum*. They had newspaper articles and drawings in the background. There was an oil painting of me on the fucking mast. But the big thing was the cake right in the middle of the case. It was made by Pastry Chef Siegfried Stolz. Everybody said it was a masterpiece of cake-making. It was maybe three feet high and five feet long and an exact model of the *Slocum*, right down to every board and nail. The East River was under it. It was on fire and sailing into the wind. It was art and not for eating. So what they did was to preserve it with a special shellac. It stayed in the case for thirty-five years, till 1939, when it just fell apart piece by piece. That was the best part of my hero days, that cake. If I had had a picture of it, I wouldn't have burned it. Twenty years ago in '64 I got *Party Cake* to make this one for me. But it was nothing like the Siegfried Stolz *Slocum*! A total masterpiece!

Cortin, glass of wine in hand, got to his feet and sang "For He's a Jolly Good Fellow" and everyone joined him.

Linda Fernandez announced that she would leave. She took a few steps toward the door, turned back, and said to Knittel, Hey, I forgot my keys.

Eddie fished a leather key container from his jacket and gave it to Linda.

When will you be back? she asked.

Not too late.

When not-too-late?

Ten, ten-thirty.

All right, Linda Fernandez said, not later'n that. My babysitter is goin' by twelve.

McHooley unlatched the door for her. She was framed by the fading June daylight.

♪2♪

Knittel wrapped a handful of ice cubes in a napkin and pressed it to his forehead. Your air conditioning stinks, Jimothy, he said.

McHooley, smiling weakly, said nothing.

Anybody here know what the *Graphic* is? Knittel asked the Companions of the Happy Hour.

Was, said Oster. One of the great New York newspapers which went belly-up.

In what year? asked Knittel.

No idea. What year?

Thirty-seven, said Knittel.

You don't know, said Cortin, you're fucking bluffing.

Knittel laughed. Never mind, he said. In 1905, May, on the green front page of the early edition—the early edition was green, y'know—there was the headline *Little Germany Is Dead*. Not much was true in the *Graphic*, but that was true. Little Germany, *Kleindeutchland*, was dead, all right. By the time I was on crutches and out on the streets the whole Lower East Side where the Germans lived was a ghost town.

The saloon door, said Joey Cortin, was flapping in the wind and the tumbleweed was rolling down 9th Street.

I hate you, said Esther Lieber, looking at Joey Cortin. No, I love you. Shut up, okay?

Knittel laughed. Don't be so upset, Esther. I thought the same thing myself many times because it was like that. Brumer's Saloon on the corner was empty except for some cops who were cooping. And the door almost flapped, y'know. On the doors and windows of the empty buildings the wreaths, the dead flowers, and the black ribbons rattled when there was a breeze. Spooky.

It was unspoken but it was like everyone had agreed to move away. It was like living in a graveyard, a deserted graveyard. All the genuine dead were already in the Lutheran Cemetery. The moving vans came and went. Some were horse-drawn and some were motor trucks. Many moved to Yorkville and to Ridgewood. Others upstate and out of state. I stayed. I thought to myself I'd move later, which I didn't do.

Why not? Oster asked.

That's another story. The last ones to move were the merchants. They tried to keep their shops open but who was left to buy something or get shoes repaired? You know how it was in the ghost towns?

Couldn't get your boots fixed? Cortin said.

And you couldn't get your pants pressed. On Avenue C even the whorehouse closed. I was going to say, in ghost towns, in the movies, dust blows. Dust is always blowing. In *Little Germany*, it was garbage blowing.

Aw, c'mon, Eddie, Vilma said. You mean chicken bones? Orange peels were blowing along the streets?

Dry garbage, Eddie said.

Refuse? Oster suggested.

That's it: refuse! Dropped out of my mind: refuse. Newspapers. Cigarette packs. Gum wrappers. Cardboard. Broken umbrellas. Pieces of discarded clothing. Blowing. Nobody there to clean it up.

Before the *Slocum,* every janitor, every store-owner, was out three, four times a day, to sweep his sidewalk. It was the German way, cleanliness before Godliness, y'know. Now everything was empty and dirty. It was the end. Except we didn't know it yet.

⸗ 3 ⸗

The dust, the refuse, was blowing. But I thought everything would turn out all right in the end.

Cortin stood up at his place at the table. Folks, he said, I want you to meet Edward F. Knittel, the hermit goldminer and last resident of Dry Gulch.

All right, Knittel snarled, you're gettin' to me now, you fag!

Stroke! shouted Esther Lieber.

I'm losing my patience with all of you! said Vilma Rakos. You're such a bunch of shits!

Hey, said Milt Oster, I haven't said a word!

You will though, you wanna bet?

I won't.

The quarrels of Caucasians are epic, Bo Wang said and, with a nod to Mindy, added, Work ethic. Let's clean up.

Together they cleared the table and carried the soiled dinnerware to the kitchen. The Companions of The Happy Hour returned to the bar.

Empty apartments, empty buildings, empty streets! Maybe only one out of five stayed behind. Those too old to move and invalids or cripples like me, Knittel said almost to himself. Ach, ach!

Louder, please, said Oster.

Little Germany was sucked away. It was like a vacuum.
Landlords abhor a vacuum. Over night the walls of the downtown ghetto crashed. Just like that, y'know, the walls came
atumblin' down. And, Knittel said, as he picked up an empty
beer bottle, if you sing it, I'm going to brain you, Joey!

He'll do it, so shut up, Joey, Vilma said. Put down the
bottle, Eddie. Put it down. Okay? Go on, please.

Knittel pursed his lips and twisted them from side to side.

I think you were saying, Mr. Knittel, said McHooley, that
the walls had come atumblin' down?

Are you still sloshed, McHooley? Esther asked.

I'm nine minutes away from total sobriety. You may
proceed, Eddie.

You're a gentleman, Jimothy, said Knittel and continued.
Spooky. One night you went to sleep, Knittel said, rubbing his
beard, and it was quiet when you woke up. Only bird song and
the sound of the river. But, a few days later when you woke up
you could hear things going on. First, I thought Little Germany
had got haunted, y'know. In two weeks the whole neighborhood
was filled up again.

The Jews, Ukranians, Poles, and Italians had taken over.
Italians were over west of Tompkins Square and going uptown.
The Poles and the Ukranians were south of them. And the Jews
who used to be on streets like Cherry, Stanton, Cannon, Hester,
Eldridge, and Delancey were now on the streets closest to the
river. On 9th Street I was surrounded by Jews. Kosher butcher
shops, a synogogue on 6th Street, Yiddish newspapers at the
newsstands. Life, life! I was surrounded by Jews. The street talk
changed. The food smells changed. The look of the women
changed. You know what? I loved it.

What's so bad about Jews? Esther asked. I like them.

I loved it but it made some problems. Like the Boys' Club
of New York. They had a shit fit, y'see. Here they had built this
great new building on Avenue A and 10th Street. Six stories,
gymnasiums, a swimming pool, a library, even a little ice cream
parlor. But what were they going to do with the Kikes, the
Polacks, and the Wops? It was a catastrophe!

There you go! Esther said laughing.

Now I got to know all about the Wop-Kike problem
because the Boys' Club arranged an honor for me. Since I was
already on crutches, it was no problem to hop the four blocks
to Avenue A and 10th.

They had a little ceremony in the library. We all got to stand at a wall where there was a cloth covering a big rectangular shape. I said to myself, Oh, shit! It's going to be like Luchow's! A big, fucking painting of the *Slocum* in flames with me shinnying up the burgee pole!

Congressman William Sulzer introduced the proceedings. It was the same old thing. Praise, hooray, and all that.

Sulzer introduces a Boys' Club member who says how I have inspired a whole generation with my courage and my modesty. Because of that, they have created an honor called *The Bravest of The Boys*. Then he pulls a cord. The cloth falls to the floor. On the wall is this black wooden board, very large. On the top in large gold letters it says, *The Bravest of The Boys*. Below that, in pretty big letters, too, it says on one line, FRANCIS EDWARD KNITTEL, and below that Hero of the *Slocum* Disaster, 1904. Ach, ach, ach!

Heros must suffer, Edward, Oster said.

You betcha, Knittel said. Every time a Boys' Club boy did a great, brave deed, an act of heroism, they would put his name on that board. And do you know what the bravest act of all was? Dying! That was the best way to be brave, die! World War I got a good listing. Each name, no matter what that boy did, would be printed in gold below mine, *smaller* than mine. Even now, I tell you, it makes me want to cry!

Knittel blew his nose. Here's the kicker, he said. Congressman Sulzer, very concerned, y'know, takes me to one side and tells me they're going to *close* the Boys' Club, shut it down. He wants me to help prevent that.

I ask Sulzer, Why do they want to close the Club?

They didn't build it for the new population, he says.

They don't want the Wops, Kikes and Polacks? I say.

That's right, he says.

Well, it's their Club, I say.

No, Edward, he says, it's a public trust. The Boys' Club is for the young men of the district. My district. The Trustees have no right to close it.

So why do they want to do it?

Prejudice. Even though you and I are German-Americans, Edward, it doesn't mean we are opposed to young men of other nationalities, right? Will you help me keep it open?

Yes, I say. Knittel scratched his beard. Now why did I say yes?

Because you were on the side of justice, said McHooley, three minutes from sobriety. And I support your position!

Thank you, Mr. McHooley. The fact is, I didn't care except that Rosy was Jewish and that's why I said yes to Mr. Sulzer. The next week there was a story in *The Times* which had a headline: *Slocum* Hero Opposes Closing of Boys' Club of New York.

I know you succeeded, Eddie, because the Boys' Club is still open to this very day, Cortin said.

That's right, Joey, and here's how they did it. A little prestidigitation!

You know *prestidigitation*, Eddie? Cortin asked with a great Jimmy Durante imitation.

Also *fuck you*, Joseph. Instead of devoting the Boys' Club to the development of German-American youth for careers and jobs in the free enterprise system, they changed the whole idea to a crusade against juvenile delinquency an idea, which got invented on the spot.

And the Kike-Wop-Polacks all cheered! Oster said.

Listen, said Eddie Knittel, where else could you get a hot shower in the winter time?

This is stupid, Vilma offered.

Well, it was one of the things that happened because of the *Slocum.* Something else happened, too. Along with the Congressman, Honeycuitt, Helga, me, and a few survivors put together The Association of The Survivors of the *Slocum* Disaster. We elected Charles Dersch and George Wunner for President and Vice-President.

Margie Ann Plunkerbrote was Treasurer, Esther said.

Yeah and she brought her pisspot to every meeting. The whole idea was to have an organization which would look into the needs of the survivors and their families. Lots of medical things. And there were people who had emotional problems, which in those days we didn't know much about. Also financial problems, lots of those. When the disaster was still fresh, y'know, we could raise money pretty easy. Teddy Roosevelt kicked in five hundred bucks. Mayor McClellan the same. But we used it up as quickly as we got it. It didn't take very long before the Association was broke. So Congressman Sulzer decided that we had to go to the government for a redress of grievances.

♪ 4 ♪

I am now sober, McHooley announced. I extend my
apologies for any embarrassment I may have caused the assembled company. I turn the floor back to our benefactor.

You're a good drunk, Knittel said. You're quiet. You're
not like Vilma there.

You've never seen me drunk, Vilma said softly.

That's because you only get whacked at the Boulevard,
baby, Cortin said.

Don't get cute with me, Joey, Somebody might take you
seriously. I don't get drunk.

I could have sworn!

Joey, be nice, Vilma said and turned to Knittel. You were
redressing your grievances.

That was an exciting time!

You find the government exciting? Oster asked.

Knittel thought for a moment. It wasn't boring, he said.
But it was not so much the redress thing. It was everything else,
y'know. I got to be sixteen. I grew a couple of inches. Helga and
I went out to the loony bin to see my father once a month. He
didn't talk to us except once in a while he'd look at me and ask,
Where's your mother? What happened to the children? Although there wasn't the old neighborhood anymore people
called me the Mayor of Little Germany. Instead of the papers
writing about the *Slocum* everyday, it was once a week or more
like once a month. Wolf, my uncle, we didn't hear from. Helga
said he was lost in the Black Forest and she hoped the wild
boars would stick their tusks into him.

Melvin kept coming around but I knew it was not for me.
They were a cute couple, Melvin and Helga. They were holding
hands but they didn't want me to see. They had good excuses
for being together a lot. The Association and the Grievances.

Who should help the survivors and their families? Not
Knickerbocker. The corporation was bankrupt. Congressman
Sulzer asked about the other boat owned by Knickerbocker.
Couldn't we seize that asset? Well, up your ass, Sulzer. The
other boat, the *Grand Republic*, was a separate corporation even
though it had Frank Barnaby for president and almost the same
board of directors, and it had committed no crime. The United
States Marshall seized the burned-out hull of the *Slocum* and

sold it for eighteen hundred dollars. That money went into the treasury of the United States.

Why? asked McHooley, It was my impression that Barnaby had sold the hull.

Maybe you're right, Jimothy. I'm confused.

When Knittel said he was confused, he slapped the bar top. I was not, *not*, confused.

All right then why did the government seize it?

I don't know why, Eddie Knittel said with a sigh. The City of New York had no responsibilty and no right to the money because the *Slocum* burned on the river. The river didn't belong to the City of New York. It didn't belong to the State of New York either. Rivers belong to the United States of America. That's why all the inspectors were U.S. inspectors. So we had no choice but to go to Washington. We were quite a troop Helga, Honeycuitt, Dersch, Wunner, and me, and we went where ever Representative Sulzer took us.

I don't know how many hands I shook--Representatives, Senators, Cabinet members, and one afternoon I saw the President himself. In his office.

Eddie, Vilma shouted, you must have been thrilled!

That's true, I was thrilled but, let me tell you, I was also scared. There he was, the Rough Rider with his funny little eyeglasses. He pushed a chair under me. I hope you received my letter, Edward.

I did, I said.

Then he talked a lot. He asked me questions but he didn't let me answer. He just went on to something else. There was only one thing he wanted me to talk about: the iron bar in the cork. Was I shocked? Was I angry? Did I warn the people on the *Slocum*?

I said you bet I was shocked, you bet I was angry, but no, I didn't warn people because there was fire all around.

Roosevelt said the iron bar was the thing that upset him most. Accidents will happen, he said, but iron bars in life jackets? Unforgiveable! The perversity of mankind is unending!

There were some papers before him and he signed across the bottom of one. This is a confidential report from the Department of Justice, about that damnable iron bar, Edward. Take it with you and, if you should ever meet a cynic, why you just show him this document.

Ah, Eddie, and it got consumed in the fire! said McHooley.

Knittel smiled. Not all of it, Jimothy. That one where Roosevelt had signed his name I've always carried with me. Not to convince any cynics, either. But to keep myself on a steady course, y'know. When I think I'm ready for the loony bin, I tap my pocket where the sheet is and say, There really are iron bars in life preservers.

He took his billfold from his jacket and removed a piece of folded plastic which contained a yellowed laminated sheet of paper. Sections of it had been taped together. It had the signature of Theodore Roosevelt across the bottom. He handed the piece of plastic to McHooley. Read it, why don't you? Knittel said.

McHooley cleared his throat and in his lilting accent read:

As to the life-preserver case: On September 29, J.H. Stone, manager, and H.C. Quintard, Charles W. Russ, and James Russ, employees of the Nonpareil Cork Works, of Camden, were indicted under section 5440, Revised Statutes, in the District Court of the United States for the District of New Jersey, for conspiring to defraud the Government and prejudice the administration of the steamboat inspection laws by putting upon the market compressed-cork blocks for use in making life-preservers, each of which blocks contained in its center a piece of bar iron about six inches long, weighing about 8 ounces. This iron was inserted for the purpose of bringing the weight of the blocks up to the legal requirement of six pounds of good cork to each life-preserver.

Since the Slocum *Disaster a large number of* new life-preservers have been placed upon passenger vessels everywhere. About 300 of these blocks containing a piece of bar iron, as described, had been shipped recently from the Nonpareil Cork Works to David Kahnweiller's Sons, manufacturers of life-preservers in New York City. A member of that firm, expert in the matter of handling cork, suspected the blocks were not right, and on breaking one of them open found the iron embedded in the cork. The discovery was reported to the officers of the Steamboat Inspection Service in New York

and then to the Department of Commerce and Labor.
The case was duly investigated by the Department
of Justice, with the assistance of the Secret Ser-
vice, and the indictment followed.

This was *after* the disaster? Oster asked.
After, said Knittel. Ain't that somethin'!
And the redress of grievances?
That was something, Miltie. After all, every member of
the Congress was one hundred percent on our side: What a
disaster! What a tragedy! What a pity and what a shame!
William Sulzer prepared a Bill and got fifty co-sponsors.
The Bill for The Relief of The Victims of the *General Slocum*
Disaster was put before the House Appropriations Committee.
This was toward the end of 1904. The Committee and the
whole House cheered. But they found a few technical errors in
the Sulzer Bill. It had to be withdrawn.
No problem! Sulzer resubmitted the Bill in the late Spring
of 1905. This Bill was better, but Idaho, Mississippi, and Maine
strongly objected to some language which might create a poor
precedent.
It went on like that till 1910! By that time, when I went to
Washington, I had no more Hero credentials. Who was Edward
Francis Knittel? The *Slocum* Disaster! Why, of course, that was
that accident in New York on the Hudson River. Was that
before the *Titanic* or after? Yes, it was a terrible thing, But it
happened a long time ago, ten years or more, wasn't it? Well,
maybe it wasn't that bad, but it sure felt that way.
Congressman Sulzer changed his strategy. He wrote another Bill, co-sponsored only by the Representatives from New
York City. This Bill was put before the Committee on Claims
and, if they approved it, they'd send it on to the House. Then
the House could pass the Bill with a dollar amount to be given
to the claimants. All of this because you can't sue the Government of the United States, y'know, not unless they agree to it.
Sounds absolutely British, said McHooley.
Sulzer got some top lawyers who knew how to deal with
the Committee on Claims. They also were *pro bono.* They
thought it was an open-and-shut case. They made a good pitch.
It went something like this: Was there any doubt that the
United States, because of its inspectors, shared a good measure
of the responsibilities and the guilt of what happened on the
East River?

Okay for that, said Vilma. But was the government responsible for the fire? Did they ever find out how the fire started?

Knittel roared with laughter. How the fire started? Christ Almighty, Vilma, I don't know. Nobody knows. Someone dropped a cigarette. Someone lit a blowtorch. Someone turned the flame up too high under the chowder. It was an act of God. No one knows, Vilma. All we knew about was the hose, the lifeboats, the cork, and the iron, and the fucking inspectors who were part of the fucking United States Government.

Congress has the right to pay any debt which, in its opinion, has been incurred by the United States. These debts can be debts of honor or debts of mercy or any kind of debt a majority of the House wants to pay, y'see? The house can call a dog a debt. And that's what the dog is then, y'know what I mean?

It's getting complicated, Esther Lieber said.

A rose is a rose is a rose, said Cortin.

Knittel winced. Look, this *pro bono* lawyer told us that once Congress had passed a law giving sugar bounties to an outfit which had the name The Realty Company. In those days, I think, a bounty was like a subsidy. The Supreme Court ruled this was unconstitutional but advised Congress they could vote to pay The Realty Company any sum it felt was owed. The San Francisco earthquake victims got five million dollars. In 1906, two hundred thousand dollars was appropriated to take care of the graves of Confederate soldiers who had died in federal hospitals. Money for the sufferers of the Mount Peles eruption, the Charleston earthquake, the Johnstown and Galveston floods, and eight hundred thousand dollars for *damages* from the earthquake caused by the eruption of Mount Etna.

The Committee on Claims refused to vote on Sulzer's Bill. That was the end of it, that was the fucking end of it!

But why? It's not fair, said Esther.

Knittel shrugged.

No idea? asked Oster.

They say it was because the Knickerbocker guys, Barnaby and the others, the Steamboat Inspectors, those crooks, the First Mate and the Second Mate, all of them were acquitted at the criminal trial. How can the Congress give the survivors money when the United States was found not guilty? Everybody was innocent. Everybody was innocent except Captain William Van Schaik. He was guilty. Sing Sing. Twenty-five years.

Oh, boy! said Esther.

Oh, boy, indeed! said McHooley.

Did Congressman Sulzer get the survivors anything? Vilma asked.

Nada, said Knittel. Seven fucking years in Washington and we scored one big zip. But there was one good thing. Helga and Melvin became an item.

That's nice, said Cortin.

Yeah, said Knittel, as I said, they were cute, walking along hand in hand, stealing a little kiss here and there, taking adjoining hotel rooms with connecting doors. Whenever I walked behind them, I giggled, y'know. There was Honeycuitt with his big ass and there was Helga with her big ass, the two of them jiggling along like two hippos in love.

That's mean and tasteless, Mindy said tearfully.

I didn't mean to hurt your feelings.

Well, you did, damn it!

Joey Cortin giggled. Don't tell me we have to add the sex life of hippos to the injustices of mankind?

You're worse than Eddie, Esther said.

She's right, Joey, Oster said. A little irony: Cortin and Knittel together at last in love.

I apologized, Knittel protested.

Well, I sure in hell won't, Cortin said, his voice rising. It pisses me off! So Mindy has fat legs, thunder thighs, and a big ass. Is that the end of the fucking world? No pun intended. Look, Helga and Melvin waddled off into the sunset. I thought it was sweet. I thought Eddie meant it to be sweet.

It was mean!

Hey, I apologized!

I'll tell *you* something, Mr. Gay Guy, Mindy said, her anger having dried her tears, homosexuals detest fat people, don't they? Don't they?

Yes, most gays do. They share the popular prejudice, Mindy. There are outsized gays, too, You know. They have problems but they find others who are attracted to them.

Only weirdos! said Mindy.

Cortin became quiet for a moment. I don't want to go on with this, Mindy.

Why not, Joey? You afraid of the truth?

Joey shook his head slowly. Listen, Mindy, I'm less afraid of the truth than Knittel. You're just a little fucked up. If someone is attracted to you, it doesn't mean he's a weirdo.

He's not wrong, Mindy, said Vilma. There's more to love than a beautiful body.

You're talking like my mommy. Out there among the stars is your Prince Charming. He's going to find you. He's going to love you just for you.

It could be true, Mindy.

You can say that, Vilma, because you're beautiful.

Oster put his arm around Mindy's shoulder. When you graduate, summa cum laude and get your doctorate, will you feel better about your life?

What's that mean? You think I hate myself because I have a big ass?

Yes, said Oster. I think you were made in Hollywood, Mindy. You don't think your ass is good enough for Robert Redford.

Off, off! Esther Lieber shouted. She doesn't need this. That's how she feels. Leave her alone.

Esther, said Joseph Cortin, is right. It's a question of love. Mindy wants to know that love exists and that love is transcendent. I will tell you, dear friends, love does exist and, alas, it is not transcendent.

♪ 5 ♪

THE TENOR'S TALE

Once I loved a woman, Joseph Cortin said.

And that was your mother, Edward Knittel said.

Cortin shook his head and smiled sadly, No, Eddie, I hated her. She was a revolting little bitch. She shouldn't have had children, she should have had vipers.

You didn't like her.

Far less than I like you, Edward. May I take two giant steps?

Joey, you may take three.

Once I loved a woman. It was the greatest mistake of my life. I was twenty-two and gay since I could remember. My career was taking off. Little Joe Cortin, the voice of liquid crystal. Ten appearances on "The Ed Sullivan Show". Co-star with Bob Hope in Vegas.

Little Joe Cortin, the handsome kid from Bensonhurst. The smile that broke hearts. The voice that made Popes weep. The flying crystal notes which brought a Sunday-night truce to the Gallo-Profaci Wars, when Little Joe Cortin sang for Ed Sullivan and the whole world.

My lover was Antoine. Antoine was his gay sobriquet. Thomas Gillicuddy was his real name. He was a construction worker who was on my payroll as my bodyguard and secretary. We had been together for five years. He was the one who had deflowered me. He adored me. He was good to me. Of course, I was also good to him.

My career terrified us. We had to be careful. I dated girls. Showed up at prizefights with the best-looking broads in the business. Once Antoine circulated photos of me in the buff with a lady whose name I won't mention. The pop grapevine, the teeny boppers of the world, spread the myth that Little Joe, hung like a horse, was America's Don Juan. And my little nubile fans were busy trapping me at the stage door or hiding under my hotel-room bed. How many panties the postman delivered! Panties with pubic hairs scotchtaped to the crotch or a spot of blood encircled by mascara and autographed: I love you, Little Joe.

Sometimes Antoine and I could not get together for weeks. When we became desperate, my PR people would put a notice in *Variety* announcing I was going to L.A. for movie meetings. Then an overnight stop in St. Louis, where Antoine was waiting.

Makeup, mustache, brimmed hat for me. Dark glasses for Antoine. Meet Me In St. Louis, Tony, a flaming night and gone! Back to the terror of the straight world.

My nerves were jumping like cats in a sack! Little Joe got onto uppers and downers and coke, of course. Now, which was worse? Being exposed as a queer or as a drug addict?

Cortin laughed and tapped the rim of his empty wine glass. McHooley filled it.

Addicts get sympathy. Queers get fucked. I mean that symbolically, of course, Cortin said as he looked from face to face. I'll tell you this. I was a good singer, a real good singer, and that's what kept me more or less sane.

You were a great singer, Joey, Vilma said, great!

Thank you, Miss Rakos. I could have been a champion. One day my father, Mario Cortina, comes to me and says, My son, Roberto Guarcello, has honored me. He came to the butcher shop today. He asked me to do him a great favor. I said to Don Roberto, Me? What is it Mario Cortina can do for you? Don Roberto said, My daughter, Claudia, has just graduated from college in Massachusetts. Smart girl! Mario, she makes her pappa feel very *stupido*. You know what she wants for a graduation present? A date with your son, the singer! She wants to show off a little.

I embraced my father. I said, Hey, Pop, you want me to take her out? Sure! You tell Don Roberto, I'm at his service.

Perfect! What could be more macho than dating the daughter of the Boss of Bosses, Don Roberto Guarcello!

Oh, boy! Esther said, this is interesting!

More interesting than I had expected. First place, Claudia Guarcello was so beautiful I wished she were a man.

I took her to Elaine's for a steak. Claudia could eat and Claudia could drink with the same kind of gusto as Antoine. After Elaine's I took her to Club 54, where the management kept the fans off my back. Claudia knew how to dance! She was bumping and grinding me all over the floor under the wild light and the deep booming of the bass.

We didn't speak while we danced. At the bar she said to me, Joey, I've got to fuck you!

Hey, I said, easy, lady!

No easy, Joey, I must fuck you now, tonight, in the next ten minutes!

I laughed. Claudia, this is just a courtesy gig.

No, it isn't. The car is outside. Don't you love to fuck in cars? That limo probably has a bed in it.

She got me by the arm and dragged me through the 54 crowd onto the street. The limo pulled up to the curb in less than a minute.

She pulled her dress off. She was naked. Her red-olive nipples were erect. I was petrified, can you believe that? I was petrified! Claudia did everything. She opened my fly, took out my tool and, like I said, I was petrified, like a rock. Even as she sucked me, I filled with fear. I never had had sex with a woman. If I lost my erection how would I explain it—me, the Don Juan of the world? I swear to you, I believed that, if I couldn't make it with her, she'd *know*.

I filled my mind with thoughts of Antoine, his hard, hairy body. Antoine coming toward me, perfumed and ready. Antoine gently turning me over, pulling my hips up toward his manhood. And as Claudia pulled my hips toward her spread thighs, I did not lose my erection. I slid into her with a little cry. And I thought of Antoine pushing deep into me.

You're making me blush, Joey, Vilma Rakos said.

Cortin smiled and pinched her cheek. I'm doing a public service, he said. You dear Happy Hour squares now know how fags get it on!

Me too, said Oster. Pretty steamy stuff.

But in that consummation I filled with a guilt and a confusion I had never had. For the first time in my life I saw an opportunity to escape my nature. To be with a woman. To spin out the heterosexual fantasies of a normal life. To live with a woman, to marry, to have children. To be able to live without that awful fear of exposure. To escape the screaming bats and hissing snakes which inhabited the closet of my life.

And I loved Claudia! She was beautiful, intelligent, graceful, knowledgeable, and blessed with exquisitely good taste. Even her sexuality: it was essentially like Antoine's. I was the desired object of forceful passion.

But it meant I would have to give up Antoine. I went through hell. I loved him as only old lovers can love: shall I count the ways? But Claudia was a love with a future. I chose her. I chose her because that would guarantee that my singing would never be endangered. Singing was life to me.

My last night with Antoine was very sweet. That special sweetness because I knew that it was a bliss which would never be repeated. Half the time as he caressed me I wept. He knew. He sensed the different quality in our loving. He asked me why I had been weeping. I wept again as I told him our relationship had to change because of Claudia. I would be with him when I could, if I could. But we would have to be even more cautious than ever. I said, Antoine, I still love you. I will always love you. I was still in his arms. I could feel the rage build in his body. He beat me unmercifully. He left me covered with blood. The broken nose was easily fixed. The open wounds above my eyes were stitched. Can you see the scars?

I told Claudia I had been beaten up by two men who had gotten into my hotel room in Vegas. They had taken my cash, my Rollex, and my diamond pinky ring. Macho stars always are at risk.

It was good to have been beaten. It made parting easier for me. I don't believe it helped Antoine. His rage remained.

Don Roberto was overjoyed when Claudia announced our engagement. He gave us a thirty-foot boat, complete with Captain. We called it *Claudia's Dream*. I canceled my bookings and we made it a Long Island summer. Ostensibly idyllic.

But it wasn't. Little by little, subtlety by subtlety, I was unable to make love to her or, much truer, I couldn't respond to her making love to me. We both needed a construction worker with sexual largesse. That's a pun, Vilma. Don't look so unhappy.

If you want to tell it, tell it!

Vilma, this is 1984. I'm telling you a love story. It happens to be my love story.

All right, Joey. Just tell it.

Cortin smiled. I sail on, he said. The media was filled with our romance. Nothing in print or on television failed to mention Don Roberto. Mafia Princess and Singing Star seek happiness together. Roberto loved the publicity. I suggested a clipping service. He was amazed to learn that such things existed. My PR company added Guarcello to my clipping service.

But Antoine, off my payroll now, let the bats and snakes escape. He also had photos! Had he always had them? Who had taken them? Who had watched us when we made love?

Ed Sullivan called me in. He told me there were nasty rumors and he had seen some awfully provocative pictures. Flat-out denial on my part, frauds and fakes. Come on, Ed, you know me, I'm Little Joe Cortin. Shared laughter. Cavalier dismissal. Not a cock-stand's bit of truth! Ed, can you believe what your eyes see? Fakes, Ed, fakes! You know they're fakes!

I never played "The Ed Sullivan Show" again.

My next album, *Claudia's Dream*, was delayed by the record company. My agent told me my bookings were being dropped. The fag thing was now common knowledge.

Very common. Claudia knew. It was a mess. But it wasn't over. I had betrayed Antoine. I had betrayed Claudia. But most of all I had betrayed Don Roberto. That meant, you see, it wasn't over. It wasn't over, not by a long shot.

Joey Cortin jumped off his stool and screamed! Look at me! Look at me! Everything was destroyed. Everything in my queer world. *Everything, everything, everything!* But it wasn't over. There was more to play out.

Ach, said Knittel, you're with friends. It's okay, Joey.

Cortin continued. I was picked up by some of Guarcello's soldiers. They pushed me into the mandatory black Cadillac. We headed for Brooklyn. I thought to myself: I'm going to die. I was scared but not unhappy. Death was the big dentist. It would hurt but I'd never have a toothache again.

They pushed me out of the Cadillac. They pushed me into my father's butcher shop. My father was there. He was trembling. The look in his eyes was a despair I had never seen there. I tried to console him. I said, Pop, it'll be all right.

The man behind me slapped me across the head. Shut up, you fag fuck.

The man to my left said, Listen, Guiseppe, we ain't got too much time. The Boss wants to see you in one hour.

Okay, but leave my father out of this. He didn't do anything.

The man to my left says, We ain't going to hurt your father, Giuseppe. We just need him to do a job here.

They pushed me into the icebox. It's an icebox made for whole sides of beef, pigs, the butcher's goods. There are carcasses hung from hooks. One of the carcasses is Antoine.

Your boy friend, one of them said. He was fuckin' you in the ass. Well, he ain't gawna fuck you no more, Joey.

Stop makin' speeches. It's cold in here. Chop him up, Pop, and let's get outta here.

Yeah, it's cold, said the third man, who stood behind my father. Get him down, Mr. Cortina.

My father, his arms around the frozen corpse, lifted it off the hook which had held it beneath the armpit. My father laid Antoine on the icebox cutting table, the frozen legs straight out beyond the table's edge.

Okay, said one of the voices. Chop him up.

Pop, I yelled, don't do it!

I gotta do it, Joey. No choice, no choice.

My father began to cut away the bloody clothes frozen to Antoine's body.

What the fuck you doin'? Cortina. You don't have to undress him. He ain't for eatin'. Slice him up, Mario. We're runnin' out of time.

My father lifted a saw down from a hook. He took a deep breath. I began to sob. Antoine, Antoine, I cried, I'm so sorry. I love you.

A gun hit me hard on the side of my head. Fucking fag, said a voice. Look what trouble you made! I passed out.

My face was swollen when we got to the penthouse where the Boss of Bosses was waiting for Little Joe Cortin.

Outside the floor-to-ceiling windows you could see the East River from end to end. When I was brought into the room, Guarcello, keeping his back to me, asked, Is he in the room?

Yes, Don Roberto.

No closer. I don't want that scum near me.

Don Roberto walked to the window. He leaned his forehead against the glass. Pain, he said. I have had the pain of humiliation. My daughter, my only one, has been put to shame. Why did you do it?

I couldn't help smiling. It was crazy. I was inside Guarcello's nut house of form and values. I asked softly, What have I done?

What? he snapped and turned to face me. You dirty little faggot, you deceived my daughter! My child who gave you her love.

I didn't decieve her, Don Roberto. I loved her.

Watch your mouth!

Why did you kill Antoine? He didn't deceive anybody.

He was pushing the pictures of you and him. Filth. How did that make my daughter look? How did that make *me* look?

He shouldn't have done it. He was angry at me. You shouldn't have killed him. You should have killed me.

Claudia begged for your life! Begged me to spare you. She's that kind of person. You shame her and she cries for you. I could not deny her this. If she didn't stand between you and me, it would have been you in the butcher shop with your father cutting you down to steaks.

You bastard, I said, you little fucking Wop bastard!

The man behind me punched me in the back of the neck. I collapsed to my knees. Go ahead. Finish me. Claudia will never know you killed me. Please. Please, do it. Kill me, please kill me.

He restrained himself. I gave my word. I don't deceive.

He had turned away from me again. After a moment he said, Bring him to the window. Guarcello pointed to a boat on the river. You recognize that? Is it too far away? My gift to you, *Claudia's Dream*. You know who's on that boat? Nobody. Just your Mick boyfriend. Just some steaks and chops. I don't want them in the world with me: not the boat and not the freak.

I hated him, I wanted to spit venom in his eyes. Make him writhe. I said to him, I loved them both. They both loved me.

On the boat we all made love together. Claudia went down on
Antoine. Claudia went down on me. I went down on Claudia.
Antoine took hold of my—

Guarcello beat my head with an ashtray. I gushed blood
for him. I smiled. I said, Kill me, you greasy, little Wop.

You are evil, you fag sonuvabitch! You are against God!

Three of my front teeth hung loosely from my gums. I
pulled them from my face. I spit a mouth full of blood at
Roberto. If you love your daughter, you monster, kill me!

The man behind me rabbit-punched me again. I collapsed
to my knees again. My pale-yellow shirt had turned bright red.
Kill me, I said, I'm begging you, please!

In agony, Don Guarcello, said, No. You will live. I swore
to Claudia on my mother's grave. You will live a long life,
Giuseppe. Now, watch the fucking boat!

Fucking is the operative word, I said.

He smashed the ashtray into the side of my jaw. I knew it
was broken. I screamed then I giggled. Guarcello's men pulled
me to my feet.

Watch the boat!

I watched. Two minutes perhaps. The boat burst into
flame. The orange-blue fire was swept back by the wind.

Full speed into the wind, Eddie. A short distance from
North Brother Island, it exploded.

Don Roberto turned to me. He was smiling. It's out of my
life, he said, out! He continued after a moment. You have told
me that, next to my daughter, singing is the love you have in
this life. There is no more Claudia for you so you have only the
singing. Only the soul which is in your voice. Now Guarcello
looked into my eyes. He cupped my swollen face in his soft
hands. He hissed at me, Giuseppe, as long as you live you will
never sing, not in the public, not in the bathroom. If I learn that
your beautiful voice is heard anywhere, *anywhere*, Mario is
dead, your mother is dead, and your fucking whore sister is
dead. Capisc'?

I stood there trembling.

Answer me, faggot! Capisc'?

Capisco, I said.

Louder, he said.

Capisco! Capisco!

Capisc, what, faggot?

As long as I live, I will never sing.

* 6 *

McHooley placed shot glasses before each of them. He filled them, spilling, as he went along the bar. Each of them drank except Cortin, who smiled at the bar surface.

Vilma, who was standing behind Cortin's stool, put her arms around his wide shoulders and rocked him gently from side to side. She held him that way for a long moment, then she kissed the back of his neck. Joey reached up and covered her hand with his own. He kissed her fingers with the lightest brush of his lips.

It's all right, Joey, she said, it was another time.

Wang cleared his throat. To be frank, he said, there isn't a Chinese proverb which is applicable. Turn up the radio, Mr. McHooley.

Mort Shuman was singing "Mr. Lee" about a black Union soldier who returns home to Mississippi after the Civil War only to get lynched.

Have you noticed that the room has become cool? McHooley asked. The air conditioner has kicked in. It works that way.

It took two hours, said Esther. Can you change the station? Some easy-listening. I know he's your favorite, McHooley, but give me a break.

I'll lower the volume.

Any one for mini-cocktail pizzas? asked Mindy. I'll make them, Bo. She went to the kitchen.

Oster smiled broadly. Look here, my drinking and crying companions, how would you like to hear the latest accounting approach to delayed debits and accelerated credits in three consecutive, non-scheduled fiscal years?

No, said Vilma Rakos. Just tell me if quarters in the meter is deductable without a receipt?

One hundred percent, said Oster.

That's life! said Eddie Knittel to no one in particular. Everything is life, ain't it? Now you would think with the Committee on Claims ignoring the survivors that it would all be over with the *Slocum*. But as McHooley has told us trials never end, and nothing else ever ends. *Ach, du lieber Augustine!*

Did somebody say my name? Esther asked. McHooley, nothing else but seltzer for me, I'm getting cuckoo.

So, said Knittel, the hull of the *Slocum* was turned into a coal barge. She was scuttling coal up and down the inland waterways until one day, carrying a full load, she sank off the Bronx coast. Would you call that the end? Well, that wasn't the end either.

It sounds like the end, Eddie, Vilma said. Now what can it be but ghost stories? Let's all go home.

Cortin looked at Vilma and smiled broadly. Was it something I said?

Bo Wang cackled.

What's the joke? Esther said.

Mini-pizzas, Bo managed to say.

Mini-pizzas are funny?

Still laughing Bo said, Caucasians have no sense of humor.

Oh, let's go home, Esther Lieber said.

Eddie Knittel, talking almost to himself, looked up toward the ceiling and said, Helga became the President of the Association of the Survivors of the *Slocum* Disaster. Helga and Melvin were living in open sin because Wolf wouldn't give her a divorce unless he got half the money from the house.

Eddie, McHooley began to say—

Don't interrupt my train of thought. Helga went around to the churches, to the Democratic Clubs, the ladies clubs, raising money. Sulzer advised them to give it up. Honeycuitt would give it up but if Helga won't, he won't. *The Times* is down to one story a year on the *Slocum* Disaster. So every June 15th I get interviewed. Not by Melvin, because *The Times* wants a fresh point of view. Before I'm done with interviews I've talked to twenty-five different reporters. None of them really gives a shit. None of them goes to the files. To each of them I must repeat the whole story.

Did you? Rakos wanted to know.

Nah. I gave each new guy a copy of the story by the last guy and I say, Anything else?

Melvin laughed at this. He said, They won't be very fond of you, Edward.

I answered him, Tsk, tsk. But the headline was almost always the same one: *The Hero of the* Slocum *Disaster Remembers.*

Mindy came through the swinging doors. Fifteen minutes to pizza time, she said.

With two spoons Bo Wang drummed on some cups and half-filled glasses he had arranged before him.

Are you starting the floorshow, Mr. Wang? McHooley asked.

Tik a tok, dah tik a tok, *You for me and me for you,* Bo Wang drummed and sang.

Joe Cortin got off his stool. C'mon, Mindy, he said. He danced her in a cartoon of a tango around the room. Isn't this the most graceful, the sexiest dancer you've ever seen?

Joey, you're crazy, Mindy said.

Very good, said Esther Lieber. You're terrific, Mindy. You're crazy, too!

Bo Wang drummed his spoons up the bar to Esther and said, Shall we dance? He pulled her from the stool and danced her in continuous circles.

You're making me dizzy, Wang!

That's life, princess, said Wang.

What the hell! said Oster to Rakos. Shall we?

Rakos slid off the stool and entered Oster's embrace. Oster led her in an awkward waltz.

You know something, Miltie?

What?

You're a terrible dancer!

True, said Oster, stopping his clumsy dance to make a deep bow.

McHooley observed the dancers. He said, 'Tis the madness of the hunger!

They've been eating like pigs, McHooley, said Knittel through the smile which lifted his beard. How about you and me, Jimothy?

I'm on duty, Eddie.

Admit it, you can't dance. You don't like dancing.

That's true. It always seemed too erotic to me. Keep in mind, Eddie, I didn't have my first woman until I was twenty-eight.

You're a poyvoyt, McHooley, said Knittel, who had left his corner and danced his hobbling dance with his cane. I learned to dance on the *Slocum.*

Oster, laughing loudly, lost control, pulled away from Vilma, and sat down on the floor.

'Tis the madness of the hunger! McHooley announced to the room. Turn, turn till you churn into butter.

Knittel and Rakos each gave Oster a hand and pulled him to his feet. Oster, still laughing, said, Oh, my God, I've wet my pants.

Vilma, also laughing, pointed to the dark spot on Miltie's gray pants. Miltie's pissed in his pants! she shouted.

'Tis the madness of the hunger!

The dancing continued. Joey Cortin released Mindy and partnered Eddie Knittel in a box-step. Mindy continued to dance alone. Joey sang out:

> *Rosy, you are my posy,*
> You are my heart's bouquet.
> You are the one who knows me,
> *Don't you ever run away.*

Cortin raised his arm and signaled the others. They all sang as they danced.

Esther Lieber interjected, Joey! Don Roberto! You'll get killed!

Fuck him! Joey Cortin sang.

'Tis the madness of the hunger! McHooley said as he shook his head.

Still dancing, Mindy asked, Is it fifteeen minutes? The pizzas. I don't want them to burn!

Let 'em burn! Oster shouted.

Cortin danced Eddie Knittel into several twirling motions. Knittel's eyes turned upward. His jaw dropped. He toppled backward and fell to the floor.

♪ 7 ♪

Knittel's head was in Vilma's lap. McHooley brought another cold towel. Vilma laid it across his forehead. McHooley put some smelling salts under the old man's nose. His head jerked. His eyes opened. What happened? Knittel asked.

Y' passed out, lad.

It was the dancing, said Vilma. You were dancing with Joey.

Sonuvabitch tried to kill me!

I did not.

It's all right, Joey, Knittel said in a weak voice. My fondest wish is to die on a *Slocum* anniversary day.

Not in my place! snapped McHooley.

Well, you could always put him outside with the garbage, Esther giggled. Now I'm into gallows humor!

Can you sit up? Wang asked.

With a grunt Knittel, pushed himself up on his elbows. Still dizzy, he said.

Have you got an Equity cot? Cortin asked McHooley.

What might that be?

A cot, have you a cot in the place?

We have a beach chaise, Mindy said, and hurried to the kitchen. She returned with the aluminum-framed chaise with its vertical and horizontal green-and-white plastic strips. She unfolded it and adjusted it to a sitting position. Joey and Vilma pulled Eddie to his feet and helped him onto the chaise. Boy, Eddie, said Mindy, you scared the shit out of me!

Ach! It's a sign of age. He looked at the ring of faces. We were having a good time, weren't we?

Great, said Esther, except for a certain party pooper we all know.

Well, said Eddie Knittel, at least I didn't die. That would have been a bummer.

Why? asked Oster. It's the eightieth anniversary of the *Slocum.* You'd have your wish.

I can't. Linda is waiting for me.

Love conquers all, said Cortin.

And I haven't finished my story. It's not over, y'know. After I tell it all, then I can die and I won't give a shit.

Vilma tugged Eddie's bearded chin. But Linda is waiting, right?

My God, what time is it?

It's a long way to ten-thirty, Mindy said and went back to the kitchen. She returned, bringing out a large serving tray covered with mini-pizzas.

It's hard to find help like you these days, Bo Wang said. Then he banged the bar witha spoon. Attention all! The story begins!

Continues, said Mindy.

Bo Wang bowed his head in her direction. Continues, he said.

At Oster's suggestion the men lifted Knittel in the chaise longue to the top of the bar. Oster said to Knittel, We are at your feet, Great Hero! Speak on.

His smile still weak, Knittel said, First I want to say, fuck you, Miltie Oster.

Sustained applause.

PART IV

1

Esther is right, y'know, when she said I was going to tell ghost stories. The *Slocum* dies and people come up from the dead to talk to you. My father still haunts me, maybe because he took him so long to die. Ach!

Dreams? Oster asked, probing.

Maybe dreams, that could be. What is it when you're looking out the window and them two black crows flap by? And you're not thinking about anything and it's a clear day, y'know? And there comes Tammuz walking up the street like nothing ever happened. Or sometimes Rosy in her lilac blouse. Not memories because I see them out there on the street. A waking dream? Sometimes Rosy sits there on my stoop, looking up, waiting for me to come down. Ach! Hallucinations must be it. Whatever it is, I can't just go to the window and order up crows or anything. I look out, I expect nothing, and there's Rosy. Oh, how beautiful that is!

Beautiful? said Esther. I'd be in the doctor's office.

Knittel smiled. He reached over and pinched Esther Lieber's cheek. You're sensitive like my Aunt Helga. After a few years Helga couldn't take the visits to the loony bin. I could understand that. It was no picnic. But I was his son so I went. Once a month. I wouldn't do more than that. A week before I had to go I would get a weak stomach, loose bowels. When I got to the hospital they were always glad to see me. I think I was the only visitor to the back ward where they kept my father. Dr. Cohen, the alienist, was a hunch back with a lame foot like mine. Quasimodo. A nice man. Always smiling, he liked his work.

He always talked with me before they brought my father out to see me. I think they cleaned him up a little because his hair was always wet and slicked back. Dr. Cohen had told me long before that Tammuz Knittel was without hope. As he was, so he would be.

They gave us the use of a small room. It had a table in it. Oak, I think. The surface was rough. There were hearts and initials carved into it. My guess was it had come from a school somewhere because they weren't going to give knives to crazies, y'know. There was always a guard outside the door in case of trouble but it wasn't necessary. I was twenty-five, something like that, and I had bulked up. Maybe two-sixty, two-seventy. I was a journeyman plumber, already working for Stimmler & Sons. I had got big but my father had shrunk, and his hands, the only part of him still big, were soft from idleness.

We sat opposite each other and played pinochle. He liked that. Crazy, huh? He's nuts saying yes and no to voices only he hears, but he's playing pinochle!

You're not going to tell us that he got the best of you, McHooley said.

Eddie Knittel, looking down from the beach chair, said, Almost all the time, McHooley. The insane don't lose their intelligence, y'know. They're crazy, not stupid.

We're playing two-handed pinochle, which is a good game, and maybe it needs the most skill. My father is listening to voices. He folds his cards and puts them down. He is having another argument with Samuel Gompers. He's always arguing with Samuel Gompers. He thinks Gompers is an enemy of socialism and had forced the United States to go into an imperialist war against Germany. My father yells, Don't tell me about the Kaiser! Don't you ever put Wilhelm's name in your mouth, you dirty Jew bastard. The Kaiser is a socialist. He's the best of the socialists!

All of this he's screaming. Then he turns back to the table, picks up his cards, fans them out, and melds a flush in diamonds.

Here it is 1915, already. The trials are long over. No one is guilty except Van Schaik, but not for starting the fire. You know who started the fire? Knittel asked with a grunted laugh. My father started the fire! He told me so. Many times he told me. He'd turn to me suddenly, his eyes hot. I'll tell you why I set the fire on the *Slocum*, he'd say. You want to know why?

I would always say, Why, Pappa?

Because your mother is a dirty, rotten whore. A cheap, two-dollar whore with a cunt full of worms!

I'd close my eyes when he repeated this. My ears I couldn't close. Ach!

I woke up early in the morning before anyone else, he said with that crazy laugh and heavy German accent, his eyes sparkling. I went down by the dock. I did a swan dive into the river. I swam up and down the river until I found the *Slocum*. They were hiding it from me but I found it. I climbed up the rope. I went straight to the pilothouse. I hid myself inside the wall so no one could see me. It was very hot inside the wall. I did not breathe too much. Someone would hear. Down on the dock, by the hundreds, people were coming. Singing, they came up the gang plank. Good German songs and "Old, Black Joe" they were singing.

Now I ask you, how the fuck did he know what they were singing? He was at work.

I hold my breath, Edward, so they shouldn't know I'm on the *Slocum*, he tells me. Then the whistles were blowing and the horns were sounding and the boat was sailing up the river.

Why should it be so hard to tell this part? Knittel asked of the ceiling.

McHooley poured the brandy into the glass, which Knittel had reached down toward him from his perch on the bar.

Don't tell it if you don't want, said Vilma, patting Knittel's leg.

Knittel smiled to her. He sipped the brandy and said, Here goes nothing.

In one minute, my father says, Pauline comes with a rush into the pilothouse. The Captain is waiting for her. He opens her dress from the back. He unhooks her corset. Her breasts come out and he sucks on them. I'm angry, but I don't say a word because I want to find out what it's all about. They can't see me because I'm inside the wall and I'm invisible.

As he speaks, is he seeing my mother and Van Schaik before him? I don't know, but his eyes are bulging. His voice is loud and the veins in his neck swell up.

She takes off her clothes piece by piece, my father says and he repeats, *piece by piece.* Now she is naked. The whore is naked! What kind of woman have I married? A whore, a whore, a whore! Now the Captain unbuttons his fly and takes out a cock like a horse. In a minute Pauline has it in her mouth. She sucks and sucks until he empties himself into her mouth. She swallows everything and she says, Good, that was very delicious! Then the Captain lets Pauline steer the wheel. He gets behind her and holds her tits and then he does it to her in the backside!

Then she asks the Captain for money. He smiles and he says, I know what the money is for. It's for socialism. You're going to give the money to Eugene Debs. Pauline says, No, not for Eugene Debs. To the Jew bastard Samuel Gompers I will give it. Then she grabs the Captain by the throat and says, Give me the money!

He gives her the money. She kisses the money. They fall down on the floor and they do it like dogs.

I come out from the wall. They don't notice me. I go down to the boiler room. With a shovel I take burning coals from the furnace and throw them all around. The floor is on fire. Then I go back up to the deck and make a swan dive into the river and swim away.

The first time I heard this from my father I went to the toilet and on my knees I puked my guts out. When I came back to the table he was shuffling the cards.

I hate him! Oh, how I hate him!

How can you hate him, lad? He's yer father and the grief stole his mind.

I know all that, McHooley. Still and all, I hated him alive and I hate him dead, and I hate his memory. He was worse than his brother, Wolf. Whatever it was, I think it ran in their family. The mind, the mind! But I guess everybody's mind is crazy. Mine is nutty and yours is nutty.

Absolutely, said Joey. Wisdom from on high!

I'll tell you one thing. I always wondered why he said her name. He shouldn't have said her name when she was with the Captain. But I'm glad in his hallucinations he never said she let her hair down. It was my memory, that: Mama on the roof, letting her hair down, pulling her inlaid comb through.

You can't hate crazy people, Esther said.

Don't make it a class action. It's my father I hate.

Oster said, I suppose he died in the insane asylum.

No, said Knittel, he died on the Brooklyn Bridge. He just walked out of the hospital one morning in December of 1915. No one stopped him. He was invisible, all right. That morning it was cold as hell in New York and all he was wearing was a thin shirt and a pair of summer pants. Late in the afternoon he got on the bridge. He walked up one of the heavy cables. He took off all his clothes–underwear, shoes and socks, everything. He hooked one of his arms around a guy wire and screamed until the night came. The cops found him there. Now I'm telling you what Sergeant Norman Brown told me.

They couldn't talk him down, y'know. By the time they found him, he had turned red and blue but he was still scream-ing. I asked Sergeant Brown what he was screaming. Brown, puzzled a little, said, Obscenities about some Pauline and a Captain. And the *Slocum* was in it. He kept yelling that when the *Slocum* came under the bridge he was going to jump down onto it.

Nothing else ? I asked him.

No. Eventually the cold took him over because suddenly he said nothing more. He had turned a dark blue. He was dead. His feet slipped off the cable. It was very eerie. He was frozen stiff, his arm hooked over a wire, and he was flapping in the wind. The wind was so strong it lifted the corpse and flipped it into the air. It was not like a stone that he fell but like a kite without a tail. The corpse rose, tumbled, sailed, and twisted in the night. Weird. We held the sailing corpse in the lamplights we had coming from the truck. We lost him going down. It was too dark to see him splash and too noisy to hear it.

✦ 2 ✦

Perspiring, Milt Oster dried his face and smooth-shaven head with a napkin. He asked, Is the air conditioner still going?

Pumping away, Mr. Oster. It was the dancing, McHooley said.

I've been asking myself, Vilma Rakos said, why is there so much death in this Happy Hour? The people on the *Slocum*, Esther's story, McHooley's story, Joey, Tammuz. Isn't there any thing nice that happens?

Puzzle, Oster said. No matter how many wonderful things exist, we cling to darkness. Darkness guides us. It's the ice inside us.

I don't want to hear that, Cortin said.

You, Joey?

Me. That's part of the meaning of being gay. There must be hope. There must be a pony in the barrel of horse shit. Life must be beautiful. Judy Garland must give another concert. There must be love. Listen to old Eddie, he floats up from the dead but it's Rosy alive who shapes his life, makes his life beautiful, makes him beautiful.

Ach, ach, ach, Rosy! Knittel cried out from his high perch. It's true! How would I have lived all these years without Rosy?

Puzzle, said Oster. No matter what, we find a way to live.

That's because we have McHooley's, Esther Lieber said with a laugh. Let's not get heavy. I hate heavy drunks.

All right then. Let us eschew heavy, said Oster. He looked up at Eddie Knittel on the chaise longue. Oh, Hero, bring us some light!

Why are you always so sarcastic, Miltie? Vilma asked. Joey, Wang, too. Always the men.

Oster sighed. It comes out that way, doesn't it? But it isn't true. If Pollyanna had been a boy, that would have been me.

Well, I don't know that, said Vilma. But look, Knittel's Helga and Honeycuitt, weren't they sweet? Eddie, weren't they sweet?

Knittel grimaced. With the back of his hand he rubbed some tears away.

Oh, Jesus Christ, Eddie, something awful? Vilma asked.

No. It's just that they died. In my lifetime everybody died. Present company excepted. Yes, they were a sweet couple. Bittersweet, said Knittel.

♪ 3 ♪

Melvin Honeycuitt was a misfit. He knew it too, y'know. He told me a lot about himself when I was still recuperating from the *Slocum.* Wolf had already gone back to the Fatherland. So Melvin peeled a half an eye for Helga. Unlike Jimothy McHooley, who didn't get laid until he was twenty-eight, I don't think Honeycuitt ever got to have a woman in a proper way until Helga.

What do mean, *in a proper way?* Esther asked. How did he have them, with a straw?

I don't know, Tootsie. It was his shape, and he was so blond he was like an albino. He was maybe thirty when he found me on the beach. To me he looked old already. My father and Wolf were older but they didn't look as old as Melvin. Bald also, with one blond strand pulled over from back to front. I always thought if he ever got laid it had to be with a hooker and even with a hooker he'd be ashamed of the way his fat wobbles. A wonderful man but always embarrassed about himself.

In those days I thought he was like that because he came from a family of people in that kind of shape, fat assed, wobbly people. From what Helga told me it was not that way. Melvin was the exception. In him popped out all those genes. What's it called?

Recessive, said Oster.

Recessive, that's right. His whole family was guys six feet tall and every one of them a general going back to the Revolutionary War. And, back in England, counts and dukes. Handsome guys. The women too.

When Honeycuitt gets born they already have him scheduled to go to West Point. His father was the adjutant commander of the school. But, by the time he's five, they have their doubts. The only things he's good at are dancing and marksmanship. But horses no. Sabers, no. And hiking in the woods? He's got flat feet and a heavy ass.

Poor guy, Vilma said.

I tell you he must have felt he let everybody down. There's a family house outside West Point with oil paintings of twenty Honeycuitt generals and Melvin can't look one of them in the eye. So he becomes a reporter.

Helga finally got to sell the house on the corner of 9th Street and Avenue D. In 1935. A fire demolished it. It was all settled with Wolf. She goes to live with Melvin in his brownstone on 74th Street between Riverside and West End. He had a garden in the back. Aside from flowers and vegetables, Honeycuitt grew corn. Would you believe that?

Oh, yes, said McHooley. Tis my experience that anything will grow in New York. There'll never be a famine

They lived there and I got a flat at 816 East 9th, the last house before the stables, the factories, and the pier.

I think the high point of Melvin's life was the *Slocum*. It made him a little sad when the *Slocum* began to lose its glamour. He sold one article to *Harper's*. That was it.

We had good times together eating out at Luchow's or going to the beach. On the beach we'd just sit on the sand. No bathing suits for us. Helga didn't want to show off her figure. Melvin didn't want to show off his figure. Anyway, if he'd ever gotten the notion to undress, he'd be burnt to a crisp, so light his skin was. And me, I didn't want to show my foot in the clumsy brace. I didn't want to show the thick scars on my arms.

So why did you go to the beach at all? Mindy asked.

Ach! The ocean, Mindy! Is there anything greater to look at than the ocean? And we made many runs to the country in Melvin's roadster. They put me in the rumble seat so I got plenty of wind. Like I told you before, I'm already six foot three and two hundred fifty pounds. I'm crammed in there.

It doesn't appear to me that y'er that large, Eddie, McHooley said.

Well, I ain't. I began to shrink at seventy-five. If I live till a hundred twenty, as the Jews say, I won't be any bigger than Margie Ann Plunkerbrote.

4

Knittel looked sharply down from his chaise lounge. Listen, he said, I'm getting a little nervous up here. This thing ain't the Rock of Gibraltar, y'know. I don't want to crash into

McHooley's sink. Whoever it was who put me up here, put me down.

Wang, Oster, and Cortin lifted the chaise with Eddie in it and lowered it to the floor. Cortin gave Knittel a hand so he could pull himself to his feet. Eddie went to his stool in the corner and said, Okay, that's better!

He looked carefully at his Comrades of the Happy Hour. McHooley, squatting down, was counting the cold beer bottles in the lower refrigerators. Esther Lieber was applying fresh lipstick to her mouth. Joey's craggy face was far away in the prairies of his thought. Knittel had never seen Joey show such a sadness. Vilma, his sweet protector, was smoking, allowing blue clouds to escape through her nose. Beautiful woman, Vilma. Oster seemed to be looking toward him but his eyes were blank. Mindy, bending over, not flattering herself, was sweeping something unseen into a dustpan. Bo Wang, black eyes alert, was locked onto to Knittel, telling him that Wang didn't like Knittel much and had little empathy for him. The feeling was mutual.

Knittel now felt that none of them was thinking of the *Slocum*. His stomach knotted. He was losing them. They had had enough of his long, burning *Slocum* legend. They were now thinking of other things.

He couldn't afford to get angry. It would give them, some of them, an excuse to walk out. But he wanted them to hear everything he had to say, everything. Even if they slept through it. Be nice, his brain voice growled.

Achtung! Eddie Knittel sang out. There ain't so much left of the story so lend me your ears!

Julius Ceasar, said Oster.

Knittel reads sometimes, said Cortin.

It's just that we're all a little drunk, said Esther Lieber, you can hear the buzz.

We'll listen, Edward, said Vilma Rakos, please continue. It's not very long, right?

Knittel nodded and, keeping his voice light, splitting his beard with a smile said, Even though the Survivors Association was getting nowhere, those were real good years for me. Except for the brace and the scars, I was healthy and strong. I was a good plumber, too, and it was just a matter of time before I'd get a Master's License. And that's where the real good money is. I was at that time, y'know, the youngest member of the Association of Plumbers and Steam Fitters, Local Seven, American Federation of Labor. Now I'm the oldest living member. In those days when I went to a meeting I got a lot of glad-handing. They knew my father had been a union stalwart, y'know. And me, I was still the hero. Gompers himself once came up to me at a meeting and shook my hand.

Popular Eddie, said Esther.

That was the upside, Knittel said, There was a downside, too. Y'see Captain William Van Schaik was also a good union member. Charter member of the Harbor Pilots, Master and Mates Association. The AFL, Gompers, they all felt that Van Schaik was sacrificed in the interests of corporations and capitalism.

Well, well, well, said Oster, his eyes now alert, a bit of weather coming up!

Oh, yes, weather, rallies, and petitions. Free Captain William Van Schaik was bigger than Free Tom Mooney, I'll tell you that. Van Schaik was on the agenda of every labor meeting in the United States. Free Captain William Van Schaik! If you listened to a single street rally, and there were dozens, you'd have been convinced that Christ had been put up on the cross again. Eugene V. Debs spoke at the Free Van Schaik Rally in Union Square. More than a hundred thousand people came out. Gompers spoke from the same platform as Big Bill Heywood, who later got himself buried under the Kremlin Wall. Hundreds of thousands of people signed petitions asking for the Captain's release. They shipped these off to President Roosevelt. Roosevelt said no. That was 1905 and the years following.

But about me, everybody is in a dilemma, y'see. The union brothers like me because I'm a good kid and I've suffered a lot.

Yes, and you're still the hero, said Oster. Heroes are not to be dealt with lightly.

That's the whole point, Miltie! I'm the hero, the good kid, but it's my testimony that brought Van Schaik down. That doesn't go down so good with a lot of brothers. And it doesn't go down so good with Honeycuitt either! Now what does he say? What can he say? I was confused? I had amnesia? How did I suddenly remember the minute-by-minute truth at the Coroner's Jury Trial? Was Van Schaik really innocent? Amnesia, confusion, confusion, amnesia.

Knittel laughed. Here's the twist. Me and Melvin, we both had to shut up. I had put the noose around Van Schaik's neck and the brothers are saying maybe Hero Eddie was a little bit confused on that point about how long the *Slocum* went up river into the wind. Every harbor pilot, every steamship captain, testifies that Captain Van Schaik did the right thing by beaching at North Brother Island and that each of them would have done exactly the same thing. Sacrificed to corporations and capitalism! But Melvin wants to believe that on that point my mind and memory were clear as a bell. So I shut up and Melvin shut up.

Did you sign the petition? McHooley asked.

I wanted to but I couldn't. What would President Roosevelt say? What would *The New York Times* say? No one pushed me. William Howard Taft took me off the hook. In his campaign for President in 1908 he promised Sam Gompers he would pardon and free Van Schaik if he got elected. So, when Taft defeated William Jennings Bryan, he kept his word. He got Van Schaik out of Sing Sing and gave him a pardon.

Peace at last, said Oster.

Almost, Miltie, almost. There was one brother who wanted my balls. An Irishman, McHooley, he was a steam fitter by the name of Morrison. Oh, he was a flaming Red! A Wobbly.

Say again, said Joey Cortin, a what?

A Wobbly, Knittel said. I told you I outlived my time, Joey. A Wobbly, a member of the Industrial Workers of The World. They advocated one big union. No more craft unions, no more AFL's, no more Samuel Gompers. No more capitalism. Pull everything down. Throw emory dust into the wheels of industry. And if that didn't work how about a stick of dynamite?

Now Jim Morrison himself was a nice guy. Big fellah, soft spoken, always helping sick members and singing Joe Hill songs. He believed in things that were best for the working class, and for those things he was ready to die. Morrison liked to use me as an example of a good brother who fell into the sin of being the boss's tool. But I only saw him at a meeting now and then. I gave him plenty of room. But when the *Titanic* hit the iceberg that's when the shit hit the fan!

Jaizus! said McHooley.

In the newspapers they were comparing the *Titanic* with the *Slocum*. So there was my name again with artists' pictures of Eddie Knittel on the mast with his pants on fire. There are drawings of the *Titanic* a blink before she smashes into the iceberg. Fifteen hundred dead. The biggest sea disaster in the history of the world. Bigger than the *Slocum* with its eleven hundred dead, with its twelve hundred dead, with its thirteen hundred dead.

What difference how many, Eddie? Vilma said. You're not going for a record.

No, Vilma, *they* were going for records. Roger Maris hits sixty-one. Hank Aaron hits seven-fifteen. More dead by far in the North Atlantic than on the East River.

But you had a greater audience, Oster said.

Yeh, but in April of 1911 Eddie Knittel got on the front pages again. And, oh, boy, didn't that ever get Jim Morrison's Irish up!

Again, he's agitating against Eddie Knittel, the capitalist *agent provocateur*. Morrison said it with a French accent. Gave more weight to it, y'know. Showed how fucking smart the mick was.

At the next meeting he puts up a resolution that I should be denounced and, as a capitalist tool, expelled from the Union.

The *Slocum* thing is almost ten years old. Van Schaik is out of Sing Sing maybe five years and Morrison is after *me*! I was afraid that I'd never get to be a Master Plumber, y'know.

Knittel became pensive. He stroked his beard.

So? said Esther Lieber.

So I defended myself. I said at a meeting where Morrison was making me look worse than Jack The Ripper, that what I had said at the trial was the truth and that Jim Morrison was telling lies.

So, Morrison, who's about my size, big fella, says if I were not a crippled, cowardly, lying, little prick he would beat my brains in.

I say, Watch your mouth, you Wobbly fuck!

Don't make me do it, he says.

Do what? I say. You afraid the cripple will knock your brains out?

Don't provoke me, Morrison yells, his face becoming red as a beet. Don't provoke me!

Provoke? I say. I'm on his ass now. I know I got him. So I just build it up. You Wobblies with your big mouths are fucking the working class and you're afraid of little cripples. I can kick your ass all over the union hall in front of a hundred witnesses. Does that scare you?

Stop! he screams.

You want me to give you the Red Flag to cry in? I say. Are you the Wobbly hero Joe Hill is always yodeling about?

The Joe Hill insult does it. Morrison becomes icy calm. He says, All right, if it has to be, it has to be. Let's get these chairs cleared away.

So that's what they do, they push the wooden folding chairs to the sides of the hall.

Cortin whistled. I always knew you were crazy!

I just got my Cherman up, said Knittel. Now, Joey, let's get these tables pushed away and I'll give a full, live version of Red Morrison versus Knittel the Kid.

Well, what are you waiting for, Cortin? McHooley said. Here's the lighthearted moment for which we all have waited! I told you Eddie's nose was the gift of fisticuffs!

Oh, stop it! Vilma said raising her voice. Eddie, you fell down when you tried to *dance*. You'll kill yourself!

Nah! I was too drunk before, that's why. The vapors of the booze have left my head.

He'll have a stroke! Esther Lieber shouted. You can stop him, Vilma. He'll listen to you!

No, he won't. He wants to die.

Cortin, Oster, Wang, and Mindy pushed the chairs and tables aside.

Mindy, don't help! Esther shouted again. He'll die and it will be your fault.

That's silly! If he wants to do it, he'll do it.

She's a psychology major, McHooley said.

Bo! Esther pleaded, don't let them!

Captain Kinipshun will be served, Bo said with a smile. Let the fool go.

Oster asked, Whatever happened to charity?

Knittel laughed robustly. I'm in better shape than any man in this room and I'm going to go ten rounds.

All right, damn it, Vilma said, her jaw tight, Go kill yourself! And give us a refill, McHooley!

Knittel laughed. Now they're interested, all right, he thought.

The tables removed from the center of the room, Edward Francis Knittel stepped forward into the clearing and bowed. McHooley lightly struck a large brandy snifter with a knife and it rang clearly through the room. Round one! McHooley said.

Knittel took off his jacket and handed it to Vilma. Hold this, I won't be long. I can beat this bum now as I beat him then.

Knittel rolled up his sleeves and bared his heavily scarred arms. With his gimpy leg in the high orthopedic shoe he shuffled forward and back, bobbed and weaved, put his thumb to his nose and snorted.

I feel sorry for Morrison right away. I can see he doesn't know anything about boxing. I had learned to box at the Boys' Club under the punch-drunk eye of a former professional welterweight.

Morrison rushes at me swinging his arms like a windmill. He surprises me with that. He bumps into me and knocks me down. My gimp gives me a balance problem.

I'm up in a minute. He rushes at me again. I'm set. I put a stiff jab into his face. Like I opened a faucet, blood rushes from his nose.

Morrison is so surprised, he stops in his tracks. He puts his fingers to his bloody nose. Maybe it was broken.

Knittel hobbled about in the cleared space, sparring with the air. His jaw calmped in a grimace beneath his beard as he jabbed and grunted.

Somebody with brains yells out, Stop this! This is the Union Hall! Knittel said as he jabbed. I think that's a good idea so I put my arms down. But Morrison, oh, he's angry! He comes right at me swinging. He catches me a good shot in the ear. My head is ringing.

Round Two! McHooley sang out.

Cheap shot, said Cortin.

Shut up! said Vilma.

I don't like fights, said Esther.

I'm annoyed. Not really angry, just annoyed, Knittel said. The scowl in his beard had become more intense. I want to teach him a lesson.

He rushes at me again. I stop him like a mule hit with a bat with a straight right then a hard jab to his nose again. More blood. He smiles like he's saying a little blood isn't going to bother him.

He comes again. My jab moves him off balance toward his left. I catch him with a hard right hook over his eye. The flesh separates and blood seeps out.

I think maybe he's got the message, y'know, but he keeps coming. I open a cut over his other eye.

Knittel hobbled and danced and threw sharp punches. His breathing became more labored.

I call out into the Union Hall, Knittel said, Somebody tell this brother to stop. He can't fight. He's getting hurt!

But no one says a word. I want to avoid hitting him but, because of my leg, I can't get out the way of his rushes quickly enough so I have to punch him to keep him off me. His whole head is swollen up like a pumpkin. A pumpkin lined with red streams.

I don't want to hit his face anymore so I switch to his body. It's easy to block what he throws and I hook and upper-cut into his belly. Maybe I break a few ribs. One hook makes him gasp. He can't breathe and he wheezes down to the floor like an empty paper bag. He sits there sucking in his wind. When he's able to breathe again he smiles up at me. You're still a fucking cripple scab! he says.

I didn't pay any attention to that. I says to him, Morrison, walk away from this. I don't want to hurt you.

I say to the others, Will you please stop this fight? The man is hurt.

No one says a word. They're smelling blood and they want it to go on.

Slowly, Morrison gets to his feet. It ain't going to be as easy as you think, Knittel. You'll punch me until your arms fall off. Then I'm gawna kill you.

Well, the sonuvabitch had a plan there, y'know. My arms *were* getting a little heavy. I smile at him and say, Not before your face falls off.

Where Morrison gets the energy or the quickness from I don't know. He rushes at me. I'm ready. But he ducks down and slides into my bad leg. I crumple. He gets on top of me and pounds away. I have my arms up, shielding my face. I roll with his punches. He beats away for awhile until his arms get tired and his breathing is like a busted bellows. When he pauses, I push him and he falls over backward.

I get to my feet. I says to him, Morrison, this is enough. One of us is going to get hurt real bad.

That'll be you, you capitalist flunky, he says as he struggles to his feet.

Why, I ask him, why?

Because of what you did to Van Schaik. He was innocent and you ratted him into jail.

I'm sorry he went to jail. But, look, he's out and pardoned, ain't he?

Makes no difference. You're a hero for the ruling class.

I think you're crazy, Morrison.

Before this fight is over, cripple, you're going to be dead.

I turn to the men standing around the space where we're fighting and ask again, Will somebody stop this fight?

Nothing but the silence. I'm angry now myself. My thought is: Knock him out. Knock him out hard. End this thing.

Knittel jabbed the air.

I just stand still, Knittel said. I just wait for him. Now, poor Morrison imitates a guy who thinks he's a boxer. He shuffles around and slides from side to side. He jabs into the air a foot away from my head. I just stand still and smile.

When he comes into range, I jab. His head snaps back. Blood runs. He smiles like an idiot and comes forward again. I jab his head back again. I could stick in ten jabs but my arm is tired and I've got to save myself for a good shot.

Boom, boom, boom, Knittel said, and jabbed at Morrison's face. I set myself this time. He comes to me and I put all my weight behind the right I throw. Morrison goes halfway across the Union Hall. He falls face down on top of someone's tool box. He opens the box and lifts out a big wrench and a claw hammer.

He staggers toward me. His face is bleeding like one red sheet.

Morrison says to me, You'll die for the working class of the world, Knittel! Rejoice! Rejoice!

He's as crazy as Tammuz.

The wrench in his left hand comes down. It's a long miss. His arm is limp at his side. I hit him so hard! I never in my life hit anybody so hard. He falls on his back. His eyes are open but he can't move. The wrench and the hammer have fallen from his hands. I pick them up and step toward Morrison to help him to his feet.

A man at the front of the crowd yells to me, Kill him, Knittel! Bust his fucking skull!

He's a short, stocky man with a big mustache. A rage comes up in me and fills my throat! I roar. I mean, I'm an animal and my throat is filled with blood. I want to kill this man! With all my heart and soul, I want to sink the claws of the hammer into his skull. I want to kill him! Kill him! Tear his mustache off his face! It's not Morrison I want to kill but this fucking bloodsucker! Full force I throw the wrench at that face with the veins popping out of its head. Miss. He runs from the hall, the bastard! That dirty little bastard!

Knittel was breathing hard. Then he started to sob. I want to kill him, tear his mustache off, kill him, kill him! His sobs were filled with the breath he sucked from the bar room air.

Calm down, Eddie, lad, there's no one here to kill, McHooley said in his most soothing bartender voice. The fight's over, lad, it's over now.

Vilma pushed a chair under Knittel. He crumpled into it. He sat there, suddenly small, weak, and very old.

⌁ 5 ⌁

I think, said Oster, we're cutting decades off the life of our benefactor.

Yes, you're overdoing it, lad. A little brandy? You're trembling.

No more brandy! Throw a blanket over him, said Esther Lieber. Is there a blanket in the house?

Mindy retreated into the kitchen and returned with a thin, pink baby blanket. She put it across the old man's shoulders. Somebody left it, Mindy said, a drunken mother.

Thanks, said Knittel, but I'll also take the brandy. A finger, McHooley.

McHooley passed the snifter to Oster. Oster handed it to Knittel. The pink blanket slipped down behind the old man. Mindy retrieved it, fixed it about his shoulders again, and fastened it at his throat with a large safety pin. Came with the blanket, she said.

Thank God, you didn't kill that guy! said Esther Lieber.

Why? I wanted to, said Knittel weakly.

Why? Don't be stupid, Eddie. If you had killed him, you wouldn't be here today. And how would we hear the story? Esther Lieber said.

Knittel snorted. You're all tolerating me, I know that. I appreciate it anyway.

Well, said Joey Cortin, you won the fight by a TKO. Would you like to go on to the next episode?

The Perils of Eddie Knittel, said Oster.

I'm winded, the old man said.

Promise me something, said Esther.

What?

You won't die. You'll finish the story.

I *must* finish the story, my dear yenta. Then I'll die in your flabby arms.

Bastard, said Esther with a short laugh.

I like the image, said Joe Cortin. What a way to end a play. He finishes the story. He clutches his breast. He dies in her flabby arms. Curtain.

La Bohème, said Oster.

La Boat Ride, said Cortin.

Romantic, Vilma said facetiously.

You're against romance? Joe Cortin said. You, Vilma Rakos, against true love? I thought you were like me when it came to love. Ready to die for it.

She lifted Cortin's hands to her mouth and kissed both of them. Oh, yes, Joey, exactly like you. Ready to die for love. Unlike you, ready to kill for it.

Jaizus! said McHooley.

You're just trying to top Joey, right? said Esther Lieber.

Vilma wouldn't do that, said Knittel.

No, you're right, Eddie, I wouldn't do that.

It was just a way of talking, right? said the old man.

No, Eddie, it wasn't just a way of talking. I killed for love and I'd do it again, too, Vilma said, her face becoming pale, her eyes blank.

Jaizus, said McHooley.

Vilma Rakos bit her lip and, wide eyed, looked from face to face. Oh, she said, it ain't what you think. I'm not a murderer or anything like that.

THE TAXI DRIVER'S TALE

I'm going to smoke a lot of cigarettes, Vilma Rakos said as she lit one. You guys don't know much about me.

How can we when you just sit around looking beautiful all the time? said Esther.

Thanks. It's in the family. I'm Hungarian, you know.

No! exclaimed Cortin. There's a tragedy for you.

Vilma punched Cortin's arm. I go to a shrink. She was in my cab and we got to talking.

It sounds unethical, Milt Oster said.

Well, we've got a barter deal. I see her once a week and I take her where she wants to go whenever she wants.

Not only unethical but a little pricey.

No, she's nice. I have no self-esteem, she's working on that.

No self-esteem? You? said Mindy.

Swear to God! Whale shit, bottom of the deep blue sea.

But you're so beautiful!

Vilma shrugged. I was only beautiful once, she said. Before that I was only whale shit. Even in grade school, a boy would say, Let's do dirty, and I'd do dirty.

There was no one I could refuse. Up went the skirt, down came the pants.

Grade school, asked Mindy?

Yeah, we didn't know how to do it but we did it.

His voice still weak, Eddie Knittel said, Vilma, I don't want to hear this.

I'm not going into details like the whores on Avenue C or stuff like that. It's the way I was, Eddie. Nobody knew about it except a couple hundred guys. My parents never caught on. We went to church every Sunday, St. Tividar's. Father Sandor said I looked like a saint with my gold hair and black-lace mantilla. In confession I only had the smallest sins. There were at least five guys sitting in the church who had done the nasty with me. It's so funny, each one of them thought that he was the only one and maybe, because of what he had done, I might be sent to hell. I don't think they confessed either.

Vilma paused to light another cigarette. You know what worried me? I was sure that one day after so many guys the silence would break and somebody would talk. Then everybody would talk. They'd talk and they'd laugh. They'd say, Here's what I did with Vilma on the roof, here's what I did with Vilma in the cellar, here's what I did with Vilma in my car. That was the kid stuff. Then it got to bedrooms and motels and stuff.

Eddie, his voice stronger, said, Vilma, I swear if you keep up with this, I'm going home.

Vilma smiled. Eddie, don't be like that. It's my story, okay?

Knittel finished the last sliver of the brandy. Okay, he said, but no details.

Gee, you're pure, said Esther.

Yes, he is, Vilma said.

And what about this housekeeper, Linda Fernandez? asked McHooley. Do you think that's purity?

Yes, I do. And I think Linda is a saint, Vilma said.

Sainthood is everywhere these days, said Bo Wang, who had been listening with his head cradled on his crossed arms on the bar. Vilma? he prompted.

I wanted to break out. End it, you know. I thought all I had to do was to marry someone, have kids, get fat. There was Christopher sitting in the church each Sunday. I had put out for him. He thought he had been the one and only. Innocent Vilma. Bad Christopher. It was easy to go from guilt to marriage.

Cigarette. Pause. Flame. Geyser of smoke.

The problem was, said Vilma, I couldn't get pregnant. I could screw like a bunny but I couldn't get knocked up. What is that, Miltie, an irony?

Oster nodded.

I felt so low! It was my fault. Christopher didn't mind it. I was giving him a good time. We were saving money. His pay from the telephone company, mine from waitressing. We could wait a couple of years.

I don't want to keep on about me and Christopher. The long and short of that marriage was that he learned of my past thing from some pole climber who I couldn't even remember. And Chris couldn't let bygones be bygones. He began to beat up on me. At the beginning, I told him I didn't blame him for doing it. And I didn't either. I deserved it. He told the whole thing to his parents. They told my parents. We separated. I went back to my old ways.

Poor Christopher! I really fucked up his life. You'd think he'd say good riddance to bad rubbish but no. He began to follow me after I got off work. Sometimes he'd just yell so everybody could hear: She's a whore! She's a cunt! You wanna fuck her, mister? She fucks for free! Then he would try to beat me up right on the street, people around and all. I would run. I was faster than him.

One night he caught me in front of my house. He ran me into the brick wall. He punched me. He kicked me. I'm thinking to myself, I deserve it. Do it, Christopher. Harder, harder. Kill me, Christopher, please.

Cigarette. Light. Smoke.

This taxi rolls up to the curb. The driver steps out and gets between us. Get the fuck lost, he says to Christopher.

Vilma laughed. Christopher said, Mind your business. This is my wife!

Gregory, the taxi driver, says, Mister, I don't care if she's your grandmother. Get off!

Christopher tried to get past Gregory. Gregory kicked him in the balls. Chris falls on the sidewalk holding his crotch. I get down beside Chris. He's moaning. I say to Chris, It's all right, honey!

Can you imagine that? He's moaning, holding his balls, and I'm calling him honey, baby, sweetheart!

Vilma laughed again. I look up at this taxi driver who's got a red beard, like a flag, and I say, You sonuvabitch, why don't you mind your own business?

He says, The guy was trying to kill you!

It ain't none of your business. Gidadda here before I call the cops!

There's human nature for you, he says and goes back to his cab.

I help Chris to his feet. The minute he lets go of his balls, he hauls off and knocks me into the wall. He's beating the shit out of me again.

Gregory comes back, pulls Christopher away from me, and whack, whack, whack, Christopher is out cold.

Well, Eddie, m'boyo, said McHooley, there's a contender for the heavyweight championship of McHooley's Bar and Grill.

Knittel snorted.

Vilma laughed.

I really don't see what's so funny, Vilma, Mindy said.

Life is funny, Mindy. You know what I did? I screamed bloody murder. I screamed for the cops. Gregory just stands there with his mouth open. The cops come and they arrest Gregory. They take him to jail! They tow away his cab. They say he'll lose his license and maybe his medallion.

Caucasian justice, Bo Wang said.

I felt very bad about it. I refused to press charges. Chris wasn't available when the court called him.

Happy ending, Oster observed.

Happier than you think, Miltie. Gregory is parked outside my building a few nights later. He stops me at the door and he says, Listen, I just wanted to thank you for getting me off the hook.

I say to him, Well, I put you on it, didn't I? Thanks for saving my life.

I turn to go in and he grabs my arm. He says, How about a cup of coffee? A week later we're living together in his place in Forest Hills.

Fancy, said Esther Lieber.

Oh, it was a ground-floor apartment with bars on the windows.

In Forest Hills?

Yup.

Cigarette. McHooley's Zippo flaring, lighting Vilma's face. Smoke. Bar sounds.

I'm getting in too deep with Gregory, Vilma said. I'm having feelings for him. I don't want to have another bad ending.

Love, Esther Lieber said, you were in love.

Not then, no. It was something which comes before love. Maybe wanting to be in love but being afraid to be in love. In my imagination I think I've fucked half the guys in New York and one day Gregory will find out. So one night I tell him. Gregory looks at me a long time. Then he says, Thanks. Can I get you some coffee?

Then everything was *so* good. I didn't even care about my family not wanting to see me. I didn't care about anything except Gregory. We couldn't have children. My plumbing was broken. I think it made Gregory sad but he never said anything.

So he was perfect, said Cortin.

Everybody has their problems, Oster said.

Listen, wise guys, said Vilma, he was *almost* perfect. The only thing was he was sad somewhere. I never knew why. I just tried to be nice and upbeat for him. One day he cut his hair short and shaved his beard. He was even handsome.

He had gone to college, Columbia. He had studied philosophy and that's what had made him sad, he said. What he liked best was going on hikes. I got to love that. We went hiking everywhere. On the Adirondack Trail we once hiked all the way down to Georgia. We hiked in the Rockies. We hiked lots of places in Europe. We were rich, right? No kids. Gregory owning the cab, hacking at night, and the day man paying all the expenses and kicking off some extra, too. We had a little money. That part of it, having money, was like with Christopher. The difference was love.

I won't sneeze at that, said Esther Lieber.

Hiking was the thing. We'd hike and hold hands. Sometimes we'd stop and kiss. I don't mean I'd grab him or he'd grab me. Something spontaneous, light and sweet, like a butterfly landing on my mouth.

Love it, Joe Cortin said.

Sometimes, if we only had a day, we'd drive in the taxi up to Sunken Meadow Park for a few hours. Beautiful, it was so beautiful.

Zippo. Flame. Smoke. Drink. Ice rattling.

Four years of paradise. Then Gregory began to cough a lot.

Hard coughing and then blood began to come up. It was cancer. He had cancer in both lungs. Four years in a perfect paradise and one year in a perfect hell.

Vilma wept, a thin crying. Esther put her arms around Vilma and rocked her. Shhh, shhh! It's all right, honey. God, what shit there is in the world! Esther said.

Oster tapped his glass. McHooley arbitrarily poured some rum into it. Bo Wang brought some chicken wings and onion rings to the bar. They ate silently and waited for Vilma to stop weeping.

When she had lit a fresh cigarette she wiped her eyes and spoke again.

Naturally, the doctors told us with chemotherapy and radiation Gregory's chances were good. We just had to go the course and have faith. I had the faith and he went the course.

Gregory didn't believe he could survive. He did the chemo and the radiation for me. I would say, Even if there's one chance in a million, we have to take it, Gregory. Sure, that's right, baby, he'd say, and he'd put that big smile on his wide mouth.

I tell you after the first chemotherapy the oncologists cheered. The tumors were shrinking! And they shrank more and more! Even Gregory's spirits went up. There was a chance.

One day the doctor said, It's all going better than we expected. The tumors are gone or negligible. Now we have the opportunity to seal off the cancer permanently with radiation treatments.

There would be eight. They'd have to zap him eight times. Each treatment he got weaker. He got these burn marks on his neck and chest. His throat was burnt sore. I had to feed him baby food. He could hardly swallow it. He couldn't get out of bed. I had to put my ear to his mouth to hear him talk. So that's how he was at the end of the fucking burning.

All we had to do now was wait for him to recuperate. He knew he wouldn't and I knew he wouldn't. I went to RC church in the neighborhood and prayed everyday.

His hair had fallen out from the chemo. His gums were bleeding. He broke out with boils. He got shingles bad, bad. He didn't smile anymore. He was a long way past being brave. And I had made him do it. One chance in a million!

One day he whispered in my ear, I can't stand it anymore. End it, please.

He told me to blend up all his pain killers in some orange juice. I did it. He couldn't hold it down. He puked.

Vilma Rakos wept again. When she was able to speak she said, He asked me to put a garbage bag over his head and hold it there until he died. I couldn't do it. I refused. I begged him to keep trying. Tears ran down his cheeks.

Finally, I crossed myself and put the bag over his head. I put my hands around his neck. I was saying Hail Marys and waiting for the courage to squeeze so I'd lock out the air. My grip had hardly tightened when his head fell forward.

He had left me a note saying what I should do when he died. There were eleven things I had to do, people to call, telephone numbers. He had arranged everything to make it easier for me. He had taken charge of his own funeral. I made the calls and said what Gregory had said I should say.

So the doctor came and said he was dead. He said he'd send me the certificate. You know the Death Certificate, to make the end of Greg's life official. His oncologist wanted to do an autopsy. I said no. The funeral parlor guys came and took him away. They cremated him the next morning. No one was there but me. He had a sister and a brother but he hadn't known where they lived. The day after that the funeral guys brought me the ashes in a gray cardboard box. I was supposed to scatter the ashes on the Sunken Meadow trail. He had thought that that would be nice. But I couldn't do it, Vilma said, tapping the bar top softly with her fist, I just couldn't do it. It's two years and I still can't.

I moved back to 95th Street. The box of ashes is on the floor in an empty closet. I never open the door. Vilma Rakos blew her nose. It's almost like I'm being unfaithful.

Jaizus! said McHooley.

Vilma, Cortin said after awhile, if you want, I'll go to Sunken Meadow with you.

Vilma started to bawl again. Finally she said, Thank you, Joey.

I'd like to be along, said Oster.

The others said they wanted to attend. McHooley said he'd close the bar on that day.

When she stopped crying Vilma said, I can only take five of you in the cab.

That's all right, said Bo Wang, I have a car.

PART V

1

Edward Francis Knittel, the pink baby blanket around his shoulders, limped rapidly downtown along Broadway. He was not at all certain why he had left McHooley's. He wasn't sure that anyone had seen him leave. Of course, when they'd set a day to scatter the ashes, he would go.

Vilma's story had moved him deeply, as it had moved the others. But why had he left the bar? The feeling he had in his stomach was the answer. But, Eddie Knittel couldn't decipher the feeling which limped along with him. Everything seemed to be slipping away. It was not the fear of Death sweeping around the corner and seizing him. Nah. It was some kind of loss, he thought. He stopped abruptly in his hurried walk. It was an image which filled his mind. He has become a tree standing in a field of snow, a tree shedding its leaves. Then a man in dark clothes puts down a handful of dry twigs and bare branches on the snow. Spontaneously the twigs and branches break into bright flame and Knittel imagined himself on fire, burning from his feet upward, unable to scream against the knife hot flame.

Knittel trembled. He walked more quickly. His hip hurt.

When he reached 86th Street he realized that he had forgotten his walking stick: his black, gnarled truncheon, his rod of anger and retribution. It was clear to Knittel that his anger was deserting him. The anger of eighty years which he had worn like armor was rusting away. But wasn't that what he had wanted? To get rid of the anger, to sink the *Slocum*?

The old man hobbled across the gutter to the esplanade which divided upper Broadway in two. He sat down on the brown bench which spanned the esplanade's width. The headlights of cars on his left, going uptown, pelted his face. On the right, going downtown, the lights bounced off the overflowing green garbage can which was before him.

A young woman crossing the street put a half of a sandwich in his hand. Times will get better, Grandpa. Don't lose the faith, she said.

Thanks, Knittel replied, not looking at his benefactor. Without thinking he took a bite of the damp white bread. It was tuna fish. Knittel didn't like tuna fish. He placed the sandwich beside him on the bench.

He was sad. If you asked Oster, Knittel thought, Oster would say depressed. It was the word they'd used in the recent years. He was *blue*. Everyone gets *blue* sometimes. But why? Vilma's story was not that bad. So once she was a floozie. But hadn't she found love in the end?

Maybe it was the foolishness of the entire evening. Who cares about the *Slocum*? Who cares about heroes, fake or real? The dumb thing was that it was he himself who had dragged the *Slocum* up from the bottom of the river where it belonged. One thing was sure, all right. The evening had gotten rid of his anger and in its place there were the white bones of eighty years of sadness.

Rosy! Knittel yelled into the noisy Broadway night. He wept. How many times he had wept this evening!

Although he had not done it in many years, Knittel found himself thinking of how Helga and Melvin came to their ends. Why had they come back to him now as he sat here in the middle of the traffic? The mind is a strange thing. Who could know how the damned thing with its coils and channels worked?

Poor Melvin! he thought. In his heart he wanted to be a soldier like all of them Honeycuitts. When they had killed that Grand Duke—or had it been an Archduke?—and the war had started, it was Melvin Honeycuitt who was the first to go to the battlefield. The other Honeycuitts, uniforms, medals, and all, had been left behind. They had to wait until President Wilson had declared war while Melvin had rushed off to be under fire even though he was just a volunteer ambulance driver for the Frogs.

But he was there on the battlefield where he had wanted to be.

Knittel, on the Broadway bench, his pink cape rising as he got to his feet, crisply saluted the air. *Allons, enfants de la patrie,* he sang. No one noticed nor heard his loud singing.

Whatever Melvin had written to Helga, Eddie Knittel could not know, of course. The one letter, a long letter, which he had received in the winter of 1916 went up with the other stuff he had burned. If he could not recall much of what Honeycuitt had written, the two photographs were clear in his memory. One was taken over the hood of the ambulance. It showed Melvin at the wheel. He held a Fatima in his fingers like a piece of chalk, like he was going to write something on the air. Smiling. In the other one he was standing alongside the ambulance. Profile. He had drawn his belt very tight to show that his belly, had been lost in France. His belly but not his rump. You could see its shape in his baggy pants. The long strand of his colorless hair, had been pulled back as always across his scalp, front to rear. On the back of that photograph there was the date: February 19, 1916. Melvin had written, *For My Hero, Eddie Knittel.*

Of the letter Eddie Knittel could recall only two things. One was the sentence: *I am writing this from Haricots Orange!* Then Melvin had explained that *Haricots Orange* was a joke. But Knittel had never gotten the joke. The other thing was that Melvin had scraped up a German soldier from the battlefield during a brief truce arranged to bring in the dead and the wounded. The poor kraut had been overlooked by the German Ambulance Corps. The German had been badly wounded and Honeycuitt had known that the infantry corporal would not make it. The soldier spoke some English and he was pleased to know that Melvin was American. What the German wanted to know was if Honeycuitt had ever heard of the *Slocum.* When Melvin said he had, the soldier reminded him that it was all Germans who had died. Then he had asked Melvin, Whatever happened to the German boy who had climbed up the *Slocum* mast? You see, Melvin had written, how important the *Slocum* Disaster was? How important you were, Eddie, to a dying enemy soldier?

How sad it was, Knittel thought, that Honeycuitt had died of dysentery. It should have been Big Bertha blowing him to

smithereens or a machine gun sawing him in half. Something
all the Honeycuitt soldiers could cheer. But in the end the
Honeycuitt tradition was upheld. Melvin had been posthu-
mously commissioned a First Lieutenant in the United States
Army. They brought his body back and buried him in the
national cemetery at Arlington. Knittel and Helga had gone
there one Memorial Day and put flowers on his grave. He was a
good man, Helga had said.

Helga herself, after being active all the years in The
Survivors Association, had died in October of 1933. And the
cause of that had been Wolfgang.

In those days Eddie had made sure that he went out one
night a week with Helga. Dinner at Luchow's and after that a
movie. It was at Loew's Second Avenue one night that year
when Wolfgang came onto the movie screen in the "Fox
Movietone News". Big as life was my uncle Wolfgang Knittel,
Eddie remembered. There he was standing with Ernst Roehm,
Joseph Goebbels, Hermann Goering, and Adolph Hitler.
Wolfgang was to the rear, smiling, but not laughing, nor dancing as Hitler and Roehm were doing. Wolfgang–in response to
what?–gave the Nazi salute and his big hand came forward on
the screen. Helga bolted upright. Wolf ! she said, It's Wolf !

Between the thumb and the forefinger of Wolfgang's huge
hand there was a tattoo: a line drawing of a boat with
paddlewheels, two smokestacks, and a mast. A ragged halo of
flames crowned the boat. Knittel knew that the crown on the
hand in the black-and-white film was red.

Knittel wondered why the Fox Movietone newsreel image
of Wolfgang had pushed her into a silence so deep that he knew
that Helga would die. Wasn't it Wolf who had gone like a ghoul
among the dead women? Wasn't it Wolf who had beaten her?
That she should jump up like that was no surprise, but was it the
shock, of Wolf leaping out from the silver screen or was it
something else, Knittel had wondered. Maybe she still loved
Wolf. No, that was impossible, it could not be that. It had to be
something else. She was sick in bed the next day. From the
"Fox Movietone News" to Helga's death it had only been a
short time, two weeks maybe.

Eddie Knittel wiped his nose with a corner of the baby
blanket. All right, let it be as Oster said, I'm depressed. Knittel
thought that *maybe* he wanted his anger back. He knew he
wanted to shout, Poyfidy, poyfidy ! He knew he wanted to

condemn *The New York Times* one more time, one more year. He knew he wanted to condemn Margie Ann Plunkerbrote, too. But now he was unable to do it. He was disgusted with himself. On the esplanade bench Knittel sighed heavily.

He thought perhaps he would go directly home, where Linda was waiting for him. Maybe she was not in love with him but she knew how to be tender, how to make an old man happy for a few minutes. The money he gave her was not for that, she was no whore. It was for her children, for clothing and for college. It was she who had insisted on cleaning the apartment in the brownstone, which he owned, because that was what he had first hired her for. Knittel smiled into the light-pocked Broadway night. She may as well clean the place, he thought, it would belong to her when he died.

Knittel nodded his head. There's no fool like an old fool. Out loud, he said, Why did I want to sell the *Slocum* to strangers? Ach, Ach! How could I pay them to listen! Shame, shame! But they took the money, all right. Except Vilma, of course. You can't blame them when an old fool gives his money away.

Too much energy, Knittel said to himself, I've been giving out too much energy. Damned fool, dancing and boxing like an idiot. Giving out that kind of energy could certainly depress a man his age. Linda had said that often. You wanna kill yourself, Eddie, she'd ask, if he tried to have sex with her more than once a week. Once he had said to her, I'm strong as a bull! She pinched his bearded cheek and said, I know that, Eddie but I don't want no dead bull in my bed.

Somebody sat down on the bench next to him. Knittel turned. It was Joey Cortin. You had us worried, Eddie, sneaking out like that.

I didn't sneak out.

Well, you were just gone. And you left your cane and your cap, Cortin said and placed them on Knittel's lap.

The old man put his cap on. He gripped the cane and put its metal-encased tip firmly to the ground. Thanks, he said. Y'know, I used to have a cane with a sword in it.

To kill someone? Cortin said.

Knittel laughed. I thought of that, he said.

You want to come back to McHooley's? Everybody's waiting for you. You haven't finished your story.

How do you know that, Joey?

Instinct.

I don't know if I have any more to tell. You got paid. I got my money's worth.

Come back anyway. Say good night.

Knittel thought for a moment. All right, he said, I don't want to add rudeness to my other sins.

Well, that's what we always say at McHooley's: If God ever created a gentleman, his name is Eddie Knittel.

I'm an old sonuvabitch and I've lived too fucking long.

That too, said Joey. Let's go.

Give me a hand up, said Edward Knittel.

~ 2 ~

Slowly, they walked uptown toward McHooley's.

Knittel stopped and looked at Joseph Cortin's handsome face with its smooth mustache and deepening lines. I like you, Joey, Eddie Knittel said.

Cortin smiled at the old man. I knew you'd come around, sweetheart, he said. I'm not going to give you a kiss but I have an important question.

What?

Do you want to keep wearing that blanket?

Knittel, smiling, stroked the pink cape. Nah, he said.

Cortin unpinned the blanket and dropped it into the first sidewalk garbage receptacle. When they reached Straus Square at 106th Street, with its vest pocket triangular park, Knittel tapped the marble bench with his cane. The bench was part of the memorial to Isidore and Ida Straus, who had gone down with the *Titanic.*

Knittel said to Cortin, There was once a plaque in Tompkins Square Park for the *Slocum,* a little plaque. You needed sharp eyes to find it. For a boatload of dead people a little plaque you can't find! Here you have a whole square and a park for the memories of just two people. Ach, ach!

Does it make any difference? Cortin asked.

No, not anymore, Joey. But I wish people remembered the *Slocum* the way they remember the *Titanic*, deck chairs and all.

If they remember the *Slocum*, Eddie, they'll remember you and you'll have to go on being the hero. Tonight your idea was to sink the *Slocum*, to let it go.

But it's so hard, Joey. Knittel sighed. Am I making a mistake?

The silhouette of Joseph Cortin shrugged in the dim lights of the park's decorative lamps. He reached behind Eddie Knittel and touched the marble wall to which the bench was joined. There are words engraved but I can't read them, Cortin said.

Eddie Knittel, without looking at the low wall, recited the engraved words:

IN MEMORY OF ISIDOR AND IDA STRAUS. LOVELY AND PLEASANT WERE THEY IN THEIR LIVES AND IN THEIR DEATH THEY WERE NOT DIVIDED - SAMUEL.

She wouldn't leave him, Joey, she wouldn't leave him. She could've been in the lifeboat with the women and children. She stayed with her husband. Rosy! Rosy! Knittel said, shaking his head.

After some moments of silence, Cortin said, C'mon, Eddie, everybody's waiting. They're worried about you.

Holding onto Cortin's arm Knittel walked slowly toward the park's narrow end. The drunks and addicts occupied the benches. On the grass some of them slept spread-eagled on their backs, their heads covered by newspapers. Some were in fetal positions, their hands pushed between their thin thighs.

A small figure, a man or a woman, stooping severely, confronted them and said, Hey, man, I'm dying! I got a fucking bellyache. Help me, man. A quarter, a dime, anything. Please, I'm dying!

Knittel gasped. The old man dug into his pocket. He pressed some small bills into the extended, dirty hand.

The stooped figure scuttled away like a crab.

Knittel wrapped his arm about the streetlamp. A long shadow fell from the brim of his cap. He pushed the cap back. It fell to the ground. He was breathing heavily. You all right, Eddie? Cortin asked.

Knittel nodded. Okay, I'm okay, he said. Scared the shit out of me! Jesus, I thought it was Mobo.

Mobo? What's a Mobo?

Knittel mopped his face with his powder-blue sleeve. A
creature, he said.

A dog?

Nah. A person if you can call him that. Scared the shit out
of me! Jesus!

⁊ 3 ⁊

A survivor, said Knittel. Mobo was the king of survivors.

Of the *Slocum*? asked Little Joey Cortin.

Of the world! said Knittel. Did you ever hear of Franklin
Delano Roosevelt?

And how does Roosevelt fit in?

You know Roosevelt invented the WPA?

I don't know everything, Eddie. Women People of
America?

You're mocking me! Every American child knows, Joey.
Anyway, it's the Works Progress Administration.

You live a hundred years, you know everything.

Ninety-five.

So I rounded it off.

Who the fuck was Mobo? Roosevelt's dog?

That was Fella, Knittel corrected. Scared the shit out of
me. I'm still shaking.

If you're finished holding up the lamppost, let's go.

No. Let me tell you about Mobo.

But hurry it up, he said, McHooley will have the cops out
looking for us.

Knittel laughed. All right, all right, he said. Pick up my
cap, Joey. Thanks. Knittel fanned his face. Scared the shit out of
me! Raised my temperature! Oh, boy! I'm having one fucking
big night, Joey!

Then the old man put the brim of his cap between his
teeth and bit into it. His eyes bulged.

Well? asked Cortin. Are you going to speak?

Yes, yes! Knittel said pulling the cap from his mouth. Don't be so damned much in a hurry. I'm arranging it in my mind. It's complicated.

Cortin shook his head. In McHooley's I could get a drink while I'm waiting. Eddie?

The old man did not respond. His head bobbed as if it were part of an inexpensive toy.

Cortin raised his voice. Eddie! he shouted. The river is dripping out of your ears! Will you, please, please, *please* speak or I'm going to take that lamppost away from you.

When Knittel still failed to respond, Cortin sighed and waited.

When the old man did speak, it was to himself. He said, You've got to figure Mobo got burned pretty bad before they threw him overboard. He hit the river too close to the paddlewheel and got sucked into it. It was the day after the *Slocum* had beached on North Brother Island that they found little Mobo in one of the paddlewheel boxes. A cry, they say it was a cry. A cry coming from the wheel. My God, think of it, Joey, this is a six-, seven-month old infant! The fire hadn't killed him. And going round and round in the paddlewheel, being dragged under the water, being knocked about in the paddlewheel box and he doesn't drown, Joey, he doesn't die! Ach, ach!

Cortin seated himself on one of the Straus Park benches. He said, Talk a little louder, Eddie.

When they got Mobo out of the paddlewheel they took him into the hospital on Leper Island. The story was told that the skin was hanging off his body in sheets. The face, they say, was like a fat, red blob. The infant Mobo is a hot bag of broken bones. But he was alive, Joey, the infant Mobo was alive! Ach!

So in the Hospital for Contagious Diseases they gave him a heavy shot of heroin and leave him on a rubber sheet. They expect he'll be dead in minutes, hours.

How the hell do you know all this, Eddie? You were in the Lebanon Hospital in the Bronx. You were in the Bronx, damn it!

Knittel snapped his head toward Cortin. Don't be such a smart fag, Joey!

Isn't that true? Maybe you read it in *The Times*? Or maybe your friend Melvin told you?

Ach! said Knittel, no it wasn't in *The Times*, wiseacre, and Melvin didn't tell me either.

You know, Eddie, you'll drive me crazy.

I heard it in the hospital, Joey. The doctors and the nurses, it was their favorite story, the miracle of the infant who wouldn't die. Doctors and nurses talking while the hero was floating, talking like I was a piece of dead meat. But I heard them, Joey. I would have heard more if they hadn't shipped me off to Helga's house.

So you kept in touch with Mobo?

No, smart ass, that's where Franklin Roosevelt came in with the WPA.

You know something, Eddie, you're not making sense anymore. No sense at all. Let's go.

Don't lose patience, Joey. This is one hell of a story!

Speed it up.

Okay, okay. There used to be piers going all around Manhattan. A pier on every street sticking into the river. In 1934 Roosevelt's WPA, with crane barges, came along the East River and began the business of pulling down the docks and scooping up all the lumber, which people had been stealing anyway for their wood-burning stoves. All of this tearing down because the WPA was going to build the Franklin Delano Roosevelt Drive.

Which stands gridlocked to this very day! Let's go, Eddie.

How old are you, Joey? You got a long life ahead of you. You can spare me ten fucking minutes!

Joseph Cortin sighed. All right. I am going to sit here forever without saying another word.

Knittel snorted. That'll be the day! he said. He fanned his face with his cap and, and ignoring Cortin, continued. When the WPA pulled down the docks they let out hundreds of thousands of water rats on the City of New York.

The plague.

That's right, the plague. You should see them, Joey! Thousands of them! Homeless now, running along the shorelines. Disoriented, swimming in the river, going in all directions. What a sight, Joey! Many of the rats made their way into the streets, into the buildings. A bunch of rats got into the lumberyards and the stables. Goddamn rats were huge! When cats saw them, the cats took the hell off! The damned things killed one lumberyard watchman's three monster dogs. Killed them and tore them apart. In the stables they wounded some of the horses and killed a pair of stable goats. In the tenements along the streets adjoining the piers, people had to stay up all night long with shovels to protect themselves from the rats. The City came out with exterminators and trucks filled with poisons to spread along the waterfront and in the basements of the buildings.

What have all these rats got to do with the infant Mobo?

I'm coming to that. Just listen, okay? Hundreds of cops came out and walked the waterfront shooting at those long-whiskered bastards. And the cops were out-numbered a hundred to one! So people came out to back them up. Kids, with piles at their feet, threw stones at the rats. They winged a lot of them, killed some. And people who had pistols, shotguns, and rifles joined in the rat slaughter. They were all along the shoreline blasting away. It was like a war. It went on for a week like that.

Dead rats floated uptown or downtown on the tide, killed by poison, stones, and bullets. Sometimes you'd see a patch of red on the river, a blood slick. I had a rifle myself, y'know. Honeycuitt had given it to me on my twenty-third or twenty-fourth birthday. So I was down on the shore shooting.

Hit anything?

A few. It was hard to miss. The rats were as big as cats and they were confused with their nests torn away. Lots of them ran around in circles, squealing.

So I'm popping them off when out of a hole in the ground, I think it was a hole in the ground, comes this creature. This Mobo. He's like a thick bundle of rags. A rope is tied around him like a belt. A dirty woolen hat is pulled down over his head. Hair hangs down his face which you couldn't see. Not a beard, Joey, long, straight, stringy hair.

Mobo is stooped over. Like he's stooped almost in half. With one hand he touches the ground. He knuckles along like an ape. The other arm is inside the layers of clothing he's wearing. Only the dirty hand sticks out. The nails are thick. They curl like claws.

And, Joey, he stinks! I mean stinks! From ten feet away he gives off the smell of an overflowing outhouse.

He comes toward me and I point the rifle at him. He sits down on the ground and growls. He can't speak. Sounds come from him.

He sees I'm not going to take the rifle off him. After a while he takes out a stained writing tablet. In red crayon he prints *Mobo* and points to himself. I point to myself and say, Eddie.

Me Tarzan. You Jane, Cortin laughed.

Knittel laughed too. Like that, he said. But Mobo is staring at me. I feel he's staring even though I can't see his face behind the hair. Finally, he points at me and writes on the tablet: *Hero*.

Then there's some rifle shots very close. Mobo scuttles away and disappears below a tangle of green, mossy poles lying on the riverbank.

You fuck, said Cortin, you're making all this up. You're putting me on, Eddie.

No, I ain't, Joey. I swear to God!

♪ 4 ♪

They walked slowly toward McHooley's in silence. When they entered, Bo Wang rattled his galvanized iron tub with a metal spoon. Pipe all hands on deck! he barked, the Admiral has been fished out of the sea! All hands present and accounted for, Sir! Bo Wang said and saluted sharply.

Knittel did not react.

What's wrong with him now? Vilma asked. What's bothering you, Eddie?

Nothing, said Cortin. He's all right. He's in his Mobo phase.

His what phase? asked Esther.

Mobo phase, monsters from the deep, said Joey Cortin and quickly recounted some of what the old man had told him.

Hate rats, said McHooley with a quick shudder. I'm thankful he told it out in the park.

Knittel remained silent.

Vilma, said Esther Lieber, I'm getting afraid of all this stuff with Eddie. I think we're wearing him out. I know he looks like a *shtarkah* but he really could die, you know.

Don't be morbid, said Oster. He'll outlive this building.

I sense intimations of mortality, said Wang.

Vilma put her hand on Eddie's shoulder. Are you doing okay, Eddie? she asked.

Knittel rubbed his beard. Why can't a man think around here? he asked.

You can think all you want, said Mindy, but you don't have to scare everybody.

Listen, when I think it's not like when you think. You have to shuffle through twenty years, kiddo. I have to spread out the files of a century.

And lots of papers get lost, said Cortin.

That's true. You don't know how true; Joey, Knittel said. He looked about the room. He looked at the faces waiting for him to speak. No one, *no one*, ever wrote a single word about Mobo. Not *The Times*, not *the Herald, the Tribune, the Sun*.

You skipped *the Post*, said Bo Wang.

And *the News, the Mirror*, and *the Graphic*, said Oster.

Stop it!, Vilma said.

It's okay, Vilma. It's true: no one. If you go to all the archives and libraries and morgues, there is no Mobo. Not a word. Not a comma. You know why? Because they'd die of shame, that's why. If they could have they'd have let the paddlewheel keep turning until the little bastard was drowned.

Knittel took off his cap and laid it top side down on the bar. He stroked his head with his large, thick hands. Like Joey said before, there are pages missing. But it doesn't matter, y'know. I knew enough and I knew it from Mobo. But if you ask me how it was Mobo told me that would be a puzzle. He did though.

He had pads. His pockets were filled with pads, crayons, pens, and pencils. I could ask him something that would take five minutes. Mobo could answer with one word. Boom! Like that. Bull's-eye without any bullshit.

Knittel brushed his hair back again. He was in the Hospital for Contagious Diseases for seven years. You got fingers, count them: seven years. For the first miracle months, they waited for the infant to die. I'm guessing they fed him with an eye dropper—his mouth had been burned down to a little hole, y'see.

They could've let him starve, said Oster, or they could've dropped a pillow over his face. I suppose ethics and Christianity prevailed.

I thought about that, said Eddie, it's one of them missing pages. But no one should ask why. There ain't any answers for the why's. When they brought Mobo into the hospital his raw arm was crossed over his raw belly and that's the way it healed. His arm got welded to his belly in these thick scars.

Where were the heaven-sent surgeons? McHooley asked.

Missing page, said Knittel. Don't ask me logical questions, Jimothy. The scars, when he healed, prevented his legs from straightening out. He couldn't walk. They put him on the floor. He learned to push himself around. His good arm got to be very strong.

Powerful imagination, said Bo Wang. How could you know? How could one-word Mobo explain it?

Right, said Eddie Knittel, I'm imagining. It's the way I explained it to myself, but it was a cripple imagining about a cripple. Here's a poser, Bo. How did they dress him?

How, do you think?

Knittel shrugged extravagantly.

But he did grow up? Vilma said. Of course! What am I saying? You found him on the riverfront!

Wasn't so easy. Every step of Mobo's way was a fucking miracle, y'know. When he was about seven years old or so, they put in the psychiatric hospital on Long Island. The same one my father had been in.

Why in the name of Jesus? asked McHooley.

Knittel chuckled. Well, McHooley, if you can't walk, and you can't talk, and you shit on the floor as you drag yourself along and you also look like you were dragged up from the bowels of hell, where should you be put? In the old loony bin. In the back wards with the most hopeless and the most helpless of God's creatures.

How awful! said Mindy.

Oh, said Knittel, Mobo didn't know the difference. His playmates were insane and most of them shit on the floors too. Mobo, while he couldn't make intelligible words come out of his deformed head and scarred hole of a mouth, learned the sounds of language and the meanings of words from his rocking, screaming insane companions.

Imagining this? said Bo Wang.

Yes. Some of it. Some of it I learned from Mobo over the years I knew him. Like his name. Is Mobo your name? I asked him once. He wrote on his pad, *Given*.

By whom?
Don't know.
Why Mobo?
Sound. In Throat.

And he touched his throat and made the sound which came out of the hole in his face like that, like *Mobo*. It took a long time and lots of questions for him to explain that he learned language from madmen and from doctors and nurses who put him on display. And he taught himself to read.

Like Frankenstein's monster? asked Oster.

Knittel shrugged. Mobo learned the alphabet from madmen when they were lucid. The insane were his primer. Then he graduated to the wrappings of toilet tissue and from there to *The New York Times*. He read every printed thing that fell before him, y'know. Books of every description. Medical texts, novels, histories, anything, everything. He only had one eye. The other had been burned away. One eye and that one grown so nearsighted he had to read with the type an inch from his eye.

Stop! said Esther, you're getting to me. I can't stand it!

You're right. It's fucking morbid, Eddie said, but it's also amazing!

Well, skip the biology, said Cortin, go back to the rat fest. What happened there on the waterfront between you and Mobo?

Well, it was because he knew I was the Hero that I got interested. How could he know? Okay, maybe like Esther said, she could remember Buchenwald or maybe Plunkerbrote could remember things.

Aha, said Oster, you allow for early memory now!

But they were three years old, Vilma said. Mobo was an infant! Six months!

That's right. Now listen. I came down to the river every day. I brought him food. Bread. Cheese. Meatballs. He'd break everything up into tiny pieces and stick them into his mouth. I suppose he had teeth because he chewed. Now here's the beauty part. After a few days he wrote that he wanted Coca Cola and *The Times*. So I made sure to bring them.

He had learned about the *Slocum* and the Hero through the anniversary stories. He had figured out—how?—that he had been on the *Slocum*. You know why we became friends? The food, sure. That was important. But it was my gimpy leg. It made me something like him, y'know. I let him roll up my pants so he could study my built-up shoe with its iron brace. One day Mobo printed on his pad: *Hero Shoe No Good For Me.*

Mobo was very intelligent. Very. When I had showed him my burnt arms he nodded his head. Sympathy and approval. We became brothers. He trusted me. It was then that he offerred me his hand, his free hand, which I shook.

I suggested that I get him an apartment. He considered the idea for a few days then he printed out: *Apartment. Frightened.*

It took a lot of talking, explaining before he agreed to my idea.

What was there to explain? Vilma asked.

A lot, said Eddie. With the docks gone, where could he live unseen in the daylight? He only came out at night to go to the garbage cans down the street to scavange, scaring the shit out of anybody who happened to see him.

I told him I would get him a basement apartment, in the rear. It would be secure. He would not be seen. He still could go out at night if he wanted.

Knittel rubbed his beard again. When I finally got the monster into this apartment, I had to convince him to let me give him a bath. It took time to convince him. When he agreed I helped him get his rags off. Filled with lice. And that poor scarred body! Ropy scars everywhere. The only places where his skin was normal was the lower part of his back, the back of one thigh, his lower abdomen, and his genitals.

Jaizus! God can be cruel, can't He? Why would he leave the man his balls? McHooley asked with open anguish.

I asked the same question, said Knittel. Why would God leave the poor bastard with a hard-on?

That's life, said Oster.

He was afraid to get into the tub. There wasn't any shower there. Took a half-hour to get him in. Then he liked it.

Bubble bath? asked Bo Wang.

Knittel laughed. I got him a bottle of that stuff once and then he'd never take a bath without it. I got him clothes from the Salvation Army. Because of the shape he was in I needed oversized clothes. Big pants, big jackets, big shirts and coats. It was very hard for him to dress himself. That's why he had avoided changing clothes when he had lived under the docks.

It was a contortionist act to do it. But the sonuvabitch loved clothes and I bought him lots of them. Took him an hour or more to get dressed. I watched him once. It was hats he loved best of all. He had more than two dozen. Derbys. Derbys were what he wore most. On special occasions–Sunday was special–he put on a derby, a swallowtail coat, and formal striped pants. So it was like he was going to a wedding or some kind of diplomatic thing.

I got used to seeing him. After awhile it all seemed normal. Even the hair hanging down across his face.

I put furniture, Salvation Army, in the apartment. I tried to show him how to cook and how to use the stove. He wouldn't do it. Because of the flame, y'know. He was terrified of fire. It was like in the B horror movies: monsters are always scared of fire.

Aargh, aargh, Cortin roared and flailed the imagined fire-filled air with his arms.

Fucking Cortin! Knittel said and turned to Esther. So, you win the bout about memory. He remembered, his whole body remembered the *Slocum* burning!

Jaizus! said McHooley.

At night Mobo went out to walk. In the wee hours he walked. It was, as he explained, a great pleasure for him. He told me a lot about walking in the night. I wish I could remember the things he wrote down. Beautiful. If I knew what poetry was I'd say that Mobo wrote poems. *The mouth of night sucks out the firmament's glow. I am a wounded star. I fall through the sky at my feet.*

He wrote that, Eddie? Vilma asked.

Yes.

What does it mean?

I don't know.

Did he know he was writing poetry?

Oh, sure. He read everything. I'd go along Fourth Avenue and buy bunches of second-hand books from the shops. Books for a penny or a nickel. I dumped them into his apartment. All day long he'd hold some book up to his eye and read, read, all the time. I wished he could talk because he knew so much. Writing out thoughts and ideas was very difficult, y'know. Once he tapped his head and wrote down: *Philosophy!*

Who knows what was locked in there? Ach, ach! Anyway I paid the rent, I bought him food. I don't think anybody knew Mobo lived in that place. The janitor thought it was me.

So it was for some years I knew Mobo. From the WPA to WW II. He stopped trying to write me his thoughts. He was glad to see me, though, whenever I came. He'd stroke my arm and I felt he was smiling behind that veil of hair which had turned gray during that time.

Every once in a while, he'd write something down and push it before me. Whatever he wrote it seemed to get sadder. Once he wrote down: *I Am A Genuine Monster. I Have Survived Tragedy And Calamity. Why?*

What did you say? Oster asked.

Nothing, Miltie. What could I answer? One day I went to the apartment. He was not there. It had never happened before. I sat there all day in the middle of Mobo's stacks of books and newspapers. All day I sat there. I knew he had to be dead. Late at night I went back to my place.

A cop came to my door the next morning. He told me they had found a small pile of neatly folded clothing down at 3rd Street and the river with a letter addressed to me. Just a few lines was all, a few lines: *Thank You, Hero. Everything Might Be Beautiful. You Are. I Am Not. The Pain Just Continues. Mobo.*

The cop wanted to know who sent the letter. I told him I didn't know. The cop said, Some kind of joke. I said I didn't know.

I never thought Mobo got undressed and piled his clothes by the iron fence there. I couldn't believe he had undressed himself naked. I couldn't believe that. I couldn't believe that he had hoisted his scarred body over the iron fence and fallen into the river. I was sure he had put the clothes together like that so that I'd be sure to get the letter, y'know.

He must have jumped in, Esther said.

Maybe.

How can it be *maybe*? asked Cortin.

They never found the body. Maybe Mobo just walked away in the night.

How can that be? He'd have been found sooner or later.

You think so, Joey?

The note, Eddie, was a suicide note, said Oster. Certainly a note of departure.

Maybe, said Knittel.

You don't believe that Mobo is alive somewhere, scuttling around? McHooley said.

Maybe.

Cut it out, Eddie! Vilma said.

Knittel laughed. I'm sure he's dead. I wish his body had been found, that's all.

Knittel drummed the bar top with his fingers. Cortin picked up the old man's rhythm and drummed as well. Bo Wang, too.

♪ 5 ♪

He was dead, right? asked Esther Lieber.

Knittel's beard opened on his smile. I suppose so, he said. He was never seen again.

Were you upset?

Not very much. Mobo had wanted to die. He had had enough.

Jaizus! Don't be so bloody cavalier, McHooley said.

Knittel ignored the barkeep. Mobo made a world for himself, he said.

He made a world in which he couldn't live, Joey Cortin said. I wish you had been upset, you old fuck!

Well, I wasn't. I knew him seven, eight years. As time passed we had less and less to do with each other.

How can that be, Eddie? Vilma asked. You were his best friend.

His only friend, Vilma, his only friend. It was a matter of communications, said Knittel. He read for days at a time with a large magnifying glass under the light of a 300-watt bulb. Sometimes he forgot to eat. Coke bottles with straws in them, all over the place. When I came to see him he'd hold up a sign that said *Hello.* That was it. When I left there was never a sign saying *Goodbye.* I don't know if he even heard me close the door.

Well, at least Mobo had a sense of humor, Oster said.

Like an undertaker, said Knittel. He never even read the funnies.

Cortin broke into laughter.

Well, said Knittel with a broad smile, I think it was because of living with the rats. Rats got no sense of humor at all, y'know.

Cortin, laughing harder, slid off the bar stool down to the brass rail. He gasped, wheezed, and wiped his eyes. Then he went back to laughing again.

I'm not the only cuckoo here, Esther said. Get up, Joey. You're making an ass of yourself.

Cortin laughed to the top of his tenor range.

McHooley reached over the bar and squirted Cortin with a jet of seltzer from the dispenser. Cortin stopped, stood up, wiped his face, and brushed his wet jacket. Thanks, Jimothy, I knew I could count on you, you asshole.

No trouble, Joey, any time, McHooley said.

You were saying, Oster said, rats have no sense of humor at all.

Right, said Knittel. He patted his jacket pocket. I'm out of cigars, Vilma, let me have one of your coffin nails. Thanks.

In the year he vanished, the bastard had given up eating for reading. I couldn't get him to take a breather. And while it was not his habit to take a bath very often, now he quit entirely. Terrible, awful stink. But he was used to stinks like that.

And his one good peeper was getting worse and worse. He read with a book hung on his nose and his head stuck right up under the lampshade.

I mean, said Esther, he was reading and reading and he didn't speak to you?

He didn't say a mumblin' word? Bo Wang asked.

How sad! Milt Oster said. Mobo was reading himself to death.

Oh, wouldn't that be good, Miltie! But he'd read for a week straight, sleeping a little on his good arm. Then he needed a Coke and food, soup mostly. Then he wanted to talk, to communicate. But there were only his writing pads although the little fuck would write on anything, y'know. He'd print on the newspapers lying around, on grocery bags, pieces of cardboard, and sometimes there would be a wooden slat or two from a box. He wrote with India ink laundry markers I had given him. Black, thick, dark, so he could see what it was he was saying. And as much as he wanted to share his thoughts with me, how could he do it? Frustrating for him. Sometimes that made him squeal like a rat. When he was excited about something, or he was very serious, he would print it and add exclamations. Or he'd put a box around something or a star. Also, he'd underline. The more important, the more heavy the underlines, three or four sometimes.

<u>Old Testament–Wonderful!! Meaning?</u>
<u>Sunday Times. Explain War. Meaning?</u>
One day he lays down *Paradise Lost*, by John Milton. He taps the book and he prints: <u>You Like This?</u>

I never read it, I say.

<u>Why Not?</u>

It's too long and I ain't into angels, I say.

<u>Satan Is An Angel.</u>

Y'don't say!

<u>Lucifer. Bearer Of Light.</u>

No!

<u>God's Best Angel!!</u>

Who?

<u>Satan. Lucifer!</u>

No! You've got that wrong, a smart guy like you. Satan is evil, Mobo.

He shakes his head: <u>No! Perfect Angel! Read. Don't Talk.</u>

On a large brown bag he printed out neat block letters. You gotta understand when Mobo got neat and careful he was talking very serious.

<u>God Made Satan First.</u>
<u>First Angel Of God Is Satan.</u>
<u>Taller Than Norway Pine.</u>
<u>Beautiful, Beautiful Was Lucifer.</u>
<u>Lucifer Sits At God's Right Hand.</u>
<u>Satan Watches God Work.</u>
<u>God Creates Angels.</u>
<u>Millions. Millions.</u>
<u>Angels From The God Magic.</u>
<u>Not one,</u>
<u>None So Beautiful</u>
<u>As Lucifer.</u>
<u>God Loves Lucifer.</u>
<u>God's Gift To Satan</u>
<u>Power!!</u>

<u>Like God, Satan can make Angel Life!!</u>
<u>Eternities, Eternities!</u>
<u>No Angel Life Creates He Them.</u>

Hero, Did You Know That?
I told you I never read it.
Sad For You, Eddie.
Satan. Eternities. Eternities.
Nothing To Do In Perfect Heaven.

Didn't he like the singing? I say. I was kidding him but he didn't get it.
Idle Hands.
One day Satan Thinks
I will Emulate God, My Grand Father.
I Will Make Life!

Out Of The Satan Head
Emerges A Woman Angel
More Beautiful Than All Angels Is She.
Satan Weeps To See Her So.
Satan And Woman
In Nakedness Make Love.
Together They Lie.
Content They Are.
Thunder!

Almighty One Comes.
Black Clouds Hide His Great Head.
Angry Is Lord God.
Thunder Voice:

What Have You Done, Lucifer, My Son?
Created A Life.
A Red Fear Like Fire Falls On Satan.
You Have Fornicated!!!!

God In Thunder Speaks:
You Have Fornicated

With Your Created Daughter!

Lucifer Trembling,
What Is It, My Father,
This Fornication? This Daughter?
Lightning And Thunder

Over Cool, Sweet Paradise.
God Lord Almighty Takes Daughter Of Satan
Plunges Woman Angel Into Hell
Hell Beyond Chaos

<u>For Daughter Angel Harlot Woman</u>
<u>God Has Created Hell.</u>
<u>Harlot's Name Is Sin.</u>

Mobo printed *Sin* very large inside a kind of star, like in the comic books.

Pow, Bam, Shazam? asked Esther.

Like that, yeah. Don't cut in now. Mobo prints out:

<u>In Hell, Sin Has Child:</u>
<u>Three Heads</u>
<u>Nine Tails</u>
<u>Oily Black</u>
<u>Boy Child.</u>
<u>Name Of Child Is</u>
<u>D E A T H.</u>

Pow, Bam, Shazam, said Knittel. That one word took up one whole piece of gray cardboard from the shirt laundry. Oh, boy, Mobo had a head of steam going. More.

<u>Death Rapes Mother</u>
<u>Sin Gives Birth</u>
<u>Three Wild Dogs.</u>
<u>Each Hour Clock Strikes</u>
<u>Dogs Go Into Womb Of Sin</u>
<u>And Chew Entrails</u>
<u>Each Hour Hounds Get Born</u>
<u>Hounds Of Hell</u>
<u>Guard The Gates</u>
<u>Barbs In Nine Tails Of Death</u>
<u>One Sting, Man Dies.</u>

Knittel paused, smiling to himself, Fucking Mobo, he said.

Jaizus, McHooley said. Was it Mobo saying all that, Eddie, or was it the poet?

I never read the book so I don't know. Mobo wrote on a shopping bag, *How Can You Live And Not Read This Book.*

I was so knocked out by the story he wrote down that I shivered. Mobo saw that and he gave out his high-whistling rat squeal. Then he printed again:

<u>Watch This, Eddie!</u>
<u>1. God Creates Lucifer</u>

2. Lucifer Creates Woman

3. Lucifer Fornicates Woman

4. God Throws Woman Into Hell

5. Sin Gives Birth To Death.

6. THE WAGES OF SIN IS DEATH!!!

!!!!!!!!!!!!!!!!!!!!!!!!!!!!!!!!!!!!

Jaizus Christ, said McHooley.

Cortin opened his mouth to speak. Before he had emitted a sound the old man said, I'll answer the question, Joey. I took all them sheets Mobo printed, even the cardboards and shopping bags. I read everything a thousand times. I knew the whole thing by heart. So it didn't matter when the Mobo papers got burned up in the famous fire in my apartment. I'll tell you this: Mobo would have liked it that way. *Finito.* Up in smoke. No dinosaur bones.

You really think he would have liked it, just being sort of erased? Vilma asked.

Oh, yeah, said Knittel, without a trace.

That's so sad, Eddie, Vilma said.

Why? said Knittel. No one even knew the little monster existed. Except for a few nurses and doctors and psychopaths, no one knew. Nobody would believe the psychos and the medical profession which had tried to kill the fuck, and they weren't going to tell anybody. He was born. He burned. He drowned. He lived. He died. He disappeared. And that, my friends, is the whole Mobo *schmeer.*

You might show a little feeling, Eddie.

The old man stared at Vilma Rakos. You don't think I have feelings?

I know you have feelings. It's just the way you say things sometimes. Like "the whole *schmeer*". You're a sensitive person, Eddie.

Didn't anybody but you know about him in all those years? Who saw him, who talked about him? Oster asked.

Let it go, Miltie. He was the phantom of the *Slocum* without an organ. Everybody gets turned on by a freak. Gives people a chill up the spine. It's a funny thing, y'know, for a long time Mobo didn't know how much of a freak he was. When he finally got the idea of himself, the pain began for him. He wanted to die. Not only die in a plain sense but die forever. Disappear.

For Honeycuitt it was different. He wanted to be remembered. He didn't want to disappear but, goddamn it, he did. I thought you said they buried him at Arlington, Cortin said. First Lieutenant Melvin Honeycuitt.

That was a different Honeycuitt, Joey, the old man said. That was Honeycuitt the soldier, off to Honeycuitt Heaven.

You're getting obscure, Admiral, said Bo Wang. A Honeycuitt is a Honeycuitt is a Honeycuitt.

And I've seen the Charlie Chan pictures—you're inscrutable, Mr. Wang. Melvin lived two lives, y'know. He died in France for the Honeycuitt dummies. But it was the fucking *New York Times* on 43rd Street that killed him.

And you find me inscrutable, Mr. Knittel?

Knittel slid off his stool and limped to the far end of the bar, where a few cold onion rings remained on a plate. He scooped them up and ate one as he returned to his place.

The Times was interviewing me in 1944. A reporter named Tad Gordina. I give him my standard handout, y'know. But he wants to do a good job so he asks me more questions, one thing and another. I'm telling him about Melvin, what a great *Times* reporter he was. The next day he comes back and tells me there is no Melvin Honeycuitt who worked for *The New York Times.* I threw the little fuck down the stairs.

Was he implying that Honeycuitt was a figment of your imagination? Oster asked.

I don't know what he was implying, said Knittel.

But Honeycuitt was really real, Eddie, wasn't he? Esther Lieber asked seriously. It wasn't like the dream on the boat with Rosy? Or like those crazy crows?

Knittel shook his head. He was real, all right. But I got so shook up and so angry I never talked to *The Times* again. Those bastards! No Honeycuitt! Poyfidy, poyfidy, poyfidy!

You're not going to leave it there, Eddie, lad, said McHooley. There was a Honeycuitt on *The Times.* The Honeycuitt who sat at your bedside, the one who went to coroner's trial, the one with your sweet aunt, the one who called you Hero.

Don't be an asshole, McHooley. Of course there was a fucking Melvin Honeycuitt on *The New York Times!* Knittel shouted.

Hey, I thought you wanted to stop being angry, Eddie, Joey Cortin said.

I do, I do, Knittel said. He clasped his hands together and brought them to his forehead. But I was so mad, Joey!

I tried to find Congressman Sulzer, Charles Dersch, and George Wunner to be witnesses to Honeycuitt's life. But they were dead. I got a lawyer to look into it. He looked into the Congressional records. No Honeycuitt. He tried to get hold of the records of the coroner's trial in the armory. Not maintained.

But there are copies of *The Times* going all the way back. Did your lawyer look there? Oster said.

Knittel nodded. He looked. He brought me microfilm copies of the whole summer of 1904 and even 1905. I cried because I read again every story Melvin had written, every fucking one. Even the report that kid Peter gave him when I was in bed at Helga's house, when he told Melvin about how they'd be firing the canon to bring the bodies up. Every fucking story in the fucking *New York Times* and Honeycuitt's name was not on one of them!

Mindy, in the ensuing silence, went through the swinging doors, returning quietly with two platters of chicken wings. These are the last, cold but good, she said.

The bar people chewed. McHooley, who was not partial to wings, found a small one and ate it. They waited for Knittel to continue. Finally it was Vilma who said, Well, I still believe there was a Honeycuitt, Eddie.

Knittel's beard moved in a small smile. Thanks, Vilma, he said. But ain't it the damndest thing you ever heard, no Melvin Honeycuitt! You know why? They didn't have by-lines for reporters until World War I and poor Melvin was in his ambulance talking to dying Germans about the good old days on the *Slocum*. Ach!

Oster snapped his fingers as the idea struck him. The payroll records! he shouted. What about the payroll records!

Knittel shook his head slowly. In 1939 *The New York Times* destroyed all its bookkeeping stuff prior to 1929.

Oster stroked his bald head in an amazed sadness. He said, They shouldn't have done that!

Esther Lieber said, What about Melvin's family? They'd know.

Nah, said Knittel. They're all gone. Last one to go was a Second Lieutenant, second or third cousin. Got himself killed on the Normandy Beach in World War II.

Knittel, sensing another silence forming, said to McHooley with a circling finger, Drinks all around, Knittel pays.

On me, said McHooley, as he poured.

Mindy said, I want champagne.

⌐ 6 ⌐

Listen, said Eddie Knittel. I was so goddamned down. They were stealing my past from me, my life! Hell, Mobo had disappeared into the river with the water rats. Honeycuitt down there in Arlington. Helga in the Lutheran cemetery, and all those who died on the *Slocum*, and no one was paying attention. I was as blue as you can get, y'know? So I decided to have a memorial service for all of them. Speeches, a moment or two of silence, a music band.

Carnegie Hall? Cortin asked

No. They were booked. All through that June of 1944, they were booked. I was lucky to get Town Hall. They couldn't give me June 15th, which was the proper memorial day. I wanted that. I had to settle for June sixth. It was the only day in June they had.

Who was the band, Bunny Berrigan?

Hah. It was serious music I wanted, Joey.

A string quartet? Oster suggested.

Nah, I got the American Symphony Orchestra with that Polish guy conductor.

C'mon, Joey Cortin said. Are you saying you got the American Symphony with Leopold Stokowski?

Yeah, that's him.

It must have cost a fortune, Esther said. Hey, big spender!

It wasn't so bad. The orchestra was high school kids and old guys. There was the war on, y'know.

I'm sure it was one glorious night, McHooley said.

Nah, said Edward Francis Knittel, it was one big flop. I had ads in all the papers. "Concert in Memory of the Victims of the *Slocum* Disaster. Leopold Stokowski and the American Symphony Orchestra. Admission Free."

Knittel shook his head.

So? Esther said.

Nobody came, Knittel said.

Oh, Eddie, you're exaggerating. Someone had to come! Margie Ann Plunkerbrote!

Knittel looked up and said, That's right. She came. Came up to me and said, Mr. Knittel, I'm Marjorie Ann Plunkerbrote. I am also a survivor. That was the first time I had met her. Good-looking then. There were a few others sitting up front and scattered around. In the last row of the orchestra there were some winos snoring. More of them than the others. The balcony was empty.

Jaizus! said McHooley. What a bloody shame!

But the music was good! They played some kind of mass and something by Dvorak!

Who did the oration? asked McHooley.

It was supposed to be that guy, the old pro bono lawyer from when we tried to redress our grievances. Also the new president of the Association of the Survivors of the *Slocum* Disaster. But the pro bono didn't show up and the president of the association had, unfortunately, died that morning.

Didn't anybody go onstage to say something? Vilma wanted to know.

Me, said Knittel. In between numbers I was standing there. I said, Everybody will stand up, please, for a moment of silence.

That was it, Cortin said, a moment of silence?

That was it, Joey. A moment of silence. A whole symphony orchestra and just a moment of silence.

But why didn't anybody come? Mindy asked. Wasn't that peculiar?

Nah, said Eddie Knittel. June 6, 1944, was D-Day. We were invading France, y'know. Everybody was home listening to the war on the radio.

7

THE ACCOUNTANT'S ACCOUNT

Milton Seymour Oster laughed, a laugh caught in the back of his throat almost as if he were gargling. He stroked his shaven head with both hands. It was D-Day all right, he said, I was seven years old. I was listening to it on the radio.

I could hear the explosions of the guns. All those cracking sounds that they've now got canned for TV programs. A reporter, maybe it was Edward R. Murrow, I don't know for sure. He was right there on the beach, describing what was happening. What he saw happening. What he thought he saw happening.

LST's were sliding up on the beach. Our boys were jumping out. The Germans were on top of the cliff shooting them down. You could hear cries as the boys got hit or cries because someone else got hit.

The reporter was not in control of his voice. It was trembling, filled with gasps. He described the Rangers placing scaling ladders against the cliff walls. In my little boy's mind I could see that. It was like a movie with the Indians on their rough ladders going up the walls of Fort Apache and the Germans chopping them down with axes and rifle stocks.

Murrow told how the sands of Omaha Beach were soaked with blood. How there were places where the sand didn't absorb the blood, which formed pools.

Airplanes came over the German-held cliffs, strafing and dropping bombs. The reporter said the 101st Airborne had been dropped behind the enemy lines. Many floated down dead in their parachutes.

Boats opened up, and tanks, jeeps, and trucks rolled out, churning up the red beach. Murrow began to weep, sob. Oh, my God, he said, the tanks are running over the dead and the wounded! Our tanks are killing our boys. They're being mashed into the sand. Oh, my God, oh, my God! The radio was broadcasting the loud crying of the voice. The dead are everywhere! There are thousands!

Then our Stromberg-Carlson went dead. I thought it had broken. I tried to tune it. I swept the red marker across the dial's little numbers. There was no Murrow.

But the war was everywhere else. Suddenly another voice was speaking, jubilant, triumphant.

Glorious victory, it said, the engagement has ended! I can see our troops lining the cliff over Omaha Beach. They are waving their iron helmets and cheering. One paratrooper on the cliff's edge is kneeling and praying. Now a white, gold-striped LST is landing on the beach.Three five-star generals are emerging from the mouth of the landing craft.

I heard all that on the radio, Oster said and finished the drink before him.

You were dreaming it, Knittel barked. There was no blow-by-blow broadcast. They didn't start that until Viet Nam and then it was color TV.

I love it! said Cortin.

I'm so surprised at you, Miltie! Vilma Rakos said. You shouldn't make fun of the war.

I wasn't making fun of it. It was all on the Stromberg-Carlson. It was what I heard.

Dreamed!

Oster laughed. If you say so, Eddie.

Jaizus, said McHooley. It's damned disrespectful, Miltie.

It was on my radio, said Oster.

Esther Lieber sighed. Will you straighten us out, Miltie? It almost sounds true until you get to the generals. But we all know that ain't true.

Tell us it ain't true, Miltie, Cortin said, pleading.

It ain't true, said Miltie.

Jaizus, said McHooley, is there anyone here who wants to buy a bar?

Bo Wang said, I'm first in line, McHooley. You promised me! I have the downpayment.

Are you serious, Bo? Vilma Rakos asked.

Sure, he's serious, said McHooley. He wants to be the first Asian-Afro-American to own an Irish-drinking establishment. Affirmative Action. Equal opportunity capitalism.

I love it! said Cortin. Delicious!

You're all nuts! said Mindy.

It's the Happy Hour! said Esther Lieber. Whoopee!

It was the Stromberg-Carlson, said Oster. It was all over the radio. Edward R. Murrow was in tears. The victory was glorious. There were more dead than could be counted. The generals who came out of the mouths of the boats all wore white uniforms.

Tell us it ain't true, Miltie! Cortin implored again.

Well, it's half-true, said Oster.

Half? asked Knittel.

Something like that. You said it yourself, Eddie. Nobody came to the concert because they were all at home listening to their radios. I was seven years old. I was listening. It was what I had imagined as I listened. It was all very thrilling. Blood. Nazis with tomahawks. Generals in white and gold. The soldier on top of the sheer cliff, praying. Inspiring. Charles Laughton, a six-star general. Beautiful.

Oster reached for Cortin's glass and drank from it.

A few months later my mother told me my father had been part of the invasion and that he had died. She showed me the medals the Army had sent. A Purple Heart and a Silver Star. My father was a hero.

Knittel harrummphed. Oster smiled toward him.

Years later, when I was fourteen, another letter came from the Army. It said my father, Walter Oster, had not died on Omaha Beach.

He was alive? Your father was alive? Esther Lieber, astonished, asked.

No. He was dead all right, Esther. But he had died in a field hospital outside Cleobury-Mortimer, a small English town. Pneumonia. His outfit, the 329th Signal Base Depot Company, had had the honor of being part of the invasion while he was in the hospital bed. His Company had gotten completely destroyed, wiped out, everyone, to a man. The Army simply had included Walter Oster with the dead 329th. My father was a clerical error, you see. And the Army delicately suggested that my mother send the medals back.

She didn't do it, did she, Miltie? Rakos asked.

Oster nodded. My mother, married again, had kept the framed medals on their maroon velvet mat, hidden away somewhere. Her husband didn't want them hanging on the living room wall.

Cortin clapped his hand to his chest and sang:

Picture the scene
Of a child in a home,
Gazing up in surprise
At a man who came in
While he was alone
With a mask over

Both of his eyes.
First he went
To the desk in the hall
But when he reached
For the medal,
Which hung on the wall,
With tears in his eyes
The little boy cried:
Please, don't take Daddy's medal,
He won it for bravery.
It was found by his side
Before he died
And sent here to my Mommy and me...

Milton Oster, listening to Cortin sing, didn't notice the tension in his companions. When Oster finally laughed, the others relaxed. I never did understand why the Army wanted its medals back, Oster said.

It's things like that drive a man to fury! McHooley said.

Maybe. It just filled me with awe and wonder. Awe and wonder! How could they find out such a thing? That Walter Oster had died in a field hospital outside a place called Cleobury-Mortimer instead of on the bloody beach? Who could have discovered such an error, such a tiny error? A private? A lieutenant?

A fucking bookkeeper, Knittel said.

Exactly! said Oster. Awe and wonder and no computers! Whoever he was had poured over lists miles long. He extrapolated. He compared. He isolated this Cleobury-Mortimer corpse from those thousands in the red waters and red sands of Omaha. Then he typed up his report and submitted it to all the proper echelons.

That's sick! Why? Why not just forget it? Mindy wanted to know.

Admire him, praise him! He was doing his job, Mindy. No errors. If there were errors, the books would not be balanced. This soldier wanted the books to balance. It was important to him. He wanted his world to be perfect.

That's shit! Knittel said.

At that time, when I had acne, before I had psoriasis, it seemed miraculous that this mole could tunnel into darkness and find my father listed in the wrong place. I admired him, this secret man who balanced the books.

I would have hated him, said Esther.

Me too, said Mindy. How unnecessary!

Oster shook his head. I absolutely admired him. I wanted the opportunity to be like him. To balance the books. To find the bottom line, no matter how obscure. That's why I loved math and science and eventually became an accountant.

Well, said Vilma patting Oster's hand, so long as you're happy, Miltie.

But I'm miserable! said the accountant. Books cannot be balanced, my friends. And nothing has a bottom line Oster said with profound sadness.

Is this man really your accountant? McHooley asked. If he is, lad, y'd better cash him in.

When you stand before the Big Bookkeeper in the sky, McHooley, won't he open the golden ledger and add up your debits and credits?

You're an atheist hooligan, Oster!

No, I'm not. I believe, McHooley, God is the last hope we have to get the books balanced, Oster said, stroking his bald head.

Jaizus, said McHooley, if you're a believer, what am I?

A Catholic, said Cortin, a Catholic like me.

You can't be a Cat'lic, Joey. You're a queen, Eddie Knittel said sweetly.

Vilma said, You know I'm a church-goer. Joey says he's Catholic but he doesn't go.

That's right, Cortin said. They kicked me out of St. Patrick's twice. But in my heart I'm Catholic.

So, said Knittel, that leaves you, yenta.

Okay, I confess, Esther said. I'm a single head of house-hold, non-virgin atheist. I can't stand vengeful Gods. I never saw a sign of a loving God. And the world's all fucked up so I'll be the token atheist at McHooley's Bar and Grill.

I'm an atheist, said Mindy.

Well, said Knittel, you're the right age for it. And what about the heathen Chinee?

Bo Wang smiled. Ah, Honorable Old Fart, China boy very confused. Too much heritage. Confucius say, in Year of Rat all atheists turn tail. All true believers get drunk.

Stories, let's tell stories, Esther said, her voice rising.

Okay, if it makes you feel better, Oster continued, my story is approximately as follows. When I found out there was no bottom line and no balanced books, I was deeply disturbed and I got psoriasis. My legs, my arms, my elbows, my chest, my buttocks. My heels split into deep fissures. I couldn't wear shoes. I filled my socks with medicated creams so I could walk. The smell of my ointments filled the air. I squished and sloshed around my office and apartment. Estelle, my wife, couldn't stand it. She moved out.

Just like that? asked Vilma.

Well, it was pretty ugly, Oster said, stroking his glowing scalp. Her attorney got a fat separation deal for her.

Because you were ugly? Esther asked.

No, because psoriasis is an *emotional* disease. Her lawyer told the court I had very ugly *emotions.* The judge who examined nude photos of me agreed. I hated him and I hated her. And my psoriasis got worse. It went to my scalp. They had to sedate me to shave my hair off.

I can't imagine you with hair, Esther said.

I'll show you a nude photo, Oster said. My mother's husband left her around the same time because my mother had developed Alzheimer's. Now she had no husband and no medals. I put her in a nursing home until her money ran out. A fortune! Then I paid her bills and I paid for Estelle. But C.P.A.'s can afford that, right? Wrong. So, more or less, I avoided paying taxes.

Hmmmm, said Bo Wang.

The IRS thinks that's not appropriate. So they attached my bank accounts and seized my business income. I had no money left. I moved into a single-room occupancy hotel with winos, addicts, and welfare people. The psoriasis spreads to my scrotum and penis.

Eech! said Lieber.

You bet! said Oster. Now, my mother, who couldn't remember who I was, was put on Medicaid. That's was a big relief. Little by little I crawled out of debt. I got a new apartment. I had suffered but I had endured! The best was yet to come. My wife's attorney, whom I still hate to this day, calls and tells me Estelle has early signs of Alzheimer's.

You see why I'm an atheist? Mindy said.

The lawyer drops her as a client for ethical reasons—that is, she's now a pain in his ass. She calls him ten times a day and doesn't remember why she's calling.

Jaizus!

He says since we're only separated, and her family doesn't want to be involved. Perhaps I would be a good and kind person and take care of her. After all, he says to me in the voice of a thousand trials, you loved her once. She needs you now to take care of her affairs. After all, you're still married.

You did it? Rakos asked.

Yes. She's in her own apartment. I manage things.

Vilma patted Oster's hand again. Embarrassed, he turned away from Rakos and looked toward Lieber. So that's my story, Esther, he said.

I'm sorry I pulled you away from the bottom line.

You did the right thing, said Knittel.

We are doomed! Oster said, staring at the old man. A vein in Oster's smooth temple throbbed.

There is no closure for anything! I told you, there's no bottom line! The books can't be balanced! Oster was shouting now. Doesn't anybody in McHooley's benighted Bar and Grill know what that means? NO BOTTOM LINE!!! NO BAL-ANCED BOOKS!!!

Oster's laugh covered the air conditioner's fitful purr and a Mort Shuman song on the bar radio.

⌐ 8 ⌐

Knittel looked at Oster and asked, Why are you so fucking happy if the books won't balance?

I'm not happy, Eddie. I'm filled with despair. What it means is that the universe doesn't work. You get it? The universe doesn't work!

The air conditioning doesn't work, said Esther.

I've leap-frogged over Newton and Einstein! Oster shouted. Do you, *can you,* understand what it means to this planet when there's no bottom line? When the books will not be balanced? The universe doesn't work and I have discovered it! Let me have a straight seltzer in a small glass.

You'll have to pay, you blasphemer, said McHooley.

Seltzer is free, said Esther.

It is not free to bald-headed accountants who blaspheme, McHooley said.

Oster took a drink from Cortin's glass.

I'm not getting something here, Vilma Rakos said. Do you know what Milton is talking about?

No, I don't, said Eddie. The whole thing is a goddamn accountant joke. Do you care if the books balance?

No, said Vilma, not really.

Do you, Esther.

No, said Esther softly.

Louder! said Eddie Knittel.

No, said Esther. I have to go home. Now I'm really cuckoo. And drunk also. And I can't pee in public toilets.

Do you care about books balancing, McHooley?

I've made myself queer. Slip of the tongue. *Clear.* Books should balance like pretzels and peanuts.

And you, Joey?

I want the books to balance, Eddie, but I know that they don't.

Bo?

Wang laughed. I'm not part of your occidental crowd, old man. They're your books. You balance them. Bring in some seals.

Heathen Chinee, Knittel mutterred.

Don't you want my opinion? Mindy asked.

No, said Knittel. Miltie, are you drunk?

As drunk as I ever get.

Okay, Miltie, what books won't balance? What bottom line is missing, Miltie?

Those of the earth and the universe.

As long as my books balance. You're my accountant. Ain't I got a bottom line?

Milton Oster stroked his bald head and nodded.

Then it's okay, Milton.

You're his accountant? You're Eddie Knittel's bookkeeper? Joey Cortin asked, thumping Oster's chest with his forefinger. How can he trust you?

He does my taxes. I can't do taxes. I can run plumbing up and down the Empire State but fucking taxes! It would be all right if I could use the short form.

Oster smiled. Millionaires can't use short forms, Eddie.

All the bar people turned toward the old man. But Eddie Knittel did not speak.

Finally it was Esther Lieber who spoke. Eddie, she said, I'm thinking of you in a different way. You wanna go out?

What would Linda say? asked Vilma, letting down her long, thick hair and shaking it out.

I love it! What would Linda say? Cortin said, batting his eyes.

Eddie reached over and took a cigarette from Vilma's pack. He lit it and blew a smoke ring. I'm innocent, Eddie Knittel said. It just grew. Two world wars, lots of plumbing, General Motors, IBM, Xerox and Microsoft. I don't buy or sell. I just grow.

Now there, said Milton Oster, is the capitalist incarnate! He grows. He just grows. I can run up his balance. I can plumb down to his bottom line. But it's the other business that plagues me.

You mean the universe? asked Esther.

Yes.

You're scary, Miltie, Esther said, and you're cuckoo. More cuckoo than me.

Why? asked Milton Oster. Tell me why? You loved a Nazi, who loved you. Is that a balance? And I believe it, too. And McHooley tells us that trials never end. That's right, trials never end. I believe that. But that's not the bottom line, is it? And Joey tells us that song is his whole life but he will not sing because he wants to live.

I've been singing. You heard me.

I mean really singing, for the world. But I believe both things at once. That you want to live and that you want to sing. And if you sing, you die. It's not what I would call a balanced proposition. And, Vilma, who, at last found love, has it snatched away from her. Should love end in the wind on a hiking trail? Is that the bottom line?

Vilma broke into tears again. Stop it, Miltie she said.

I'm sorry, Miltie Oster said, I'm sorry, Vilma. But your proposition isn't balanced, is it?

Ach, said Eddie Knittel, this is plain bullshit, Miltie.

Right on! said Esther.

She put her cheek down on the bar top.

Vilma pulled a small red comb through her hair. The cigarette protruding from Knittel's white beard was dark with his saliva. He rolled it from one corner of his mouth to the other with his tongue.

You know what? asked Eddie Knittel, My story is over.

Explicit carmen, said Oster.

What the fuck is that? Knittel asked.

Latin, darling. *"The song is over"*, Cortin translated.

Let's get out of here, said Esther.

Oh, no, said Bo Wang, not before the accountant philosopher gives us the bottom line on the *General Slocum*. And I've waited all night to hear the end of the Honorable Old Fart's story. I will not be denied.

What about your story, Confucius? Knittel asked. You may as well tell it. Everybody else has come on board.

You forgot Bo and me, said Mindy. But that's okay. We're just the help.

Actually, old man, I have no story. What I have is a condition.

And what might that be?

A.A.A. Asian-African-American. Fatal.

And all the time we thought you were an architect, said Esther.

You don't like my cooking?

Aye, lad, yer New Zealand Irish stew is first class.

Thanks, boss. Eddie, I want you to know that your story is the saddest and grandest story I have ever heard.

The old man stroked his beard. He stared at Bo Wang resentfully and without trust. Inscrutable, he said.

What is the story's end, Eddie? Bo Wang asked.

The old man's eyes closed slowly as if he were absorbing a pain.

Maybe, said Joey Cortin, it has no end, no bottom line.

You said, *Explicit carmen*, said Vilma.

Miltie said that. I translated.

Vilma turned to Oster. Is it over, Miltie?

He shrugged.

Vilma Rakos turned to Eddie Knittel. I guess it's up to you to say, Eddie.

Edward Francis Knittel opened his eyes, which were glazed over and bloodshot. He looked at Vilma Rakos but addressed himself to Milton Seymour Oster.

I'm sorry about your psoriasis, he said. You're a good guy and a good accountant, Miltie. No balance? No bottom line?

I'm tilting toward agreeing with you even if I don't want to. There should be some order in life, shouldn't there? Mobo said God created everything out of chaos. The universe, the earth, us, everything. You got to figure, Miltie, that a lot of chaos was left over. Still and all I miss Rosy. I feel her near me when I go to sleep. I miss my mother. I hardly remember my brother and my sisters. I remember my father but I don't miss him. Honeycuitt and Helga, when I talk to myself, which I do a lot these days, I also talk to them. They were good people. I loved them very much. There's no way I can talk to Mobo because he was always flashing his printed pads and telling me to be quiet. My two wives, Jesus, they're perfect blanks. The second one, I think she was a nice lady, died in Disney World on the Terror Mountain ride. Ach, ach, Rosy, Rosy, we could have had a life, y'know!

Knittel drew his sleeve across his eyes which had filled with tears.

Vilma put her arms around the old man and kissed his flat nose. We all have lives, Eddie, she said. C'mon, your life's not been too bad.

He scratched his beard. I wish Van Schaik had lived longer, he said. I would have apologized to him. I was too disrespectful when I saw him up there in Cohoes.

Cohoes? asked Vilma. What's that?

A town. Upstate New York, near Albany. I was too young then and he was too old. It was 1937, no '38. Maybe '36. I was in my late forties. Van Schaik was maybe ninety. Whatever year, it was summer when his letter came.

It was a polite kind of letter. A little stiff like the Captain, y'know. *Honorable Sir* and stuff like that. He wrote that he knew that I had not forgotten the *Slocum* although the rest of the world may have. Van Schaik said he remembered me from the trial days in the Bronx armory and that I had conducted myself very well. There were some things he had wanted to tell me. *Things I have long wanted to share with you about the ship of my last command.* Formal. Poetic. I had the letter on my bureau for two weeks before I answered it. Why the hell I wanted to see him I didn't know, but I wanted to. It bothered me that I wanted to see him. The long and short is, I wrote to him and said I'd be at his farm—he had a farm—y'know, in a few weeks. .

ᶜ 9 ᶜ

Those days before I went to visit him I was very nervous. Smoked too much, drank too much schnnaps, made sloppy mistakes on my jobs, snapped at people.

What else is new? asked Cortin.

Knittel didn't seem to hear him. He was on my mind, Van Schaik was. Remembering him on the *Slocum* and at the Coroner's Jury Trial. Such a good-looking man, dignified, proud. The trial—so many years I could still hear Van Schaik's voice. It was like an actor's voice, big and smooth. Those dark specs on his nose. Now he was an old man living out his years in the country, and I was getting close to fifty myself.

In your case that's early middle age, said Bo Wang.

Knittel didn't seem to hear Wang any more than he had heard Cortin. Ninety was very old to me then and I wondered how the years had changed him. He hadn't had an easy time of it, jail and all.

They indicted him in 1904. His lawyer, who was put up for him by the American Association of Master, Mates and Pilots, got Van Schaik enough delays so he didn't get to trial until the beginning of 1906. January. The jury took only thirty minutes to find him guilty. The judge gave him ten years. His lawyer appealed and it wasn't until 1908 that they carried the Captain off to Sing Sing. He was over sixty. The Socialist Party and the AFL fought for him. And the Wobblies, of course. More than a quarter of a million names on petitions: Free Captain William Van Schaik.

My Aunt Helga was furious with all these anarchist scum. When I said I thought maybe it wasn't all his fault and that I'd rather see Barnaby in jail, did she yell! He murdered your whole family! she said.

But Honeycuitt, I think, was more on my side, although he never said so because of his business with Helga.

Anyway, as I told you before, President Taft, kept his word after he beat William Jennings Bryan for The White House. Van Schaik was in Sing Sing three years when Taft got him parole. And a year later Taft pardons him. That's 1912. After that Van Schaik more or less went into seclusion. The years pass, then the postman brought his letter. Ach!

So, I gassed up my LaSalle and got on the road to Cohoes. It was a good car, the LaSalle. Sturdy. Heavy. It had a self-starter.

The weather was very good that day. The air was fresh and it was warm enough so I could keep the window rolled down and have my arm half out. I started off just when it got light. The trip would take six hours or so, a hundred fifty miles. You could make good time with a LaSalle, even stopping for something to eat.

Van Schaik was living in the caretaker's cottage behind a big house built around the Revolutionary War time. The main house had white columns that went up maybe three stories. You could see it once had been a grand place. But it was old. There was very little glass left in the windows and the veranda sagged all around. It was on a big spread of land. The trees, which had been planted in rows along the driveway, needed care. The branches had grown until they touched each other, grew into each other. The lawns all around had become meadows, mainly grass but with big patches of wild flowers.

Knittel gripped his beard. *Rosy, you are my posy*, he said under his breath.

Three or four hundred yards past the big house was Van Schaik's cottage. It looked small by comparison but it wasn't. It was white with green trim on the windows, and the front door was green. A meadow fronted the cottage and it was filled with flowers. I pulled up on the road alongside the meadow. I walked toward the house and I yelled as I walked, Ahoy, there! Captain Van Schaik, this is Eddie Knittel. Are you home?

There was no answer for a couple of minutes and I thought it was a wasted trip. Maybe he wasn't home or maybe I had come to the wrong house.

But the door opened and standing there was an old man. It was Van Schaik, all right. He was wearing his uniform and his naval cap. Smartly pressed, the creases of the navy-blue pants sharp. Around his white collar was his black bandanna. He was still wearing those little black lenses.

Ahoy, Master Edward Knittel! he calls out. I welcome you to my home! I can't see you in the sunlight. Come forward!

I didn't think he was able to see me until I reached the stair to the porch. Then his face lit up with a smile. He shook my hand, a real firm handshake, and he took my elbow and led me through the door into the parlor.

It had the smell of an old man, y'know. I hate that smell. It ain't to be found in my house. It's the smell of death. I won't have it and Linda, she's terrific, makes the place smell like a forest.

Pine Sol, said Cortin.

Why do you always do that, Joey? Vilma asked. Let him alone. He's into the story.

Cleaning his house is not part of the story, Vilma.

Knittel didn't seem to be aware of the low-key exchange between Cortin and Rakos. He continued.

All the windows in the parlor were closed. The room had a pink wallpaper with yellow daffodils. It seemed new. That surprised me. I expected it to be faded, y'know. Over the fireplace there was a big painting of the *Slocum*. Not with me climbing up the mast and not on fire, either. The *Slocum*, its paddlewheels churning up the water, the two tall smokestacks sending up gray smoke, its name in gold, and the hull so white! It was the best painting of the *Slocum* I had ever seen.

All around the parlor walls were other pictures, some paintings, mainly photographs. I didn't get a good look, but most were of boats. Many of the *Slocum*.

There was a small oval table in the middle of the room with a large bowl of flowers. They were so nicely arranged that I thought they were artificial. I felt one of the leaves.

They're real, Van Schaik said. The woman who cleans always fills a bowl. If my sight were better, I might enjoy them more. The *Slocum* damaged my eyes, Mr. Knittel, if you remember. Would you care for some lemonade, freshly made?

That would be nice, Captain.

He left the room. I could hear his sound in the kitchen. He returned with a large cut-glass pitcher and two glasses. We sat at the table and had the lemonade. He asked me if my trip was good and did I come by train. I told him I had a car.

After the lemonade he showed me his fruit orchard. He walked slowly, sometimes sliding his feet along the ground where he thought there might be a high root sticking out.

Are your eyes that bad? I asked him.

Bad enough, he said. In the shaded sections of the orchard I lose contrast. I trip over the roots if I'm not careful. When the sunlight is bright it's worse. I see nothing at all in the glare.

I had never been in a place where fruit grew. On the walk I picked apples, pears, mulberries, cherries, and ate them. Juice ran down my chin. Everything I ate I was saying, Mmmmmm. Van Schaik laughed at my sounds. From the grapevine Van Schaik cut me a small bunch of muscatel. That was really good!

Back in his parlor we had some more lemonade. I was beginning to feel uncomfortable. Why the hell had I come? Why had he asked me to come? I began to think of when it would be right for me to say it was a real good visit and all that.

Van Schaik took off his dark glasses. He put on clear glasses. To see me better he turned his head to the side as if his sight might be better from the perimeters, y'know.

Well, he said you're not the boy I remember, Mr. Knittel.

It's been a long time, Captain.

I went to prison, Mr. Knittel.

Yes, I know. The President pardoned you. That was good.

He shook his head. No, he said, it wasn't good, Mr.Knittel. It wasn't good at all.

It was a pardon, Captain, you were forgiven. Your slate was wiped clean.

That's not what a pardon is, Mr. Knittel. It's a ritual begging. One must say, put into writing, that one has come to realize now the nature of the crime of which one was convicted. The one to be pardoned, Edward, says that he realizes that his conviction and the sentence meted out were just. He must profoundly regret, in writing, to having committed his crime. If the President will be good enough to forgive the criminal, the criminal promises he will become a model citizen and he will never do such foul deeds again. You see, Mr. Knittel, when one accepts a pardon, his slate does not become clean. With his own words he has confessed to his crime. In this way he has engraved his guilt in stone. Worst of all the criminal, dog that he is, sits up on his haunches and begs his master to pardon him for his sins. I sat up on my haunches, Mr. Knittel, I did that shameful, shameful thing. I have often thought that my soul would have been more at ease if I had stayed in my prison and completed my sentence. My debt to society paid. Don't you think so, Mr. Knittel?

I can't agree to that, Captain, I said. Everybody was happy about the pardon.

They didn't understand. It wasn't a pardon I needed. It was exoneration I needed.

Your friends worked very hard to get you pardoned.

You too, Mr. Knittel?

No. It would have been embarrassing. But I was glad when it happened. In those days I had a reputation. I had a name.

You were the Hero.

They called me that. It's too complicated. I was a kid.

I can understand that, Captain Van Schaik said. You had been given a reputation. As you said, you had a name.

Yes, sir.

Did you ever think, Master Knittel, that William Van Schaik also had a name?

Yes, sir, you were respected in the whole country. Especially New York.

Van Schaik is an old and honored name. My people came here with Peter Schuyler. There were still savages in Manhattan. We built the city in which you immigrants came to live. Van Schaik is an *American* name, Mr. Knittel. I have shamed it. Do you understand that?

I think so, I said.

Van Schaik is a name that was in New York before George Washington was born. It is not easy for a man to suffer the loss of such a name. In spite of what has passed, Mr. Knittel, I will fight until my death to retrieve my name and my honor. No Van Schaik would do less, you see.

I shifted in my chair but I didn't speak. Suddenly he smiled and relaxed. He almost seemed to have become warm, y'know.

He gets up from his own chair and he says, I have some very good local beer from Utica. You must have some. He comes back from the kitchen with two pewter mugs with great heads on them. I drained half in one swallow. It was a raw beer. I got a little buzz on. Thanks, I said, I enjoyed that.

Do you know what stands between us, Master Knittel? he says.

Now I'm real edgy. I feel a change in the weather. No, I say to him.

Six or seven minutes, Van Schaik said, six or seven minutes.

Oh, I say.

Let me bring the pitcher, he says. He goes to the kitchen and comes back with more of the Utica beer. He fills my mug. He says, Drink up, drink up!

I take a swallow. I don't understand, I say.

At the Bronx armory I said it was two or three minutes to North Brother Island. You said seven. Do you remember that, Mr. Knittel?

You know how sometimes when you feel real danger coming you get very calm. Well, I got very calm and as icy cold as the beer. I remember that, Captain, I said. I said six or seven. It could have been eight. I remember that.

You were so dead sure, Mr. Knittel.

Dead sure, Captain, dead sure.

He smiles and nods. I have no more beer to offer. Would you like some lemonade?

No.

Tell me, sir, do you think it was fair that I was the only one to be convicted of a crime? Indeed, sir, of several crimes?

No, I said, I think it was rotten. Because Flanagan and the man who had helped him had run off. The whole crew went overboard except, maybe, the black man. I forget his name.

I forgive the mates and crew. They were not genuine seamen, they were day laborers. But the others!

Especially Barnaby, I agreed. He was a rotten liar. He let you swing for him.

I cast no blame on Barnaby, sir. We dined together often. He was a gentleman.

He lied. It was everybody but him who was to blame.

We each had our responsibilities.

Are you saying you were responsible for the people who died?

Yes, I am responsible, he said softly, responsible if you allow the seven minutes to which you swore, sir.

As this point I thought I'd like to have the lemonade or even a glass of water but I wasn't going to ask for it. Captain, I said, I testified under oath.

You were mistaken. You had been badly hurt, Mr. Knittel. There is no doubt you had been confused. And you were only on the threshold of your manhood. You were the darling, the Hero of the nation. On your hospital bed you basked in the adulation of the mobs. The berserk and drooling mobs. Somebody had to be sacrificed on the altar of injustice.

I could see that he was getting agitated. There was spittle at the corner of his mouth. And it was you on the altar to be sacrificed? I asked.

Yes, Mr. Knittel, I was on that altar and you quite calmly cut my throat.

Is that why you asked me to come here, Captain? To tell me that? All right then, I've heard you. I thank you for the lemonade and for the beer. It's a long trip back to New York. I've got to get going.

Not yet, he said. There is something I want to show you.

Van Schaik went to the fireplace, where he took a paper from the mantle. For a moment he stood before the painting of the *Slocum.* The Captain came to my chair, stood behind me, and put the sheet of paper before me. I want you to read this carefully and then affix your signature to it.

He walked back to his chair. He replaced his clear eyeglasses with his little black specs.

I stared at him. I began to feel my blood warming. My heart was loud. I was angry and I was afraid. He smiled at me across the small oval table. The spittle at the corner of his mouth blew up into a little bubble. I looked away from his fucking eyeless black specs. I looked down at the sheet of paper he had given me. It was all typed out, y'know. Like a lawyer does.

I can only remember the first part, which I swear burned into me.

Knittel looked from face to face along the bar. They were locked into his story and only McHooley moved, his damp bar rag following his hand in its silent circling.

Knittel continued, I remember this much verbatim.

Verbatim? asked Cortin.

Verbatim, said Knittel.

Knittel stroked his beard and recited. *I, Edward Francis Knittel, of my own free will, state that the testimony made and given by me in all courts and at all hearings and in all depositions in re the time of the outbreak of fire on the Excursion Boat General Slocum on June 15, 1904, was in error.*

Was in error, Knittel repeated. It went on to say that Captain William Van Schaik's stipulation of the time the fire started, the exact time, two minutes to North Brother Island, was correct. Other versions of the time expressed by me were wrong.

And why was that? Well, the paper said I was only fifteen years old and that, because of the panic on the *Slocum* and because of my wounds, my burns, my fractured skull, and the influence of malevolent parties, I was confused and in grave error as to the time it would have taken to reach North Brother

Island. Then there was a line on which I was supposed to put my signature.

I looked up from the paper. Van Schaik was getting tenser. There was white spittle in the other corner of his mouth. You know something? Like a man who was about to die, the whole *Slocum* business passed in front of my eyes. I felt sweat on my forehead. A trickle of sweat ran down my sides from my armpits, It was not two minutes, I said in a voice so low you could hardly hear it. It could never have been two minutes! The Prosecutor had allowed as much as nine. It was forever! It was fucking forever going to North Brother.

You were positive? Oster asked. Eighty years later, Eddie, and you're one hundred percent sure?

Miltie, Miltie, on the head of Rosy, I swear: eight minutes! It had to be eight minutes!

Knittel rubbed his beard and continued.

Those black specs were drilling holes through me. Sign your name, Van Schaik said, sign your name!

When I smiled it made his face jump.

Sign! he said.

I ain't got a pen, Captain, I said.

He sucked in his wind and he says, There's a little desk behind you. If you go to it and let down the dropleaf, you'll find an inkwell and a pen.

Why don't you get it for me, Captain? I said and I was smiling.

I don't know where it came from but Van Schaik is holding a long-barrelled pistol in his hand. It's pointing right at me. Maybe he's half-blind, but he knows exactly where I'm sitting.

I say to myself this is fucking serious. So I get up very slowly. The pistol barrel follows me as I back away from the table to the desk. I open it. I see the inkwell and the pen. I pick them up, one in each hand. I show them to Van Schaik.

Sit down, he says. Sign it.

I sit down. I look at him. The pen is between my fingers. I don't move. I hear the gun cocking. I dip the pen point into the black ink.

Sign, damn it! he says.

I dip the pen in the ink again. With my left hand I swoop up the inkwell and knock it to him. It hits him in the face. The ink runs down his nose. I throw the pen like a dart. The point goes into his neck, right below his ear. The gun goes off. It's like someone hit me on the head with a two-by-four. I fall to the floor.

I'm thinking to myself, This is the end and why am I such a *weisenheimer*? I should have signed the fucking thing! Later I could've explained how he had held the gun on me. But right then I thought he was going to blow my head off.

I crawled away like I was Mobo, like a fast crab, heading for the door. Van Schaik's gun was blasting at me. Big splinters were exploding out of the floor.

The door was closed when I got there. But like in many old houses the door is badly hung. The outside daylight comes underneath it. Maybe an inch on the side where the latch is. I got my fingers under the door.

Knittel held his arm up. He clenched and unclenched his fist. In those days this was one fucking strong hand. I could bend horseshoe nails with it. And I'm scared, I'm terrified! I pull the motherfucking door right through its latch. I'm on the porch. I roll off onto the grass. And I run like a big, brown, gimpy bunny into the field of wild flowers maybe a hundred yards away.

Cortin laughed. I'd give a week's pay to see that, Eddie!

Me too, said Edward Francis Knittel. That's what I thought as I ran. How can you be scared to death and be thinking how funny it was at the same time?

⤙ 10 ⤚

I'm lying there, red and yellow flowers all around me. I'm wondering why the flowers smell so bad. In a minute I know. I've shit in my pants! I'm stinking up the whole beautiful world. Now I hate Van Schaik. How I hate that fuck!

I'm looking up at the sky. It's so blue! It's almost as if I'm floating in the river again. But there are no seagulls, just some small birds. The air is filled with bird songs and a stink you wouldn't believe.

What can I do now? I ask myself. Are you going to lie there in your own shit? I swear to you, I thought it would be better to die. So little by little I squirrel out of my pants, which ain't easy because the pant leg gets caught on my brace. I have to arch my back and try to get the leg through. It won't work and all the crap is dripping on to me.

I stand up. I see Van Schaik on the porch. He's got a shotgun now. He's looking from left to right, from right to left, like a lighthouse beacon. He can't see me, I know that.

So, I'm standing there, first on my good leg and then on my gimpy leg, taking off my fucking shitty pants. The stuff is loose and all over my brace and legs. I struggle my BVDs off and, with the clean part of it, I wipe myself as well as I can. What a mess! What a stink!

I'm standing there naked from the waist down, stinking, and my head hurts. I touch my scalp. My hair is caked with blood. The blind bastard creased my skull! And I'm angry. I was never so angry in my life. I wished I had a gun.

I look at him sweeping his head from side to side. Van Schaik! I yell out, You're a fucking maniac!

His head jerks quickly in the direction of my voice.

Where are you? Knittel, he shouts. I'm going to kill you, you liar! Coward!

I'm here, you blind bastard! I yell again. I'm here among the roses, Captain Van Schaik. If you can find me, you can kill me.

He cups his hand above his black lenses and slowly, slowly he searches the field before him. I hold very still when he seems to be looking in my direction, but he sweeps by without seeing me.

You can't kill what you can't see, Van Schaik! I yell.

Sign the paper, Knittel, I beg you, sign the paper! What can it mean to you?

It's a lie! I will not sign a damned, rotten lie! You understand that?

Please! he shouts, Please! The word bounces off the trees.

I can't do it, Van Schaik.

Please! he says again.

I want to tell you this, Captain. I was not confused, I was never confused! You and your men, you were the ones who lied. You're no better than Barnaby!

You bastard! Son of a whoring bitch, Edward Knittel!

Are you talking about my mother, Captain Van Schaik? She was burned up on your boat!

Liar! Liar!

Hundreds, hundreds, burned alive on your boat! You know why, Van Schaik?

Liar! he yells with all his force.

You know why, Van Schaik? Listen to me, I'm going to tell you why! Because you didn't take the fire seriously, old man. You thought someone would come along and piss on it or throw an old tarp on it. That's how fires were always put out on the *Slocum* and the *Grand Republic.* You fucking maniac!

Sign the paper!

Ask Samuel Gompers! Why didn't you head her into the Manhattan shore?

It was the wrong course, Knittel! You know that, Knittel!

I laugh. I just stand there with my balls hanging out and I laugh. Loud and hard, I laugh.

North Brother Island was the only course! Every river man knows that! The only course!

The only course, yes! It was the only course you wanted to take, you maniac. The *Slocum* was in full blaze when you took her into the wind. Maniac! Maniac!

Stand up and let me see you, you coward!

I am standing, you sonuvabitch!

For a few minutes it's quiet across the field. He's turning his head, searching for me. I'm standing, still catching my breath. If he lets off a shot, it will only be by luck that he hits me.

Where are you? he says. His voice is very tense now. Where are you?

After a while, I say in a calm voice, without yelling, because I realize that the sound would carry very well across the field, I know what it is, Captain. I know what it is you have done.

He almost screams, You know nothing, nothing, you kraut!

I know something, Captain, my Captain! I know why you didn't run the *Slocum* onto the shore even as late as Sunken Meadows!

Fool! The river bottom is rocky there!

I laugh. And you'd wreck her? Tear her bottom out? Bust her up?

Yes! he yells, yes! Then he's silent for a while. He's in thought. He has stopped hunting for me and he lowers his gun.

When he speaks again, his voice is calm and strong. Did you know, Knittel, he said, there were oil tanks all along the shore there? Did you know that? If I had run her onto the shore there, the oil would have gone up? I could have set all New York on fire. Did you know that? North Brother Island was the only course!

I know all that, Captain! Damned lie!

North Brother had a good sand beach!

Wouldn't tear her bottom out? Is that it, Captain?

Two minutes. Two and a half minutes, he says, shouting again.

Liar! Eight minutes and I'm giving you charity about that, Captain. Eight minutes into that headwind! It was murder!

North Brother Island was the right destination, you bastard, Knittel!

And it had a good, smooth, sandy shore! Is that right, Captain Van Schaik?

Yes, he said, swinging the shotgun in a jerky arc, you know that's right!

What good was that smooth, sandy bottom, Van Schaik, when you couldn't bring her in sideways to the shore? You hit the beach nose first with everybody caught behind the flame in front and the flame behind. They were afire and still jumping! And the paddlewheels were still spinning, chopping up those babies! Six hundred more died in that single minute, Van Schaik. That minute on your lousy smooth beach! Right there, right there, in the river off the island, off the smooth fucking beach, six hundred more died!

Liar! Liar! I couldn't bring the boat in because a fierce current came up suddenly! You know nothing of these things, kraut!

I laugh. Here's the truth, Van Schaik. You beached at North Brother to save the goddamned *Slocum* for Barnaby and Knickerbocker! That was your job, wasn't it? Save the *Slocum* for Barnaby and Knickerbocker?

Liar! he shouts. There's a sob behind his cry. It kicks off the trees and the hills in a weak echo.

Now I yell again, all out, top of my lungs. You got away with murder, Van Schaik! You get no medals from me! It was eight minutes, you fuck!

Boy, does he scream! He lifts the shotgun to his shoulder and fires off both barrels! Bam! Bam! The kick of the gun knocks him against the door of the cottage and, still screaming, he slides down to the porch floor. He's sobbing and I feel no pity for him.

And once I had almost believed him. I had wanted to believe him. But those terrible minutes were there. Seven of them. Eight of them. And others did believe him in the *Slocum* days. Why? Because he had such a sharp sailor suit, such a nifty mustache, a voice that came out of the Old Testament, and those little black specs on his beautiful nose.

I reach down for my pants lying there among the flowers but they were too soiled. I leave them there with my BVDs. I pull the tails of my shirt down as much as I can. Well, they cover my crotch and my ass. I walk through the field to my car. I drive slowly back to New York, taking my time because I don't want to get home before nightfall. There's still an awful stink to me.

I sit in the car in front of my building for an hour maybe. After midnight, when I don't see anybody on the street, I jump out of the car, hop up the stairs, and go in.

⚹ 11 ⚹

Vilma Rakos gathered up her dark-blond hair with her small, square hand. She slipped a red rubberband over the thick fall which reached below her hips. She twisted the hair into a bun. Loose strands fell over her ears and a few, light and dark, rested on her cheeks.

Oster stared at her.

Something wrong, Miltie?

You're beautiful, he said.

Oh, cut it out.

No, I mean it, you're very beautiful.

I know that look, Miltie, Rakos said with a smile. Are you hitting on me?

Oster ducked his bald head. Of course not, he said and turned away from Vilma, who smiled softly.

Don't get bent out of shape, Miltie. I take it as a compliment, she said. Even though you're a little bit drunk.

I never get drunk, Oster said without looking back to Vilma.

Look at Knittel, said Joey Cortin, he's gone out into space again. He's pissed beyond belief. Bubbles are coming out of his ears.

He's rocking up and back, said Esther Lieber, giggling, so we know he's alive. Eddie, stop rocking. It's no good for you. Oh, am I cuckoo!

It is my considered opinion that old Edward has finished his story, McHooley said. He snapped his fingers in front of Knittel's eyes. Have you finished, old man?

I don't know, said Knittel, still rocking. I'm scouting around in my memory banks to see if there is anything left worth saying.

Well, you just take your sweet time, said Cortin. The night belongs to you.

Thanks, said Knittel. What did I leave out? The old man looked from face to face, seeming to wait for an answer.

How would we be knowing that, Eddie? McHooley said. It's your tale and we have all night.

I haven't, said Knittel. I've got to be somewhere.

Oh, we all know that, Esther said. Linda is waiting.

Cortin tittered.

Don't! said Vilma. I'm going to get mad, real mad!

Sorry, said Cortin.

Oster said to Eddie Knittel, What happened to Van Schaik?

Knittel stopped rocking. Ach, he said, poor man! He died in a nursing home near Utica a couple of years after my visit. There was an obit in *The Times*.

Big one? Oster asked.

Six, eight lines, Miltie. *Captain of the Slocum Dies.* Standard shit.

I wish you wouldn't use that word any more, Eddie, said Mindy.

Knittel's beard split on his smile. You don't like it? he said.

It isn't pleasant.

Knittel's beard swallowed his smile. No, it isn't, he said. That part of the story with me in the meadow? It was hard for me to tell that part. It was so humiliating. Ach, the stink has never left, y'know. Whenever I think of that day my nose fills with that smell. Shit and wild flowers. Hero!

Even heroes have bad days, old man, Bo Wang observed.

Yeah, even heroes, Knittel repeated. You know something? I'm inebriated but we don't call that drunk on 9th Street.

Knittel slapped his bearded cheeks with both hands at once. Ach, ach, ach! he said. Before he went off to die in France I asked Honeycuitt what the meaning of the *Slocum* was, y'know.

Please, said Esther, why should it have a meaning? It was an accident. Somebody's cigar ash in that barrel of straw.

Honeycuitt took a couple of weeks on that one. He said it was a kind of manifest destiny. It had been written. That's why no one lifted a finger to stop it. They all knew about the storeroom, about the lifeboats, about the life vests. The mates knew, the crew knew, the government inspectors knew, Barnaby knew, and goddamned Van Schaik knew! They had to let it happen, that's the thing! Helga believed what Honeycuitt had said. But she didn't say anything herself. And fucking Mobo, he said it was God who did it because He was angry at someone over at St. Mark's Lutheran. He did his rat-squeal whistling laugh when he printed that out. A Mobo joke!

I don't believe it was God. God is not that way, said McHooley.

Who done it then? asked Joey Cortin. In this case we know it wasn't the butler.

It's history as a game, said Oster, stroking his scalp. Pin the tail on the fading donkey of memory.

Nothing fades for me, nothing, said Eddie Knittel. Ask me anything.

Tony Lazzeri's average in May of 1931? Cortin said.

Fuck you, Joey.

McHooley, did I ever tell you I was a Jewish alcoholic? Esther asked.

It's better left unsaid, said McHooley as he filled her glass with wine.

Everything just tumbles on, doesn't it? Oster asked the group. It's impossible to hold onto anything. You grab something, you grab it by the throat, and it slips away from you. You grab hold of a bear and it turns into an eagle and flies away. It's numbers, it's numbers! Numbers should be real, the certainties of the world! But they are not. They are bears and eagles and all make believe!

Oster stroked his bald head with both hands. The books can't be balanced! he shouted. There's no goddamned bottom line!

Who cares? said Joey Cortin. Who needs a bottom line?

I need a bottom line, Knittel said quietly. I want to know that I have lived my life for something. Something definite. Something that had a beginning somewhere and will have a fucking end somewhere. Life is not just garbage floating on the tide.

No bottom line, said Oster.

I'm with Eddie, said Vilma.

I am too, said Mindy.

Who cares, said Cortin, as long as there's love? Love is the river.

Esther said, Did I mention I was an alcholic? I'm so cuckoo, I'm so cuckoo! I'm very inebriated.

McHooley, I have to know this, said Bo Wang. Do we open tonight for the young beer drinkers or does this go on forever?

That, Bo, is up to your friend, the Admiral.

Admiral? Bo asked the old man.

Knittel laughed. It goes on forever.

Bo Wang shrugged. Okay, he said, it's your boat ride. Say on, old man.

I'm thinking, Knittel said. I'll think of something.

What about Linda? Vilma asked.

Oh, Jesus! What time is it?

Ten and ten, McHooley said.

I still have a few minutes. She doesn't like me to be late. She has the babysitter waiting, Knittel said.

He turned suddenly to Oster and said through clenched teeth, You ain't my accountant anymore.

Suit yourself, Oster said.

Now why did you say that, Eddie? Vilma asked. Miltie is your friend, isn't he?

I need a bottom line!

Give him his stupid bottom line, Miltie, Esther said. What difference does it make? Give him a bottom line if he wants it.

No, said Oster.

No? asked Cortin.

No, Oster repeated.

Why? said Cortin.

Principle, said Oster. I have entered a new law into the universe: no bottom line!

The universe is all law and order, lad. Galaxies and galaxies of bottom lines.

Yeah, McHooley? So why is it going to blow up? Or collapse. Whatever, Esther Lieber postulated.

Does that mean there is a B.L. or there ain't a B.L.? Cortin asked.

Stop! said Vilma. If Eddie says he needs a bottom line, then he'll just have a bottom line and let's stop all this wise-guy bickering, okay?

Okay, said Milton Oster, I'll let it go. Eddie you've got a bottom line.

Okay, you're my accountant again. I wasn't serious, Miltie. You'll always be my accountant, said the old man.

Get paid right away, Milton, said Cortin.

You know why I'm not going to scramble your fag brains, Joey? Knittel said.

Why are you not going to scramble my fag brains, Eddie?

It was what you said before: Love is the river. That was beautiful.

You're a ninety-five year old asshole, Eddie. What I meant was that there was no bottom line. The river goes on and on with its flotsam and jetsam. A moving condition. Infinity. No end. No bottom line. Just because you want a bottom line, Eddie, doesn't mean there is one. Now, why don't you fire Miltie again!

Knittel leaned against the wall in his corner. He stared at Joey Cortin and said nothing. He drummed his fingers on the bar.

You certainly find a way to pick on him, Joey, Vilma Rakos said.

He's gets on my nerves, Vilma. We've given him his money's worth. I have a few problems of my own.

He's old, Vilma whispered, he's very, very old.

Let him stay home. Let him lie down and die. He's like an old, second-rate actor showing his hit reviews, reviews he got in a small-town newspaper on the road somewhere. Reviews which have turned yellow and are crumbling. The *Slocum* closed in New Haven a million years ago.

You are one mean sonuvabitch, said Oster. Have you been waiting all night for this, to stick a harpoon in his back?

Joey Cortin began to weep silently. I'm sorry, he said, I'm so sorry! I'm just a lousy, bitchy queen. From my heart, Eddie, I apologize. I didn't mean a word of it. God, Eddie, I know how much pain you've carried all these years.

Knittel drummed the bar but did not respond. Cortin blew his nose several times. He looked directly toward the old man. Please, he said, I don't want to cause you any more pain, Eddie. Forgive me, please.

Knittel, saying nothing, stared toward the back of the room.

Don't worry, Joey, Vilma said. He'll come around. You know, he really likes you.

I know that, Cortin said, that's why it's so awful. How can I behave so badly? I love the old fuck. I love you, Eddie.

The old man didn't respond.

I'm just a whore-bitch and I'll get what I deserve and I'll deserve it when I get it. He set his jaw and stared silently toward his craggy image in the mirror at the back of the bar.

All right, said Esther, enough already! What's eating you, Joey? Drop the shoe.

All right, Cortin said.

He stared at his hands then looked up. I don't know whether I'm negative or positive, he said. *I don't know if I'm negative or positive*! Tomorrow, I'll know tomorrow. Oh, please, God, be kind, help me! Forgive me, Eddie!

The air conditioner made its small rattling sound. Muffled traffic seeped into the room. McHooley poked into his cold boxes and rattled bottles.

Oster broke the silence. It'll be all right. You'll see. We always see the dark side when we're afraid.

I thought he was just a virgin child, Little Joe Cortin said as he wiped his eyes. He told me his father was an MD, his mother a school teacher. He showed me a photo of them with him, his father's arm around him, his mother at the piano, singing. They were all so apple pie American. In bed he whispered into my ear how much he wanted to be in theater. He played me like a fiddle. He even said he was a virgin, that I was his first. I believed him. I really did. Love always wants to believe. That's how he came on to me. Sweet face, musical voice. I spent so much money on him to keep him happy. He was a hooker! A 42nd Street cocksucker!

Jaizus! said McHooley. And he's got it?

Cortin nodded. He blew his nose. He didn't tell me until he began to show. He got so skinny. Anybody could see it except his lover.

It'll be negative, Vilma said. I have such a strong feeling.

I'm praying to God, Joey said. I went to St. Patrick's yesterday. The day before, too.

Eddie Knittel came into focus. Flotsam and jetsam on the river of love, he said.

Yes, yes, Eddie, but it's so awful, so awful! Will you forgive me? Let me off the hook? I don't want to be beat up anymore!

Edward Knittel nodded his head. Don't worry about it, Joey. It's all right. Everything is all right.

I hope you really mean that, Eddie, Vilma said.

Does it make a difference, Vilma? I feel bad for Joey but, one way or another, does it make a difference? For his sake I hope he doesn't become one of those blankets, a statistic, Knittel said. He lit the cigarette he had taken from Vilma's pack. Nothing makes much of difference. Numbers in Oster's ledger.

I don't get it, said Esther. What about the *Slocum*?

Do you think the *Slocum* makes a difference, yenta?

Yes, I do. Didn't it change your life?

Knittel laughed softly. Yes, it did. I survived. Eleven hundred died. Bo was right. It wouldn't mean much in China. What's eleven hundred souls mean in China?

I didn't mean it exactly that way, Eddie, Bo Wang said.

Don't apologize, Wang. I'm getting perspective, said Eddie Knittel. Everything could be the same or different. It all depends how you look at it, right?

Edward Francis Knittel suddenly felt cold. He wished Joey hadn't thrown away the pink blanket. He wished the air conditioner would stop. He wished McHooley would turn on the heat. But it was not really the cold that disturbed him, although he felt himself trembling. It was the emptiness. It was the profound emptiness.

He could hear Vilma saying, Are you all right, Eddie? You look as white as your beard.

And Knittel could hear himself saying, I'm all right, Vilma.

Why are you shaking? Give me your jacket, Miltie, she said and placed Oster's seersucker over Knittel's shoulders, over his own light-blue jacket.

I'm so empty, Eddie said to Vilma Rakos.

You'll warm up in a minute, she said, standing behind him and massaging his neck. How does that feel? she asked.

Good, Knittel said, good.

It was the emptiness sucking away inside him. His friends, he thought, The Companions of the Happy Hour, were not a bad bunch. They had all made their journeys but they were not empty the way he was empty.

The *Slocum* had sunk to the bottom of his emptiness. The flames had been extinguished. The paddlewheels had stopped turning. The charred bodies were gone. The *Slocum* was broken but it was clean. The smashed decks had been swept. Immaculate. Sterile. No one was down there. Rosy was not there.

In the emptiness Knittel heard his gravelly brain voice say, You shouldn't have told the story. You needed it inside, the flesh of memory and regret. Emptiness had sucked everything away. Edward Knittel reached over his shoulder and touched Vilma's hand.

He was submerged in the river again. Gray. Green. Cold. Floating upward to the masked light. Floating upward to the fat lady who stared down. River air bursting into the drowned boy's lungs. The beach of pain. The burgee of pain. Melvin. The Hero. Sucked away.

Edward Francis Knittel heard his speaking voice say, Ach! The Companions were looking at him intensely.

All right, Eddie? Vilma asked.

I'm all right, sure, Knittel said. I'm going to outlive Margie Ann Plunkerbrote and her goddamned lies by a thousand years.

He turned to McHooley and asked for two fingers of brandy. McHooley put it before him. Knittel sipped. When he had finished, he got unsteadily to his feet. He paused for a moment to drink the clinging remains in the wide-bottomed glass.

Then he felt the old anger rise up from his legs to his stomach to his chest to his cheeks. Geronimo! he shouted.

And with no warning Eddie Knittel threw the empty snifter at McHooley, who ducked. The snifter shattered a cluster of pyramided glasses on the first shelf of the back bar.

Give that man a kewpie doll! said Cortin, still attending to his nose and eyes.

What's got into you, lad? the startled McHooley asked.

Eddie! shouted Rakos. That's enough!

Get hold of him, Bo! McHooley called to Wang.

Wang took a step forward as Knittel lifted his briar shillelagh over his head.

I don't get paid for things like this, Jimothy, Bo Wang said
with a smile and kept his distance.

Knittel picked up a heavy glass ashtray and scaled it like a
disk at McHooley, who leaped out of the way. A bottle of Wild
Turkey flew apart and splashed over the back counter.

It's on your bill, Eddie! McHooley shouted.

Good to know! yelled Knittel and pitched a beer bottle
past McHooley's ear, bringing down a cluster of liqueurs together with the glass shelf which supported them.

Bo Wang now took some quick steps toward Edward
Knittel, who grabbed his black-briar walking stick and swung it
at Wang's face. Wang pulled his head back and stopped. Take it
easy, old man, he said. I won't hurt you.

You heathen Chinee creep, you couldn't hurt me on your
best day! Knittel said laughing. He whirled the stick above his
head and let it fly from his hand. One of the ceiling-high
mirrors cracked zigzag along its length. The walking stick
bounced out into the bar room.

Edward Francis Knittel shouted: Damn it! It was just a
picnic! There was laughter and there was dancing! There was
all of us on that day going up the river to Locust Grove!

We all know that, Eddie, Oster said trying to issue a
soothing sound.

Was you there, Miltie? When the ship sailed, when the
band played, was you there? Knittel said and threw another
beer bottle. More glass crashed. More booze spilled.

Jaizus! shouted McHooley. You'll pay!

Boy, oh, boy, is he angry! Esther Lieber said with a joyous
smile. He's still on the *General Slocum*! *The boy stood on the
burning deck ...*

Eddie, I want you to stop this! Vilma demanded.

Knittel laughed. There was no one there to redress our
grievances!

That's the way it is, Eddie, said Esther.

If only we had graves for them! There must be a way to
balance the books, Miltie, there must be!

Calm down, Eddie, I'll balance them. I'll figure it out,
calm down.

Knittel took the wad of currency from his shirt pocket and
threw it into the air. The bills separated and floated down like
the green celebratory paper of Wall Street on parade. The

Companions of the Happy Hour were decorated in hundred dollar bills, which they did not touch.

I lived my whole life in one month, y'know that! In one month! There *was* a Rosy! You all know that! There *was* a Rosy and that's the bottom line!

The old man lifted his bar stool and threw it with all his strength at the back of the bar. The remaining glass and bottles came crashing down.

Jaizus! cried McHooley.

EPILOG

1

Four cops, guns drawn, crashed through the locked doors of McHooley's Bar and Grill. They surveyed the wreckage. Sgt. William Jefferson picked up a long shard of mirror glass and stared at the sliver of his dark face reflected in it. Eddie Knittel and Joe Cortin still sat at their places at the bar. Esther Lieber, Vilma Rakos, Miltie Oster, Bo Wang, and Mindy were a few steps away from it. Esther Lieber plucked two one-hundred dollar bills from her hair.

The sergeant said, What's happenin', McHooley?

McHooley didn't answer. The sergeant slipped his .38 back into its holster. The other cops did the same.

Somethin' happened, McHooley. The precin't got a bunch of phone calls. One said there was a robbery. Another said an explosion. One asshole said it was a massacre at McHooley's and the blood was seepin' out under the doors and then the building collapsed.

Cortin looked toward Sgt. William Jefferson. He brushed some glass off his shirt. Did you get a call in a chirpy little voice saying, The sky is falling?

What're you talking about, Joey? Jefferson asked.

Never mind, Cortin smiled. You can't believe that chick anyway. She lies, she lies, she always lies.

The sergeant picked up some currency from the floor. Did Brink's make a delivery? he asked.

The cash belongs to Mr. Knittel, Billy Boy, said McHooley.

The sergeant turned to Zabinsky. Check the toilets and go down to the cellar.

Right, Sarge, said Zabinsky. He walked briskly toward the rear.

There's wine down there! McHooley shouted after him. Now don't ye go knockin' things down! I've had enough of that for one day.

Luis, Jefferson said to the thin officer, try the kitchens. Don't steal anything. If you see money around, don't touch it. See if anybody is hiding in the fridge.

Wait one minute there, bro! Bo Wang said to the beefy sergeant. You can't go into my kitchen without a search warrant.

Yes, I can, Wang. I got probable cause.

I want to see your search warrant!

Sue me.

You're a vigilante, Jefferson. Why are you harassing these poor, pasty, ice people? I'll have your ass up before the Civilian Review Board.

Fuck off, Bo! What happened? Will somebody, please, tell me what the hell happened? McHooley?

McHooley dropped the shard of glass he still held. It splintered and tinkled into the glass rubble which covered the duck board at his feet.

Kristall Nacht, said Esther Lieber, shaking her head to get the glass out of her graying hair. I'm afraid to touch it.

Talk to me, McHooley, talk to me! said Jefferson. What the hell happened?

I think, McHooley said, it was sort of a spontaneous crashing, lad. We were talking about the old times when, with no provocation, it came down.

Y'don't say!

A sort of immaculate conception crashing.

Jefferson studied the shining carnage behind the bar. What's the bar stool doing there, McHooley?

Why, it was there for me to sit upon, Sergeant Jefferson.

And did you kick it over?

I do not quite recall.

Here's a black walking stick, said Officer Mulholland. It's Knittel's shillelagh.

I see it, I ain't blind, Mulholland, Jefferson said tartly and pulled his stomach in. All right, Eddie, that's your stick, ain't it?

Stop picking on him, Esther Lieber said. He's a very old man!

Very, very old, Oster added.

Jefferson released a long sigh. Okay, okay, wise guys. Nothing happened. No complaints. No charges.

I'm bringing you before the Civilian Review Board, Bo Wang said. You're being brutal!

Oh, shut up, Wang! Jefferson barked.

Did you hear that? I want witnesses! He threatened me! That was straight forward verbal abuse!

Jefferson ignored him. All right, I'll accept what you said, McHooley. It just happened. The glasswork crashed all by itself.

That's right! said McHooley, without provocation. And I don't want your cops making off with Mr. Knittel's money.

Jefferson asked, All right, did anybody get hurt?

No, Mindy answered, we're fine. Really, everyone is fine.

Vilma Rakos pointed to Oster. Miltie's got a cut on his head. Look, it's bleeding!

Milton Oster explored his bald head. His long, thin fingers found the wound. The blood had already begun to cake. Shit! he said.

Don't touch it, Miltie, Vilma said, removing his hand, Don't touch it. There's a little piece of glass.

She reached carefully to the cut and plucked the glass out of the wound. She reached over the bar to one of the chrome-plated dispensers. Is this one water, McHooley? she asked.

Beer, said the bartender. He brought up one of the flexible soda-dispenser hoses and squirted. The napkin in Vilma's hand turned brown.

That's Coke, she said.

Best thing in the world, lass.

At the open doors a crowd of young people, McHooley's night-time regulars, pressed forward. They were barely inside the room. They studied the scene silently until some one in the crowd shouted out, Somebody got killed!

It was a fight! another voice said.

A dealer got killed!

Lookadat! The bald guy's bleeding!

I know him, all right, he's a pusher!

Get back! Jefferson shouted at the crowd. Mulholland, get 'em outta here! On the sidewalk, on the sidewalk!

Mulholland confronted the partyers. All right, all right, back up, back up, outside!

When will it open? a young red-headed woman asked.

I don't know, said Mulholland, just step outside.

Will someone tell us?

We don't know, Mulholland said. He took her elbow, turned her gently, and edged her outside. He closed the double doors and put his back against them.

Luis Moyano returned from the kitchen.

Anything? asked Jefferson.

Nothing, said Moyano, nothing. Not even one little cucaracha.

The cupboard is bare! said Miltie Oster. The final chicken wing has flown!

Zabinsky returned from McHooley's cellar, brushing some dirt from his shoulder.

Zabinsky? asked Jefferson.

Like he said, said Zabinsky, cases of wine and whiskey.

That's all?

Well, said Zabinsky, that's all except for the rats. There's plenty of rats down there.

Mindy looked angrily at McHooley. Damn it, she said, damn it! You told me there were no rats, McHooley! I don't have to work with rats! I quit!

Mindy threw her apron in the general direction of McHooley. It fell over Cortin's head. She walked quickly across the room. Mulholland opened the door to let her out.

Jefferson took out a thick, deeply worn leather-bound pad, opened it, and positioned his ballpoint on the page. I need an explanation, he said, anything. Any kind of bullshit just so I can make an official report.

Smiling, his white beard glistening with glass, Eddie Knittel said, I did it.

Well, that's no surprise, Eddie, Jefferson said. Somebody get you pissed off again?

No, said Esther Lieber, it's the *Slocum* Disaster. Eightieth Anniversary.

Writing in his pad without looking up, Jefferson asked, A celebration? Eddie?

A celebration, the old man answered. The *Slocum* is sunk. I sank the *Slocum.*

You know something, Eddie? I'd like to lock you up, Jefferson said, and turned to McHooley. No charges? No complaints?

From under Mindy's apron, which still covered his head, Cortin said, Peek-a-boo!

No charges, no complaints, said McHooley. You may take yer constabulary and leave the premises.

Jefferson shook his head. The Liquor Board will get you if you don't watch out, McHooley. Make sure the little bastards have ID's.

You won't go out of yer way to report me, now?

Listen, word gets around, McHooley. Some of the kids out there have come up from the Village. Some from the Bronx. Just cover your R'yal Irish Arse and check the ID's. Do you want me to let them in?

No, no. I'll be ready for them in a while. Take yer posse now and go. I'll let them in.

Out on the sidewalk Jefferson's voice boomed: McHooley's will open in twenty, thirty minutes. There was an accident and they're cleaning it up. Make sure your ID cards are okay because Officer Mulholland will be coming around to check you out.

Oh, no! cried a voice from the crowd. Not Mulholland! He's an incorrigible statutory rapist!

High girlish laughter.

A voice: Fuck you, Mulholland!

You, too, Jefferson!

Laughter.

We'll be back! Jefferson boomed over the heads of the young crowd. Behave! I mean it, you behave!

Jefferson and Moyano got into their police car, Zabinsky and Mulholland into theirs. Their sirens came up to pitch, their lights flashed, and they rolled away.

♪ 2 ♪

Esther Lieber stared at Bo Wang when he emerged from the kitchen through the swinging doors. Look at him! she said. The Sheik of Araby!

In his gray, custom-tailored Armani suit, Bo Wang bowed and turned in a slow circle to display his splendor. His necktie was black and patterned with pink rosebuds the same color as his shirt. Pink enamel rosebuds were gripped in the gold settings of his cufflinks. The shoes were black alligator.

McHooley, deadpan, asked, Tell me, Mr. Wang, would ye be helping me clean up this glass now?

Shift is over, boss. I've got a date.

Now Bo, lad, Mindy has left my employ. There's a crowd of IDs out there. You've got to help me.

Sorry, boss. When you see my date you'll forgive me.

Heathen Chinee, said Eddie Knittel.

Wang smiled. Your beard is filled with glass, Eddie. The *Slocum* is sunk and it's time for you to go home.

Jesus, what time is it?

Ten nineteen, said Miltie Oster.

Oh, said the old man, it's okay, poifect! I'll be home in time.

In time for what? Cortin asked.

I ain't going to take the bait, Joey. And give me my money, Knittel said, taking the currency Cortin held in his hand.

With your troubles, Joey, how can you keep on joking? Vilma asked as she fixed an adhesive bandage to Oster's scalp.

Joey shrugged. If this is my last ignorant night on earth I'm going to enjoy it. That's what I tell myself, he said, and blew his nose into a bar napkin.

Esther Lieber picked up Mindy's discarded apron and put it on. Listen, McHooley, I haven't anything to do. I'll give you a hand. How do I get behind the bar?

McHooley lifted the bar gate and let her in. He gave her a shovel and a broom. He pulled a trash can from beneath the bar and put it in the center of the rubble-strewn floor. You don't have to do this, you know, he said.

I know, Jimothy. Let's say I have an overwhelming need to volunteer.

They filled the trash can quickly. McHooley rolled it away and put a second in its place.

Outside a voice yelled, Lady coming through! Start the floor show!

Mchooley responded to the insistent tapping on the door glass he opened the door narrowly. A very tall, slender, blonde squeezed into the bar. What the hell's going on out there? she asked.

Kiddie night, said Eddie Knittel. Smiling his appreciation of the sensual blond body. Don't tell me you're Bo Wang's date!

That's right, she said. Why is your beard filled with glass?

Because I don't know how to get the shit out, said the old man.

His name is Eddie Knittel, Wang said to the tall blonde.

Pleased to meet you, Pop. Let's get out of here, Bo, before the mob comes in.

If you're smart, Miss Longlegs, you'll wait for the mob to come in and then go out, Esther Lieber said from behind the bar. You've already got a run in your pantyhose.

The woman looked back over her shoulder at the leg she lifted behind her. Goddamnit! Shit!

Also, you don't want me to hurt my Armani, do you, darling? said Bo Wang.

Well, what are we going to do, Bo? Just stand here with your forlorn friends?

The cover of *Vogue* has spoken!

And who the fuck are you?

Name of Joe Cortin, m'am, Cortin said with a Western accent.

Little Joe Cortin! My mother's favorite singer! Did anybody notice the C-notes on the floor?

Joe Cortin got off his stool, bowed, and said, May I have this dance with you? He took the woman in his arms and said to McHooley, Music, maestro, please.

McHooley turned the radio up and The Temptations filled the room. Joey Cortin and the blonde, moved around the tables and chair in great dancing strides. The blonde was as tall as Cortin, but her legs, spiking down from under her short, black skirt, were much longer than his.

Bo Wang cut in. The blonde towered over him. Oh, she said, I adore short men! They're so nice and comfy!

McHooley and Lieber went through the room, sweeping up broken glass and hundred-dollar bills. Although the bar floor still had a patina of embedded glass, McHooley announced, That's good enough. Let them little beer-guzzlers in.

Joe Cortin opened the doors. The young men and women rushed into the bar. In a minute all the chairs and tables were occupied. The bar front was embraced by a line of new customers. McHooley was squeezing off beers from the dispenser. Esther served bottled beer from the refrigerators below the back bar. Hey, this is nice! she said.

The jukebox is broken, a youth in a Nike tee-shirt yelled.

Another youth switched on his ghetto blaster. The heavy metal rattled the windows and drowned out the purring of the air conditioner. The crowd shook their bodies as they danced. The beer went so quickly, McHooley couldn't wash glasses fast enough. He switched to papercups. Esther ran out of bottles. Why don't you go down to the cellar and get some wine, Jim?

They don't drink wine. They'll have to make do with draught. I have enough of that to make them piss all night.

Bo Wang and the blonde danced out the door.

The used beer glasses covered the tabletops. The paper cups covered the floor.

Ah, to be young! said Oster.

Boy, said Vilma Rakos, looking at the bobbing dancers, we never did that when I was a kid.

How old are you, Vilma? asked Oster.

Well, Vilma said, ducking her head to hide her embarrassment, I haven't hit the big four-oh, yet. I'm only thirty-three.

God, said Oster, you're not that much younger than I am!

Does that mean anything?

You're so beautiful, Vilma!

Miltie!

If I could dance to this stuff, I'd ask you to dance.

Oh, it ain't that hard, Miltie. You feel the beat and you go up and down and forward and back and stuff.

I can't do it! I like touch dancing. Do you know what I mean?

You're hitting on me, Miltie!

I'm trying to get to know you.

I'm a taxi driver, that's all.

That's not what I mean, Vilma.

The ghetto blaster fell into silence in the middle of a guitar scream. Oh, shit, it's broke! They say Japanese stuff is the best and this is the top of the line. Shit!

Hey, Mr. McHooley, you know how to get the jukebox going?

No, I don't, McHooley yelled as he served another beer.

Maybe they'll get the hell out of here, said Eddie Knittel. How can they live like that? Don't they die from the noise?

Noise doesn't kill, mister, said a young woman smoking a joint. It's silence that kills. Can you fix that fucking thing, Arnie?

The doors to McHooley's slammed open. A man on rollerblades, wearing a red bulbous clown nose, skated gracefully around the bar room floor. He was in his sixties.

Comrades! the skating clown shouted. The revolution is coming and nothing and no one can stop it! Lenin is dead but Castro is alive! Don't let capitalism and imperialism fuck you over! Humor is the most important thing! The revolution can't be won without humor! Everybody laugh! Everybody sing!

Joey climbed up to the top of the bar. All together now! he shouted to the crowd. *Arise, ye prisoners of starvation*, Cortin sang. C'mon, kids, I can't hear you! Low voices to the left, high voices to the right, baritones in the middle! On the downbeat! Sing out! *Arise, ye wretched of the earth!*

The young crowd, in silence, stared at Cortin. Someone said, McHooley's is a nut house for old people!

So what else is new? Esther laughed from behind the bar.

The red-nosed revolutionary skated once more around the room then out the door.

Joey Cortin, his arms extended and open, announced, My name is Little Joe Cortin, your mother's favorite singer from the Golden Oldies days! I'm going to sing! I'm going to sing for you! I'm going to sing for the whole world! Open the doors! Open the windows!

Joey Cortin looked across the upturned faces and smiled. His white teeth gleamed. He inhaled slowly. A soft melody arose and reached all parts of the room at once, filling it with no effort.

It was an Italian song, a Neapolitan street song.

Eddie Knittel looked up at Cortin. Fucking Joey, you sure can sing!

Cortin, finished the song, and looked at McHooley. This one's for you, Jimothy, he said.

And the sweetest "Danny Boy" ever sung came out of him. Not out of his mouth, not from his lips, but *out of him*. Cortin seemed to float on the sound he made. *Oh, Danny Boy, the pipes, the pipes are calling*.... And the sound he made was a disembodied sound which filled McHooley's Bar and made it holy.

The tears rolled down McHooley's face. He stopped pumping the beer and softly sang beneath Cortin's silver voice. I know yer Irish, Joey. There is a truth no one can deny, Joey boy!

Then Cortin sang "McArthur Park", about a cake melting in the rain. The crowd applauded. Then "The Snows of Fifth Avenue", a song no one had ever heard before. A song Little Joe had saved for this night. Someone sobbed. The crowd applauded. Then he sang some Al Jolson songs. One after the other he sang them. And after each, Cortin's voice throbbed in the air.

When he ended with *Rosy, you are my posy, You are my heart's bouquet...* Eddie Knittel said, Oh, you fucking Joey, how you can sing!

Then "Mad about The Boy" and the house applauded for a very long time.

Cortin stopped. He stood on the bar top, trembling, unable to move. Miltie Oster and Vilma Rakos helped him down. He fell into Miltie's arms and wept. It'll be all right tomorrow, he sobbed, won't it, Miltie?

You know it'll be all right, Joey. Don't worry, it'll be all right. I know it. I heard it on the radio.

Vilma kissed Miltie on the neck.

Eddie Knittel tried to put his head down on his arms but the glass in his beard hurt his face. Jimothy, he said to the bartender, while Joey was singing I was dreaming, y'know. A waking dream, Jimothy.

And what did ye dream, ould fella?

No crows in the sky. No crows on the windowsill. No coal in Rosy's mouth. A good dream. A soft dream. I was all naked in bed with Rosy and my gimpy leg was good and I had no scars on me. The *Slocum* is sunk. Jimothy, tell me the truth. Do you think I still can get a hard-on with all the anger out of me?

If anyone in God's world can do it, you can do it, Eddie.

I'll find out tonight, Linda willin'.

The silent ghetto blaster snapped back to maximum sound. It works, it works! Arnie shouted although he could not be heard. Half the room got up and danced.

Emotionally drained Joey Cortin, his wide shoulders sloping down, sat, and watched the dancers.

Miltie Oster said to Vilma Rakos, You kissed my neck. Why did you do that?

I wanted to, she said.

But why? Tell me, why?

You were tender with Joey.

Yes, but that's not it. Is it?

You're pushing me, Miltie.

I have to. I want you.

I know that. Life's too complicated.

It's true, Vilma. God, I love you.

You don't even know me, Miltie.

I've always known you.

You're crazy.

You were on my radio.

Miltie! I know you're not really married but you're still involved.

Only for a little while. Forget her, Vilma.

I can't, Miltie. Please, don't push me. I can't!

The clown on rollerblades came through the doors again. He skated twice around the room, crushing empty paper cups beneath his wheels and then, on one leg, he zipped out to the street.

Esther said, Did you notice, McHooley, no one's ordered beer in the last five minutes?

Take my word for it, lass, they will again. Nothing known to man has ever stopped beer when it flowed. There's a line waiting at the latrine door.

Tell me the truth, McHooley, said Esther Lieber. When we were their age did we piss that much?

♪ 3 ♪

Mulholland and Zabinsky parked their patrol car and posted themselves inside the bar entrance. Before calling for the attention of the beer drinkers, Mulholland smoked a cigarette. Then he shouted, Listen up everybody! This is your friendly police officer. On the count of three I want to see IDs held in your right hands reaching for the ceiling.

Zabinsky took over. And a one, and a two, and a three! he yelled.

Extended arms and IDs pierced the smoky air of McHooley's.

Mulholland and Zabinsky moved from table to table checking the cards. Mulholland asked two young women and a young man to get up and move to the bar. Zabinsky made the same request of two other young men.

You're sisters, ain't you? Mulholland said to the girls.

No, we ain't! the taller of the girls protested.

You're fifteen. She's fourteen. You're the Constantino girls.

No, we ain't. This is a frame-up, the younger of the two said.

We got you last month at Kincannon's, said Zabinsky. You're babies. Who's this squirt with you?

The girls remained silent.

You know Sergeant Jefferson's rule, girls, Mulholland gently admonished. One more time and we take you home to your parents.

The younger of the two said, Fat lot of good.

Where'd you buy these? Zabinsky asked the young men. They hung their heads. Where? he repented with an edge to his voice.

A guy on the street. In the Village. He said it was all right, the chubby boy answered and began to whimper.

The other boy said, What's the big deal? You gawna arrest me?

Zabinsky jabbed him with his night stick. Listen, wise guy, you're just an illegal yout'. Tell me where you got your ID.

ID, Eddie Knittel mused, did we have IDs when I was a yout'? Do you remember IDs, yenta? Do you remember yout'?

Esther came over to Knittel's corner. With a vengence, Eddie, she said. I was too little to have an ID. But all the big people had them. Millions and millions of them, Eddie.

Esther Lieber put her arms on the bar before the old man, palms up. See, she said, no numbers.

Mulholland and Zabinsky ushered the under-aged kids out of the bar. Zabinsky, over his shoulder, called to McHooley, Commence firing, Jimothy. We got the poipertrators.

The boom box hit its maximum again and the feedback was a knife-sharp squeal. Arnie lowered the sound. It's okay now, he said.

Then the tape jammed. Everybody laughed. A well built jock with heavy-framed glasses said, *A cappella*, now we all boogie *a cappella.*

Hearing the word Joey Cortin looked toward the young man. He was appealing, Joey thought. But tomorrow had to happen first.

Knittel picked at the glass in his beard. He pricked his finger and stopped. Ach! What kind of barber takes out glass?

McHooley announced, Whoever is smoking that funny stuff had better stop it. The gendarmes will be back and it's me they'll bust.

Fuck you, McHoo! said a joyous voice.

Show some respect! Eddie Knittel said.

Shut up, asshole!

Esther, reach over there and give me my stick.

Handing it to him, Esther Lieber said, Don't kill him, Eddie.

Knittel put his stick over his shoulder. All right, he said, which one of you pimples called me an asshole? Show your face!

Laughter.

A young woman's voice: I don't believe this!

Well, asked Knittel, where's the tough guy?

Fart! said a voice toward which Knittel turned. From another direction, another voice, Fart!

More voices: Fart! Fart! Old fart! Go home, Fart head!

McHooley put his shotgun into view. All right, lads and lassies, I don't like the temper yer showing tonight. It would please me if you all decided to leave of your own accord.

Fuck you, McHoo!

McHooley cocked the gun and pointed it toward a tall, young man with a thin mustache and a light, stringy beard which seemed to have been built one hair at a time. I do believe you want to tell me how sorry you are, lad? Well?

I'm sorry, said the tall young man.

You're very sorry, said McHooley, sincerely now, if you like your knees.

I'm very sorry.

You're very, very sorry.

I'm very, very sorry.

I hear the voices of angels calling you home, lad. Step lively now!

The young man snaked through the crowd of his peers, who laughed and hooted as he found his way out.

Oh, well, said a young woman, win some, lose some. Someone buy me a beer?

And there's another difficulty, lass. The well's gone dry, McHooley said.

The bar became quiet.

Yer all welcome to stay as long as y'like, now. McHooley has never turned a guest into the street.

In the silence the young men and women seemed nervous. There were patches of conversation, bursts of polite laughter. The boom box issued no sound. Singly and in groups they drifted out into the street.

Esther Lieber surveyed the bar room. Empty beer glasses crowded the tabletops amid patterns of dried foam. Almost every paper cup had been thrown to the floor.

Esther smiled. She said to McHooley, What is it? Is McHooley's against saw dust?

Just more to sweep up. No one spits on the floor anymore. A spittoon would go dry for a month.

Watch where you're pointing the gun, McHooley, Eddie Knittel said. Put it away. You're probably as bad a shot as Van Schaik.

Not at all, Edward, said McHooley. I've never seen a wall I couldn't hit. Anyway it's empty.

♪ 4 ♪

How quiet it is! Vilma Rakos, said uneasily. She was more comfortable, when there was sound. She could do a long shift in the cab because the city streets were always talking to her and her radio was playing classical music, Gregory's music. Finally she said, Jim, put the radio on, will you?

A string quartet played softly.

That ain't Mort Shuman, McHooley, said Eddie Knittel.

The tribute is over, said the barkeeper. I'm giving you my second best.

Poyfect! said Knittel. I'll admit to you I'm tired. He closed his eyes. He spoke so softly that even the muted string quartet masked his voice.

Knittel mumbled along until Cortin said, Speak up or shut up, Eddie.

The old man opened his eyes for a moment. He looked at Cortin and said, Thanks.

I was trying to dream of Rosy again. It ain't happening right. I squeezed my brain but I couldn't get my old feelings about her. Like on the Fifth Avenue bus with me and her going uptown. Her lavender blouse. Her curly brown hair. Her breasts. Her voice. I'm squeezing, concentrating. I can imagine her but it's all dry, y'know? It's the first time Rosy ever was cold to me. She's not floating out of my heart anymore.

But before you said you dreamed your leg was better and you had no scars and you were naked and stuff, Vilma said.

Ach, Vilma, I'm ashamed to say, I made that up. I thought that would stop her from fading away from me. I would cry but I'm out of tears.

Oh, Eddie, I'm sorry! said Vilma Rakos.

She'll return in all her glory, lad! McHooley said, smiling and reaching across the bar, slapping Eddie Knittel on the shoulder.

Eddie smiled. They're all fading. Maybe that's the way. Maybe I'm getting to my time.

If you say that again, I'll be very angry at you, Eddie! Vilma said.

Me too, said Esther.

Knittel sighed. Maybe it ain't so important, he said. What the hell!

Oster shook his head. Eddie, he said sternly, it's the most important thing in the world!

Miltie, said the old man, it's history!

No, it's not history! Oster said.

So what is it, asked Esther, if it isn't history?

Memory, said Miltie, it's memory.

I'm not getting it, Esther said.

History kills, said Oster. History is bones. Bones we find in deep graves, on lonely beaches. Memory keeps everything green and alive. In memory you can hear your father speak, breathe, feel his hand stroke your head. In memory you can smell the odor of a lover, her secret perfume. History will not give you those things. Memory is always alive.

Well, said Joey Cortin, that's very profound but what'll we do with Eddie's *Slocum* when Eddie dies? Which is maybe in the next five minutes.

His memory will join the billions of memories in the collective memory, the universal gene pool, said Oster.

But, Miltie, is that enough? Joe Cortin protested.

We listened to his story, Joey, said Esther Lieber. So now it's in our memories, too, right?

Stop that pollyanna shit, Esther, Cortin said. It's all going to be dead. It'll die with us. None of us is going to deposit anything into other memory banks. No fucking progeny! No, no, my blotto friends, all the memories die with us. Even if we have memories when we sober up.

Is that true, Miltie? Because we don't have children? Vilma Rakos asked anxiously.

Miltie stroked his bald head and stared up at the ceiling. After a long moment, he smiled brightly. No, Vilma, Oster said. It is not true.

Thank God! Vilma said.

How'd you figure that? Joey asked, a little annoyed.

There were a few hundred survivors. They had children. So it's into the pool!

But Eddie's memory! What happens to Eddie's memory? What happens to Helga and Melvin?

Eddie Knittel's laughter roared through the bar room. When he finished laughing, he said, I shouldn't have done that. It hurts my beard. How am I going to get the glass out of my beard? That's a real thing.

One of those little vacuum cleaners, Esther Lieber suggested.

Mindy was right, said McHooley. This isn't a Happy Hour, it's a nut house.

Listen, said Oster, the *Slocum* goes into the gene pool of memory. Let's take a vote on it. All those in favor of Knittel's memory of the *Slocum* going into the racial memory pool, raise their hands!

Only Vilma put her hand up.

Only Vilma and me vote for the gene pool? Oster asked, looking from face to face. You people are voting for history? I tell you history stinks, history is dead.

Listen, Miltie, history balances the books, said Eddie Knittel. There's the bottom line, for you, Mr. Accountant.

No, Eddie, no. History is the bones. The bones point back to memory, Oster said, his voice sharp and tense.

Well, lad said McHooley, there's no way to tape-record everybody who ever lived. Why, in many parts of the world there's no electric power, not even a wee drop.

Those without electircity don't count, Cortin said somberly.

Why not? Oster asked. It's the only way to save the world. All our memories into the Jungian pot! he shouted.

Cuckoo, said Esther, Miltie is getting cuckoo.

In that caldron is the old chaos out of which God created Heaven and Earth. If you had read the book, Eddie, you could have asked Mobo. He knew, didn't he?

He was as crazy as you, Miltie, said Knittel.

In the caldron of chaos the memory of the *Slocum* floats, Oster said. All existence roils. Nothing dies. In that cold viscous soup everything exists and there is no purpose for it. The ledger can't be balanced. A bottom line cannot be conceived.

Wow, said Esther, maybe we should take another vote?

What the fuck are you talking about, Miltie, *Slocum* soup? I don't want soup! I don't want history and I don't want memory, either!

Tell the truth, Eddie, Oster said in a level voice. do you really want to forget everything? Remember nothing? Obliterate the *Slocum*? Obliterate Rosy?

The old man pushed his stool from the bar. He walked to the doors and stared out at Broadway.

How did you get so smart? Vilma asked Oster. She lifted his hand to her mouth. She kissed each of his fingers.

Oster, stunned, said, I love you, Vilma.

I know, she said. I've been thinking about it, Miltie. Later, we'll drive around in the cab and talk, okay?

Oster smiled, his eyes filling with tears.

True love strikes at McHooley's Cortin said to the bartender. James, I have a proposition for you.

I like you, Joey, said McHooley, but not that way.

Funnee! said Cortin. Proposition is, why don't I go down to the cellar and bring up some wine and booze?

How can I refuse, lad?

We don't have to vote on that, said Esther.

Knittel returned to the bar. He was smiling.

Is the feeling back, Eddie? Vilma asked.

Nah, he said, but I had a thought. I'm in pretty good shape, y'know. I eat pretty good. I move my bowels pretty good. Once a week I have a sex life. There's no reason for me to die, is there? I'm only ninety-five.

What're ye sayin', lad? Will you be trying for a hundred?

For the hundreth anniversary of the *Slocum* Disaster, Knittel announced.

You'll be a hundred fifteen! said Esther Lieber.

Don't knock it! the old man said. A hundred fifteen and pull the plug!

Cortin returned with a carton of mixed bottles. Esther and the barkeep washed some glasses. McHooley poured.

♪ 5 ♪

Eddie Knittel bolted upright on his stool. Oh, my God! The time! What time is it?

Eleven fifteen, Oster said.

She'll kill me! Joey, you come home with me and tell her about the accident.

What accident?

How I fell down, y'know. Come on, Joey, come on!

Both the entrance doors opened violently and Linda Fernandez stepped inside. Following Linda was an old woman carrying a wilted bouquet of red roses.

Sonuvabitch! said Knittel. I had an accident, Linda. Ask *him*!

Linda Fernandez smiled coldly, Hey, it's all right, Eddie. You don't have to lie to me.

I ain't lying, Linda. I fell down.

You fall on your face? What's the shiny stuff in your beard?

Glass.

Your face fell in glass?

That's right. My face fell in glass. Ask anybody.

There's a technicality here, said Oster. Actually the *glass* fell *into* his *face*.

You're the accountant. Eddie told me the bookkeeper had no hair on his head, Linda said, smiling grimly. Eddie, I ain't pissed or nothing. My babysitter is sleeping with the kids and this here nice old lady, she come to the door with a bunch of flowers. She got a funny gringo name, Eddie, and she's looking for you. We sit in the living room and we talk.

Eddie Knittel looked suspiciously at the old lady in the wrinkled, beige-linen dress. The old woman's mouth lifted in a closed smile. Her blue eyes, young, tried to engage him but Knittel turned toward Linda. That's very nice, Linda, very hospitable, he said.

You like the glass in your beard, Eddie?

No, it hurts. I don't know how to get it out.

Somebody got a comb? Linda asked.

Vilma passed Linda her comb.

Thanks, Linda said. To Eddie she said, This is the one you like, old man?

She's a friend, Linda.

Linda stepped close to Eddie's stool. Pretty nice-looking friend, she said. Put your head back, Eduardo. She placed her own hand over Eddie's beard and pushed his head back roughly.

Eduardo, is it? said Esther. I'm glad you haven't got a razor in your hand.

Linda laughed. You think somebody so old like Eddie wouldn't have something on the side? He's an old bull. Put your head back more, Linda said to Eddie.

She combed gently through his beard. The light bounced off the glass bits as they fell. Those which the comb held, Linda tapped out against the bar. The bar people observed Linda as she combed Eddie's white and yellowed beard. When she thought she had finished, Linda, took Eddie's chin and moved his head from side to side. I don't see no more shinings, she said. You got a little blood on your neck.

Olé! Esther Lieber said. Good job!

You his friend too? asked Linda.

He never flirted with me, said Esther. I'm not his type.

Linda, don't embarrass me. I've had a big night, Eddie said.

A very big night, lass, said McHooley. He sank the *Slocum* you know.

I know that, Linda said. She pinched Eddie's cheek. How come you never tell me about the *Slocum* shit, Eddie? Everybody knows about the *Slocum* shit but not Linda Fernandez. Funny, hah? I'm just a housekeeper, hah?

For Christ's sake, Linda! I didn't think you'd want to know. It happened a long time ago.

A hundred years, Linda said, I know that.

Eighty, it was eighty years ago, the old lady wth the roses corrected. Eighty years ago on this day in June of 1904, when Eddie was a boy, a young man, a handsome young man.

Above his beard Knittel's cheeks blushed. You ain't Margie Ann Plunkerbrote? Eddie asked.

The old lady smiled. Yes, I am. And I've brought these roses for you. There are eighty of them.

Oster asked, Margie Ann Plunkerbrote, the poet of the Angry Squire?

Yes, said Miss Plunkerbrote and nodded curtly.

She came to the house to bring you roses and say happy birthday, Linda said.

Anniversary, said Cortin.

Whatever. So I tell Miss Margie to wait, Eddie is back at ten-thirty the latest.

I had an accident! Knittel blurted out through his tight beard.

And you ain't got no quarter for the phone? Linda asked, her cold smile grown colder.

You saw my beard! You saw the blood!

Hey, cool it, Eduardo. I ain't bent outta shape. Margie told me all about the *Slocum* and them poor dead people on the ride. Margie told me. It's true?

Yes, it's true.

Now you ain't lying, Eduardo?

Why should I lie?

You lie a lot, Eduardo.

Don't embarrass me, Linda! Knittel said, his voice rising. All you have to do is read *The New York Times.*

I don't see it in *La Prensa*, Eddie.

Linda, why should Margie tell you about the *Slocum* if there was no *Slocum?*

I think she's nice. I ain't against her but you got these funny gringo friends, Eddie.

Linda! I'm going to get fucking mad!

Don't talk to me about fucking, you old shit! You said no later than ten-thirty. Then you send this old witch to mess with me!

Eddie slapped Linda across the face.

For a while only the purring of the air conditioner was heard. Then Linda, walked quietly out of McHooley's, paper cups crunching under her sneakers. From the street they heard a shriek.

Oh, my! said Marjorie Ann Plunkerbrote.

Was that Linda? Vilma asked.

Yes, said Eddie Knittel, that was her. Ach, ach! I try my best not to let her get my goat but she knows how.

She wasn't very nice, Vilma Rakos said.

I shouldn't have hit her.

I never would have thought..., Marjorie Ann Plunkerbrote began.

Oh, shut up! Knittel growled.

If you ask me, lad, she wanted to be struck, McHooley said.

I didn't ask you, you fool! Sorry, Jimothy. She's sensitive. Have you any smokes left, Vilma?

All gone, Eddie.

Eddie Knittel looked at Marjorie Ann Plunkerbrote, her head down, as she slowly smoother the wrinkles on the skirt of her dress. I apologize, Knittel said, I sincerely apologize.

After a heavy, quiet pause filled with his sighs, Knittel said, The thing is, I got her involved, which I shouldn't have done. I got her involved with me. I got her into my bed. It's confusing for her. She's my housekeeper. I pay her a week's salary for a day's work. There's money in this old goat and she smells it. She's got two nice little boys and no husband. From welfare to middle class in one bounce. Confusing. She sees I ain't a bad guy. I don't shame her.

Knittel looked at the faces of his tired companions. He looked away from the stern eyes of Marjorie Ann Plunkerbrote. He cleared his throat.

You know what confuses her most? the old man asked. That I could still get it up and give her a good time. Maybe I'm the only man to bring her on, y'know. She likes it, y'see. She likes me.

Maybe the confusion is that she loves you, Joey Cortin said.

Knittel nodded his head sadly, heavily. That's it, he said, she loves me, Joey. She loves me.

But that's nice, isn't it? Vilma said.

This is no way to speak of Miss Fernandez in public before strangers. I do not hear the voice of love, Mr. Knittel.

I didn't solicit your nosy opinion, Miss Plunkerbrote. He turned to Vilma Rakos and answered her question. No, it ain't nice, Vilma. Here she is, balling an old man for his money and what happens? The worst thing! She falls in love with him! And she hates herself for it. She doesn't know if she's doing it for love or for money. She doesn't know if she's a good woman or a whore. She knows she can't explain it to her priest, her parents, or her friends. And what if her kids find out?

Awful! said Esther Lieber.

A can of sperms! said Cortin.

That's right, said Eddie, that's right! I know all this is going on in her, but I want her! Not hundred-dollar whores, her! And the more I try to do for her, the more she feels like a whore. I even told her when I die, the house will be hers. I set up trust funds for her kids.

Very generous ones, too, said Oster. All the rest of his estate goes to the Hebrew Orphan Society of Ohio.

But that makes her feel all the worse! She's a good Catholic woman and she's living in sin! Sin for gain, y'know.

Jaizus! said McHooley.

I've been ready to make an honest woman of her, said Knittel. Many times I told her, I'll marry you! She said she knew that. And wasn't it true, marrying a man who should have been buried twenty years before, would only make things worse? Why would a woman still to the near side of forty want to marry a man who, taking the odds, should die next year, if not before? What would her priest, her parents, her friends say then?

They'd say smart, Esther Lieber observed, nodding her head.

That's right, yenta. They'd say she married that old shit for his money. Smart! Poor baby! That's why she's so angry with me. It's as if *I* did it. Trapped her.

But you didn't! Vilma said forcefully.

Ah, Vilma, but I did.

Do you think she'll be waiting for you, Eddie, when you get home?

Oh, yes, said Eddie Knittel, that's the damned sad part, she'll be waiting for me.

Marjorie Ann Plunkerbrote stood erect, clutching her small purse. In a soft, sad voice she said, Mr. Knittel, I think I'm intruding here. I think I'll go and leave you with your friends.

Eddie Knittel stared at her. He did not reply.

Esther Lieber said, Please stay, Margie Ann, I like you. I want you to stay. I'm really glad you came. Many times tonight when I wasn't cuckoo, I thought about you. I even wondered what kind of dress you wore on the *Slocum* that day.

⭑ 6 ⭑

Margie Ann pursed her lips. After a moment she smiled and said to Esther Lieber, Well, all right, I'll stay if you want.

And have some tea, Miss Plunkerbrote, McHooley said passing a heavy white cup across the bar. Mr. Knittel is not himself today.

I had written a poem for this occasion, Miss Plunkerbrote said, but I don't think it would be appropriate to read it now.

What occasion did you have in mind? Joey asked.

The Eightieth Anniversary, of course, she said, I don't like sarcasm, young man.

Well, that will be over in a half-hour, Cortin said. We've been celebrating it all night.

Mr. Knittel, said Margie Ann turning away from Joey Cortin, will you please accept these roses? I purchased them for you.

Knittel did not respond.

Miltie Oster took the dying bouquet from her arms. He laid them across Eddie Knittel's thighs. Snap out of it, Eddie, be a gentleman.

I shouldn't've hit her!

When you go home you can kiss and make up, Vilma Rakos said.

Eddie sighed. Yeah, he repeated, kiss and make up.

Would you care for a little wine, Miss Plunkerbrote? McHooley offered, holding up a green bottle. Wonderful after hot tea.

I thank you, no, the old woman said with a girlish laugh, I'm a teatotaler.

Now, I haven't heard that expression in this place in years and that was from my landlord when I tried to bribe him.

And failed? Oster asked.

And failed, said McHooley. He turned to Eddie Knittel. Now be civil and thank Miss Plunkerbrote for the roses.

Thanks for the roses, Margie Ann. I appreciate the thought, Knittel said. He held his bearded chin in his hand. His eyes blinked brightly in the direction of the old woman. Can I ask you something?

Certainly, Mr. Knittel.

You were only three years old, what could you remember?

Marjorie Ann Plunkerbrote's face grew narrow and stern. I can assure you, sir, I can remember a great deal. By the age of three I was out of McGuffey and into books which were quite advanced!

Well, don't lose your knickers, Margie. I'm only asking because you're standing here and it means a great deal to me.

Sometimes you can be real rotten, Eddie, said Esther. How would you behave if Margie hadn't brought you the roses?

Knittel pulled his hand across his beard. Sorry, Margie, he said. It's just been a lousy night.

I understand, said Margie Ann, but you can still be civil. Without civility what would become of the world?

Sorry, Eddie repeated, forget it.

I thought you wanted to know if she remembered, said Esther.

It's not important, said Knittel.

Well, said Marjorie Ann Plunkerbrote to the others, heroes, you see, among their other traits, are always stubborn, aren't they?

Knittel thought if he hadn't liked Marjorie Ann Plunkerbrote before, he certainly didn't like her now. No lectures, please, he said. Tell it to *The New York Times.* You're always telling somebody.

That is correct, Mr. Knittel. I often have been interviewed by *The Times* and other periodicals five years ago and five years before that over a period of forty years.

I noticed that, said Eddie Knittel. Can you tell me why *The New York Times* would want to interview a three-year-old child?

That was your fault, Mr. Knittel. You had refused to talk to them so they turned to me. I believe it was because of a poem I had written on the *Slocum* subject. I'm a very private person, Mr. Knittel, but I gave myself gladly to these interviews because I did not want the memory of the *Slocum* to disappear.

It was none of your three-year-old business! Knittel shouted. Not one ever asked you!

That does not matter a fig, sir. In that year, 1944, you had withdrawn your presence and prestige.

Because of Honeycuitt! Knittel yelled. Do you know how those bastards treated Honeycuitt?

I do not know who this Honeycuitt was but the whole world knew who Edward Francis Knittel was and you refused to keep the *Slocum* alive. It became my job, my burden, and I took it on!

Cortin applauded.

Sarcasm, young man! Margie Ann snapped.

She got you there, Joey! said Miltie Oster. So you've kept the memory of the *Slocum* alive?

And the memory of Edward Francis Knittel too, the Hero of that awful event! There was never an interview issued by me where the Hero was not mentioned! I daresay with reverence.

Ach! blurted Knittel.

Is that true, lad? asked McHooley.

Ach! said Knittel. What's true? What isn't true? Just tell me this, Miss Plunkerbrote: how is it you described the boiler room so well, so clearly, in *The Times* today? What the hell would you know about the fucking boiler room?

Someone will have to wash your mouth out with Fells Naptha Soap, Mr. Knittel!

Ah, said Oster, snapping his fingers, a school teacher!

For more than sixty years.

The boiler room! Knittel prompted. What about the boiler room?

My mother, a school teacher before me, prized my education. She took every opportunity to expand my mind.

The boiler room, Knittel gargled, the boiler room!

My mother walked me all over the *Slocum*, from stem to stern, all three decks and below decks, too.

The boiler room, Margie, will you please get to the goddamned boiler room!

I will if you can control yourself. You can be certain that I will speak of the boiler room. May I continue?

Knittel nodded with angry exasperation.

Thank you, Miss Plunkerbrote said. I was awe-struck to see that great machinery moving, the huge arms turning, turning the shafts which turned the paddlewheels propelling the great white hull up the river! There were two fire men, naked to the waist, shoveling coal into flames inside the boiler. Red and orange and blue were the flaming coals. Remember that? How could a child ever *forget* that?

All right, all right, Knittel mumbled as Margie Ann continued.

And the utility cabin, I remember that just as clearly, with its filth and corruption. The floor covered with bits of food, cigar butts, wood shavings, spittoons fashioned out of empty cans and, lying in one corner, a dead black rat. The barrels filled with straw, I see them clearly in my memory. And I can see the oil lamp burning on the rude cabin table. And one of the crew lighting his cigar with an acetylene torch!

She was there, Eddie, she saw all that, said Esther. That's exactly the way you told it.

Knittel, exasperated, waved his arm at her.

Yes, Mr. Knittel, my mother took me around the Main Deck, too. I saw you there. I saw you standing to the wind at the prow with your arm around the waist of a very pretty girl. You were being sprayed by the river. And even then, Mr. Knittel, I knew you were in love.

Stop! Eddie Knittel shouted.

I will not! said Marjorie Ann Plunkerbrote. Let me explain to you how I knew you were in love with that girl. I knew you were in love with her because in my three-year-old heart I was in love with you.

Vilma Rakos put her hand to her mouth to suppress the sound which filled her throat. It was very quiet in the bar room.

They all looked toward Margie Ann except for Knittel, who was staring down at the roses in his lap.

Am I shocking you, Edward? I have always wanted to tell you how I felt on that day. Perhaps I would have told you at the Town Hall concert but you were so distracted. Did I bring you roses that day, too? I think I did.

All right, Margie, I apologize. It's enough.

No, it is not enough. I've wanted to tell you all of this for so very long. I had hoped perhaps under different circumstances. Not in this place, not before strangers.

You're blaming me for breaking your three-year-old heart. That's not fair, Margie!

As they say, nothing is fair in love and war, Edward. Of course, I'm not blaming you! You have no idea what thunder you hurled into my breast!

Jaizus, said McHooley, it's the poetry spilling out!

Margie Ann smiled at McHooley. Sir, she said, Edward Knittel was the most handsome boy I had ever seen. He was quite tall, broad shoulders, his face the model for Greek and Roman sculptures. Oh, I held my mother's hand but I was looking for Edward!

When the fire came I saw Edward come up the stairs in clouds of smoke. Like a god rising. I waved to him, hoping he'd see me! Then the fire spread. It was everywhere. But in my mother's arms I was unafraid. I was looking at Edward. I watched him as he climbed up the mast and signaled to the shore. I was very calm as long as I could see my hero prince. Only the pounding of my mother's heart informed me that something was terribly wrong. My mother's dress caught fire. Quite calmly, she said to me, I'm going to throw you into the river, Margie. Splash and kick as if you're swimming. Then I flew through the air for a very long time.

The water was so cold. Some men leaning out of a skiff pulled me from the river. I never saw my mother again.

The men put a dry shirt about my shoulders. The river was filled with people from the *Slocum*. I remember boats and shouts, the gray powder floating on the water, the heat of the burning vessel making the air hot. I saw you there in the river, Edward. You were pushing a board, a large piece of jagged wood, with two infants on it, crying and screaming with pain.

Knittel jumped from the stool. The roses fell to the ground. They were dead, damn it, Plunkerbrote! he shouted. They were goddamned dead!

Not as I remember it, Marjorie Ann said calmly.

McHooley poured some scotch into a water tumbler and put it before Knittel, who swallowed it.

Those were some of the memories of the three-year-old child, said Marjorie Ann Plunkerbrote. And, through all those early years, your fight for the *Slocum* survivors. I followed your struggle. I followed your trips to Washington. How you stood before Congress and bared your wounds in the names of all the victims. It was there in *The Times* for the whole world to read, Edward. And I read it too.

Well, Miss Plunkerbrote, every word you read was written by Melvin Honeycuitt.

I am unfamiliar with him. I was heart-broken, completely heart-broken, when you retired from the scene of the *Slocum.* that was forty years ago, Edward. Town Hall was your last public appearance.

The Hero is dead, Miltie Oster said, lifting his glass, long live the Heroine!

McHooley and Cortin joined in the toast.

The front door opened. Sergeant Jefferson put his head inside. Everything okay? How'd you get rid of the noisy bastards, McHooley?

No beer, McHooley said.

Have a good night! said Jefferson as he withdrew.

Will somebody be kind enough to call me a taxi? asked Marjorie Ann Plunkerbrote to no one in particular. I have to teach tomorrow. I have not yet retired.

Hey, said Vilma, I'll take you home, Margie!

♪7♪

Everybody got into Vilma's taxi except James Timothy McHooley, who often slept in the small room in the back, where he kept a change of clothes.

At the first red light, Milton Seymour Oster, who was sitting up front with Vilma Rakos, put his arm around her shoulders and kissed her mouth. She responded.

Am I turning you on? he asked.

For a very intelligent person you're very dumb. I just hope I don't fall in love with you. I can't help myself when I fall in love. When I fall in love I just go all the way.

He kissed her again. The light changed.

In the rear of the cab Little Joe Cortin sat with his face at the open window. His eyes were closed against the soft breeze.

Esther Lieber sat in the middle. She thought if Mindy really had quit she might ask McHooley for her job. There wasn't much pleasure in being a receptionist in a dental office. At McHooley's Bar and Grill there were always people and liveliness. You didn't have to think too much or remember too much. And Bo Wang was nice, although she was sure he was destined to be an architect or a gigolo. And she'd save a good deal of money on wine. Her forehead creased. Would McHooley get pissy about it and keep her from having any? That might be a trouble spot.

Next to Esther sat Edward Francis Knittel. He was angry. He was angry about several things, and he was trying to sort out what it was he was most angry about.

He was angry and disgusted with himself for slapping Linda. And in front of everybody, too! He had never minded it when she got on his case at home. That was private. He could manage that, was even amused by it. Although he had slapped her a few times, and then only because her angers and her nagging had somehow made him feel that he was betraying Rosy. How could that be, he wondered.

Was it because of the *Slocum*? Margie Ann telling Linda all about it? Had Linda gotten pissed off because, not knowing about this important thing, this *Slocum* thing, it made her feel like a little tramp he didn't care about?

All these years, Knittel thought, and no smarts at all! No answers. Just questions which irritated him more and more.

Had Honeycuitt been right all along? Had Van Schaik been right? The bad head wounds. The loss of consciousness on the North Brother Island beach. The opium, the heroin, the laudanum. Could they have caused confusions? Honeycuitt had argued over and over again that he had been confused, that he had forgotten some things and made up others.

And there had been those dreams, which had made everyone's eyebrows go up. And the crows on the windowsill, which, even now, Eddie Knittel believed had been real, as real as his brace and his scars.

Eight minutes or three to North Brother Island? Who was right? Van Schaik or him? At the Coroner's Jury Trial he had been absolutely sure, positive.

Now Marjorie Ann Plunkerbrote, with her just-so English and school-teacher voice, announces that he, *he* had climbed the burgee pole and saved those infants from the sea! Memories, memories, memories. Miltie was counting on the truth of memories. But Knittel knew that memory could be as false as the cold bones of history. Had he not manipulated his memories at will? In his day dreams and in his night dreams, if you could say dreams are memories, Rosy had made love to him. Sometimes like a whore. Sometimes like saint. As he had wanted her, as he had commanded her.

And in his memories he could argue with Melvin Honeycuitt, make him sweat with doubt, make him change his mind.

And, in his memory, he could call up Teddy Roosevelt and ask him what he was going to do for the survivors. And the President would say, "I'll give each of them one million dollars."

Sometimes Roosevelt would say ten million. And Roosevelt would punch his fist into the palm of his hand and shout, "I'm going to hang that Barnaby by his big greedy balls!"

Edward Knittel could see that memory had more faults to it than history. At least in the tombs of history, bones are bones.

Knittel wondered now if he needed to sink the *Slocum*, or the other way around, keep it afloat?

A feeling flooded Edward Knittel's chest and stomach. Sink or float, he thought, maybe the *Slocum* was not important at all.

Knittel also thought, *knew* more than thought, that it was very unlikely that he would live to celebrate the hundredth anniversary of that ancient tragedy. And that, too, was unimportant.

Fuck it! the raspy voice in Knittel's brain said. What I have to do is be nice to Linda, make it up. And the raspy voice offered another thought: What if Linda is not in the house when I get home?

Eighty years rolling and now he was no longer sure of anything that had happened in his life. Edward Francis Knittel rubbed his beard and pricked his finger on a tiny remaining piece of glass. He sucked in a mouthful of air on feeling the sudden pain.

Is there something wrong, Mr. Knittel? asked Marjorie Ann Plunkerbrote.

Everything, said Knittel. He had to giggle. There was Margie Ann sitting on his lap, holding the bouquet of eighty roses. He had forgotten she had been there on his thighs. Margie Ann had no weight to her at all. Are you comfortable? he asked.

Very. This is something I never imagined, to be sitting on your lap. The lap of a hero.

Well, when there ain't room on the seats, ladies wind up on one kind of lap or another.

Eddie resumed his thoughts. Was anything real? Of course! In the first place, there *was* the *Slocum*, ain't that true? And he had been on it. Marjorie Ann Plunkerbrote was, after all, an unimpeachable witness to that. Marjorie proved, one hundred percent, that there had been a Rosy Farkas. And if not from the fire and the railing gate how did he get his gimpy leg and the thick, ropy scars? In his wallet, of course, there was the yellowed report about the life jackets with their rotten cork and iron bars. And it had been signed by President Theodore Roosevelt, with whom he had once sat. It was an open and shut case, open and shut!

Eddie Knittel now took a deep breath. He said to himself, No, sir, I was never confused!

He looked at Marjorie Ann's face, her thin, wrinkled mouth very close to his. I never climbed the pole, Margie, he said firmly.

Edward, I saw you with my own eyes!

It was some other kid with red suspenders. And the babes on the board, they were dead. I swear to you, they were dead! Did you see me floating on the fat lady? Did you see the ghoul in the rowboat?

You're confusing me, Edward, Margie Ann said.

Knittel's beard split into a great smile. He patted Marjorie Ann's thigh. Thank you, he said.

The taxi swerved sharply. Vilma put her head out the window and yelled, Learn how to drive, you motherfucking bastard! Go back to New Jersey!

Miltie Oster smiled. He pressed his fingers into her arm.

Esther Lieber said, If you got us killed, Vilma, darling, I wouldn't mind so much. But such a dirty mouth!

It wasn't my fault.

It wasn't her fault, Oster said looking over his shoulder, smiling still.

Are you all right, Marjorie? Knittel asked Plunkerbrote. Break anything?

A few roses, perhaps. No, I'm quite fine, Edward.

Joey Cortin, still looking out the window, suddenly turned to the others. He was smiling broadly. I know I'll be all right, he said, I know I'll be all right.

You're gawna be so negative, Joey! Esther Lieber said. Tomorrow when you tell us, we'll be flying! We'll have a party! Eddie will pay!

Yes! Yes! Joey said. He was filled with joy. It's going to be all right, Eddie!

No one in this cab has a single doubt! Knittel said.

Sitting next to him, Esther could feel Joey filling his lungs with air. He began to sing. *Rosy, you are my posy, you are my heart's bouquet.*

Esther joined in. Then Vilma and Miltie.

That's a very familiar song, said Marjorie Ann Plunkerbrote. Where is it from?

Although there was no weight to her at all, her boney bottom had begun to make Eddie Knittel feel uncomfortable. He shifted his position.

When Joey stopped singing, it became very quiet in Vilma's taxi.

Eddie Knittel reached into his jacket pocket and took out the plastic-encased copy of "The Slocum Waltz". Can you sing this, Joey?

Cortin scanned it. Very nice, he said, very pretty. Where'd you get it?

Washed up on the beach of North Brother, Knittel said.

Under his breath Joey Cortin hummed the tune.

Where are we going? Eddie Knittel asked Vilma Rakos.

Just taking everybody home, Eddie, the taxi driver said. Margie lives downtown. Then we'll go back up.

It's very kind of you, said Margie Ann.

You're okay for a school teacher, Margie, Esther Lieber said. Any time you want, you can come to McHooley's and have a few with us.

Remember I'm a teetotaler, said Miss Plunkerbrote, laughing. Thank you, all the same.

Out loud, in his sweet tenor voice, Joey Cortin sang.

Unheard by the others, Edward Francis Knittel, sang the song into his beard.

When you waltz on the deck of the Slocum
when you dance on a rare day in June,
leave your cares in a basket at home
and you'll laugh at the waves and the foam,
yes, you will...
Oh, you'll sing and you'll dance
to the fiddler's tune,
yes, you'll sing and you'll dance
and you'll laugh like a loon
and you'll whirl and you'll twirl
and your skirts will all swirl...
Oh, your long hair will throw off its comb
and you'll wish you'll never go home,
and you'll wish you'll never go home.
On the Slocum,
on the Slocum,
on the merry ship, the Slocum,
one, two and three
we're waltzing
on the very, merry
Slocum